O9-ABI-830

Nest of
Vipers

Nest of Vipers

Linda Davies

DOUBLEDAY
New York London Toronto Sydney Auckland

PUBLISHED BY DOUBLEDAY
a division of Bantam Doubleday Dell Publishing Group, Inc.
1540 Broadway, New York, New York 10036

DOUBLEDAY and the portrayal of an anchor with a dolphin
are trademarks of Doubleday, a division of
Bantam Doubleday Dell Publishing Group, Inc.

Library of Congress Cataloging-in-Publication Data
Davies, Linda, 1963–
Nest of vipers / Linda Davies.
p.   cm.
1. Floor traders (Finance)—England—London—Fiction.
2. Commercial crimes—England—London—Fiction.   3. Women in
finance—England—London—Fiction.   4. Conspiracies—England—
London—Fiction.   5. London (England)—Fiction.   I. Title.
PR6054.A887N47   1994
823'.914—dc20   94-27269
                                                 CIP

ISBN 0-385-47596-9
Copyright © 1995 by Linda Davies
All Rights Reserved
Printed in the United States of America
February 1995
First Edition in the United States of America

10   9   8   7   6   5   4   3   2   1

Acknowledgments

I have a wonderful group of people to whom I am enduringly grateful. Family and friends provided much love and support. My parents, as always, were unstinting in every way.

I have the two best agents that anyone could wish to have: Toby Eady in London and David Black in New York. I can't thank them and their colleagues, Victoria Hobbs and Susan Raihofer, enough.

Everyone at Doubleday has been a joy to work with. David Gernert is a wonderfully clear-eyed editor who unclouds my own vision. Stephen Rubin, Ellen Archer, Jayne Schorn, and Jackie Everly overflow with creative ideas and have given me superb backing. Amy Williams organizes everything with great efficiency and humor.

Yvonne Thomas' and John Cutts' practical comments and advice have given me great encouragement. Chris Fagg, Rosie Collins, and Andrew Neil did much to get things moving. Eric Kohn's brokerage services are unrivaled.

Andrew Hyslop and Rupert Allason shed bright light on the intelligence world.

And the City of London gave me inspiration.

To my parents, Glyn and Grethe, for all their love and support.

Prologue

"She's perfect."

"What makes you so sure?"

"She has the right cover. No one would ever suspect her. She's intelligent and discreet, and she's ambitious—the challenge would appeal to her. She's idealistic—she would break the law if she thought she was justified. And she'd probably enjoy it."

Bartrop began to look interested. "Why's that?"

"There's a look of controlled sedition about her."

Bartrop frowned. "That's a double-edged quality, don't you think? You seem to forget, we can't afford to make a mistake. If any of this got into the papers . . ."

"It won't," Barrington assured him. "She'll be on our side, and anyway, I've done my homework. She knows how to keep secrets. She'll gossip as much as the next woman, but not about things that matter."

"You're fond of her, aren't you?"

"It's hard not to be."

"You know this could be very unpleasant for her. If things go wrong, we'll have to drop her."

"Don't you think I ought to tell her that?"

You'll tell her what I decide she needs to know, thought Bartrop. He said, "Tell her not to get caught, but explain that if she does, she's on her own. The question is, can she live with it? I don't want her crying to the police."

Barrington thought for a while. "She'll be all right."

Bartrop spoke slowly and deliberately. "It wouldn't be in her own interests to speak out anyway."

The director of Counter-Narcotics Crime at MI6 and the governor of the Bank of England smiled confidently. There was no reason why either of them could have known then that Sarah Jensen, if wronged, was capable of blind irrationality, that if they ever betrayed her, she would, like Samson, pull the pillars down around them all.

Chapter One

Sarah Jensen returned from lunch at two-thirty. She took her seat at her trading desk and studied her four trading screens intently for five minutes. Then she picked up her telephone handset and executed a quick trade, closing out a position. It took thirty seconds. It made half a million pounds.

With a smile and a flourish she switched off her screens, gathered up her handbag, and prepared to leave. David Reed, her colleague who sat next to her, looked up in surprise.

"You can't leave now. It's just two-thirty."

Sarah laughed and blew him a kiss as she headed off.

"Watch me." And they did. Half the trading floor followed her progress as she crossed the room and disappeared into the lifts.

At twenty-seven, Sarah Jensen had all the trappings of a normal life, albeit at a rarefied level. She was smart and beautiful. She was one of the top foreign-exchange traders in the City of

London. She lived in a big house in Chelsea with her brother and her boyfriend. She had looks, love, and money. But she also had fear.

The life that she had so carefully constructed was fragile. Just as her childhood in New Orleans had ended one sunny after-noon with the death of her parents, so her new life could end suddenly. In seconds. A glittering impact of steel on skin, an act of violence—there was no rationality or justice to sudden death. The fear never left her. It burrowed deep, it hid itself in distor-tions, denial, and lies, but it never went away. And its shadow showed in everything she did, from the blithe risk-taking as she staked hundreds of millions of pounds at her trading desk to her careless, casual affairs, to security now with her boyfriend, Eddie, to her whisky and her glorious laughter and her uninhibited en-joyment of life, of the moment.

The fragility was, in its own way, strength. Her awareness that everything could be lost in an instant gave her a rich life, well lived. It gave her an edge.

She wondered sometimes if anyone suspected, if anyone saw the shadows behind her sunny exterior. No one really *knew*, she was sure of that. Her two closest friends, Jacob Goldsmith and Mosami Matsumoto, might have glimpsed the hidden side, the fear and the risk-taking it engendered, but they never discussed it, never went beyond the image Sarah had created for the world. They knew something else was there, but they knew to leave it alone.

The money screamed across the wires, its provenance fading in a maze of electronic transfers that shifted it, hid it, broke it up into manageable wads, which would be withdrawn and redeposited elsewhere, obliterating the trail. Antonio Fieri, the mastermind of this operation, smiled with pleasure. He loved the foreign-exchange markets—massive trades, huge profits, a river of gold.

Fieri left nothing to chance. His willingness to take risks was matched by a readiness to eliminate them, with extreme violence, if necessary. These skills had guided him to the top of organized crime in Italy, and rendered him almost invulnerable to threats from rivals or the judiciary.

To the uninitiated, there was nothing in his physical appearance to suggest his power or ruthlessness. He was middle-aged, short, overweight, with a lumbering gait and thinning hair, dyed black. Still, a sense of menace oozed from him, from the limpid, watchful eyes which seemed to calculate and predict every nuance of human behavior, penetrate every protective screen. In other circumstances he might have been a student of the humanities, a psychiatrist, or a detective, so keen were his powers of perception. But, devoid of empathy, driven by greed and ambition, he had become instead a murderer, and a brilliant financier for the Mafia.

These days he killed by proxy, the thrill of direct involvement having waned. He preferred to occupy himself with the clinical business of laundering and making money, and of all his schemes, this, his latest, was unsurpassed.

He replaced the telephone. His fat fingers left sticky imprints on the plastic. He calculated his profits and smiled in satisfaction. Seven million dollars in three hours. Easy money. And clean. So much cleaner than blackmail, extortion, drugs, or murder. Just voices on a telephone, numbers on a screen, a few squiggles on scraps of paper. And quick, too. All it took was a few seconds, and the money hurtled round the globe.

Fieri grinned, his face splitting into a wide crack like the gash in a Halloween mask as he pictured pounds, dollars, deutsche marks, and yen flying through the sky. Four hundred million dollars' worth. How far would they stretch end to end? he wondered. Rome to New York in tenners? He laughed, eased out of his chair, and waddled over to the fridge in the corner of his office. Four hundred million dollars in ten months. He poured himself a glass of champagne and drank to easy money.

Had Fieri known where his paper trail led, the champagne would have turned to bile in his mouth.

On a sweaty trading floor in a merchant bank in the financial district of London, known as the City, a young foreign-exchange trader put down his telephone, resisting the urge to whoop with delight. Another $3 million for the numbered account. And a quarter share for him. It was becoming a bit of a problem, he thought, laughing to himself, spending so much money surreptitiously.

James Bartrop, director of Counter-Narcotics Crime at MI6, sat in his office in Century House, a twenty-story tower at 100 Westminster Bridge Road, southeast London. Designed in 1961, it was typical of office buildings of that period: gray, grim, characterless, dreary, unpopular with its occupants. The only distinguishing feature was the anti-bomb netting that protected the first eight floors.

Soon MI6 was to move to its new building in Vauxhall, just south of the River Thames, less than half a mile diagonally from the Houses of Parliament. The building, which had cost £240 million to construct, could not have been in greater contrast to Century House. It was a product of the self-aggrandizing style of eighties architecture. It had been tagged the Towers of Babylon by the press, which gave it a vaguely ludicrous air. It was de-

several interesting calls. The first call is from someone who does not identify himself. He just tells Calvadoro to buy dollars and sell sterling. Six hundred million dollars, broken up in installments of twenty-five. Then Calvadoro calls three different brokers here in London and gives them orders for two hundred million apiece, telling them to break it up between the usual accounts in bundles of twenty-five."

Bartrop sat inhaling deeply, waiting for the punch line. Forshaw leaned forward slightly, his back still ramrod straight.

"Mauro, the head of station in Rome, thought that he recognized the voice of the anonymous caller." Forshaw paused for effect. "He thought it was Fieri."

Bartrop raised an eyebrow in a gesture of refined interest which, many times and always unsuccessfully, Forshaw had tried to emulate.

"I'm having the voice checked. But the interesting thing is that whoever it is seems to want to disguise the size of his trade. It is possible that he is managing money for twenty-four different accounts, but I doubt it. More likely the trade is suspect. In the foreign-exchange market, six hundred million attracts attention. Twenty-five million does not. All the records will show will be a series of trades for twenty-five million dollars, with no apparent connection."

Bartrop exhaled loudly. "What time did this happen?"

Forshaw smiled. "As you just guessed, half an hour before the Bank of England announced it was cutting interest rates by one point."

"So we have a leak somewhere in the central banks, possibly even in the Old Lady?" For centuries the Bank of England had been referred to colloquially as "the Old Lady of Threadneedle Street."

signed not to blend in with its environment but to bellow its individuality, to trumpet its presence from every buttress, tower, and green-tinged window—not, perhaps, the most appropriate home for MI6, or the Secret Intelligence Service, as it was formally known. But then, SIS was on the point of being "avowed"; in other words, its existence would soon be recognized by Act of Parliament, and this new building in its shameless way seemed to announce the fact to every even casually informed passerby.

Along with a new building, MI6 had a new role. One of the side effects of the end of the cold war and the ensuing "peace dividend" was a need for self-justification on the part of the security services. Assets formerly tied up with fighting communism had to be redeployed. Great new threats to national security—primarily drugs and terrorism—were identified. MI5, under its new director general, Stella Rimington, won additional areas of responsibility in the fight against terrorism, particularly the IRA, and now coordinated the intelligence-gathering activities on the Provisionals.

MI6 stepped up its activities in the realms of illegal narcotics, economic intelligence, money laundering, and organized crime. This process had been under way for some time. The Counter-Narcotics Crime Section (CNC) had been established in 1987. MI6 now had a major international role in this area, working with the FBI, the U.S. Drug Enforcement Agency, and British and American customs. It also liaised with the Financial Action Task Force, which was specifically targeted at combating money laundering.

A high percentage of the illegal drugs entering the U.K. were controlled by a sinister alliance of the South American drug barons and the Italians, who acted as the South Americans' European agents. James Bartrop was under intense pressure to infiltrate this alliance and the networks it spawned, in order to intercept and reduce the importation of drugs into the U.K. One of the prime movers behind this international cartel was, Bartrop suspected but could not yet prove, Antonio Fieri.

Bartrop had first become aware of the existence of Fieri ten years earlier, when he had been head of station in Rome. Fieri, a suspected lieutenant in the Sicilian Mafia, was rumored to be suborning national and local politicians, ensuring that lucrative building contracts were handed to Mafia companies. There was never any proof, just suspicion. Fieri had always managed to outsmart the various authorities who were on his trail.

Bartrop had kept his eye on Fieri while rising through the ranks of Six, or the Firm, as it was known to staff, or the Friends, to informed outsiders. Now he was director of CNC, and according to intelligence reports, Fieri was one of the top men running the Mafia's drug and financial operations. If Bartrop were to allow himself anything as simplistic as a single target, Fieri was it.

Bartrop rose from his desk, walked to the window of his office, and looked out at the Thames flowing dirtily by. He squinted at the sunlight dancing off the river. It was a perfect May day. He stood immobile, his palms against the window, staring out.

He made an angular silhouette against the sunlit glass; nervous energy pared the fat from his bones. He wore a dark suit, elegantly tailored, which emphasized his slimness. His physique was that of a man in his twenties. Only his face betrayed the approach of middle age. The skin was tawny from too many cigarettes, and deep lines spread out from his eyes and around his mouth.

His face was extraordinarily mobile, questing and expressive. But it could also shut down into cold inscrutability. He was a consummate actor. He combined calm reflection with an almost computer-like speed of analysis. This produced a mind of real

brilliance, and hastened his progress through the Firm. Some said one day he might be chief.

He was widely respected but had a sizable contingent of detractors, who said that perhaps he was just a bit too clever. He had heard such criticism, and laughed it off disparagingly. He turned his acute powers of observation outward. He avoided introspection whenever possible.

His intercom buzzed. He returned to his desk and hit the on switch. His secretary, Moira, announced that the deputy director of CNC, Miles Forshaw, wanted to see him.

"Send him in," said Bartrop.

Seconds later Forshaw appeared. Bartrop gestured to the seat opposite his desk. Forshaw sat down and began to speak.

"Something came in last night." He scratched his chin, speaking in the slow, measured tones that never failed to irritate the more mercurial Bartrop. "A report from the Italian desk. You know that financier we've been investigating, Giuseppe Calvadoro?"

Bartrop nodded.

"Well, we picked up a most interesting snippet of information. Got some gardening services people in there yesterday to replace some withering plants. They wired his office and telephone for half a day, got the bugs out of there before the next sweep."

Bartrop laughed. Calvadoro was a pillar of Milan society, eminent and respectable, almost above suspicion—the perfect broker for a crime boss. Bartrop had no proof that Calvadoro had Mafia clients, but whoever his clients were, they possessed secrets worth protecting. Twice a day a security firm swept Calvadoro's lavish offices on the Via Turati, even checking mail in case a bug might be found lurking in the spongy interior of a brown Jiffy bag.

Forshaw continued. "Anyway, Calvadoro made and received

"It looks that way." Forshaw propped his chin on his hands and looked pensive.

"And Antonio Fieri might be our insider trader?"

The two men smiled in unison. Bartrop's eyes became opaque as he sat silent for a while. He turned to Forshaw.

"It's almost unthinkable that the leak, if there is one, is coming from the Old Lady. Information on sensitive topics like interest-rate cuts is known only to the men at the top. I've known Barrington, the governor, for years. He might be a fool, but he's never a criminal."

The intercom buzzed in Moira's office. Bartrop's disembodied voice filled the room.

"Get me the governor of the Bank of England, would you, Moira?"

The governor was just leaving for his monthly meeting with the chancellor. He had got as far as the vaulted hallway when his secretary caught up with him.

"Ah, Governor, I'm pleased I caught you," she announced, catching her breath. "A James Bartrop is on the line. He says it's urgent."

Anthony Barrington paused for a second and frowned at the name Bartrop, then turned with reluctance and walked sedately back to his office. No official of the bank ever hurried anywhere. The Old Lady of Threadneedle Street was an oasis of grace amid the noise and perpetual motion of the City. Scurrying down corridors was undignified. Leave that to the American investment bankers in their glass-and-marble towers.

Barrington shut the door to his office, sat behind his desk, and waited for his secretary to connect him.

Chapter Two

At seven o'clock that evening, Bartrop's black Rover pulled into the courtyard at the rear of the Bank of England. Bartrop disappeared through a door off the courtyard, followed by his Royal Corps of Military Police bodyguard, Munro, who doubled as his driver, and took the lift up to the governor's private flat.

Barrington waited in his study, wondering what the meeting was all about. At least he had got Bartrop to come to him. He had been irritated that morning by the other man's suggestion that he go to Century House. It was customary for the world to go to the bank, and that included an MI6 director, as Bartrop well knew.

The ring of the bell interrupted Barrington's thoughts. He walked over to the door and peeped through the spyhole. He saw Bartrop standing some way back, with another man behind him. *Bodyguard*, thought Barrington, opening the door and greeting Bartrop loudly. He held the door open questioningly toward the bodyguard, who gave him a grave nod, thanked him, and said that he would wait outside. Barrington led Bartrop through to the sitting room, grateful that he did not have to be shepherded in this way.

Barrington got drinks. The two men sat opposite each other in covered armchairs. Barrington was relaxed, his long legs stretched out before him, his right hand hanging limply down the outside of the chair. In his left hand was his second gin and tonic of the day. He was ten years older than Bartrop, and looked it. His hair was thinning, peppery gray. The evidence of too many good dinners and bottles of claret was clearly visible in the jaw and waistline. But unlike Bartrop's, his skin was almost unlined, and his features were a study in contentment. His eyes were smiling, benign. He expected no more surprises from life. Bartrop, studying him, felt a twinge of contempt. He sat sideways, legs back, nursing a whisky, and listened to Barrington's small talk. After a while his impatience must have become obvious, for Barrington drifted into silence.

Bartrop drained his whisky and shifted fractionally in his chair.

"Governor, I was wondering if you might explain to me the procedure you went through yesterday when you cut interest rates by a point."

"Quite simple," said Barrington, rising to refill their glasses. "We wanted to give the economy a bit of a boost. Inflation is under control. We'll watch it carefully, of course, but at the moment it's not a problem. No adverse circumstances, need for a cut, so the chancellor and I agreed on a one-point cut, as soon as practicable. The markets were steady yesterday afternoon, so we decided to do it then."

"Who knew of the decision in advance?"

Barrington paused for a second. "All the main central banks, apart from the Japs, who were asleep." He handed Bartrop his glass. "Why do you ask?"

Bartrop watched the flicker of irritation in Barrington's eyes. Understandable, since it was a question loaded with unpleasant implications, especially when asked by an intelligence man. Bartrop prided himself on his perceptiveness. Yes, it was irritation, nothing more, he was sure. Anyway, Barrington had too much to lose and little to gain by passing on inside information. A successful career as a merchant banker, which had added to his already considerable personal wealth, ruled out money as a motive. So what was left? Bartrop smiled slowly. Barrington was hardly a subversive. Intelligence reports had given him a sparkling bill of health when his appointment as governor had first been suggested. If there was a leak from the central banks, Bartrop felt confident that it didn't come from Barrington. He drank some more whisky and told Barrington about Antonio Fieri and his suspected gambles in the foreign-exchange market.

Barrington agreed that Fieri's trades looked suspicious. And he had news of his own to confide to Bartrop. A week ago, he had taken a call from Jonathan Gilbey, the head of the accounting firm Dawson-Lane. Gilbey had informed him that a junior employee of DL had reported suspicions that something funny was going on in the foreign-exchange, or FX, proprietary trading department of a big American bank in the City. Proprietary trading, Barrington explained to Bartrop, was where a bank assigned a certain amount of its own capital to specialized traders who would use it to "take positions," that is, to gamble in the markets on the bank's behalf. This contrasted to more run-of-the-mill FX market-making, where banks merely acted on behalf of clients— insurance companies, pension funds, industrial companies, or other banks—buying and selling currency on their instructions. Proprietary trading was riskier for the bank concerned, but potentially infinitely more rewarding.

Barrington explained that the Dawson-Lane employee had been one of a team working on an audit of Inter-Continental Bank, known as ICB. He noticed that the profits made by the FX Prop Department, as it was known, had recently leapt to unusual heights.

When Barrington asked Marcus Aylyard, the head of the Markets Supervision Department of the Old Lady, to look at the monthly profit-and-loss statement of ICB's FX Prop Department for the past year, it became evident that there was substance to the young auditor's suspicions. Aylyard saw a pattern. Substantial profits were earned in the immediate aftermath of intervention by the central banks in the FX markets, or after market-sensitive actions such as changes in interest rates. Up to a point, that was normal. Intervention and interest-rate changes were both cause and consequence of volatility in the markets. It was during periods of volatility that the biggest profits were made, and losses taken, by speculators in the FX markets. But it was the size, the consistency, and the sudden onset of ICB's profits that gave cause for concern, for they raised the possibility that someone in ICB was trading on inside information. If that was the case, the inside information could come only from the highest level.

Bartrop and Barrington agreed, it looked as if there was a leak at the heart of the financial system. A leak that would appear to link one of the most senior members of the Italian Mafia with a seemingly respectable City bank.

Barrington began to worry. He could ill afford trouble on his watch. But Bartrop felt the adrenaline of possibility. This was the best news he had had in weeks.

He got to his feet. "I must go, Governor." He extended his

hand. "I'd appreciate it if you would leave the ICB problem alone for a few days. I have an idea that might address your concerns and mine. I'll call you tomorrow or the next day."

The governor shook Bartrop's hand and saw him out. Then he retook his seat on the covered armchair and stared thoughtfully out over the City skyline. He couldn't make up his mind about Bartrop. The man had a certain mercurial charm, and the leaps and turns of his mind were amusing to observe, but inevitably he was discomfiting. They had met on several occasions, mainly at Financial Action Task Force meetings, and each time Barrington had felt conscious of a keen purpose in Bartrop beyond that of the obvious task at hand. What it was, he could never discern, but that did not diminish its power. Again today he wondered what role that brilliant mind was devising for him. Bartrop had, in abundance, imagination and the power to manipulate. Barrington, despite his position at the apex of the City, was not by nature a cynical man, but he was extremely wary of James Bartrop.

What was the idea the other man had alluded to? Something brilliant and devious, requiring his connivance in some way. Well, he would cooperate, within reason. Antagonizing the Friends was not wise, and anyway, in this case they had common interests, or so he thought.

Had Barrington possessed the power of foresight, he would have followed a very different course from the one that Bartrop at that very moment was mapping out for him.

The two men met again the following evening at eleven-thirty, after Barrington had finished an official dinner. They sat opposite each other in the governor's flat. Bartrop spoke bluntly, seemingly without guile.

"About our mutual problem, Governor—I have a proposition for you that might suit us both."

Barrington sat listening.

"It looks as if there might be a link between Fieri, whom I am chasing, and ICB, which is your responsibility. But link or no link, you need to investigate ICB." He paused. Barrington nodded.

"Now, if my understanding is correct, many of these City frauds vanish into thin air if a team of outside investigators or regulators is sent in."

"Yes, that can be the case," said Barrington. "Ideally, you need to be on the spot, catch the fraudsters red-handed. Then you have better evidence and a much stronger case. Incriminating evidence can disappear very quickly when the investigators go in." Barrington warmed to his theme, detecting a note of sympathy for the difficulties faced by the bank in policing the City. "Then, of course, there's the problem of the invisible victims of fraud. Supposedly sophisticated organizations or individuals are often reluctant to admit they have been duped. They would rather swallow their losses than their pride. So sometimes it is incredibly difficult to get them to cooperate with the investigators."

"Yes, I can imagine," said Bartrop. "So what would be ideal, as regards catching the miscreants red-handed, not frightening them off, would be to have a colleague work as an investigator." He paused, carefully studying Barrington.

"You mean an undercover agent?" Barrington said sharply.

Bartrop smiled. "Yes, that is exactly what I mean. And we don't have any FX traders in the Firm, so what I would like very much for you to do is to come up with suggestions." He paused to let the significance of his words sink in. Barrington sat with his head tipped very slightly to one side, wary but interested. Bartrop continued. "You need to find someone who is a very good trader and who is curious, inquisitive, but above all, trustworthy and discreet."

Barrington let out a bark of laughter. "First of all, that is a very rare combination. Traders are among the most garrulous, untrustworthy people I know. Lying is an essential part of their job, and they are almost congenitally indiscreet. Second, even if I could find your perfect spy, how are you going to get him into ICB?"

Bartrop looked straight ahead, in a pose that suggested that while Barrington's understanding was defective, he would do his best to ignore it.

"First of all," he said, emphasizing "first," lacing it with the faintest ridicule, as if Barrington had been caught using his fingers to count, "I am sure that with your innumerable City contacts you shall be able to come up with a suitable candidate. And second, these traders seem to flit from bank to bank more often than I change my shirt, so it shouldn't be long before a vacancy arises."

Barrington, to his regret, could find no fault with this argument.

"Why not use someone already in ICB?" he ventured.

"Well, it would be the obvious thing to do, wouldn't it, except that we don't know who to trust. Much better to bring in an outsider, don't you think?"

Of course I bloody well think, thought Barrington, not missing the implication. He wondered why Bartrop felt it necessary to be so gratuitously unpleasant. He wanted to stamp his authority on the meeting and bring it swiftly to an end.

"Your idea sounds reasonable, Bartrop." He got to his feet in dismissal. "I'll look into it."

"I'd be grateful, Governor. Also, if you could engineer a lunch or dinner with the most suitable candidates, to feel them out, as

it were . . . I'm sure you will think of a way to do it discreetly."
Bartrop glanced at his watch. It was twelve o'clock. He rose to
leave.

Barrington was silent for a while. "When we find your spy"—
he stressed the last word, knowing it would annoy Bartrop—
"what happens then? How do we proceed?"

"That very much depends upon what sort of person he is."
Bartrop paused, as if mulling something over. "Actually, Governor, I'm glad you brought that up. As far as procedures go, do
you want to do this directly? You might prefer to use a cutout."

Barrington wondered if Bartrop was using jargon deliberately
to irritate him. "A cutout?"

"The deputy governor, perhaps, or your supervisory chap,
what's his name? Aylyard?"

"Why would I want to use someone else?"

Bartrop shrugged. "Common practice . . . in case anything
goes wrong."

"What could go wrong? Are you telling me that you foresee
some kind of trouble?"

Bartrop laughed. "No. Not at all. As I said, it's common practice. We're not clairvoyants. If anything does go wrong, you're
protected. Someone else takes the fall. That's all."

Barrington took a step closer to Bartrop. "Let's get this
straight, Bartrop. If there is any likelihood of anything going
wrong, we can forget this whole thing now. I'll find another way
of investigating ICB."

Bartrop said levelly, "I don't read palms, Governor, but I do
know that there is no reason why this operation should run into
trouble. I wouldn't have put it to you if I didn't think it would
work, if it wasn't controllable."

"And you'll control it, will you? You'll make sure nothing does
go wrong?"

Bartrop hid his rising impatience behind a mask of geniality. "That's my job, Governor. I'll do everything in my power."

Barrington smiled. "Good. Well, that's all right, then. You do your job, I'll do mine. And as for the deputy governor . . . well, between you and me, there's a perception in the markets that he's not up to the job, too lightweight. I'm not quite sure about his shelf life. And Aylyard, well, I just don't think he has the *gravitas*. He's very good at his job, but he's not what you'd call a people person."

Bartrop moved toward the door. "Fine, Governor. I'll leave it to you, then."

The two men shook hands and said goodnight.

Bartrop took the lift down to the courtyard, followed by Munro, who slipped in front of him to open the door to the Rover. Bartrop stepped through the open door and sat back on the cloth seat. Munro drove quickly along the deserted City streets. Bartrop gazed through the window, pensive. At this stage, it might be courteous to notify the Security Service, MI5, of his planned activities, but it would be better not to have any complications. No need to indoctrinate any more people than was strictly necessary. And he wanted Fieri very badly . . . and anyway, this was not an operation for Five, or even for Six. It was a City affair, run by the governor of the Bank of England. If it yielded information that proved useful to him, that was just good fortune. He smiled at his reflection in the bulletproof window.

Chapter Three

When the phone rang, Sarah Jensen was in bed, entwined with Eddie, making the most of his last few days in London before he flew off on his latest expedition. Sarah stretched out a naked arm and scooped up the receiver. It was her colleague, David, and he was worried.

"Sarah, look, it's half past eight, you're an hour late already and Carter's looking for you, in a bit of a steam, unlike him . . ."

Sarah let out a peal of laughter. "So what did you tell him?"

"I said you had a doctor's appointment first thing."

"Brilliant," said Sarah. "They never see anyone before nine. Half an hour for my appointment, three quarters of an hour from Chelsea to the City—I'll see you about ten-fifteen." Before he could say anything she had dropped the receiver back in its cradle and turned her attention back to Eddie.

At ten o'clock she finally eased free of Eddie's arms and

slipped out of bed. Eddie watched her walk across the room. She was tall, about five foot nine, slim, with long, elegant muscles, and curvaceous. She walked lazily, unselfconsciously, enjoying her nakedness. She took a long shower, bunching up her long brown hair and holding it aloft with one hand, out of the reach of the water. A trail of shrinking puddles lay in her wake as she stepped out, wrapped herself in a thin cotton kimono, and walked across her bedroom and out onto the roof terrace. She loved it best in June, colored and scented with roses, six-foot palms, gardenias, and geraniums.

She lingered for a moment, letting the warm air dry her damp skin, before returning inside, rifling through her wardrobe, and picking out a lilac linen dress and tan shoes. Slinging her bag diagonally across her chest, she kissed Eddie and, smiling, let herself out. She hailed a taxi ambling down the King's Road and made it to her desk in Finlays, one of London's oldest and most prestigious merchant banks, by eleven o'clock.

John Carter, the chief executive and Sarah's former lover, came by five minutes later.

"Nothing wrong, I hope?" he said with a courteous smile.

"Oh, no." Sarah smiled. "Just one of those regular checkups, you know."

Carter's face colored slightly. David Reed, sitting on Sarah's left, suddenly suffered a violent coughing attack. Sarah glared at him.

"I wonder," said Carter, ignoring Reed, "if you would like to come to a client lunch tomorrow. They would like very much to have an FX person there," he added.

Sarah checked her appointment book. "Wednesday the tenth." She looked up and smiled again. "Yes, that's fine, John."

Carter returned to his office and called Barrington.

"It's all fixed, Governor. We'll see you tomorrow."

"Well done. Incidentally, do you have a résumé for this girl Jensen?"

"I'll dig one out from Personnel and have it faxed to you this afternoon."

"Actually, I would rather have it biked, if you don't mind," said Barrington.

"By all means." Carter, puzzled by the secrecy, wondered again what this was all about.

It had started ten days ago, when Carter's secretary, in that special nasal tone of hers that sought to convey that she, Kate Smithson, was impressed by no one, announced that the governor of the Bank of England was on the line. Carter took the call, wondering whether it was business or social. He had known Barrington for almost twenty years, they were neighbors in Surrey, and they had developed strong social and professional ties. Since Carter's divorce, Barrington's wife, Irene, often invited him over to dinner on weekends.

But this was not a social call. After the usual pleasantries, Barrington had started chatting about the FX markets, finally coming round to asking Carter what his own FX traders were like. There was only one worth talking about, Carter had told Barrington, describing Sarah Jensen. Barrington had then deluged Carter with questions about her—what was she like, just how good was she. Finally, he suggested perhaps they could all have lunch together sometime. He was, he said, particularly interested in talking to real live market practitioners.

Carter had not attached much significance to the call, which he put down to an attack of ivory-toweritis. The governor was probably fed up with the company of other central bankers, most of whom were rather dry individuals. He had probably decided on the spur of the moment to do a bit of slumming, and who better than a foreign-exchange trader for that? The governor would be in for a surprise, Carter thought to himself, if he ever did meet Sarah Jensen.

Carter then forgot about the call, and so was surprised when the governor rang again that morning to announce that a free lunch had suddenly come up. The governor of the Bank of Romania had, God bless the man, canceled on him, something to do with domestic problems, so perhaps he and Carter could have a spot of lunch tomorrow, and incidentally, would Carter like to bring along that foreign-exchange trader he had mentioned, what was her name, Jensen . . . ?

So, filled with curiosity, Carter had arranged it. The governor probably wanted to hire her, he thought, looking over Sarah's résumé before taking it to his secretary and asking her to bike it round to the bank for the governor's personal attention.

Fat chance, thought Carter. The bank couldn't afford to pay her half what she was making at Finlays. Since Sarah had started work with them four years ago, rival banks had regularly tried to lure her away. Neither Carter nor the head of the trading floor, Jamie Rawlinson, had any intention of letting her go. They would pay whatever was necessary to keep her.

She was the best of her generation, without a doubt. She had an instinctive feel for the markets and a flair for taking risks. She took great delight in her successes, but if she lost money, unlike many other traders, she never took it to heart. Carter felt that she was in some peculiar way ambitious, driven, certainly, but she had no time for office politics. Unlike most of her contemporaries, who publicly pledged allegiance to their employer of the moment, Sarah made it plain that she was only working long enough to save up her running-away money. All she was really interested in was going climbing and exploring with her brother, Alex, or her new boyfriend, what was his name . . . Eddie. Yes, that was it, thought Carter ruefully.

Sitting in the quiet of his office, Carter gave way to the clamor of thoughts that assailed him almost daily, and from which he found no refuge. He first tried the anesthetic of rationalization. It was only natural, he told himself, that Sarah should want to go out with someone her own age. He had always suspected that she first slept with him because she felt sorry for him. It certainly wasn't for career advancement; her talents needed no help. No, it was compassion, a gentle desire to help that led her to him. His wife was divorcing him. She never saw him, she claimed. If he was not at his office, he was at a boring client dinner, and she had long since given up attending those. So Carter began to take his star trader, Sarah Jensen, to the business dinners. The clients loved her. And it wasn't long before he did, too, pouring his heart out to her, a woman who understood both sides of his life, the personal and the professional. And beautiful, too. She was irresistible.

They were together for six months. His confidence and his faith in life were restored by her. He had wanted to marry her; he had never said so, but was sure that she could sense it. She had told him, ever so gently, that she was not right for him. Stripped of vanity by age and the paring attacks of his wife, he knew that what Sarah really meant was that he was not right for her. So, with great sadness, he let her go.

They still saw each other, and they had dinner together about once a month. He couldn't resist asking about boyfriends. For a while there had been no one, she said, but then she had met this friend of her brother, Alex's. That had been a year ago. Carter was, he thought, about as reconciled to it as he would ever be.

While John Carter was reflecting on his relationship with Sarah Jensen, her résumé was speeding through the City on the back of a motorbike, on its way to Anthony Barrington. Half an hour later, after having passed through the bank's mailroom, where it was security-screened, it landed on Barrington's desk, leapfrogging his in tray. Barrington sliced open the package and read with interest.

Sarah Louise Jensen, nationality British, had been born in New Orleans in 1966, which made her twenty-seven, Barrington calculated. She was educated at Hampstead School for Girls and Trinity College, Cambridge, where she took a double first in maths. Her interests included jazz, reading, skiing, mountain climbing, and traveling. After graduating, she spent a year traveling around the United States before starting work at Finlays.

Barrington turned to the reports written by the Personnel Department at Finlays. The first, in abbreviated note form, described her professional abilities. Outstanding trading record. Highly and consistently profitable. Cool, professional trader. Last year made £6 million for her department. Less consistent attendance record. Perhaps feels her contribution to profits earns special dispensation. When confronted about attendance irregularities, cheerfully owns up. Barrington laughed as he read a handwritten note scrawled above the last comment: "At least she is honest."

The next section was made up of various administrative details. Barrington skimmed over bank account numbers, mortgage subsidy, health insurance. He paused as one set of figures leapt from the page. Last year, total earnings: £400,000; base salary £100,000, bonus £300,000. Even by inflated City standards, that was spectacular. It made her one of the highest-paid women in the City, one of the highest-paid traders.

There was no doubt, thought Barrington, that Sarah Jensen was perfectly qualified as far as her professional abilities went. The only question now was whether she had the psychological makeup of a spy. That, of course, could only be discovered face to face. What qualities he was supposed to look for, he wasn't entirely sure. But one thing he did know was that he was looking forward very much to meeting Sarah Jensen.

He began to push her papers back inside their envelope, wondering as he did what she looked like. Before he sealed the envelope and locked it in his safe, one last detail jumped out at him. He noticed that her next of kin were listed as her aunt and her brother. That was strange, he thought. She was only twenty-seven. Surely her parents could not be dead. Perhaps there had been a rift? Not a good sign, he thought. He buzzed his secretary and asked her to get Carter on the line.

Five minutes later the two men spoke. Carter explained that there had been no rift. Sarah's parents had been killed in a car accident in New Orleans when she was eight, in a collision with a drunk driver.

"It must have scarred her, something like that," said Barrington.

Carter was silent for a while, as a succession of memories and unasked questions invaded his mind. All surmise, he told himself, dispelling them. All he said was, "I think she's come to terms with it, in her own way."

Barrington, satisfied, rang off. As far as he was concerned, Sarah Jensen was still the perfect candidate.

Chapter Four

Sarah cursed under her breath. Why was it that whenever she wanted to leave early, the markets all of a sudden became frantically busy? She glared at the columns of numbers on her trading screen, which seemed to flicker more vehemently under her gaze. With another curse, she snapped off the power, and her screen died with a wheeze and a flash of silver. Her neighbor, David Reed, looked up in surprise as she gathered up her handbag.

"You can't leave now, Sarah. It's only two o'clock. It's not even as if the market is quiet." He feigned annoyance. This was a regular game, greatly enjoyed by both parties. He enjoyed the vicarious rebelliousness, she his collusion.

"Yes, I can," she fired back. "The market's putting me in a bad mood, and when I'm in a bad mood I lose money. You know that." She shrugged as if in resignation. "So I have to leave." Her straight face began to crumble and she turned away quickly. "If anyone wants me, tell them I'll call them tomorrow."

David sat back, defeated by her logic. "Don't forget," he yelled at her departing back, "you've got lunch with Carter tomorrow." He knew from experience that her "bad moods" could last for a couple of days.

Waitrose on the King's Road was filled with mothers and babies, old-age pensioners, and the scruffily artistic, who Sarah had always thought dressed to depress. It was altogether a different clientele from that she would have encountered if, like the multitude of wage slaves, she had fit her shopping around the nine-to-five, or for her what should have been the seven-to-five. She much preferred the catholic crowd of two-thirty, she decided. Shopping after six, you always ran the risk of being mowed down by hyped-up pinstriped types let loose from their desks, taking out their frustrations at the wheel of a cart.

She lingered at the meat counter, examining the plastic-covered joints of beef, turning them this way and that, watching the blood run. She picked out the juiciest she could find, a rich dark red fillet steak, oozing blood. She then picked out potatoes for roasting, tomatoes for baking, clumps of sprouting broccoli, and a handful of red and green lettuces. Wheeling her cart over to the dairy section, she heaped in single and double cream and half a dozen free-range eggs.

Her purchases from the supermarket complete, she lugged her bags around to Chelsea Farmers' Market, just off the King's Road. Then she bought a packet of vanilla beans from Neal's Yard, a health-food shop, and popped into the off-license, ducking as she went through the low entrance. The off-license was a glorified hut, but it had a good selection of wines and a variety of friendly, if not always well-informed, assistants. She took her time picking out three bottles of 1982 claret and two of champagne. Then she clattered home.

Sarah lived in a house in Carlyle Square, a leafy garden square in Chelsea. She had bought the house a year ago for £800,000, borrowing half that amount and plundering her savings to finance the remainder. Her borrowings were huge, but sustainable, as long as she kept her job. The notorious instability of her profession she tried to ignore.

Until relatively recently, she could not have handled financial insecurity, but the wounds of childhood were being papered over by adult successes, and while she was not happy with the precariousness of her position, she refused to worry, and told herself that she found in it a gambler's thrill. A few more good years in the City and she would pay off the mortgage. She would then start to save up what she called her running-away money.

Intelligent, successful, popular, and beautiful, Sarah was never truly lighthearted. Her life now was in many ways as good as it could be, but when she chose to analyze it, which was rare, she always feared that her current peace was something in the nature of a lull. This feeling, always latent, had come to the surface with the imminent departure of Alex and Eddie. They were due to leave the next morning for a three-month expedition to the Himalayas.

She let herself into her house and walked upstairs to the sitting room, where she found the two men sitting cross-legged on the floor, poring over a large, rumpled map. They were so engrossed by it that at first they were unaware of her presence. Sarah watched them in silence. Alex, her baby brother, twenty-five, brave, kind. She always thought of him as an innocent—bright, but totally uncynical. He was predisposed to being happy.

From the ages of eight and six, Sarah and Alex had been brought up by their father's sister, Isla. When their parents died in the accident, Isla went to America and brought the children back to England to live with her in London. With the security of childhood shattered, Alex almost crumbled. Sarah grew up overnight and held him together. He suffered grief, he missed his parents, he was lonely and afraid, but he limited himself to the normal range of human emotions. And he had Sarah and Isla to look after him. He took comfort from them, and after a few years he was a happy, normal child.

He directed his energies to the outdoors, specifically to mountains, with which he became obsessed. Like Sarah, he went to Cambridge, but he spent most of his time climbing and graduated with a third. He didn't care. As long as he had time and money to climb, he was happy. Time he had, and money Sarah had. Alex spent nine months of the year climbing and lived the remainder in Sarah's house. It was the perfect lifestyle for him, and Sarah reveled in his happiness.

Just over a year ago, climbing in the Alps, he had met Eddie, a twenty-nine-year-old Australian. They teamed up on the mountain and came home to Sarah's house together. A friendship grew slowly between Eddie and Sarah. After four months they became lovers.

Like Alex, Eddie was tall and slim, with the powerful but unobtrusive muscles of the rock climber. He made documentaries for Australian television, and in between he climbed. Like most of Sarah's men, he was dark. Unlike most of them, he was kind and gentle. His sense of humor was sharp, almost caustic, but that was a product more of intellect and nationality than of malice, for he was almost devoid of ill feeling or any kind of unpleasantness. The only drawback to their relationship, thought Sarah as she walked forward to kiss him, was that with all his climbing and traveling, they saw each other rarely. Parting was always a nightmare, as Sarah reconciled herself to missing him and fearing for his safety on the mountain.

The two men smiled as she approached. Eddie reached up and took her hand, pulling her down for a kiss.

"So you managed to sneak out, then?"

She laughed and sat down between them, her bags tipping over. Containers of cream and bottles of wine rolled out, ignored.

"So show me again where you're going."

Alex traced a route through Bhutan.

"So you reckon it will take about six weeks for the trek, and then what, a few weeks of general exploring, a stop-off in Katmandu, then another month rooting around in the jungle?"

"About that," said Eddie.

Sarah stretched out her arms and hugged the two men to her.

"I can't believe you're going tomorrow. What am I going to do for three months without you two?"

Her tone was light, but both men knew she was sad. They had seen it often enough before when they left her. Alex, and Eddie increasingly so, knew that behind the confident exterior was a searing vulnerability. Sarah did her best to hide it, probably would never acknowledge it to them, but all three knew it was there.

Alex tried not to think about it. It worried and disconcerted him, as it always had. She was his big sister, had always looked after him. She was supposed to be the strong one, but there was a precariousness to her that sometimes made him afraid to leave her alone. She had been better since Eddie came on the scene. She had calmed down a lot. For the first time in years, maybe the first time ever, Alex thought she was happy, secure even. He gazed at her. No. Not secure. He wondered if she would ever be secure, if she could ever let herself be. He watched her laughing with Eddie. She was happy, though, of that he was sure.

"Come out and join us," said Alex spontaneously.

"Yeah. Why don't you?" asked Eddie.

Sarah smiled, got up, and carried her bags through to the kitchen. Not this time, she thought to herself as she unpacked them, but soon. Very soon.

The alarm went off at six. Sarah leaned over, shut it off, then rolled back to Eddie and clung to him. He hugged her tightly, burying his face in her hair, kissing her neck, her face, her eyes. After a few minutes he moved away slightly and gently stroked her hair back from her face.

"I meant it last night—you could come and join us. It is feasible logistically at several points, and you know how much we both want you to come."

Sarah smiled into his earnest eyes. "I know, and I will sometime, but not just yet. If I went with you and tasted all that freedom, I don't think I'd ever be able to go back to work again."

"That's not so terrible, is it?"

"I can't give up yet," Sarah said simply.

Eddie pulled her to him and kissed her again. He knew he couldn't win this argument. She would say it was the money, that she needed to work for another year or two, then she would have enough to stop. But he felt it was more than that. He suspected that for all her rebelliousness, she had a desire to act out the motions of a normal life, that she in fact took comfort from her routine, and from the constraints on her time that she so railed against. It was, he supposed, the orphan's desire for security and regularity.

Given what he knew about her, it was a reasonable analysis—incomplete, but as far as it went, correct.

They left at nine. Sarah stood on her doorstep and watched their taxi disappear. Her ballast was gone. She turned, went back inside, and took a long hot shower.

They hadn't gone to bed until five. After plates full of fillet steak, then lashings of crème brûlée, they had sat up drinking, talking, and laughing, playing noisy rounds of backgammon. Sarah and Eddie had probably slept for half an hour.

She stepped unsteadily out of the shower, weak with exhaustion and emotion. She glanced in the mirror as she stood drying herself. Her eyes were hollow, dull. She stared at her reflection for a long while, then smiled faintly and turned away.

They had gone. They would come back. She had to believe that. But it was an absence laced with uncertainty, and it was that which turned her stomach, filled her with fear, and, perversely, fulfilled some secret longing. For even though she fled from uncertainty, she needed it, was drawn to it by a subconscious desire to master it. It destabilized her more than anything else, but still she sought it out, invited it into her life.

Sarah looked through her wardrobe, wondering what to wear. Remembering her client lunch, she picked out a smart but severe black linen suit, perfect for her mood, she thought. The black drained the color from her already pale face. She went into the bathroom and added color to cheeks and lips, smearing concealer cream beneath her eyes to cover the black rings. If she drank enough coffee, she should manage to fool them, she thought.

Anthony Barrington was chatting to John Carter in one of the private dining rooms in Finlays when Sarah Jensen walked in. He watched her walking toward him. She was about five foot nine, probably six feet with those shoes, he reckoned. Her stride was long and confident. She looked to him like a splendid Amazon, albeit one seeking to mask her charms. She was somberly dressed, her outfit almost funereal, and with her hair scraped back off her face, the overall effect should have been clinical, even threatening. But in his eyes it was anything but.

It was, he decided, the face that did it. More particularly, the eyes and mouth, the curve of jawline, cheek, and eyebrow, a rich voluptuousness poised to overflow from every feature. The severity of hair and outfit merely acted as a foil. But as she came closer and stopped before him, he was surprised to see a web of lines around her eyes—fine lines, not quite wrinkles, but unusual for a woman of her age. As she extended her hand to him, she smiled, and the lines seemed to pull upward. It was a brave face. Her eyes lit up, she took his hand, greeted him in a deep, rich voice, but for a fraction of a second there was a void in the beautiful face, an emptiness of emotion. It disappeared quickly. He returned the handshake, looked into her smiling eyes, but took with him the impression that she had not the slightest interest in meeting him.

Out of the corner of his eye, Barrington noticed Carter looking at him strangely. Quickly he turned his attention to his old friend, who he realized had been speaking to him. He decided honesty was the best policy.

"Sorry, old boy, I was quite distracted by Miss Jensen here. You hadn't prepared me."

Carter shot Sarah a wry look. It wasn't the first time this had happened. "My fault entirely," he said, smiling. "I understand completely."

Sarah laughed politely, as if at a well-worn joke.

"Drink?" asked Carter, moving toward Sarah.

"Bloody Mary." She smiled gently.

He gave a slight nod and turned quickly to Barrington, who asked for the same. Carter busied himself with the drinks as memories assailed him. Saturday mornings, Bloody Marys. A long time ago. He mixed the drinks: usual measures for himself and Barrington, extra Tabasco for Sarah, with her impervious Cajun palate. He laughed to himself and turned to the others with a brisk smile.

Barrington watched Sarah, who drank rather than sipped. She stood beside him, looking out the window at a sea of rooftops below. They were on the top floor of the Finlays building, a modern tower block, and the older City buildings, including the Bank of England, lay below them, exposed.

"Quite a view," said Barrington. "One of the best views in the City."

Sarah turned. "Isn't it? I love standing here just gazing out. The buildings look so different, vulnerable almost, from this an-gle—no bustle, no security guards, just yards of exposed roof-top." She grinned suddenly. "If I were to rob a bank, I'd definitely start from the roof."

Both men burst out laughing.

"Well, thanks for the tip," said the governor. "Any rooftop break-ins and we'll know whom to suspect."

"Oh, don't get too excited, Governor. You'd never catch Sarah," said Carter. Both men laughed again. Sarah smiled at the window and lit up a cigarette.

The headwaiter appeared at the door to signal discreetly to Carter that lunch was ready.

"Thank you, Fred. Go ahead," said Carter, gesturing for Sarah and Barrington to sit down. He sat at the head of the table, Barrington to his right, Sarah to his left. Fred brought in a warm chicken-liver salad.

"So you were at Cambridge," said Barrington, swallowing a mouthful.

Sarah nodded, feeling a wave of tiredness and boredom, and answered mechanically, "Eighty-five to eighty-eight. Maths. Trinity."

"Double first," added Carter.

"Out of our league." Barrington laughed.

Sarah smiled politely.

"Pure maths?" continued Barrington.

"Yes, but I took a few philosophy papers."

"What a mixture."

"Perfect combination," said Sarah. "Heart and mind."

"And now the City?" Barrington leaned across the table to her, raising an eyebrow.

"Yes. It doesn't really follow, does it?"

There was a silence as both men waited for her to elaborate. She shrugged her shoulders. "Isn't it obvious?"

Barrington looked mildly embarrassed. He coughed. "Yes, but apart from the money. Isn't there any other reason? Don't you enjoy FX trading?"

Sarah laughed, then quickly smothered it out of politeness. "Well, I wouldn't say I enjoyed it. That's a word I'd use more about climbing, skiing, or reading a book. It interests me. I like gambling, and strangely enough, the markets are a mixture of heart and mind, the logical and the emotional. On Black

Wednesday, or the night when Gorbachev was deposed, emotion played as great a part as logic. Market sentiment, psychology, the attempts to manipulate the market, or at least other traders—yes, that's fascinating. It's like a great game."

Barrington was silent for a while. Carter watched him watching Sarah. Then Barrington said, "A game? It has serious consequences."

"Oh, I never said it didn't. Yes, fortunes are made and lost, hundreds of millions, billions, government economic policy smashed, political careers ended . . ."

"You speak as if that's not your concern," said the governor, slightly agitated.

"It's not," replied Sarah. "Or at least not in my capacity as an FX trader. My job is to make money for my employer. Pure and simple. As an individual, of course I care about economic policy and people's careers being destroyed, but that's what happens if you're in that arena. It could just as easily happen to me. If I got it wrong a few times, lost a few million pounds, John would have no hesitation in firing me, and he'd be right."

"You don't seem to be worried by the prospect," said Barrington.

"What's the point?" Sarah shrugged.

Carter spoke suddenly. "As far as I'm concerned, Sarah's just about the best FX trader in the City. She's the last person to worry about being fired."

Barrington sat back in his chair. "She's that good, is she?" he asked with a smile.

"She's that good," replied Carter.

Courses came and went. Fred brought in a chocolate mousse. Sarah, to Barrington's delight, attacked hers with relish.

"I was very curious to learn from John that you were born in New Orleans," he said, turning to her. He noticed with dismay that she gave a slight start at the mention of New Orleans, and he remembered that her parents had been killed there. He cursed himself inwardly. How could he have been so insensitive? However, her face recovered almost instantaneously, leaving him wondering if he had perhaps imagined her reaction. She smiled as she answered.

"My mother was from New Orleans. Her family were early French settlers who had come across from Nova Scotia. She was beautiful, my mother, darker than me, black hair, deep brown eyes, smaller, daintier . . . My father went to New Orleans on holiday, met my mother, and never left." Sarah spread her hands. "There you have it." She looked down, reached for her glass, and drank some red wine.

"Ah, that explains it, then," said Barrington, anxious to inject a light note.

Sarah raised a quizzical eyebrow.

"Your coloring," said Barrington, as portentous as Poirot.

"The original Cajuns, the French and Spanish settlers, all intermarried," explained Sarah, and with the Italians, probably with the Negroes, too. So we're darker than the run-of-the-mill French." She smiled, as if at a memory. For the first time the whole of her face lit up, and Barrington noticed, almost with a jolt, the intensity in her eyes.

Lunch was over. Barrington nodded to Carter and shook Sarah's hand warmly. She smiled, said goodbye. He was pleased to see that she looked slightly puzzled. She made no effort to conceal it. She was letting him know that she knew she had been some kind of exhibit, and that she also knew there was no point in asking him what the real purpose of the lunch had been. She had almost a patient air, as if she would find out anyway in time, as if sooner or later she always found out.

A most extraordinary woman, he thought as he made his

way back to the bank. In the quiet of his office, he called Bartrop.

"I think I have found your spy for you."

Bartrop ignored the taunt. "Good, tell me about him."

"He is actually a she, with brains, wit, and beauty. Deeply serious, too, and apparently one of the best FX traders in the City."

"Sounds promising. What's her name?"

"Sarah Jensen."

"Full name?"

Bartrop heard a rustling of papers. "Sarah Louise Jensen."

"I presume she's British."

"Well, she's a British citizen, but her mother was American, and—"

"Her mother's dead?" interrupted Bartrop.

"Yes, and her father, killed in a car crash when she was eight."

Bartrop fired off a round of questions at this.

"She's not what you would call ordinary, is she? New Orleans, orphaned, brought up by an aunt, Cajun blood. It sounds like a recipe for disaster, Governor."

"You might think that, Bartrop, but you haven't met her. She is as normal and well-adjusted as anyone you could hope to meet."

"Well, if you say she is, then I am sure you are right. But we'll just run a few checks first. Exotic women often seem to have more than their share of skeletons."

"You go ahead and vet her. I'll send round a copy of her résumé. It might help."

"Thank you, Governor. It will give us a bit of fodder to be getting on with." Pleased with his closing blow, Bartrop rang off.

Chapter Five

Bartrop rang the governor back the next evening.

"You're sure about this girl, then?" he asked.

"I was sure yesterday and I'm still sure today, unless of course your spies have found any of those skeletons you talked about."

"No skeletons. We ran a check. Nothing known against. She seems a normal enough young woman. Works hard, seems to play quite hard too, drinks her share, but it's not a problem. Lots of boyfriends at Cambridge, but she seems to have calmed down now. You knew she went out with Carter for a while, did you?"

"Of course I knew," lied Barrington. "So what?"

"So nothing in particular. Anyway, Governor, the long and the short of it is, she'll do."

"What do you mean, she'll do?" barked Barrington. "She's perfect."

"All right. She's perfect. So you're happy to go ahead."

"Yes. I'm happy."

"I mean you personally."

"Look, Bartrop. We've gone over this. I have your assurances, and what's more, having met Sarah Jensen, I can tell you for a fact that Marcus Aylyard, or anyone else for that matter, wouldn't work. She's a very cool customer. I don't think she'd be very impressed by Aylyard. The whole point of it is to impress her, to win her confidence, to get her to do what we want, no?"

"Correct."

"Well, then, no cutout. I'll do it myself."

"Right. That's very good, Governor. Now we'd better deal with the indoctrination of Miss Jensen."

Barrington recoiled at the other end of the telephone. Disgusting word, *indoctrination*.

Bartrop continued. "The most important thing to bear in mind at all times is that the indoctrination be limited. We need to tell her a good story, Governor, to convince her, to get her on the hook, but nothing that could compromise our operations with Fieri. She is absolutely not to learn anything about that. As far as she is concerned, this is just a City fraud. If we need to tell her more later, we'll cross that bridge then. Let's just see if she takes the bait. Then if she gets the job, we can see how she performs, how good she is, how reliable, and take it from there."

"Sounds reasonable," said the governor.

"Good luck," said Bartrop, and the two men rang off.

The governor reached into his desk drawer and pulled out a hip flask of whisky. He took a quick nip and called Carter. He wanted, he said, to see Sarah Jensen the following morning, say at nine o'clock at the bank. Could Carter arrange it? Just as smoothly, Carter replied yes, of course. So, still, was much business done in the City—simple requests, questions unasked until a decent time had elapsed and the matter was deemed to have passed. Favors sought and granted invisibly. A resilient way of doing business, casual, supremely effective, oiled by connections and tradition.

Carter rang Sarah at her trading desk. There was no reply. She had left early and was at that moment walking from the tube to Carlyle Square. She let herself into her house and wandered slowly through the silent rooms. She paused in her bedroom, looking around listlessly. She felt the absence of Alex and Eddie like a physical pain. She decided to go for a run. It was only a partial antidote, but it was something. She took off her clothes and began to rummage around in an old oak chest of drawers for her running kit. She pulled on baggy denim shorts and a white T-shirt. She found her jogging shoes, sturdy with thick corrugated soles, airing on the roof terrace.

She did five minutes of stretching exercises, her hamstrings straining after a few sedentary days. Then, with her house keys clenched in her right hand, she jogged across the bustle of the King's Road, down Old Church Street, and left onto the Embankment. The rush hour had already started, and the fumes were strong. Sarah ignored the cars, nose to tail in places, and ran with her eyes fixed on the river. She watched a riverboat delicately maneuver around Cadogan Pier and drop off a score of tourists before roaring off to Chelsea Harbor, half a mile farther west. She took the boats home from work sometimes, from Swan Lane in the City. It was out of her way, but worth it for the view, especially of the Houses of Parliament, and for the change.

Breaking into a slight sweat, she crossed over the pink-and-white confection of Albert Bridge and turned into Battersea Park. The sunbathers were packing up for the day, to be replaced by a horde of joggers converging from all sides. Sarah ran quickly, overtaking some of the slow joggers but sticking to the grass. She circled the park, sprinted the last hundred yards, and then walked, breathing hard, across the bridge. She had run for half an hour, and, very slightly, she felt her spirits lift.

She walked west along the Embankment, the Lots Road power station looming like some theme park creator's dream, only real. Delicate orbs of white smoke hung in the air above it, testaments to the life within. Sarah visualized a riot of glorious cogs and gleaming copper wire inside, despite having once peered in and seen only rows of what looked like giant radiators.

The outside was definitely better than the inside, as was true of its sister station, sadly defunct, which towered over Battersea Park. That really was in danger of being turned into a theme park. Much to Sarah's relief, the developer concerned had gone broke in the late eighties, and the power station had returned to a state of graceful limbo.

Cooling down nicely, Sarah turned off the Embankment and walked back up Old Church Street to the King's Road. There she encountered a procession of bankers filing along in starched shirts, lugging briefcases. Half the City seemed to live in this area. She saw a couple she recognized and ducked quickly into Carlyle Square. Every time you went out, you bumped into someone you knew. Anonymity was impossible. It drove her mad.

The phone rang as Sarah was walking through the door. She ignored it. The only people she wanted to speak to were far from telephones, in an inaccessible land. John Carter spoke to her answering machine; could she call him, please. It was urgent.

Sarah picked her way through the echoing house. It was six-thirty; she was exhausted. Whatever it was could wait till tomorrow.

She retrieved a bottle of whisky from the sitting-room floor and took it to her bedroom. She had a shower, then headed for bed. It looked stark and empty, the bedclothes in disarray. She put on an old pair of pajamas and snuggled into the rumpled sheets. She was pouring out a generous whisky when the phone rang again. She picked it up with an irritable "Hello."

It was John Carter again. He asked apologetically if he was interrupting and said he was sorry, he didn't want to plague her, but he had to get in touch with her.

"Don't worry," said Sarah, reaching for her drink.

"You seemed tired yesterday at lunch."

"Oh . . . sorry. Was I unbearably dull?"

Carter laughed. "Not remotely. The governor found you absolutely charming."

"Did he? That's nice. But you know, I didn't have a chance to ask you, why bring me along to meet the governor? The whole thing struck me as a bit peculiar."

"It was peculiar," admitted Carter, "but it was his idea, not mine. He said he wanted to talk to an FX trader, so I suggested you." He paused for a while. "Now he wants you to go to a meeting with him at the bank."

Sarah was bemused. "What's all this about, John?"

"I honestly don't know. Perhaps he wants to hire you."

"I can't believe that the governor of the Bank of England wastes his time on staff recruitment."

"You're right. But look, Sarah, all I can do is pass on his message. He said he would very much like to see you at the bank tomorrow morning at nine o'clock."

"All right," said Sarah. "See you there at nine."

"Oh, no!" said Carter. "You will be going alone. It will be just you and the governor."

At 9:00 A.M. Bank station was thronged. The Northern and Central lines converged here, disgorging a stream of sullen faces onto the streets. Carrying the *Financial Times* or the *Sun* like passports, they traipsed to Birley's for muffins and cappuccino and carried them off in white paper bags to fill the lifts of a hundred financial institutions with the smell of breakfast.

Sarah Jensen walked out of the Underground station and took ten paces up Threadneedle Street. Dazzling sunlight bounced off the tall white buildings and made her squint. She ran up a short flight of stairs leading off the street, her high heels clicking on the smooth stone. She smiled at the tall man in a black hat and pink three-quarter jacket who stood sentry at the doors to the Bank of England. The vivid pink was called Houblon Pink, she remembered, after Sir John Houblon, the first governor of the bank after it was founded by Act of Parliament in 1694. The color of his manservants' outfits, it had been retained ever since by the gatekeepers and parlor stewards who acted as butlers. Years earlier, when she had first started work in the City, Sarah had taken a guided tour of the Bank of England. She hadn't really seen much. The most interesting areas were out of bounds. She felt a quiet thrill to think that today she would see the inside of the governor's office.

Sarah smiled at the gatekeeper and walked across the large, vaulted entrance hall on a floor covered with mosaics depicting coins through the ages. She approached the messenger who sat at the inquiry desk. She announced her name, adding that she was there to see the governor.

The messenger smiled; he had been warned to expect her. He picked up a telephone, dialed, waited, and then announced that Miss Jensen was on her way. He nodded to a gatekeeper, who turned to Sarah, uttered a courteous "This way, madame," and escorted her to the area known as the Parlours, the grandest, most imposing area of the bank, which housed its governor, deputy governor, and directors.

Out of a perverse habit, Sarah tried to memorize the route, but she was soon lost, distracted by her footsteps echoing on the mosaic floors, the rich paintings hanging on the walls, the high ceilings, the fine cornices, and the distant sounds coming from behind closed doors.

The gatekeeper stopped before an oak-paneled door and tapped respectfully. A secretary opened the door. The gatekeeper ushered Sarah inside, announced her name with gravity, and withdrew silently. With a polite smile, the secretary led Sarah through to the governor's office.

Barrington stood with his back to her, gazing out the window to the internal courtyard. With his hands clasped behind his back, he seemed to be reflecting on the scene of calm and order that lay before him. The courtyard was ringed by the offices of the senior officials who ran the Bank of England. It was a matter of some pride among them that they looked in on themselves rather than out over the world outside. It was seen as a symbol of Olympian objectivity. The bustle of the Underground station with its grubby traders seemed a long way away. The atmosphere was civilized, refined, like the men who inhabited the offices.

The governor turned, smiled broadly, walked over to Sarah, and shook her hand. "Hello, Sarah. How nice to see you again." He gestured to an armchair by the wall, under a painting of a traditional seascape. "Won't you sit down?" He smiled and sat down opposite her, his eyes resting lightly upon her. Just as yesterday, Sarah felt she was being sized up.

"First of all, I'd like to thank you for coming at such short notice." He paused, crossed one long leg over the other with an elegant sweep, and leaned toward her. She gave a slight smile and waited for him to continue. His confident smile flickered for a moment, while he seemed to call on some internal reinforcement, then returned, stronger than ever. "I would ask you to bear in mind that what I am about to discuss with you, you will not be at liberty to disclose at any time. If you feel unable to comply with this, then it would be inappropriate for me to continue." The smile faded, and he watched her eyes closely.

Sarah paused for a second, trying to silence the curiosity raging in her mind. She answered in the same measured tones. "Of course, Governor. Whatever you have to say I shall treat in the strictest confidence."

Holding her eyes steady with his, he began to speak. "As you know, there have been a number of scandals involving City firms over the past few years. They have done a great deal of damage to our reputation."

Sarah nodded. There had been Guinness, Blue Arrow, Barlow Clowes, Maxwell, and BCCI, as well as a string of lower-profile cases. BCCI, the Bank of Credit and Commerce International, otherwise known in the City as the Bank of Crooks and Criminals International, had been particularly embarrassing for the Bank of England. It had been the center of the biggest fraud in banking history, and the Bank of England, as chief regulator, had come under direct attack in the Bingham report for its handling of the multibillion-dollar fraud and the eventual shutdown of the bank.

The governor frowned. "There is growing pressure for Parliament to enact anti-City legislation, which would weaken us even more and wouldn't necessarily do anything to help us with the fraud problem."

Sarah understood his concern. The City abhorred being told how to behave by what it regarded as ignorant outsiders. It preferred self-regulation.

"I fully appreciate that in some respects the existing system doesn't work as well as it could—for instance, those fraud trials which collapse after years of investigation, costing tens of millions of pounds." The governor glared at an invisible enemy. "It's farcical, and highly embarrassing."

Guinness, thought Sarah, and Blue Arrow. The Guinness case had been notorious for what looked like an uneven application of justice between defendants, some having their cases dismissed for reasons that were not fully understood or appreciated, particularly by those who received prison sentences. Blue Arrow had been something of a problem for the Serious Fraud Office. The case had taken two years and £37 million of taxpayers' money to come to trial. The list of charges was long and overcomplicated, and the patchy convictions that had been secured were overturned on appeal. The previous governor, although not responsible for the conduct of the SFO or the trial proceedings, had come in for indirect but wounding criticism by virtue of his position as the effective chairman of the City.

Seeing signs of solidarity in Sarah, Barrington warmed to his theme. "Of course, there has always been fraud in the City, but there was a time when it was possible to deal with certain cases discreetly, when the governor would be informed of transgressions and have a quiet word with those concerned, who would then retire gracefully. It was quite clever, really. The City policed itself, the fraud was cleared up, and no damage was done to the City's reputation. A sort of self-regulation. So much more effective than public washing of dirty linen, don't you think?"

"It has its merits," said Sarah, "as long as the self-regulators are incorruptible."

The governor shot her a sharp look. "Someone has to play God."

"I thought that's what the courts were for."

"Ideally, yes," said Barrington, slightly irritated, "but my point is that in certain, admittedly very rare cases, the system doesn't work." Sarah held herself in and waited for him to continue. He shrugged. "You see, we can't afford any more high-profile scandals. The fraud won't go away, but we have to come up with a new way of dealing with it, without relying too heavily on the existing system of prosecution by the SFO. Of course, the SFO will continue to play a prominent role, especially in advanced cases of fraud. And after the publication of the Bingham report, we created a new investigatory body, which has helped. But I can't help feeling that when the investigation teams go in with sirens wailing, as it were, some of the fraud just goes underground."

Sarah nodded. "So what you're saying, and correct me if I'm wrong, is that there are some frauds that can't be detected after the event—that you need to be there at the time, unobserved, almost, to catch the culprits red-handed. Otherwise the evidence is just circumstantial."

"Exactly," said Barrington, leaning across his desk toward her with a smile of triumph. "That is exactly it. And it is just this kind of problem I would like you to help me with."

Sarah felt her pulse quicken, the exhaustion of the last few days forgotten. She sat forward in her chair and listened intently.

"Are you familiar with Inter-Continental Bank?"

"Who isn't?"

The governor smiled. "Indeed. They have quite a reputation. Sharp, highly profitable, flamboyant—you know, work hard, play hard—but there's a bit of a whiff about them." The blue eyes narrowed. "Particularly their foreign-exchange department. Their trading record looks too good to be true, and rumors are circulating." He paused, studied her for a few seconds, then committed himself. "They're looking for a new foreign-exchange proprietary trader. I think you would be perfect for the job, if you want it."

Barrington smiled. Sarah sat very still, her legs coiled around the legs of the chair, her fingers clasped together. She stared past Barrington's head, out the window and into the courtyard beyond. She felt a surge of excitement. She had always wanted to work at ICB; ICB on your résumé was an accolade of sorts. If you could survive there, you could survive anywhere. It was the elite of the City, hard and ruthless, but it paid well. Blood money, thought Sarah.

She smiled at Barrington. "I'd love the job. But you had better tell me what I have to do first."

"First get the job. I'll arrange for a head-hunter to call you this afternoon to arrange an interview. With your record, you should have no trouble impressing them. Then, if you get the job, as I am sure you will, just watch and observe. Carry on just as you would normally, but keep a lookout for anything suspicious. Anything that seems to you even remotely out of the ordinary about the trading behavior, you report back to me. If ICB's traders do turn out to be breaking the law in some way, then I will deal with them."

"How?" asked Sarah.

"Very simply. I shall inform them that unless they resign quietly and stay out of the City, I shall arrange for them to be prosecuted. If they have any sense, they will accept my offer, don't you think?"

"Well, yes, I suppose so, if they are guilty and we can prove it."

"Don't forget, under my plan we shall never see the inside of a courtroom. We don't need courtroom evidence, just enough to satisfy me that they are committing a crime. The evidence would seem to suggest quite strongly that a crime is being committed at ICB. All you need to find out is who exactly is committing what kind of crime."

"You make it sound simple," said Sarah.

The governor laughed. "Sorry. I'm sure it won't be simple, but I think with time and care and quiet firsthand observation you should come up with something. Of course, it will be an experiment for both of us. We'll have to feel our way, as it were, make it up as we go along . . ."

Sarah leaned back in her chair and was silent for a while. "Aren't there professionals who do this kind of thing? I mean, I'm hardly qualified."

"That's just it," said the governor. "We can't use professional investigators. They'd scare the quarry. And as I said, what we need is a FX trader, a colleague, to watch firsthand. Someone who understands the business, who understands what is normal and what is suspicious, and someone who can observe without attracting any suspicion whatsoever." He leaned forward again. "We've looked around, Sarah. And you're perfect."

"We? Who's we?" she asked sharply.

Barrington inwardly cursed. He smiled. "John Carter, of course. It was he who recommended you."

"Oh," said Sarah. "John, of course. So he knows all about this, does he?"

"Well, no. Not everything. Some of it. But I would ask you not to discuss it with him. I've said the same to him. So he might feel awkward if you raised it."

"All right," said Sarah, vaguely irritated. "If you ask me to keep it secret, naturally I will." She frowned slightly. "But tell me, how did you come to suspect ICB, and how did you decide to investigate in this way?"

Barrington swallowed the urge to sigh heavily. She was relentless.

"An auditor became suspicious, reported it to his superiors. The chairman came to see me," he explained matter-of-factly. Then he smiled as if to instill confidence. "Then it was a question of deciding the best way to investigate. I thought about it for a couple of weeks, decided on this experiment. Then it came down to finding the right person, and that's where John Carter and you come in."

Sarah sat back in her chair and lapsed into silence for a while. The governor waited. Finally Sarah spoke.

"It sounds interesting, intriguing. I'd be willing to give it a try, but tell me, who are the suspects, and what exactly do you suspect them of?"

Barrington smiled, delighted. "You remember I said that the FX department's profits looked too good to be true?" Sarah nodded. "Well, those profits took off when a character called Dante Scarpirato arrived. It seems to me that he is either a genius or a criminal."

"And how do you think he makes his money if he is a criminal?"

Barrington smiled and shrugged. "That's the problem—trying to understand the criminal mind. They are much better at thinking up crimes than the regulators are. I really don't know what it could be. I could hazard a few guesses, but then I might send you off in the wrong direction."

"What fun. So now I have the license to think like a criminal." For a brief moment Barrington looked horrified.

"Don't worry," said Sarah, laughing. "Just a joke." She hurried on. "This Dante Scarpirato—do you know him?"

"I've met him once," said Barrington, almost with distaste. "He's full of himself, icily arrogant, smooth—you know, Annabel's, Mark's Club, permanent suntan. He's supposed to be utterly ruthless, acts like everyone's his enemy. Gets away with it because he makes so much money. He's not a very likable character." Barrington paused and looked intently at Sarah. "Although I'm told he has a way with women."

Sarah laughed again. "Don't worry about me, Governor, I can look after myself."

"I'm sure you can, very well." He began to stand, and then, as if remembering something, sat down again. When he spoke, Sarah thought he seemed slightly ill at ease.

"Oh, yes, that reminds me. There is something I must tell you. You might decide after I have told you this that you no longer wish to proceed. If so, I shall understand completely, so you must be honest."

Sarah tilted her head to one side and watched him, saying nothing.

"This operation—well, you do it at your own risk. You might think it necessary to sail just a little bit close to the wind, you know, in getting your information. As far as I am concerned, that's fine. The information is very important to us. Worth a few risks, if you're willing to take them. I don't want to know exactly how you would work, what you would do, if you got the job. Your methods would be your business. But I have to warn you that if you are caught out in any way, while I will give you all the assistance I can behind the scenes, I cannot come to your aid publicly. You will be undercover, and you shall have to stay that way. The best thing you can do is not get caught." His face had reddened slightly, but not noticeably. He delivered his lines well, his veneer of confidence smoothly intact.

Close to the wind. Don't get caught. Isn't that always the way in the City, and everywhere else, for that matter? thought Sarah. She started to voice her thoughts, but decided on reflection that this would be one joke that the governor would probably not find funny. She stayed silent and forced herself to think seriously about what he had said. After a while she spoke.

"As I said, Governor, don't worry about me. I can look after myself. I understand the rules." She added almost as an after-thought, "Just as long as they don't change as we go along."

He wasn't quite sure why he found that remark slightly omi-nous. It was just a throwaway remark, perfectly innocent. He was, he decided, seeing too much of James Bartrop, catching from him a suspicious mind.

"Good. Well, I think that's it, then." The governor looked vague for a second, then remembered. "Ah, the file." He retrieved a buff folder labeled ICB from his desk drawer and slid it across to Sarah. "You had better take a look at this. There are some annual reports, press cuttings, and an internal report prepared by our Banking Supervision Division. It shows ICB's FX trading profits shooting up over the past year, ever since Scarpirato started working there." He rose to his feet, the meeting over. "So, Sarah, good luck with ICB. Let me know how you get on." He scribbled on a slip of paper. "Here is my personal number at the bank, and my number in my little flat here, in case of anything particularly urgent." He gave the paper to Sarah, shook her hand, and said goodbye.

Sarah walked through the echoing corridors and out into the bustling streets. There was something that didn't quite satisfy her. She felt as if the governor were holding back. It was probably just his suspicions about the nature of the fraud, she decided. After all, if he had only vague guesses, it made sense that he kept them to himself; otherwise he might prejudice her investigation. She might end up chasing red herrings and miss the true fraud.

The excitement of her task drove the worries from her mind. She was committed. The governor had hit upon her weakness. She loved secrets and excitement. The covert or taboo exercised a strong appeal. In many respects, the governor couldn't have picked a better candidate.

Sarah could have declined politely, forgotten their conversation, and gone back to her desk at Finlays. But she hadn't, and her life and many others were to change irrevocably as a result.

Chapter Six

Sarah glanced at her watch. It was ten o'clock. The thorough-
fare at Bank was quieter—most people were well into their
morning's work—but there was still an air of bustle and urgency. Threadneedle Street, Princes Street, Cornhill, King Wil-
liam Street, Queen Victoria Street, and Poultry all converged at
Bank, which is both functionally and geographically the heart of
the City. Sarah had never been able to walk through those
crowded, windblown streets without feeling a pulse of excitement. She always seemed to walk faster, to look around more
sharply. Now she felt more than ever as if she were at the center
of something. Feelings that had perhaps been based on illusion in
the past were now grounded in fact: she had been approached by
the man at the heart of the City; she was working for the governor. As facts go, it was of course invisible. Not that that mattered

to Sarah. She had met the governor, come to an agreement with him, and that was real enough for her.

She turned off Threadneedle Street into Old Broad Street and walked the few hundred yards to Finlays. Inside she flashed her pass at the security men and took the mirrored lift up to the trading floor. She ran her pass through the automated security check, and the doors clicked open onto a large, overcrowded, open-plan room, which looked as if it were staging a high-tech jumble sale.

The first thing that hit her was the noise, then the chaos. Three hundred traders, salesmen, and assistants sat cheek to jowl like battery hens. They clustered on either side of a gridlike maze of desks, which filled the room. Some lounged around, then suddenly, as if struck by an electric current, reached for their phones, leapt to their feet, shouted and gesticulated wildly before lapsing seconds later into temporary apathy. Sarah walked into the maelstrom. There were few landmarks—a flag here, a porno calendar there, nothing more personal. Nothing soft—no plants, no deep armchairs or luxurious carpeting. Computer screens, stacked high-rise on top of each other, jostled for space with coffee cups, phone handsets, and bond calculators on minimal desktops. Piles of documents, annual reports, and bond prospectuses balanced precariously at thigh height. The floor was raised to house the miles of cables that fed the hundreds of computer terminals. The ceiling was dropped to accommodate the viciously efficient air conditioning system needed to cool the battalions of machines and the overheated traders. People sat elbow to elbow in the claustrophobic gap between.

Sarah picked her way through noisy greetings. "Hey, big night tonight, Sarah?" She had dressed for the governor, slightly more smartly than she did for the trading floor. She couldn't help laughing. The traders never missed a trick. They were just off by a few hours this time. Acute observers of fashion, they could read chapters into the cut of a skirt or the length of a hemline.

Sarah guarded her private life jealously, which only fueled the speculation. Occasionally she would invent tidbits to keep the traders happy, but, sharp judges of human nature, they rarely swallowed her stories. She had an elusive quality, and although the traders found it impossible to understand her, they never gave up trying.

Hiding behind her laughter, Sarah took her seat and switched on her screens, tuning in to a vast electronic world where stories were told in the movement of numbers. The machines woke up with a whine, then began to chatter nervously. Their flickering green cast a sickly pall on pale faces that never saw enough daylight. Sarah read the announcements that scrolled over the bottom of her Bloomberg screen, a computer terminal that provided constant news updates as well as a wide variety of historical financial information: "London coffee largely recoups losses"; "European veg oils subdued by uncertain Chicago"; "Boxing— Eubank and Benn spar with words"; "Wiesenthal slams world indifference to Yugoslavia."

Same old news. Nothing happening.

At two-thirty David Reed yelled to Sarah from his seat two feet away: "Sarah Jensen! Head-hunter. Line one."

Various heads swiveled, and a group of traders laughed.

"Oh, do something useful, will you?" said Sarah, exasperated. She hit line one. "Hello."

"Sarah, it's Sue Banks."

"Hello, Sue." Sarah smiled. All the traders knew all the head-hunters and the aliases they used in a futile attempt at confidentiality. Blowing their cover was a game the traders never seemed to tire of. Sarah was called almost every week by recruitment consultants trying to lure her away from Finlays, and each time the traders would make a huge joke out of it. So this time they listened, but not too closely. They had heard it all before, they thought. Sarah turned her attention back to Sue Banks.

Sue was the founder of Placements Unlimited, probably the most prestigious of the recruitment firms in the City. She was a six-foot blonde brimming over with confidence and charm. The two women had met three years ago, when Sue first attempted to lure Sarah from Finlays. They hit it off instantly, and shared a high personal and professional regard for each other.

"Look, Sarah. I know you don't want to move, but hear me out." Sue raced ahead before Sarah could say anything. "There's no point in being coy, or having you round to brief you, so I'll dispense with the formalities. ICB proprietary FX trading. Big-ticket. They're the top payers in the City, as you know. You'll be able to name your price. Time for a change, Sarah. Four years at Finlays. You'll start getting rusty."

Sarah broke in, laughing. "All right, Sue. I don't need a lecture. But tell me more."

"Well, that's it, really. The only downside as far as I can see is the head of the department."

"Oh, you mean my prospective boss?"

"Yes, if you want to put it like that. Dante Scarpirato. He's an interesting one, Sarah. Scares the shit out of me . . ." Sarah heard voices in the background and imagined Sue's secretary walking in with a fistful of messages. "Sorry, Sarah, I've got to dash. Seven o'clock tomorrow is convenient for Scarpirato. Can you make it?"

Sarah smiled in anticipation. "I can make it."

Sarah got home at six. She bolted the door behind her, walked into her bedroom, tore off her clothes as if they were burning, and wrapped herself up in an old dressing gown, belting it loosely at the waist. Peering into the bathroom mirror, she took out her contact lenses, then put on some smudgy glasses which she cleaned on the hem of her dressing gown. On bare feet she padded into the sitting room, poured herself half a glass of whisky, filled it to the brim with water, and stretched out on the sofa. The phone lay next to her on a carved Moroccan table she had picked up a few years ago in Marrakesh. She switched on the answerphone and turned off the volume—no disturbances, no tempting voices to interrupt her.

The heavy briefcase lay on the floor by the sofa. Sarah unlocked it and took out the file on ICB. It was about two inches thick, filled with magazine and newspaper cuttings, annual reports for 1991 and 1992, and the Bank of England's internal report.

Sarah flicked through the annual reports, but as she expected, they told her nothing she did not already know. ICB was a U.S.-based investment bank with ten subsidiary offices in the world's major financial centers. It had the range of activities common to international banks: corporate finance, fund management, private clients. All were profitable and well respected, but it was for its trading activities that ICB was best known.

ICB was one of the largest traders of financial assets in the world, dealing in equities, bonds, currencies, and a mind-boggling array of derivative products, swaps, options, and so on. The firm employed four thousand people worldwide, seven hundred of these in London. Sarah dropped the annual reports on the floor. It was the Bank of England's internal report she was really interested in. That contained information that would never appear in a public document.

The statistics in the bank's report certainly made ICB look suspicious. In 1992, ICB's net profits were £300 million. Proprietary FX trading, headed by Dante Scarpirato and comprising three other traders, operating on an opening capital base of £28 million, made £45 million. It was a spectacular return. Sarah, used to the monopoly money of the City, was staggered. Finlays, which employed five people on its proprietary desk, with an opening capital base of £15 million, made £18 million in 1992, and that was deemed impressive.

The other intriguing thing about ICB's proprietary trading profits was their direct correlation to Dante Scarpirato. In 1991 they were £9 million. Scarpirato joined in 1992, and they shot up to £45 million. Barrington was right. Scarpirato was either a genius or a rogue.

Sarah finished reading at nine. She rose stiffly from the sofa, bunched up the papers, now scattered across the floor, put them into a plastic bag, and locked them away in a drawer. Then she made her way out into the kitchen and examined the fridge warily. It contained a few remnants of her dinner with Eddie and Alex. She counted back. Three days ago they had all been together. She felt a spasm of gnawing emptiness. Taking a deep breath to calm herself, she retrieved tomatoes, onions, and garlic from the fridge. She attacked the onions and garlic with a razor-sharp knife, losing herself for a while in the contemplation of the herbs and spices lined up in jars on a two-foot shelf above her head.

She had learned to cook as a child. Anything was better than her aunt's infrequent and creative offerings. Isla was a brilliant woman, ahead of her time and in many ways an excellent role model for Sarah, but she was not in the least domestic. Alex and Sarah were left to their own devices for long stretches of time. Isla would regularly become entranced by her research, carried out in a dusty room at the top of the house. Mealtimes would come and go. Isla's next-door neighbor, Jacob Goldsmith, was often out in his garden, tending his plants, a friendly presence. Soon the children took to spending much of their free time with him. His wife had died ten years earlier, and he had no children of his own, so the three of them, over the years, developed a happy symbiotic existence. He regaled them with a limitless supply of stories, from his days with the Royal Dragoons in the Second World War to his travels after the war and then his career back in London.

He regularly cooked for the children, teaching Sarah along the way. Isla came to rely on him, and an unofficial division of labor was worked out between them. Isla helped the children with their homework and gave them extra lessons in their favorite subjects; Sarah's was maths, Alex's geology. Jacob fed and entertained them, became a kind of surrogate uncle. Sarah smiled at the memories. Jacob she still saw regularly, but Isla she hadn't seen for some time. She was teaching at a university in the States now, living on campus, with someone else to cook for her. Perhaps now there would be some flesh on her insect-like frame. If she remembered to eat.

Sarah thought about Jacob again and wondered if she ought to say something to him about her meeting with the governor, but somehow it didn't seem real, seemed more like a product of her imagination than a reality to be discussed, dissected. For the time being she decided to tell him nothing, to keep her own private mystery.

She stirred the tomato sauce and left it to simmer. After half an hour it was ready. She boiled some water, threw in fresh pasta, drained it after one minute, and smothered it with her tomato sauce. She piled the mixture high on a plate and carried it through into her bedroom. She sat down on the bed, plate on her lap, and turned on the TV just in time to hear Nicholas Witchell bid her goodnight. She switched the channel to ITV, content to wait for *News at Ten*, to find out from the sonorous Trevor MacDonald if there was anything new under the sun. There wasn't. Her pasta finished, she phoned ICB's Tokyo office to check on the markets, but there was nothing new there either. They rang off, promising to call her if anything came up.

Yawning broadly, Sarah headed for the bathroom. The ICB cuttings had left a trace of newsprint on her hands. She scrubbed it off vigorously with vanilla soap, splashed her face with cold water, and layered on a swath of the latest miracle cream. Dropping her dressing gown on the bedroom floor, she turned on her alarm and slipped into bed. She fell asleep dreaming of Alex and Eddie.

She awoke at six, scoured her wardrobe, and for the third day in a row dressed with care, in a sober navy linen suit with gold buttons and a crisp white blouse. Perfect interview garb, but by the time her interview came round at seven that evening, the suit bore the creases of a hard day's work.

ICB's offices were on Lower Thames Street, in a modern tower block. It glowered beside the river, its windows shining malevolently. The interior was starkly modern. A huge atrium was cut into the center of the building. It was empty except for the receptionist's desk, two sofas, and a collection of angular metal sculptures which seemed to glare at Sarah as she approached them. A brittle receptionist told her to go to the third floor.

Dante Scarpirato sat in a dark suit in a dark office on a deserted trading floor. He got up as she walked into his office. He stood very still and straight, legs planted firmly—a proprietorial stance. He was slight, fine-boned, the perfect weight for his height, she supposed. His suit too was perfect, as were the white cuffs that jutted below his jacket sleeves and the dark, highly polished shoes. He showed none of the signs of weariness or disarray that characterized most traders after twelve hours in the office. Everything about him appeared calculated, controlled. He moved toward her and shook her hand. They were the same height, she observed, eye to eye.

"Please, take a seat."

Sarah sat down opposite him. Unsmiling, unreadable, he watched her.

After a disconcerting silence, he asked, "So why do you want to work at ICB?" He turned to the row of trading screens flickering in front of him, so that Sarah spoke to his profile. From time to time he punched in a command, calling up another page on the screen, seemingly oblivious to her. He asked another question when he had to, going through the motions.

Sarah knew the technique: affect indifference, cast the other person in the role of supplicant, make him or her work for your attention. It was an ego trip, boringly predictable, and she had expected more from this man. But she had to admit that he played the game well, and she found herself willing him to turn to face her. After five minutes of this treatment she began to feel unnerved; after ten minutes, annoyed.

"Forgive me for asking, but are you interviewing me or that machine?"

Scarpirato swung around to face her, for the first time holding her gaze.

"How important is money to you?"

The question knocked Sarah off balance, first because he so successfully neutered her barb, and second because he asked the one question that pervaded City life but was never asked directly. Only innocents worked in the City for anything other than the money. Everyone dressed up their primary motivation in terms of challenge, excitement, experience, all of which was true but peripheral. To confront venality head-on was taboo. The question was almost obscene.

Sarah took her time. She studied Scarpirato's face before she answered. It was not a conventionally good-looking face, but it was arresting. The skin was well tanned, with a dark glow of stubble. The forehead was high, slightly domed before a receding hairline of wiry dark hair. The lips looked almost blue in the half-light. The nose was long and straight, but it was the eyes that held you.

There was no life in the stilted body that sat across the desk. The whole force of Dante Scarpirato was concentrated in his eyes, so much so you'd think he would die if he closed them. They were large, round, shining brown. The pupils were swollen and the cornea almost filled the eye. The rim of white was a narrow, brilliant circle. They were contemptuous eyes, jaded and bored. Suddenly and shockingly, they lit up with a gleam of mania that flared back out of sight so quickly that Sarah wondered if she had seen it at all. Abruptly, she ceased her contemplation and concentrated on her answer. There was no point in hiding behind a broken taboo.

"Money is the primary motivation."

A faint smile curved his lips. It was the only reaction he bestowed on her.

"Good. It's the only reason for doing this job."

No, it isn't, thought Sarah.

Scarpirato rose from his chair. "I have to go."

Sarah glanced at her watch: seven-thirty. It was the shortest interview she had ever had.

Scarpirato escorted her to the elevator doors. He walked beside her, hip, shoulder, and head on a level with hers. She watched his wrists, which protruded from his cuffs as he reached up to press the button to call the lift. They were delicate, almost like a woman's, except for the thick black hair that covered them. The hands were finely veined, the fingers long and thin. The lift came. Sarah rode down alone.

Chapter Seven

Sarah waited for a while on Lower Thames Street, looking in vain for a taxi. She walked along Upper Thames Street and turned into Suffolk Lane, then onto Cannon Street to try her luck there. It was Friday night. For what seemed like an age all the cabs were busy, ferrying City workers home or on to the bars, cinemas, theaters, and restaurants of the West End. Finally she saw a cab with its orange "For Hire" sign lit up and furiously flagged it down. She jumped in with relief.

"South Audley Street, please. Mayfair." She sank back in the seat, closed her eyes, and dozed.

The taxi dropped her off halfway down South Audley Street. Sarah walked along in the evening sunshine, enjoying the warmth on her face. She loved this area—the hidden streets, the opulent antique shops, the imposing townhouses, the heavy-curtained secrecy. It was quiet now. The office workers had left for home, or for the wine bars closer to Piccadilly, and it was still a bit early for the brightly jeweled, slightly overdressed women to appear. They would start to emerge around nine o'clock, stepping from their mews houses into the back of the expensive cars that purred up and away in seconds.

Sarah stopped outside a delicatessen to admire the rows of salami hanging like stalactites from the ceiling. The rich smell of newly ground coffee wafted out and lured her in. She found row upon row of Italian goodies and bought two tubes of Baci, delicious chocolate and nut concoctions from Perugia, and a pound of gleaming coffee beans. Armed with her packages, she turned right into Mount Street, then, a few hundred yards down, right again, and made her way into Hay's Mews. She stopped in front of a large house whose brilliant white walls were adorned with climbing roses. She rang the bell and waited. She felt herself being observed; then the door flew open.

Sarah's closest friend, Mosami Matsumoto, a fellow trader who worked in the City at Yamatoyo, stood in the open door in folds of white linen, barefoot and smiling.

Sarah had known Mosami since Cambridge. They had been undergraduates together at Trinity. Both were attractive, intelligent, outgoing, but they had been drawn together more by a latent loneliness which somehow remained impervious to the clamor of college life. Each recognized in the other a quiet determination, a separateness, and, more profound, a desire to escape. Mosami's pursuer was clear enough: life as a conventional Tokyo housewife, the destiny expected of her by Japanese society despite her Cambridge education, which was merely intended to be a hiatus, at best a means of getting the desire for freedom out of her system, as if it were a case of tuberculosis. Sarah, in contrast, had no obvious destiny, or history, from which she was attempting to flee, but Mosami still recognized in her the signs of flight:

intense ambition, restlessness, a lack of stillness, a reaching out, a propensity for taking risks and damaging herself, as long as that damage meant progress. An excess of work, men, and occasionally travel were their vehicles; they approached each with uncommon intensity, disappearing, hiding, reemerging weeks later.

Now, five years on, with established careers in the City, both women had a certain calmness, although it may well have been an illusion. Insofar as it was there at all, it was probably the product of fatigue, of familiar experimentation and a lack of discovery. The attraction to risk, often self-destructive, had stayed with them, and they watched closely over each other for any sign of its reemergence. They talked on the telephone every day and usually saw each other once a week. This weekend was to be a special treat for both of them; they had arranged to spend two days together, generally indulging themselves in food, wine, and shopping.

They kissed warmly. Sarah handed over one of the tubes of Baci. "Here, for your sweet tooth."

Mosami ripped open the tube and took out a couple of chocolates.

"Wonderful. My favorites." She handed the tube to Sarah. "Here, have one yourself."

Sarah took one, followed Mosami into the kitchen, and sat on a high stool, watching her friend open up a bottle of red wine.

"So what's been happening?" asked Mosami, handing Sarah a glass of wine. Sarah took a sip and led the way back into the sitting room. Mosami followed with her glass and the bottle.

"Well, it's a bit strange with Eddie and Alex gone." Sarah shrugged. "Takes a bit of getting used to. Sometimes I wonder why I bother. Perhaps I should play safe, pick an accountant next time."

"Safe!" Mosami snorted. "You think that's safe? You'd go out of your mind in five minutes. You know you would."

"Yeah. Probably. But all the same . . ."

"I know, sweetie. It's tough. Never mind. We'll have a lovely, relaxing, men-free weekend. I've got lots of plans for us."

Sarah smiled. "You're an angel."

"I know. Anyway," Mosami said, trying to lighten things up, "what other news?"

Sarah paused. "Well . . . I'm thinking of changing jobs." She waited for Mosami's reaction.

"Why?"

"Four years. Time for a change, you know."

"And that's a reason?"

"Reason enough."

Like hell, thought Mosami, getting up to pour another glass of wine.

The weekend passed in a haze of self-indulgence. Sarah returned to her own house on Sunday evening. She walked through the silent rooms, sat down by her answering machine, and replayed the messages, hoping for some news from Eddie and Alex. There was nothing from them, nothing at all exciting save a message from Sue Banks, asking her to call.

Sarah looked up the number in her book and dialed.

"Sue, it's Sarah."

"Oh, Sarah, hi, how are you?"

"Fine. Had a long, lazy weekend. How're you?"

"Dreading Monday morning, as usual."

"Not the only one."

"Now, listen. ICB."

"Mmmm."

"What d'you mean, mmmm?"

"Well, I suppose I mean 'Oh dear, fucked it up.' I don't think I'll be moving on there."

"And why not?"

"Well, Dante Scarpirato gave me all of thirty minutes, then booted me out. That's why."

Sue laughed. "Listen, Sarah, if he hadn't liked you, he would have thrown you out after five minutes. He'd done his research. He trusts me. He knows how good you are. All he had to do was see if he liked you. And he does." She paused triumphantly.

"Strange way of showing it," muttered Sarah.

"Look, don't act like a queen. You can't expect everyone to fawn over you."

"Like a queen! I hardly—"

Sue drowned her out. "Listen. Scarpirato just called me. He's at home at the moment. He wants you to call him to arrange to meet the other members of his team."

"That's a bit unusual, isn't it?" said Sarah. "Direct contact, I mean. A bit informal."

"Oh, come on, Sarah. You don't need me for a chaperone."

Sarah laughed. "No. I suppose I don't. So what's his number?"

Sue reeled it off. Sarah said goodbye and dialed immediately. It was, she noted, a Chelsea number, the same exchange as hers. So they were neighbors.

"Dante, it's Sarah Jensen."

"Good evening, Sarah."

The voice sounded rough, staccato, even more unyielding than when she had met him, and there was a note of mockery. She ignored it and waited, picking her nails in the silence.

"Can you come to my office at six-thirty tomorrow?"

"That'll be fine."

"See you then." With that he hung up.

The short exchange left her troubled. There was a coldness in its brevity, a disregard for the conventions of conversation. Many traders were like that, but this was not rudeness or a lack of small talk. It seemed, oddly, that he was dispensing with formalities.

Sarah spent the next day trading haphazardly, wishing she could go home, waiting for six o'clock. When it finally came, she hurried from the trading floor and headed for the ICB offices.

The same dark office, another immaculate suit. Scarpirato walked slowly toward her as she entered his office, extended his hand, shook hers firmly. His eyes held hers throughout. He was smiling slightly, not out of friendliness or welcome but from something that Sarah couldn't quite identify. She looked away. There were two other people in the office, lounging on cloth-covered chairs by the desk. Scarpirato nodded to them.

"Sarah Jensen, meet Matthew Arnott and Simon Wilson."

Wilson jumped to his feet, smiled, and shook her hand warmly. Arnott half rose, held her hand for a second, slumped back into his chair, and looked past her. Scarpirato pulled a chair round from behind his desk and sat between Arnott and Wilson, who quickly made way for him. Flanking him, glancing at him as if waiting for a lead, they appeared to Sarah as neophytes. She took the empty seat opposite and laid down her bag. She sat back, unbuttoned her jacket, took out a packet of cigarettes, and casually lit up. She smiled at the watching faces. "You mind?"

Scarpirato shook his head and passed her an ashtray.

"I'll have one, too," said Arnott. He walked from the office and returned with a packet from his desk. He lit up. Clouds of smoke drifted toward the ceiling and mingled with the smell of freshly smoked cigars.

Sarah drew on her cigarette and glanced casually at the two newcomers. Arnott looked like he should be advertising shirts on the glossy pages of GQ. He was a good-looking American in his late twenties. Square-jawed, with blue eyes and brown hair cut short, he was almost airbrushed to perfection. His accent had been polished, too, Sarah noticed. Twangs of New Jersey had been straightened into a Boston drawl but emerged in odd words. The image could have been wholesome, if slightly pretentious, if not for his eyes and the set of his mouth. His eyes were hard and cynical, every expression colored by a sneer at the expense of the world. And the lips were set in a faintly pursed, contemptuous look. Not the most endearing character Sarah had ever met. Nor one likely to hire her.

Simon Wilson, by contrast, seemed sweet, eager to please. He was younger, about twenty-four, had only been working in the City a couple of years, Sarah guessed, and had so far avoided the cast of jaded complacency worn by so many of his fellows. He was sandy-haired, gently freckled, dressed unlike the others in a creased suit off the rack. He caught her eye and smiled as she was studying him.

She smiled back, then glanced at Scarpirato, waiting for him to begin. He just watched her, saying nothing, making no move to do so. He half turned to Arnott. The two men exchanged a look, then Arnott sat forward in his chair and asked, "So where d'you see Cable?"

Sarah gave a slight, amused smile. "What time period are we talking about? The next five minutes, twenty-four hours, a week, a year?"

"Five minutes."

"I don't know." Sarah smiled expansively. "At five past six, when I last looked, it was 1.4930, 40. I don't know what the market's done in the last forty-five minutes, and I'm not in the habit of making blind prices. But I'd say the dollar's strengthening marginally."

Arnott whipped from his pocket a Reuters pager, a three-inch by two-inch gadget which gave twenty-four-hour updates of crucial financial prices and news. He tapped out a command and peered at the tiny screen.

"1.4910, 20. I guess that's up," he drawled. He tried another tack. "So why're you leaving Finlays?"

"Who says I'm leaving?"

"You're here, aren't you?"

"I'm here so that you can find out more about me and I can find out more about you."

Arnott glared at Sarah. She stared back, unperturbed. There was a tense silence.

Wilson broke in with a smile. "You work with David Reed, don't you?"

"Yes, I sit next to him. Friend of yours?"

"We play football." Wilson laughed. "Or at least we try to. He's injured most of the time."

"Tell me about it. He seems to spend most of the time hobbling around with some part of his anatomy covered in plaster."

"What a pain for you," said Arnott.

Sarah looked at him in silence for a few seconds, then turned away. She caught Scarpirato's eye. He had taken a cigar from his pocket and was methodically lighting up, glancing at her between puffs. He leaned back in his chair and held her gaze, playing the part of the detached observer, looking mildly amused. Sarah looked away in annoyance. She was the evening's entertainment. As far as she could see, there was no purpose to be served by this meeting save that. Wilson liked her, Arnott hated her. As for Scarpirato, she wasn't sure how he felt, didn't particularly care at that moment.

She glanced at her watch, then calmly and coolly said, "Listen, this is all very enjoyable, but I have to be somewhere in fifteen minutes, so if you don't mind . . ."

Scarpirato's faint grin was replaced by a momentary look of surprise. He swung forward in his seat.

"Of course. Sorry, we didn't give you much notice for this meeting." He got to his feet. Arnott looked up in silence and watched her walk out of the office. Wilson followed her to the door.

"Goodbye. Nice to meet you." He shook her hand.

Sarah smiled. "You too." She walked beside Scarpirato across the trading floor to the lift. Neither spoke along the way. As the lift doors opened he shook her hand.

"Thanks for coming in. We'll be in touch." He smiled slightly, then turned and walked away as the lift doors closed.

"Fuck the lot of you," muttered Sarah, alone in the lift.

Chapter Eight

Sarah walked out onto Lower Thames Street, waited for a gap in the traffic roaring by, then sprinted across. She wondered what Jacob would make of all this. Deciding to go see him, she headed for Cannon Street, stopping by a telephone box next to Bush Lane. She picked up the receiver and tapped out his number. After a few rings, his faintly quavering voice answered.

Five minutes later he put down the phone with a smile and picked up his cat, ruffling her sleek black fur. "It's about time she paid us a visit, isn't it?"

Ruby preened in his arms, closing her eyes with pleasure as he stroked her, opening them wide in indignation when he put her down again. Tail snapping back and forth in irritation, she watched him slip on some shoes, pick up keys and wallet from the hall table, and close the door softly behind him. Three deadbolt locks encased in a sheet of metal hidden within the pine of the door clicked loudly behind the old man.

He crossed the street carefully, his head full of recipes, and headed for the supermarket on Golders Green Road. Jacob Goldsmith was seventy-three years old. He had all the subtle wisdom of fulfilled age, of a life well-lived. He was full of charm and sweetness to those he loved, chief among whom was Sarah. He had always been kind and gentle, but age added a quality of intense thoughtfulness and a lightness of touch which instilled in those around him a sense of well-being and joy. You would never damn him with the faint praise of calling him "nice," for he was much more than that, and anyway, it was a description that lay badly on him; he was far too clever for that, and there was still in him a rebelliousness, which showed itself for the most part as a twinkle. He was sprightly and fit. When he dressed up to meet his old business partners, he switched into another gear, and could easily pass for sixty. But he saw little of them these days; he had retired twelve years ago, and his life now was very different.

Before retiring, for thirty years, after his return from fighting in the Second World War, Jacob had worked in London as a safemaker. And cracker. He was one of the best in the country. He worked at his illicit trade rarely, always successfully. He had never been caught. After several years of hiding his avocation from Sarah and Alex, one day, after much quizzing from an already suspicious Sarah, he revealed to the children his secret life.

Sarah was fascinated by his disclosures. He reveled in her interest, saved his more outlandish stories for her, and, after being repeatedly pestered, taught her how to pick locks and crack safes. At age eleven she was adept at gaining entry to her own house without keys, and at picking Jacob's and Isla's safes. She did that only for its own sake. She had no interest in the contents; in fact, she would add to them. Whenever Jacob opened his safe, something he did perhaps every couple of months, he would find a succession of little notes from Sarah.

Jacob's influence, and the intense pain of early childhood, forged in Sarah and Alex a curious morality. They developed fierce personal loyalties, to each other and to Jacob, and regarded with indulgence what others would see at best as misdemeanors. Jacob's little robberies were all right, because the victims were not harmed—the insurance company picked up the tab—and because Jacob himself was patently a nice, kind man. He took care of them, loved them, amused them, and helped to feed the development of their personalities, which grew largely unchecked by the constraints of convention.

Sarah's love for Jacob, undiminished by the knowledge that he was what was commonly called a criminal, produced in her at an early age the awareness of a layered morality, in which single acts in themselves were not necessarily right or wrong. She grew up with a passionate and idiosyncratic sense of morality and justice.

Although Jacob had never been caught, never came close to prison, the young Sarah always feared that he would be taken away. It was only when his semiretirement became complete and he swore that he would never go back that her fears subsided. But she grew up with the sense that it would have been a travesty of justice for him to have been imprisoned.

Her fears had hastened Jacob's retirement. He knew of her vulnerabilities, and he did everything in his power to allay them. Certain things he could not control. He worried that Sarah had a certain self-destructive streak, and he watched over her carefully. He knew of her taste for gambling, both professionally and personally, and how she sometimes deliberately raised the stakes, just for fun. Like the way she bought her house, using up all her savings and taking out a huge mortgage, all the while hating financial insecurity. If for whatever reason she couldn't work, lost her nerve or her skill, she would lose her house. There was no way she would be able to keep up her mortgage payments without her hefty six-figure salary.

But Jacob had contingency plans. Except for the worry it caused her, he was not unduly concerned about her financial position. For her eighteenth birthday he had given her an antique ruby and diamond ring. When she got her double first, he gave her matching earrings. He was keeping back for another occasion, though he did not know what, a diamond and ruby necklace, currently hidden in his bedroom, which if called upon could pay off her mortgage at a stroke. It would be difficult to sell in this country, he knew that, but he also knew of certain buyers who had an expert eye for fine jewels and could live without certificates of provenance.

He didn't tell Sarah about the necklace—she would have been annoyed at what she would have seen as his lack of confidence in her. It was not that. The necklace was a precaution against hostile fortune, a beautiful insurance policy.

Sarah walked briskly toward Bank station. She was tempted to go home and change, but all that extra traveling was a waste of time, and Jacob liked to see her looking smart. If she went home, leggings and loafers would be irresistible. She might as well keep on her City suit, get to Jacob's early, and laze around while he cooked. She bought a *Standard* at Bank station and joined the crowds heading for the Northern Line. A train turned up after ten minutes, just as the crowds milling on the platform were becoming intolerable. Sarah fought her way on, deftly maneuvered herself into a seat, and lost herself in the paper for forty minutes.

She got off at Golders Green and took a detour along Golders Green Road to the off-license, where she selected two bottles of red wine. Jacob rarely drank white, and he had passed his love of red wine on to her. Years before she started going on expensive dates to smart restaurants, she was an expert on wine.

Swinging the bottles in a plastic bag, she made her way down the hill and back past the station, then turned off the bustling main street onto the calm of Rotherwick Road. Red brick houses two and three stories high lined the street, cushioned from the road by well-tended gardens, most of them blooming with roses.

Jacob's garden was particularly fine. Since she had first known him, he had always lavished time and attention on his garden. Roses were his favorite. There were wild tea roses, lofty Copenhagens, and, best of all, big red Alexanders dripping with scent. There were lots of others too. When she was a child he taught her all their names, but she had forgotten most of them now.

Sarah opened the gate, which creaked a little. Jacob refused to oil it, keeping it as some kind of early warning system. The creak attracted Ruby, who trotted around the corner and wound herself around Sarah's calves in a figure eight. With one hand Sarah picked her up; with the other she rang the bell, the bottles clinking gently against the brass handle plate.

In a few seconds Jacob was at the door, grinning broadly. "Hello, sweetie." He hugged her, squeezing Ruby in between them, then kissed Sarah's cheeks and eyed the plastic bag hopefully. "What have you got for me? Something decent, I hope?" He opened the bag and examined the bottles. His grin deepened. "Not bad. Glad you've learned something."

Sarah laughed. "Everything I know, and all that . . ." She

lowered Ruby gently to the ground and followed Jacob into the kitchen. He took down two fragile, voluptuous glasses from an old oak dresser and opened the wine. The two glasses took nearly half the bottle. Sarah had adopted Jacob's habit of counting her consumption by the glass.

"I've nearly got everything ready. You just go and watch *Coronation Street*. Tell me what happens. I'll give you a shout."

Sarah took her wine into the sitting room and flopped on the sofa in front of the television. *Coronation Street* was halfway through. She sipped at her wine, flicked through channels, picked up an old copy of the *Spectator* and tried to read.

After twenty minutes, Jacob stuck his head round the door. "So what happened?"

"Hmm?" Sarah looked up, vague.

"*Coronation Street*. What happened?"

Sarah laughed and looked sheepish. "I'm sorry, Jacob. I wasn't concentrating."

"Concentrating. Don't be daft. You don't have to concentrate to watch *Coronation Street*." He peered at her sharply from across the room. "Anyway, better come and have something to eat."

Sarah followed him meekly into the kitchen. She sat down while he doled out a huge portion of poule-au-pot.

Jacob picked delicately at his meal and watched Sarah for a while before asking, "So what's wrong, then?"

Sarah paused to swallow a mouthful. She put down her fork. "What d'you mean, what's wrong?"

Jacob looked exasperated. "What's wrong. What's wrong. What do you think I mean?"

Sarah sighed and took a drink of wine. "Look, Jacob. I can't always tell you everything. And I'm just not sure this is any of your business." She saw his eyes register the hurt and could have bitten off her tongue. "Oh God, Jacob, I'm sorry. I didn't mean to say that. It's just with Alex and Eddie leaving I've been a bit upset. Haven't been sleeping too well . . ."

Jacob took a long drink. "It's all right, sweetie. Don't worry." He was silent for a while. "But that's not it, is it? That makes you sad. I've seen you like that before. But you're rattled, aren't you?"

Sarah studied his worn face, creased in worry. "No chance of hiding anything from you, is there?"

Jacob leaned back with a slight sigh of relief and waited.

"Well, I might as well tell you," said Sarah. "I don't see what harm it could do. There's something very strange that I'm about to get mixed up in. That I am already mixed up in." She paused for a while. "It's just a bit weird, that's all."

Jacob eased it out of her bit by bit—Carter, Barrington, the suspected fraud, and Scarpirato.

"So you see," she finished, "I want the job, Scarpirato's job and the governor's job. I just feel a bit uneasy, that's all. Things have been good at Finlays. And with Eddie. Everything's nice and calm now."

"And you just can't leave it alone, can you?"

"No," said Sarah. "I can't."

"So what are you going to do?"

Sarah smiled. "Take the job if I'm offered it."

Jacob was silent for a while. He gazed out at the garden, his face thoughtful. Then he grinned across the table. "Should be manageable. If you're careful. And clever. Could even be a bit of fun."

Sarah eyed him warily. "I've seen that look before, Jacob Goldsmith. What have you got up your sleeve?"

"Let's wait and see if you get the job, shall we?"

Chapter Nine

For two working days Sarah heard nothing from Sue Banks or Dante Scarpirato. On the first day she felt almost relieved, free to surround herself with her familiar life. On the second day she began to worry; perhaps the job had gone to someone else. At that point she decided that she wanted the job badly. Going home that evening, she tried to put it out of her mind, and affected a studied indifference that almost convinced her that she could take or leave the job, the assignment . . . Of course, perversely, that was when Sue Banks chose to call.

Sarah arrived home at eight-thirty. She had just been to the gym, and to compensate had bought a packet of chips wrapped in newspaper from Johnny's Fish Bar at World's End. Angrily she grabbed at the receiver, greasy fingers fighting to get a grip.

"Hello." It was more a challenge than a question.

"Well, excuse me." Sue laughed.

"Sorry, Sue," said Sarah, swallowing a handful of fries. "Animals eating—do not disturb, and all that."

"Don't I know it. Shall I ring back?"

"No, don't worry. I'll just munch away."

"Yuck, disgusting. Anyway, listen, Scarpirato's just been on the phone again. Would like to see you tomorrow, if possible."

"Would he now?" Sarah held a chip suspended halfway to her mouth and smiled broadly. "Well, there's a thing." She popped it into her mouth and chewed in silence for a while.

"Well," said Sue indignantly, "do you want this job or not?"

Sarah ignored the question. "How far has he got with his interviewing?"

"He's seen eight other candidates besides you," answered Sue patiently. "He's got another two to see."

There was another long pause.

"Sarah, do you want this job or not? You seem a bit uncertain."

Sarah smiled to herself. "Let's just see what Mr. Scarpirato has to say, shall we? Tell him I'll see him at his offices at six-thirty tomorrow, would you?"

"Yes, ma'am."

At six-twenty the next evening, Dante Scarpirato sat in his office with Matthew Arnott and Simon Wilson discussing the last candidate they had interviewed, an American of twenty-nine, a close friend of Arnott's—the two men had been at Brown University together.

"Well, I think he's pretty good." Arnott glanced at Scarpirato and away again. "He's a good trader, and he fits in." He paused awkwardly, adding rather lamely, "Well, he gets my vote, anyway."

Scarpirato took a long puff on his cigar, and turned to face

Arnott. "The man's an idiot. Sometimes you can be so fucking unsubtle."

Arnott's face turned red. Simon Wilson looked at his shoes. Arnott lit up a cigarette, held it between forefinger and thumb, and jabbed it in Scarpirato's direction.

"So who do you want, then?"

Scarpirato exhaled heavily. "That's just what I propose to discuss with you, if you'll just calm down for a second."

A secretary appeared at the door, cutting off Arnott's reply.

"Sarah Jensen's in reception. Shall I send her up?"

"Yes, would you? But take her to my trading desk. Ask her to wait there for a few minutes. I'll come out and collect her when I'm ready."

The secretary turned and disappeared down to reception. She returned a few minutes later with Sarah and installed her at Scarpirato's trading desk, about fifteen feet from his office.

Sarah sat sideways at the desk, holding a copy of the *Evening Standard* in front of her and appearing to read while trying to listen to the conversation in Scarpirato's office. Only a faint murmuring escaped. She gave up and concentrated on the newspaper instead. There was no point in trying to watch the three men for clues. The glass walls of the office and the glass door were covered with blinds. Only jagged images were visible from the outside.

From inside the office, the view was much clearer. Scarpirato watched Sarah through the blinds as he sat talking with his colleagues. He listened to their voices, his eyes trained on her. Arnott lounged back in his chair, stretching his arms high above his head in a posture of calculated indifference. He lit up another Marlboro.

"Can't we do this tomorrow?" he asked.

"I would like your opinions now." Scarpirato kept his eyes on Sarah's profile as he spoke.

"Why? We've got plenty of time. We have one more candidate to interview, and we don't have to make any sort of decision now."

Scarpirato continued staring at Sarah. He answered very calmly.

"Because I propose to offer her the job."

"Oh, for fuck's sake, Dante. You know what she'll be like. She's an arrogant bitch who'll cruise in, cruise out, fit in a little work between her social engagements, and just be a general disruption."

Scarpirato drew his eyes from Sarah and turned to face Arnott. "How much did you make for us last year?"

Arnott looked awkward. "Why don't you look at this year? I'm a couple of million up, as you well know."

"And you were a couple of million down last year, when, incidentally, Sarah Jensen made six million for Finlays. We all know her reputation. She might cruise in and out, as you say, but in one hour she's a fuck's sight better than you are in a week." Scarpirato smiled at Arnott. "So you have my decision. McPherson quit weeks ago. We need a replacement. We could spend months trawling through the City and we wouldn't find anyone as good as her."

Or as good-looking, thought Arnott bitterly.

"Now go out there and invite her in, would you? Then disappear, both of you."

Glowering, Arnott marched out, followed by a silent Simon Wilson. Arnott gave Sarah a twisted smile.

"He wants you in there."

He nodded to the office, swiped his jacket from the back of

his chair, and walked out. Wilson said hello, goodbye, smiled, and ambled after Arnott.

Scarpirato sat smoking a cigar. He looked at Sarah intently as she walked into the office, then gestured for her to take a seat. She felt uneasy under the intensity of his gaze. A faint smile creased his lips. A touch of defiance entered Sarah's eyes as she looked back at him, which seemed almost to deepen his smile. She wanted to reach down to her bag for a cigarette, turn away from his eyes, and veil her own, which she feared were revealing too much, but, compelled, she kept her eyes on him. They sat, saying nothing, looking at each other, each unwilling to be the first to speak, the first to look away. Finally he leaned forward, and suddenly the intensity was gone. It was as if he had assumed a different guise as he spoke—the prospective boss, official, detached, businesslike.

"O.K., Sarah, we've all agreed that you would be a useful addition to the team."

Sarah, recalling the look of spite on Arnott's face, almost laughed out loud.

"So welcome to ICB."

He seemed to take it for granted that she would accept, pausing only fleetingly for a look of assent.

"I want you on the floor as soon as possible. When can you start?"

Sarah blinked hard at the suggestion and looked away. His voice had been slow and deliberate, the words spaced for emphasis. The terminology was normal enough, but coming from him . . . She studied his face. Again there was the faint smile. She felt almost as if he were taunting her. She met his eyes and gave him a slow smile.

"I want a package of £500,000 guaranteed for the first year, and I'll start on Monday."

Scarpirato leaned toward her and studied her through narrowed eyes.

"Half a million? That's a bit more than I had in mind."

"Take it or leave it."

"O.K., Sarah, but I hope you know what you're doing, upping
the stakes. You'd better be good."

Better for you if I'm not, she thought.

Scarpirato stood and walked around his desk. He paused by
her chair. She got to her feet and stood facing him. He was
disconcertingly close. She reached down for her bag and stepped
back. He watched her as she prepared to leave.

"Just one question," she asked as they walked from his office.
"Matthew Arnott doesn't seem to like me very much. I find it
hard to believe he wants me on the team."

Scarpirato laughed. "Don't worry about him. He's an awkward bastard. But he's an inspired trader. He makes a lot of
money for us, thinks he's entitled to be a shit. You know the
type."

Sarah smiled ruefully. "Oh, yes. I know the type."

They walked across the trading floor, quiet, almost empty
now, toward the lifts. He paused there and turned to her.

"I'll get contracts to you first thing tomorrow morning."

Sarah nodded. "Send them to my home address, would you?
I'll wait there till I get them before going in to Finlays."

Scarpirato reached inside his jacket pocket and took out a pen
and a slim diary. He turned to the back—the address section.
Sarah told him where she lived, watched him write it down. He
returned the diary and pen to his pocket. Then he smiled at her.

"See you on Monday, then," he said.

"Yes. See you Monday."

He looked at her quizzically, as if something in her tone had
surprised him, then turned and walked away. Sarah watched him

disappear through the maze of desks. The lift came. She rode down alone. Sweat pricked her back.

She walked up Idol Lane to Eastcheap and caught a cab. Sinking back on the seat, she lit up a cigarette. She had got the job. Two hours ago she had looked no further than that. Now she wondered what she was getting herself into.

The next morning she stayed at home waiting for the ICB contracts to be biked around. Two copies arrived at ten. She signed one copy, sent it back, and kept the second for her files. Then she rushed to the telephone and called Anthony Barrington. He was in a meeting, said his secretary. She left an urgent message. Ten minutes later he called.

"Governor, thanks for calling back. Good news. I've got the job. I start on Monday."

"Well done, Sarah. That's excellent news. Really is. Quite a tribute to you!" He paused theatrically, then spoke with mock seriousness. "But I hope you didn't take them for too much. This will probably take a while, and we don't want your credit running out."

They laughed together. Both knew that she could pay her way. The risk lay in her being discovered before she had sufficient evidence. That's if Scarpirato turned out to be guilty. Then she would be fired, at best. Thirty-five million pounds a year would be worth defending ruthlessly.

The governor put down the phone and asked his secretary to get him James Bartrop. Bartrop came on the line seconds later.

"Governor."

"Bartrop. She's got the job."

"Excellent. It's all falling into place." He paused. Barrington could almost feel the cogs turning in his mind.

"We ought to solidify it a bit," continued Bartrop.

Barrington frowned. More riddles. "Solidify?"

"Yes. Financially. Give her some money, cash, for expenses."

"Expenses? What kind of expenses?"

"Oh, I don't know. That's not the point."

Barrington waited for the point.

"It's to bind her in. Symbolic, really. Again, common practice. It makes it more real. Makes them take it more seriously."

"Yes, I can see that. How much?"

"Oh, a few thousand."

"That's peanuts, you know, for a girl like her."

"That doesn't matter. Don't want to give her too much. Looks suspicious. Just a token. We'll pay. I'll bike it round in half an hour. Arrange to see her, if you can. The sooner you hand it over, the better. Sets the tone."

"All right. I'll expect your package. I'll see what I can arrange."

Sarah walked into Finlays with feelings of excitement and trepidation. Resignation time. Best to get it over with quickly. Bypassing her desk, she walked straight into Jamie Rawlinson's private office. Most of the bosses had private offices as well as a seat on the trading floor. Trading floors offer no privacy; they rumble with secrets, so private offices are essential.

"Good morning, Jamie. Could I have ten minutes?"

He tried to persuade her to stay. Tried, unsuccessfully, to get hold of Carter, who was in Paris on business for the day. Sarah was adamant. It was time to move on.

She returned to her desk and picked up a few personal items she had left lying around. She moved briskly, unwelcome now, unwanted. Resignations of star people were always seen as a betrayal of the firm. The atmosphere as Sarah packed her things was tense, hostile. She was now the competition, and business was too sensitive to let her hang around. She picked up her bag and began to walk across the trading floor. David Reed's voice stopped her in her tracks.

"Call, Sarah. Urgent. He won't say who he is."

Sarah cursed under her breath. She wanted to get out of the building as fast as possible. She turned in annoyance and walked back to her old trading desk, snatched up the telephone handset, and hit the button for line one.

"Hello."

"Ah, Sarah. I'm glad I caught you. It's Anthony here."

Sarah frowned, recognizing the voice but puzzled by the name.

"Oh, it's you, Go—"

He cut her off. "Yes, it's me. Sorry, not much time to talk. Could you pop by my office? Say half an hour?"

"Yes, that's fine."

"See you then." And the line went dead.

Sarah picked up her bag again and walked out of Finlays for good. She felt uneasy. Leaving after four years would never be fun. She felt the familiar rot of uncertainty in her stomach. And then the strange phone call, with the governor so keen to mask his identity. It brought back unpleasant memories. She had once had an affair with a married man. He never liked her to use his name when they spoke on the telephone, and he would never announce himself. His reticence always seemed to her like sense- less paranoia. She resented him for it, and considered him doubly disloyal. She left him after three months, determined never to repeat the experience.

She pushed the memories from her mind, but the unpleasantness lingered. She walked out onto Old Broad Street, into the warm June sunshine. The bank was two minutes' walk away, and she had half an hour to kill. She walked up to Finsbury Circus and paced around the leafy park, trying to walk away her unease. Why the urgent phone call? Why did he want to see her? Had the whole thing been called off?

She suddenly felt a wave of sick trepidation. She had resigned from Finlays. That was irrevocable. She would never have done that if not for the governor, if he had not given her a special role. Perhaps, unaccountably, he had changed his mind. Perhaps he thought she was not suitable. Panic filled her. Perhaps he had discovered something.

She sat down on a park bench and fumbled in her bag for a cigarette, then lit up and puffed furiously. She felt the nicotine flood through her system. She smoked the cigarette down to the butt, inhaling deeply.

Suddenly she laughed to herself. She was paranoid now. Stamping out her cigarette, she stood up, muttered "Fuck it" under her breath, and turned and walked back toward Threadneedle Street and the Bank of England.

"Ah, Sarah. Thanks for coming around. Short notice again, I'm afraid. Anyway, well done. Very well done."

The governor reached inside his desk and brought out an envelope, which he pushed across to Sarah. She left it where it was.

"It's yours. Something to be getting on with, cover any expenses. I'm sure you'll find good use for it."

"It's really not necessary, Governor."

"Come, come. You never know when you might need it. It's part of the operation. Please take it."

Sarah shrugged. She reached out and picked up the envelope. Without opening it, she tucked it into her bag. She looked across at the governor. He was smiling benignly, like a father dispensing pocket money. Only it didn't feel that way to her.

The governor glanced at his watch and rose to his feet. He stretched out his hand to her.

"Well, goodbye, Sarah, and good luck. You're pretty much on your own now. Of course you'll have my full support, but I'll be very much in the background, invisible almost, for your own sake, eh? Bit suspicious otherwise. Telephone if you need anything, won't you."

The broad smile was there, but the warmth was toned down. Sarah felt a slight distancing, as if she were being put away into a compartment. So that was the way it was. All right. She could see the logic. And she could do the same. She shook his hand.

"Goodbye, Governor."

She didn't look in the envelope until she got home. Then, sitting at her desk, she slit it open with a knife and pulled out £3,000. She returned the notes to the envelope and locked it away in her desk drawer. Three thousand pounds. Expenses. For what?

Chapter Ten

James Bartrop sat drinking an extra-strong espresso in his office in Century House. The office had the austerity of the ascetic. The walls were painted white; the carpet was gray. There were no pictures, no photographs. Bartrop was not a man overly concerned with his surroundings. He depended more on his interior landscape for those comforts he did allow himself. He was happy, or at least he functioned well, if he had an overwhelming purpose that gave structure to his life and form to his thoughts.

But this was not the image he presented to the world. Outwardly, he was as hedonistic as most forty-five-year-old bachelors fortified by inheritance. He ate well, drank discerningly. He lived during the week in a large house in Chelsea Square. At weekends he drove two and a half hours to his country house in Gloucestershire, or flew to the South of France or the Alps, depending on the season, almost always with female company. Professional interruptions apart, it was a regular life, peopled by irregulars.

None of the women lasted. But it didn't matter; there were always enough to fill the void. The obvious hazards of being a bachelor approaching middle age only thinned the selection, for in addition to being wealthy, Bartrop was physically appealing—six feet tall, with a firm body, a strong face, wavy brown hair, blue eyes only slightly dimmed. Wry, amused eyes, at least for public consumption. His natural cynicism he kept veiled, as far as possible.

Then there was the psychological appeal, the challenge of historic unattainability heightened by the inscrutability fostered by his profession. In short, he was attractive to women, or, more particularly, to certain kinds of woman—the ambitious, or those who were perhaps not too careful of themselves—and there were enough of those . . . Bartrop lived what many would describe as an enviable life, and he enjoyed it, too, as far as it went.

The problem for him was that it just didn't go very far. It was a distraction. His career was also a distraction, but at least it offered some value, and he gripped that. He was not evangelical. Such a quality would have rendered him dangerous and probably unsuitable for the service, but he had purpose, and he was willing to sacrifice the presumed stability and permanence of married life to fulfill it. That, simplistically, was the philosophy he had invented for himself. And it seemed quite workable.

At times his work gave him a quiet, cerebral pleasure. That morning, as he thought about Sarah Jensen, he found himself enjoying one of those rare moments of satisfaction coupled with anticipation. He often felt this way at the beginning of a relationship, but then, invariably, these feelings were clouded by the certainty of the less pleasant sentiments and emotions that would inevitably follow: impatience, disillusionment, and bitterness on the part of the woman; on his part, resigned acceptance that another relationship had run its course. But with operational matters, with Jensen, there was no such certainty. This distant, vicarious relationship did not need to end in tears. It would not, if it was well run and enjoyed a fair distribution of luck, or at least suffered no unduly bad luck. It was tricky, he acknowledged that, to himself anyway, but as he had assured Barrington, it was controllable.

At first he had had reservations about Sarah Jensen. He distrusted beautiful women. A surfeit of admirers and too many choices were not always conducive to stability. But by all accounts she was solid enough, despite her tragic childhood. And her beauty could prove to be useful in getting close to the suspects.

Bartrop found himself wondering what she looked like. He would, of course, never meet her. As far as she was concerned, he didn't exist, or if he did, he was a distant irrelevance, with no connection to her undercover role. Bartrop smiled to himself. He telephoned his deputy, Miles Forshaw.

"I'd like some photographs of Miss Jensen. Talk to the watchers, would you?"

On Monday morning, the metal statues of ICB greeted Sarah coldly. The sound of her heels ricocheted in the gray marbled foyer, and the face that looked back at her in the mirrored lifts was taut. At seven-thirty in the morning, the trading floor was packed. A sea of hard faces watched her progress. With relief she sat down in the empty seat between Arnott and Wilson.

Wilson looked up and smiled. "Morning. Welcome aboard."
Sarah smiled back. "Good morning. And thank you."

To her left, Arnott grudgingly looked up. "Yeah. Welcome aboard." Before she could answer he turned back to his screens.

At that moment Scarpirato emerged from his office and walked by the trading desks. Arnott and Wilson turned from their screens to face him. He glanced down at Sarah. "Team meeting," he announced. He was the boss, the proprietorial boss again, in tone and stance, Sarah noted as she watched him walk briskly toward a conference room at the side of the trading floor. Arnott, Wilson, and Sarah got to their feet and followed him.

Unlike the vast expanse of the trading floor, the bulk of which lay under a sickly green pall, the conference room was bathed in natural light flowing in from a window that overlooked the Thames. Tower Bridge was visible if you craned your neck. Sarah admired the view, taking her time. The others sat around a scratched black-topped desk, Arnott and Wilson sipping at steaming cappuccinos. Sarah turned with a smile and took a seat opposite Scarpirato.

Arnott and then Wilson analyzed the previous week's markets and meticulously outlined their trading strategy for the next few weeks. Sarah wondered if they always laid it on so thick. Scarpirato stared out at the river, saying nothing, then turned to Sarah when Wilson had wound up. If he hoped to put her at a disadvantage by having her speak after the others, he would be disappointed. Sarah leaned back in her chair and smiled across the table at the three of them.

"I'm not particularly interested in ivory towers. I prefer to trade by instinct." It was the kind of comment Scarpirato himself might make, and Sarah was rewarded by a barked chuckle from across the table.

"Better let those instincts loose, then. You can start to trade today. Your position limit is two hundred million dollars."

Sarah masked her surprise. She had expected fifty to begin with. She could hang all of them with two hundred. Scarpirato was laying a spectacularly inviting trap. Sarah kept her smile nonchalant.

Scarpirato continued matter-of-factly. "Stick to the usual crosses—nothing exotic for the time being. If you want to do anything else, or go above two hundred, come and see me."

Sarah nodded.

"Trade at your own discretion, but keep Matthew fully informed." The words slowed to staccato. "I'll override you if I choose, as I do with the others, but most of the time you'll be on your own." He smiled benignly. "I like people to trade as individuals, so they benefit from their own successes and suffer"—he emphasized the word—"the consequences of their own errors." He stood up, nodded briefly at her, wished her good luck, and walked back to his office.

Sarah's smile lingered as she returned to her desk. ICB's reputation failed to do it justice. It was clearly impossible to be too much of a prima donna in this place. Unfettered arrogance was not merely tolerated, it was rewarded. She had not expected to be tested so quickly, nor so extravagantly. Her trading limit at Finlays had been two hundred, but she was one of their top traders, and she had proven herself over four years. She had come to ICB with glowing references, but she was still a risk. The maxim in the market was that you are only as good as your last trade. It was one of the stresses of the job that you had to prove yourself daily. It seemed that Scarpirato was taking a willful gamble on her. She had called his bluff with her arrogant disdain.

Sarah rubbed her chin thoughtfully. It was an unsound trading practice to make decisions based on ego. Do that too often and you'd be dead in the red. But it was probably uncharacteristic of Scarpirato, she reasoned. Wilson had seemed surprised at the size of her limit. It was almost certainly much higher than his, but he showed no jealousy. Arnott's face, however, had contorted into a vicious grin. There was no disguising the pleasure he would get if she messed up big-time, and he clearly expected her to. Sarah smiled sweetly at him and reached across and helped herself to one of his full-strength Marlboros.

Smoking it, she thought about Scarpirato's trading policies. A distant head trader who reserved the right to play his own game, otherwise giving his people complete autonomy, within sky-high trading limits . . . a money-making hothouse, heaven for the talented—and the unscrupulous. She stubbed out the cigarette in a deep glass ashtray stamped ICB in heavy black, and swept up her handset. Time to talk to her regulars and test-market sentiment.

Sarah spoke daily to a community of about ten other traders, most of whom she had been dealing with for the past four years. All of them zigzagged wildly around the City, hopping up the career ladder. The only things that changed were salaries, scenery, and trading limits.

Sarah checked the dashboard, about a foot square, which had more than twenty phone lines on it, some of them direct links with other trading houses. To contact them, she would press just one button. The system worked almost like an intercom. The button, referred to as a line, would be marked ICB at the other end and would flash when she rang. After three flashes, the line would start to ring audibly. The first three silent flashes were designed to reduce the cacophony on the trading floor. It was deemed unprofessional to answer after the ringing had started, so traders and salesmen were constantly glancing between their three or four trading screens and the dashboard to pick up incoming calls.

Sarah found the button with BdP on it, Banque de Paris, where one of her favorites worked.

Fifty yards away, on the north side of Lower Thames Street, Johnny McDermott, an irascible Irish FX trader at BdP, saw the ICB line flashing on his dashboard. With a grin, he hit the line.

"Lemme guess. Sarah Jensen."

"Morning, Johnny."

"So you're working with Matthew Arnott." Johnny's voice was particularly mischievous.

"Yes."

"He's a shit." Johnny spat out the word with glee.

"Mmmm."

"And Dante Scarpirato?"

"Yes."

"He's a prize shit."

Sarah stifled a laugh. "Mmmm. And I'm working with Simon Wilson, too."

Johnny got excited. "Now, he's a nice guy."

"Mmmm. Thanks, Johnny."

"My pleasure, Sarah. Happy listening, you bunch of shits."

Sarah burst out laughing. "Johnny, you bastard, you wait."

They both knew that Scarpirato, and probably his sidekick Arnott, would listen to the tapes of her first few days of trading just for fun, and to spy a little into her private life. On a trading floor, every phone call is taped, both as a precaution against trading disputes and for supervisory purposes. Automatic access to the tapes was a privilege widely abused by senior management.

"So anyway, Johnny," Sarah said, letting her laughter die down, "seen much?"

After an hour, she had talked to all ten of her regulars, who, with their customary blend of lies, inadvertent truths, and the occasional bit of straight talking, had confirmed her own feeling that for today at least, the market was going nowhere.

In theory, traders at other firms were adversaries, aiming, in the parlance of the market, to screw each other. Everyone expected that, and was pleasantly surprised, if a little suspicious, when it didn't happen. Within limits, it was their job, and a bit of sport on the side. Sarah knew that, and accepted it without question. But the rivalry with traders on the outside was nothing compared to what she was experiencing within ICB. Arnott had marked out his opposition to her from their first meeting. At least she started with no illusions.

Arnott, she sensed, was desperate to see her fail. Scarpirato too, in his own measured way. He dangled her trading limit before her, willing her to show him what a big swinging dick she was by using it to the full, and quickly. Well, he and Arnott would be disappointed. She had no intention of trading just for the sake of it. Let them think she was intimidated by the size of her trading limit, scoff at her for doing nothing. It was all part of the game.

There was no disguising the fact, though, that they were playing hard. That was the character of the place, the famous reputation, but Sarah couldn't help feeling singled out and wondering what was behind it. She laughed at herself. The City was peopled by conspiracy theorists, but she had never thought she'd become one of them.

The day passed quietly, and at five-thirty Sarah prepared to leave. Arnott, who had spent much of the day closeted with Scarpirato in his office, swaggered by as she was switching off her screens and retrieving her bag from under the desk.

"Done anything?" He knew she hadn't. Her instructions were to keep him informed of any trades she had done.

Sarah showed her teeth in a wide smile. "Not a thing." She swung her bag over her shoulder and said a cheery goodnight. Waving a farewell to Simon Wilson, she joined the five-thirty rush. It was bad politics to leave before your boss, but important to set your precedents early. With the spring of defiance in her step, Sarah skipped into the lift, catching it just as the doors were closing.

Arnott watched her disappear, then got up and walked into Scarpirato's office. The two men exchanged a few words, then Arnott cocked his head around the door and called Wilson in. Wilson surreptitiously pushed a copy of the *Racing Post* under a pile of papers and joined his colleagues. Scarpirato was lounging back in his chair, the second cigar of the day dangling from his fingers. Arnott lit up a Marlboro. Wilson, a marathon runner, wrinkled his nose. Occupational hazards. The two men leaned toward their boss, eager courtiers. Scarpirato smiled at them.

"Well?"

Arnott took a considered draw on his cigarette. "Bit of a prima donna, isn't she?"

"Well, I suppose with her reputation, she feels entitled to act the way she likes," said Wilson.

"Yeah, and she's certainly making that clear, isn't she?" said Arnott dismissively. "She does fuck-all all day and then leaves at five-thirty."

Scarpirato stretched his arms above his head and stared at the ceiling for a few seconds. His eyes tracked down the wall to Arnott.

"Did you trade today?" he asked casually.

Arnott shifted slightly in his seat. "Yeah, I did some Cable."

Wilson kept a smile out of his eyes. Scarpirato raised his eyebrows.

"And did you make any money?"

Arnott's jaw jutted fractionally, his neck contracted into his shoulders, and his voice went flat. "No, I lost fifty K."

"Well, shut the fuck up, then," spat Scarpirato. "Save us all some money and go home."

His cheeks burning, Arnott marched out. Wilson followed him, laughing softly. Out of earshot of Scarpirato, Arnott whirled on Wilson.

"What's so fucking funny? Just 'cause you made some money today. What d'you think you are, fucking cock of the north?"

Wilson kept laughing. "Go home and take it out on your dog. You're stuck with Sarah Jensen, like it or not."

A string of expletives followed him to the lift.

On Cannon Street, Sarah hailed a taxi. She dozed fitfully, waking as the driver slowed with squealing brakes on the King's Road near Carlyle Square. She paid him off, got out, and walked through the square. She didn't notice the dowdy, unremarkable woman who glanced briefly at her as she approached her house. Letting herself in, she walked upstairs, poured herself a whisky, and lay down on her bed.

Outside, the woman turned and headed for Sloane Square. She was one of MI6's watchers—surveillance personnel. Built into the briefcase she was carrying was a camera, now holding twelve photographs of Sarah Jensen, which would shortly be developed and handed to James Bartrop.

Chapter Eleven

arah arrived at ICB the next day keen to trade. Luck was with
her, and the markets came alive. It all started quietly enough
—too quietly, she thought, calling her gang. Nothing going
on for the second day in a row, and they were bored, dangerously and promisingly bored. It wouldn't take much to make
them bite today; they would be easy prey to rumor. Sarah just
had to get there first, tap into the rumor before the crowd. She
set about ringing some of her prized contacts. Now that the
European exchange-rate mechanism had all but broken down,
the currency markets were much more volatile and susceptible to
rumor.

It was ten-thirty, and the markets were in torpor when she hit
inspiration. An old friend from Cambridge, Manfred Arbingen,
now a journalist with *Die Zeit* in Frankfurt, called for a gossip.

"Just spoke to Finlays. Told me, very pinched-lipped, you'd

gone to ICB. Said it like a curse." He laughed. "Not the most popular bank in the City, is it, your new employer?"

"No. But there are compensations, and anyway, who's in it for popularity?"

"You're right there. Bankers are just about as hated as journalists."

"We're a pair of pariahs," teased Sarah.

"Pariahs," barked Manfred. "Don't talk to me about pariahs. I've just been trying to dredge up an economics story, trudging around to various Bundesbank council members, but no one was saying anything. I'm not greedy. I'd have settled for a little leak, but nothing, *niente*. They were all po-faced and smug-looking."

He continued with his diatribe. Sarah stopped listening, her mind turning over his comment about the smug-looking Bundesbankers. After a while she heard silence. Manfred had dried up. "You still there?"

"Sorry, Manfred, boss was wandering around. Distracted me."

"Who is he?"

"Well, I'm glad you assume it's a man. Good to see that political correctness hasn't polluted Germany."

"All right, all right," he interrupted. "I'm sorry. Anyway, you were saying?"

"Italian. Dante Scarpirato."

Manfred let out a screech. "Ah! What a fruitcake! Mad as a hatter. Friend of mine worked with him a few years ago. God, you really are in it, aren't you?"

But Sarah wasn't listening. She was dreaming up a trade. She said goodbye and hit the line to BdP. Johnny McDermott picked up immediately.

"Johnny, where do you have dollar-mark spot, in a hundred?" What she meant was "What is the dollar-mark exchange rate for a transaction of $100 million, to be settled (paid for) in two days' time?" Her curtness, which would have sounded unspeakably rude anywhere else, was customary on the trading floor. Traders were schizophrenic creatures, sometimes calling up and gossiping idly for half an hour, other times launching straight into business.

"1.7745, 55," McDermott replied. He sold deutsche marks at a rate of 1.7745 to the dollar, paying out DM 1.7745 and receiving $1, and bought them for 1.7755, paying out $1 and receiving DM 1.7755. The difference, known as the spread, in this case was ten "ticks," and was the profit made on buying and selling.

McDermott was a market-maker, whose job was to buy and sell currencies. He was obliged to quote prices for buying and selling without knowing the intentions of the other trader. Trading blind in this way was one of the elements that gave the profession its unpredictability and spice. Sarah, as a proprietary trader, did not make markets in currencies. She bought and sold what she wanted when she wanted. She was never at the mercy of other traders in the way that McDermott was, but the risks she took were infinitely greater than McDermott's. He bought and sold currency all day, but rarely ran a position, that is, took anything other than very short-term gambles. Sarah, in contrast, sometimes ran positions for days, weeks even, buying up, or short-selling, huge volumes of currency.

"I give you one hundred," announced Sarah, meaning she would sell $100 million and buy the deutsche mark equivalent.

"O.K. Done. I buy one hundred dollar-mark at 1.7745," recited McDermott.

"Done," said Sarah.

The tone of their conversation and the language they used

sounded deceptively simple. But almost every word was carefully chosen and had a distinct and legally recognized meaning. Errors and misunderstandings could cost hundreds of thousands of pounds, so concentration was always intense.

The trade completed, Sarah followed the settlement process meticulously. First she scribbled out a trade ticket on her book, where she kept a record of all the trades she made. The ticket covered all the details of the trade: currencies, price, size, counterparty, date of trade, form of settlement, and settlement date. Then she tore off the top section of the ticket, a thin, pale pink slip, and stuck it into the mouth of a small machine that stamped the time on it. Then she dropped the ticket into the settlements tray. Five minutes later it would be picked up by the settlements department, which would ensure that in two days' time $100 million would be deposited in the relevant BdP account in settlement of the trade. Simultaneously, the settlements department at BdP would be making the preparations for 177,450,000 deutsche marks to be delivered to ICB's account in two days' time.

Sarah now had a large deutsche-mark position, which she had acquired in the belief that the deutsche mark would rise against the dollar. If it did, she would cut her position—that is, sell her deutsche marks for dollars—and make a profit, which, with even a small movement in the exchange rate, could be substantial.

Her records complete, she informed Arnott of her trade, as instructed.

"Any particular reason?" he asked sneeringly.

Sarah just smiled. Feminine intuition; nothing he'd understand.

For the next two hours she stared at the screens, waiting, willing the deutsche mark up. Nothing happened. The rate hovered obstinately around 1.7745, 55. She hoped lunch would loosen things up.

Wilson watched her concentrating. It was obvious to him she wasn't going to move, even for something to eat. "I'm off to Birley's for a sandwich," he announced to the air. Scarpirato had sauntered out half an hour ago, followed by Arnott. Sarah was left alone on the desk.

Ten minutes later Wilson returned with two paper bags swinging from his hand. He dropped one on Sarah's desk.

"Avocado and prawn, and orange juice." He smiled broadly. "You look like a healthy eater."

Sarah smiled delightedly, tore open the foil wrapping, and took a hungry bite. "You'd be surprised." She reached for her purse, but Wilson waved her down. It was customary to take new arrivals out for a proper lunch. He'd had one when he arrived a year ago. A Birley's sandwich was the least he could do, and he felt embarrassed at that.

He watched her eating. After a few mouthfuls, the sandwich was gone.

"So you traded?"

Sarah nodded, sipping her orange juice.

"Dollar-mark, like huge?"

Sarah nodded again. Wilson tipped his head to one side and looked at her quizzically. She laughed.

"All right. I think German inflation is better than the figures suggest. I think it might filter out into the markets this afternoon."

"Why?"

"Well, the figures come out tomorrow morning, and from what I gather the Bundesbankers are looking a trifle smug."

Wilson burst out laughing. "A trifle smug? What you mean is, smugger than ever."

Sarah grinned. "I didn't say that. Anyway, I thought it was worth a punt. Hopefully, the DM will rise a tad this afternoon and I'll clear up."

"Why this afternoon, if the figures don't come out till tomorrow?"

"You watch. Very often the market rises or falls in advance of the figures. Somehow or other someone gets an advance sniff."

Intrigued, Wilson watched her for a while, then peered at his screen, picked up his handset, sold $10 million, and bought 17,755,000 deutsche marks at a rate of 1.7755. He dropped the handset back on the desk and grinned at her. "I've got a feeling, too." They were both laughing as Scarpirato and Arnott strolled back from lunch.

At two-thirty, just as Sarah was beginning to get edgy, the deutsche mark began to tick up against the dollar. Each hundredth of a pfennig rise in the value of the mark against the dollar—say, from 1.7745 to 1.7744—gave her a nominal profit of $5,636. What this meant was that if she were to sell her deutsche marks and buy dollars at that moment, at that rate, "cut her position," she would receive $100,005,636. Since she had to pay $100 million for the deutsche marks she had originally bought, she would clear the difference, $5,636, in profit.

After five minutes, the rate was 1.7700, 10; ten minutes later it was 1.7650, 60. In three hours, the dollar-DM exchange rate had moved eighty-five ticks her way and she was sitting on a profit of nearly half a million dollars—$481,314, to be exact. She felt Wilson eyeing her nervously. He wanted to sell, to cut his position and take his profits, but he also wanted to hang in as long as possible while the trend was right and Sarah ran her position.

Sarah waited, staring patiently at her screens, the adrenaline galloping around her system as the minutes passed. At three-thirty, with the rate at 1.7640, 50, she cut her position for a profit of $538,243. Seconds later, Wilson followed her, making $59,490.

Sarah reported back to Arnott, who had watched every move. He said, "Well done," with a taut smile. Then he ostentatiously opened up a copy of the *Financial Times* and buried himself in it, as if indifferent. Sarah and Wilson shrugged and grinned at each other, savoring the high.

On making half a million, some traders would let out a victory whoop and strut around announcing their triumph to a trading floor of five hundred. Sarah never did. She enjoyed her successes quietly. The FX prop department was somewhat cut off from the other trading desks. It was possible to make half a million dollars almost invisibly. Word would filter out, but Sarah never advertised or gloried in her triumphs. Her serenity, win or lose, had given her a certain mystique in the eyes of her fellow traders at Finlays. That reputation followed her to ICB. Wilson watched her with admiration and followed her lead. He sat quietly, a look of satisfaction in his eyes.

Sarah felt like celebrating. She rang Mosami at Yamatoyo Bank. One of Mosami's colleagues answered, and when Sarah asked for her friend, Arnott, two feet away, listened with interest. Mosami Matsumoto—he knew that name. It came to him: friend of his girlfriend's. Small world.

Mosami came on the line. "Hi, darling. Sorry about the delay. Damn business."

Sarah laughed. "Yeah, me too. Listen, how about a drink tonight?"

"Sure. I haven't got anything planned." She was silent for a moment, then asked sharply, "Why?"

Sarah laughed. "News. Celebration. That enough?"

"Plenty," said Mosami suspiciously.

———

At five-thirty Sarah switched off her screens and prepared to leave. She thought she saw Scarpirato watching her through his blinds as she bent to pick up her bag, so she glared at the blinds. Arnott had been in and out of that office all afternoon. He couldn't have failed to have told Scarpirato about her trading success. Any normal boss would have come out and congratulated her straight away, taken her out for a drink at least. But Scarpirato just sat there in his office, impassive behind the blinds. She wasn't going to hunt out his praise. She swung her bag over her shoulder and walked out.

As she walked along Lower Thames Street, she felt, despite her trading success, a tinge of frustration. She was beginning to wonder how she was going to get close enough to Scarpirato to see whether he was up to anything. Most traders like to gossip away the time when the markets are quiet, unroll their personal lives for the past five years in embarrassing detail. As a breed, they are incapable of secrecy. But Scarpirato said little, gave nothing away. He never stopped for a casual chat. Even on business issues he was curt. Arnott was the only person able to drag more than a sentence from him. Sarah wondered what Scarpirato was like with friends, girlfriends, and if he ever dropped his guard.

"So?" asked Mosami, leading Sarah into the sitting room. "What's all this news, then, and what are we celebrating?"

Sarah sat down on the long cream sofa, kicked off her shoes, and stretched her legs out. "New job. ICB."

Mosami let out a hiss. "Good Lord." She took a packet of

cigarettes from a sidetable and lit up. "I hope they're paying you well."

Sarah shrugged. "O.K."

"Well, come on. Why would anyone work there apart from the money?"

Sarah smiled and helped herself to a cigarette.

Mosami watched her with a frown. "Well?"

Sarah laughed. "You've answered your own question. Why would anyone work there apart from the money?"

Mosami shrugged. "Anyway, what is it like? As bad as its reputation?"

"Worse." Sarah laughed. "My boss is pretty distant—an inscrutable Italian, of all things. But at least he's tolerable. His number two is an absolute shit. Matthew Arnott." Sarah said his name with distaste. "Cocky American. He makes it obvious that he hates me. He's probably desperately trying to get me fired before I can show anyone that I might be better than him."

"I've met him a couple of times," said Mosami quietly. "Must say I didn't warm to him."

Sarah drew her legs in and leaned forward. "How do you know him?"

Mosami smiled. Now Sarah was the curious one. "I know his girlfriend. She goes to my gym. Carla Vitale. Italian, terribly beautiful, quite wild." She laughed. "Makes us look like nuns."

Sarah raised an eyebrow. "I don't know about you, but I practically am these days."

"Yeah. Give it time, darling . . ."

"Anyway," said Sarah through laughter, "if she's such hot stuff, what's she doing with Matthew Arnott?"

Mosami looked conspiratorial. "Well, Carla's rather keen on the good things—you know, nice clothes, nice flat, nice trips.

Once, at a party she gave, we both got very drunk. I asked her that very question—what was she doing with Arnott? Apart from anything else, they're always arguing when I see them, never very happy. Carla just smiled and said, I quote, 'He's a goldmine.' " Mosami leaned back in her chair with a smile of satisfaction.

Sarah looked puzzled. "ICB pays well, but I doubt he gets more than about a quarter of a million, three hundred thousand tops."

"Yeah, it's strange. To a girl as greedy as Carla, that's really not a hell of a lot of money. He must have family money. In fact, I'm sure he does. Got a huge house in Holland Park. Must have cost him at least a million. That's probably not care of ICB."

"No," said Sarah, twisting a ring on her finger. "I don't think it is." She looked up. "Anyway, enough of Matthew Arnott. How about that drink?"

Mosami wandered off to the kitchen and returned with a bottle of red wine. She poured out two glasses. Sarah drank hers quickly, then glanced at her watch. She got to her feet. "I'd better be off. Got a lot to do this evening."

Mosami shot her a quick look, said nothing, followed her to the door, and kissed her goodbye. She returned to the sitting room and sat sipping her wine. Man trouble, she decided. Eddie gone; that comment about being a nun. *Methinks she doth protest too much,* thought Mosami.

Sarah walked out of Hay's Mews down Charles Street and into Berkeley Square. She found a phonebox and called Jacob. The phone rang and rang. Sarah could imagine Jacob ponderously laying down a book and making his way to the phone. His movements had slowed in recent years. Finally he answered.

"Hello, Jacob. Can I come round? I think I might have something."

She caught a cab and was in Rotherwick Road half an hour later. Jacob invited her in, sat her down at the kitchen table, and made a cup of tea. He would give her wine only if she stayed to dinner; she drank too much of the stuff as it was. He poured the tea and offered her a plateful of rich tea biscuits.

"I've got some supper on. Casserole. You can stay if you like, but have this for now, eh?"

Sarah smiled and took the tea. Jacob sat down opposite.

"Now, sweetie. What have you come up with?"

Sarah sipped the tea, then put down her cup. "It's not much, but it sounds a bit suspicious." She told him about Arnott's being a "goldmine." "And he spends so much time closeted away with Scarpirato. If there is anything going on, it wouldn't surprise me if they were in it together." She sipped again and looked across at Jacob hopefully.

"It does sound suspicious." He paused and grinned conspiratorially. "But I don't think you're giving yourself a fair shot at all this."

Sarah looked puzzled. "What do you mean?"

"I mean you ought to try some other methods."

Sarah waited for him to expand.

"Bugging, my dear, is what I mean."

Sarah raised her eyebrows and grinned back. "I wondered about that. Ruled it out as too far-fetched."

"Far-fetched? Don't you believe it. It's done all the time, especially in the City—industrial espionage, financial espionage. It's big business. I've got a friend who—"

Sarah burst out laughing, stopping Jacob in his tracks. "I bet you have."

"Well," said Jacob indignantly, "do you want me to get in touch with him?"

Sarah stared into her teacup thoughtfully. "I don't know. I am not sure how all this fits in, or what the governor would say."

"What do you think he'd say?"

"Well, he was distinctly coy about what methods I should use. I got the feeling that I was to use my own discretion. In fact, he said that I was more or less on my own. He implied that he didn't need to know about my methods, just the results. He suggested that we would have to sort of make things up as we went along."

"And what else?"

She shrugged. "That he wants proof, though less rigorous than would be required in a courtroom, that a crime is being committed. But he didn't say how I was to obtain that proof, other than to observe." She smiled. "I suppose bugging is just a more efficient form of observation, isn't it?"

Jacob nodded, and Sarah continued. "The only thing he really did stress, that he was quite explicit about, was that I must not be caught. He said that if I was caught, he would be unable to come to my aid publicly."

Jacob looked up sharply. "What exactly did he mean by that?"

"I suppose he meant that I would be operating in a gray area, possibly outside the law."

This, she realized, was not strictly within Barrington's mandate as governor of the Bank of England, but circumstances justified a little flexibility. She had long believed that various shadowy practices were carried out in the name of government, so she felt no qualms or fears about her task. She would just have to make sure she was not caught.

"Oh, and he gave me three thousand pounds, in cash. Said it was for expenses."

Jacob raised his eyebrows. "Did he say what kind of expenses?"

"No. Just that he was sure I'd find a way of making use of it."

Jacob sat still for a while, saying nothing. Sarah looked at him quizzically.

"What's up? You look worried all of a sudden."

He answered slowly. "No. Not worried. Curious. I'm trying to figure something out."

"What?"

Jacob frowned. "Trying to see where all this fits—the governor's involvement, not coming to your aid publicly, three thousand pounds in cash, untraceable."

"Well?"

"Well, I suppose it doesn't really fit, at least not into any framework I know of." He shrugged and smiled across at Sarah. "I'm probably getting old, behind the times. I'm sure it all makes sense. We'll just have to be a little careful, that's all."

"Careful? Why, particularly?"

"Oh, no specific reason. Just what you said yourself, about the governor warning you not to get caught. Anyway, we're in it now. Committed. The more we find out, the better. So how do you feel about the bugging idea?"

Sarah smiled. "I think perhaps you should get in touch with your friend."

Jacob nodded. "I'll do that, then. I'll go and ring him now." He got up and walked into his study. Sarah, looking out the window, missed the expression on his face as he turned away. It was determined, combative, underscored with worry. He picked up the receiver and began to dial.

After a few rings, a male voice answered. Jacob spoke quietly.

"Charlie, it's Jacob. How are you? Good. Got a few favors to ask. First of all, I want you to find out about a character called Dante Scarpirato. Works in the City at ICB. Has he got any form, any organizational contacts? Second, I need some equipment."

In the kitchen, Sarah sat deep in thought. In the course of one hour she had transformed her role from passive observer to . . . what exactly, she was not sure, but she knew that a boundary had been crossed. She did not at the time question the wisdom of pursuing such a path. By that stage, she was following the Pied Piper of her curiosity. And there was nothing, as far as she knew, to alert her to the presence of danger. The unease she felt was purely a function of uncertainty, of the unknown. That was a familiar sentiment to her, and she passed it off as normal.

Chapter Twelve

S weat was moistening the palms of Giancarlo Catania. He had quickly wiped them against the seat of his trousers before shaking Fieri's hand in farewell. But he feared that that simple gesture had been noticed, and there was no disguising the hotness of his palms in the arctic coolness of Fieri's office.

He felt, almost as keenly as the fear itself, the indignity of fear. This at least produced the mercy of anger, and it was, as always, in his anger that he sought refuge.

His driver and his bodyguard made convenient targets. Both were lounging against his official car, smoking in an attitude of almost studied nonchalance. What good would they be, he screamed, if he was set upon by assassins? Not much, they thought, smiling to themselves.

A bodyguard went with the position of governor of the Bank of Italy. Many senior bankers in Italy had bodyguards. They had become for many as much an instrument of status as of protection. For Catania, the dubious status they conferred had long since ceased to impress, and as for protection, he knew that if he ever came to need it, if perhaps Fieri turned against him, not even a legion of their number would suffice. So loyalty in those he had (four, who revolved duties) was not something that he felt inclined to cultivate. Better instead that they should serve as therapy, as receptacles for his anger.

After his public tantrum, he collapsed into the back seat of his Lancia with relief. The car pulled away with a discreet roar of its powerful engine, slid out of Via Appia Antica on the outskirts of Rome, and joined the traffic on Via di Porta San Sebastiano. Catania checked his watch. Eight forty-five. He should just make it home before his children's bedtime if that imbecile Paulo got a move on. He yanked open the partition and barked out an order. His driver looked warily at his boss's reflection in the driving mirror. Something was really eating him. He saw in his boss's anger a chink of fear.

Paulo overtook a red Fiat on the inside, accelerated away from a furious honking, and wondered for the hundredth time what a nice woman like the signora was doing married to such a pig. He looked all right for his forty-nine years: thick dark hair, not overweight, quite fit-looking. But he was still a pig.

Hunched up in the back, Catania lit a cigar and went over the meeting he had just had with Antonio Fieri. Fieri had been tense, suspicious, demanding. Worse than ever. It was, Catania tried to reassure himself, a sign of the times. It was nothing personal. Everyone was having problems. It seemed as if half the government and much of the financial and business community were being investigated. It was like an inquisition. A sick feeling rose from the pit of Catania's stomach. Perhaps it would be his turn next.

Everyone was worried, even the innocent ones. Senator Amalfi had killed himself last week. His department had become embroiled in a construction scandal. No one who knew him believed for a minute that he was guilty, but he couldn't bear the damage to his reputation. So he took his hunting rifle and shot himself. Catania stared out the tinted windows and tried to control his mounting panic.

He had expected to be in and out in an hour, in time to have a long, lazy evening with his wife and children, but Fieri had kept him there for over two hours, quizzing him about the finance ministers and central bankers of the G7, the Group of Seven Industrial Nations, and the meeting in Frankfurt next week. Catania had little to say and kept trying to tell Fieri to wait until after the meeting, when he'd provide a full report. But Fieri wouldn't let up. He wanted to know why this meeting had been called so suddenly. The regularly scheduled meeting was in two weeks in London. Why did they have to have the Frankfurt meeting as well?

Doing his best to hide his concern, Catania explained that he didn't know. The Germans said only that they would explain everything at the meeting. Everyone grumbled, but of course they would attend. No one snubbed the mighty Bundesbank.

Catania tried to sound casual, nonchalant, but Fieri's persistent questioning and ill humor shook him. Perhaps Fieri suspected something. Catania exhaled loudly. No, he couldn't. It was impossible. There couldn't be a leak. It would be like killing the golden goose. Catania shivered at his own analogy. He tried to shut off his mind. How long would he last if Fieri suspected? Fieri would show no hesitation, no mercy, no remorse. Catania knew that. He would decide, issue an order, and men would materialize, as if from the shadows. Hours. Minutes. Catania started to count.

A jolt shook him as the car screeched to a halt in front of his apartment building on Via di Sant'Eustachio, next to the Pantheon, in the heart of old Rome. He got out without a word, glanced quickly over his shoulder, and walked into the building. He ran up the four flights of stairs to his top-floor apartment. The sound of his shoes on the old stone rang out, muffled by his heavy breath. He stopped outside his apartment and rang the bell. Clara, the housekeeper, let him in. He could hear Donatella's laughter coming from the drawing room as she played with their children—a son and two daughters. Catania hurried into the drawing room and the warm embrace of his wife.

Together they played with the children for ten minutes, then Donatella took them up to bed. Left alone, Catania resumed his worrying. He went into his study, where he sat and stared unseeing through a darkening window. Unable to tolerate inaction, he snatched up the telephone, flicked through his official address book, and called the governor of the Bank of England in his penthouse flat above the bank. It was eight o'clock in London; perhaps he would just catch him before dinner.

Barrington, enjoying a rare evening with no official functions, was just about to sit down to dinner with his wife when the telephone rang. He glared at the receiver as he picked it up. Who on earth could be so stupid as to ring at eight o'clock? It was probably one of those idiots at the Treasury who, if they weren't working late, would have dinner, which they would call tea, at six.

He was surprised to hear a strong Italian accent, and listened to Catania's imperfect English with thinly concealed impatience. By the time Catania came to the point, Barrington's irritation had been transmuted into condescension, which he enjoyed more.

"My dear Governor," he said, "I know it's annoying having two meetings in as many weeks. I can sympathize with you. We are all of us rather occupied, but as I don't know what the Frankfurt meeting is about myself, I am not in a position to say whether it could wisely be combined with the London meeting." He laughed, as if dressing up a secret in a cloak of particularly fine humor. "All I can say is that if the Germans call a meeting, you can rest assured that it will be for a very good reason. They do nothing without intent. They will have given the matter, whatever it is, great consideration and will be comfortable in the knowledge that it will be for our own benefit to attend."

Barrington was not surprised that Catania seemed not to get the joke. He had always thought the Italian a rather dour, humorless individual. He often wondered how Catania had managed to become governor of the Bank of Italy. Persistence, he suspected, and cunning. Dismissing the irritating Italian from his mind, he returned to the dining room, where his wife was waiting.

While Barrington sat down to dinner, Catania remained immobile in his study. Barrington's humor, which the Englishman clearly thought so fine, had done nothing to console him. The contrast between Barrington's easy complaisance and his own unease angered him further. He cursed himself as he got to his feet. He was becoming feeble-minded, easy prey to groundless suspicions. Nothing had happened. If it had, he knew, he would not be sitting here now.

Sarah awoke the next morning with a sense of excitement. Spying on Matthew Arnott was going to be a pleasure. She took her seat next to him at seven twenty-five and began to watch him closely. She wondered about his house in Holland Park, and about Mosami's suggestion that he had family money. Sarah thought that unlikely. People with large private incomes rarely slaved away in investment banks. They might play with it for a few years, but only those with an obsessive desire to make their own pile hung around longer than that. Arnott was approaching thirty, Sarah reckoned. He'd probably been in the markets for about eight years, and anyway, he didn't fit the profile of a rich kid. He was too hungry and insecure. Sarah felt certain that any money he had, he'd made for himself. Quite possibly illegally.

But why hire her, then? If he and Scarpirato were in cahoots, trading illegally, why take risks by taking on new people? Why hire Simon Wilson? Unless, of course, he was up to something too.

Sarah leaned back in her chair, letting her eyes drift over her colleagues. She lit a cigarette and watched the wreaths of smoke curl up to the ceiling. Perhaps hiring outsiders was a cover. There was always pressure from senior management to increase the personnel in a profitable department. If Arnott and Scarpirato were up to something, it would look suspicious to refuse to take on new staff. She laughed inwardly. Perhaps she was not the only one with ulterior motives. Still, that hardly made it any clearer. And Barrington had given her few clues. He had been deliberately opaque—didn't want to prejudice her inquiry. It was obvious that she would have to use her own resources to pursue that inquiry. Hers and Jacob's. She glanced at Arnott sitting sullen-faced at her side. The bugs would definitely turn the tables. His and Scarpirato's cold mysteriousness would be exposed as posturing or concealment, perhaps both.

Scarpirato left early, at four o'clock, Sarah soon after. It had been a quiet day. She had done a small trade, made £15,000, then left well enough alone. Wilson and Arnott dabbled; both lost small amounts. Wilson was sanguine—he never seemed to get worked up—but the losses did nothing for Arnott's mood.

Sarah had been planning to get him talking, pump him about his background, but it would have to wait.

The taxi dropped her off on the King's Road. She popped into the local newsagent's to pick up an *Evening Standard* to check on the City pages and her horoscope. She could have bought one in the City to read in the cab on the way home, but she preferred to gaze out the window at the teeming streets, and to dream. She fumbled in her purse for thirty pence, and, negotiating past red double-decker buses and kamikaze messengers, she skipped across the road, crossed the pavement, and turned into Carlyle Square.

The roar of traffic subsided, and Sarah could hear children playing in the garden that filled the square. Their squeals pierced the air. She watched them chase each other through the trees and bushes. Sarah loved the garden, a green refuge, ideal for sunbathing in summer, always well tended, full of color all year round.

Looking over the gate, she saw her neighbor Mrs. Jardine, overrun by children. Sarah waved and shouted hello over the din. Mrs. Jardine waved back with a long-suffering grin. The local mothers never let their children play unsupervised, and it was Mrs. Jardine's turn on duty tonight. Sarah took over some-times, but now she wasn't in the mood. The atmosphere at work had left her nerves frazzled. She crossed back to the pavement and stopped in front of her house. It was a joy, never failing to lift her spirits.

It was large and airy, four stories high, with an elegant facade in pale brown stone. Including the basement, there were four bedrooms. Sarah's had its own roof terrace, about thirty feet square. Alex had the largest room, which overlooked the garden and acted as a repository of climbing ropes, crampons, rolled-up tents, and all the Day-Glo paraphernalia of serious mountaineering. The third bedroom Sarah had turned into a study, lined floor to ceiling with books; hers were a mad assortment, Alex's all on climbing and mountains. The fourth bedroom, in the basement, was the guest room.

The sitting room occupied the entire first floor. Light swept in from four tall windows overlooking the square and from two smaller windows which looked onto the private gardens at the back. There was a small ornamental balcony beneath these windows, filled with pots of geraniums and sweet williams, which waved through the glass at the greenery within. The walls were covered with a delicate amber-colored glaze, and the floor was dark wood strewn with old Persian rugs. The ceilings were high; Sarah always felt she could breathe in that room.

An eclectic collection of paintings covered the walls: faces of Afghan fighters next to a Scottish mountain landscape; a Nepalese sherpa next to a detail of the African bush below Kilimanjaro; mountain ranges that Sarah could name and recognize from both sides. They made a figurative map of Alex's travels around the world. The record continued in the kitchen and bathroom, where the walls were covered with enlarged photographs of what looked like make-believe Chinese mountains, whose peaks rose like daggers to the sky. Sarah would lie in her bath gazing at them, imagining herself there.

Today the house was tidy. Barbara, the cleaning lady, had made one of her rare visits. Sarah relished the order, kicking off her heels in the hall and dumping her suit and shirt on the bed. Someone had rung when she was out. It was Pierluigi di Rivana, a former colleague from Finlays. A few days previously, Sarah had rung him, suggesting they get a group of people together for dinner tonight. He was calling to confirm and to say that he would come by to pick her up at nine. His voice was slightly sharp, inquiring, aggrieved. Possessive still. Sarah knew he had long harbored a proprietorial interest in her. When, a few days earlier, she had established that he knew Marco Scarpirato, Dante's brother, and suggested that he invite him to dinner, Pierluigi had run through a range of excuses not to invite him, each rejected by Sarah. Reluctantly he had agreed to do his best to bring Marco along. Conveniently for Sarah, he had put her interest down to sexual intrigue, and, much amused, she did not try to disillusion him. She gathered from his message that Marco could come. She smiled to herself. She wondered if the brothers were alike.

She took a long, luxurious shower, washed her hair, and lay on her bed. The windows were open, and a gentle breeze wafted through the muslin curtains and cooled her. She read fitfully from a paperback, dozed until nine, then dressed quickly in a blue-and-white cotton button-down dress and high navy slingbacks. She brushed out the tangles in her hair, dabbed on some scent, and at nine-fifteen, predictably late, Pierluigi arrived.

"Ciao, Sarah. How are you?"

Sarah kissed him on both cheeks. "Ciao, Pierluigi. Fine, thank you. How are you?"

"Oh, I'm fine. Busy." He shot her a questioning look. "And curious."

Sarah smiled. "Don't be."

They went to Scalini's, in Walton Street. It was packed and noisy. It was the last thing Sarah needed after a day on the trading floor, but the Italians loved it, and she'd already had one favor; no point in suggesting somewhere spacious and quiet. Pierluigi led her up to the table. Eight of them were there already, and there was room for two more. Sarah knew them all except one. For what seemed like an age she was caught up in a flurry of kisses and hellos, but she finally turned to her right and to the stranger who was sitting quietly, watching the performance, a smile of amusement on his face. Pierluigi made the introductions with a stiff bow.

"Sarah Jensen, Marco Scarpirato."

They shook hands. Sarah slid into the empty seat next to him. Pierluigi sat across from her, watching her. Sarah smiled and turned back to Marco. He was shorter than his brother, and younger. The face that smiled at her was full and unlined, the voice and posture relaxed. He was dressed casually in jeans and a T-shirt that did nothing to hide a slight paunch. No one would have taken them for brothers.

"So how do you know Pierluigi?"

"Finlays. We worked together."

"No longer?"

"No, I left just a few days ago."

"Oh, where to?"

"ICB." Sarah dropped it casually. For a moment Marco seemed not to react. His face was impassive, then, strangely, it flickered with annoyance before returning once more to polite impassivity.

"My brother works there. He's called Dante."

"You're kidding! He's my boss." Sarah chuckled. Small world and all that.

"Poor you."

"Why's that?"

"Well, evil genius, you know."

Sarah allowed herself to look intrigued. "No. I don't know."

The impassivity cracked and Marco looked genuinely annoyed. "C'mon. My brother's brilliant, everyone knows that. But they don't pretend to like him."

Sarah began to feel uncomfortable. "He seems perfectly all right to me. Inscrutable, perhaps, but not unlikable. Certainly not evil."

Marco turned in his chair and flashed her a huge smile that didn't reach his eyes. "You don't know him."

The attempt at humor only served to increase Sarah's discomfort. So two brothers didn't get on, superficially didn't like each other. They would call each other bastards; that was acceptable brotherly friction. But Marco clearly felt the need to attempt to disguise his feelings. That he was unsuccessful only reinforced Sarah's impression that his feelings ran particularly hard and deep. She wondered what Dante had done to his younger brother.

Sarah shrugged. "Anyway, I've had quite enough of the City for one day. Let's talk about something else." She watched his shoulders ease slightly. "You're not in the City, I take it?"

He laughed. "No, thank God. I did it for three years, hated it, and quit. I'm an art student now."

"That's quite a change. What made you pick art? Artistic blood in the family?"

"No," he answered stiffly. "It's my own thing entirely. My father was a banker. He was delighted when both his sons followed him." He shrugged. "Dante was a great success. I was a great failure. There's no in-between, really, is there?"

"Not in the City, no. It has a tendency to polarize things."

Marco turned again and for the first time seemed to look at her properly. "What are you doing there?"

Sarah laughed. "You might well ask. I'm not sure. It's just something to do in the meantime, isn't it?"

Marco smiled and seemed to warm to her. "That's not very committed, is it?"

"Yuck, disgusting word. 'Are you committed to this business, to this firm? That's very important to us you know, commitment.'" Sarah mimicked the spiel that was repeated across the City a hundred times a day. Marco burst out laughing.

"Better not tell your brother that."

The laughing stopped abruptly. "Why should I?" The question was abrupt, and once more Sarah felt Marco's tension. She shrugged.

"That's all right, then." She smiled, and turned to talk to her other neighbor.

At twelve-thirty, just as Sarah was about to fall asleep at the table, the bill was finally paid and everyone rose to leave. They all said goodnight, and Sarah walked to the car with Pierluigi.

"So, satisfied? You wanted to meet Marco Scarpirato. Got what you wanted?"

Sarah was surprised by Pierluigi's tone. She glanced up at him, slightly annoyed. One hypersensitive man a night was quite enough.

"I didn't want anything, Pierluigi. I was just a little curious, that's all."

"Curious. Well, I'm rather curious, too." He drove in silence for a while, then turned into Carlyle Square and double-parked outside Sarah's house. He walked her up the steps to her front door, kissed her goodnight, then hesitated, the annoyance gone, replaced by a look of awkwardness.

"Look, Sarah, I just want to know what's going on. First of all you ask if I know Dante Scarpirato. Only by reputation, I say. But I know his brother Marco well. Bring him along to dinner, you say." He looked at her gravely and said in his melodramatic Italian way, "I don't know what you're up to, but whatever it is, you must not go out with Dante Scarpirato. Do you understand me?"

Sarah laughed in amazement. "What on earth makes you say

that? Why should I want to go out with Dante Scarpirato? I've got a wonderful boyfriend, whom I love, and even if I didn't, I wouldn't go out with Scarpirato."

Pierluigi was unmoved. "You're his type," he said, his words like slow drumbeats.

Sarah jutted her elbows out, hands on hips. "And that's it, is it? I have no say in the matter?"

Pierluigi broke into a smile at the image of resistance. "Well, you might be all right." But he added quietly as he turned away, "They all give in, sooner or later." He looked back at her standing on her steps. "Call me in a week."

Sarah let herself in, mulling over Pierluigi's words. She had been so busy defending herself that she hadn't asked the obvious question. What was so terrible about Dante Scarpirato? Why did Pierluigi feel it necessary to issue such a dire warning? Jealousy, perhaps? No, for all its power, this was more than that. As she undressed and got into bed, she felt uneasy again. An image of Scarpirato, silent in his dark suit in his dark office, filled her mind. Her conversations with Marco and Pierluigi had done nothing to improve her confidence in the man. More than that, they had left her actively worried. She had always thought of so-called white-collar crime as almost clean, painless. But around Dante Scarpirato there was an aura of pain, of fear.

Chapter Thirteen

"You made quite an impression on my poor brother." Dante Scarpirato smiled and leaned toward Sarah, his elbows on the desk, as she sat in front of her screens. "It's unfair, you know, to pick on someone like him."

Sarah looked up and met his glance. "So who should I pick on?"

His eyes widened fractionally. Before he could answer, Arnott came up and slapped him on the back.

"Morning, Dante." He sounded even more full of himself than usual.

Scarpirato ignored Arnott and walked into the conference room. Taking their cue, the others followed, Wilson arriving just in time. For the first time, Scarpirato gave them a trading axe— an order. He wanted them to buy sterling. He felt that the pound was undervalued. He thought that economic recovery was under way in the U.K., but that because it had taken so long in coming and been falsely hailed too many times before, the market was reluctant to believe the politicians, who claimed that this time a strong upturn really was in sight.

Scarpirato also thought that the representatives of G7, from the United States, Japan, Germany, France, Italy, and Canada as well as Britain, all agreed that sterling was undervalued, and that they would probably get together and mount a support operation. The only question was when. Scarpirato thought it would be soon.

Sarah listened with interest. She agreed with her boss's analysis, on the whole. The joker in the pack was the timing. Scarpirato said he wanted them to build up a substantial position, say £300 million, which would mature in a week's time. He instructed his team to buy sterling futures, against dollars, of a one-week duration. This meant that they would enter the market today and agree to buy from other counterparties in the market a certain amount of sterling in seven days, paying for it with dollars, at the exchange rate that today's market thought would prevail in one week. They would be betting that in the meantime the pound would rise in value against the dollar, so that the pounds they received in one week could be sold immediately to yield more than enough to buy the dollars they needed to satisfy their side of the bargain. The pounds left over afterward would be pure profit.

It was like agreeing to buy three apples in return for three oranges in a week's time, to find after receiving the apples that you could sell them for four oranges. Only in this case, if Scarpirato bet correctly, they could make millions of pounds.

For every hundred million pounds' position they held, ICB put up ten million in capital. The rest was borrowed. Speculating on borrowed money, otherwise known as margin trading, was a risky business, but if you read the markets correctly, the returns could be spectacular. That was the attraction of leverage. You put up only a fraction of the stake, but you took all the profits.

On a position of £300 million, a small movement of the market in the right direction could yield millions of pounds in profits. But it cut both ways. You could also lose millions, wiping out your entire capital backing. So if you held a £300 million position backed by £30 million of capital, and the market moved against you, you could lose your entire £30 million capital. Having the right idea was not good enough. You needed perfect timing as well.

On Scarpirato's calculations, sterling was going to rise against the dollar within the next week. It was a very precise gamble, requiring pinpoint timing, and it contradicted the short-term market view. You needed to be very brave, or very sure of your facts, to make such a gamble. But there were no facts, only surmise. Sarah wondered what made Scarpirato so sure.

The team spent the next day and a half building up their position, a skillful exercise in itself. Market-makers, the people they would be trading with as they did so, were ultrasensitive. If they suspected that ICB was building up a major sterling position, they would increase the rate against the dollar at which they offered sterling. On a position as big as three hundred million, that could mean tens of thousands of pounds of lost profits. So Sarah, Arnott, and Wilson moved stealthily in the markets, building up the position bit by bit, in small trades of about £10 million a time. By the close of business on Friday, the position had been filled without arousing the other market-makers' suspicions.

At five o'clock, Scarpirato, who had spent the whole day closeted in his office, walked over to the trading desks.

"How's it going?" he asked Arnott.

"Fine." Arnott swung in his revolving chair to face Scarpirato. "We've filled the position, and there wasn't a whisper. We got great rates."

Scarpirato smiled. "Good. No fuck-ups. Well done. You know my mania about secrecy."

Sarah turned slowly to look at Scarpirato. He glanced at her, turned, and walked back into his office. Sarah watched his back, got up from her desk, and followed him. She walked over to the shuttered office, knocked on the glass door, and, before waiting for an answer, let herself in. Scarpirato was just sitting down at his desk. He looked up in surprise as she pulled up a chair and sat down across from him. He raised his eyebrows and coolly scrutinized her, waiting for an explanation with a slight look of triumph on his face, as if he had goaded her into coming to him. She ignored it. Leaning back in her chair, she fixed him with a quizzical look.

"I'm curious, Dante, about how you came up with this idea about sterling." She waited for a reaction. It came almost instantaneously, as if she had pushed a button. The faint smile vanished from his lips, and his eyes narrowed so that the white was almost covered, leaving only a dark glare. Sarah studied his face, horrified, fascinated. Concentrated in the almost black eyes and the rigid set of his mouth were rage and disdain, uninhibited and unconcealed. Emotions common enough on a trading floor, they were rarely worn so explicitly. As Sarah watched him, his expression remained fixed. Here was the deliberate disregard of the conventions of behavior that she had seen before, in his curtness of speech, in his gaze. Then it was desire, now hostility, equally intense, equally intimate. Sarah looked into the dark, angry eyes. When he answered her, he spoke haltingly, as if it pained him.

"I thought I explained that yesterday morning. If you didn't understand, why did you slavishly follow my instructions for a day and a half?"

But for the look in his eyes, Sarah would have laughed. The taunt was crude, but somehow it worked. She bit back an answer and studied him in silence, wondering whether his reaction was prompted by a latent insecurity, which made him dislike any implied threat to his authority, or by sensitivity to this particular question. Either way, it was revealing in a man who clearly regarded himself as the epitome of confidence, who should have been inured to a gentle barb, even if he did have something to hide.

She shrugged. "Perhaps I missed something. You explained why you thought sterling would rise, and I happen to agree with you, but why now?" She crossed her legs and asked levelly, "Was there some kind of trigger, or were you just punting?"

The anger flared again in his eyes as he registered the insult, confirming Sarah's impression that he was a man whose professional acts were carefully calculated, governed by the intellect. Punting was a game of chance, justified by instinct. The charm of recklessness, which punting held for many traders, he would regard with disdain. The dark eyes regarded her for a few more seconds. Then he blinked once, as if to banish the hostility, and opened up.

"I just read my newspapers, read between the lines, watch the finance ministers when they are televised together. You can tell a lot just from their reactions to one another, and I keep my ears open for gossip." Scarpirato leaned back in his chair, interlocking his hands behind his head. He said nothing for a few moments, then swung forward in his chair and leaned across his desk toward her. "Satisfied?"

Sarah stood, walked to the door, and leaned against the frame.

It was a conventional answer, and she wasn't satisfied. She gave a quick smile.

"Not very original, but plausible." She felt his eyes on her back as she returned to her desk.

There was nothing left to do in the office and she had a full evening ahead, so she switched off her screens, picked up her bag, and left.

When she arrived home she found Jacob sitting at her kitchen table drinking tea. He had a spare set of keys and let himself in from time to time to do a bit of handiwork, hang pictures, wait around for delivery men and meter readers, or sometimes just to check that Sarah was all right.

She grinned when she saw him. "Jacob." She leaned down to kiss his cheek. "What a nice surprise."

"I just popped by with some news. Can't stay. I'll just tell you, then I'll be off. Friday night, you'll probably be going out on the town, won't you?"

Sarah fetched a mug and poured herself some tea from the pot on the table. "No big night out. I'm too tired, to be honest. So why don't you stay to supper? It's about time I treated you."

He laughed. "Well, if you're sure."

Sarah smiled. "I'm sure. Now what about your news?"

"Well, that can keep. You're probably all in, getting up at six. Don't you want to have a nap first? Then I'll tell you. I can get supper ready in the meantime."

"I'm fine, Jacob. Come on, tell me. The suspense is killing me."

He took a long sip of tea, enjoying her curiosity. "Well, I saw my friend today. About the bugs." He shot Sarah a triumphant look. "He says he can do it. But he needs some information first."

Sarah grinned. "Brilliant. Fire away."

He didn't tell her about his questions about Scarpirato, nor about the answers that were beginning to come back. He didn't think it was relevant.

Later that evening, after she and Jacob had eaten supper and he had driven home, Sarah called Mosami.

"Hi, it's Sarah. Listen, darling. I need to ask you something. Is it all right if I come round now?"

"Yes, of course. See you in a bit." Mosami put down the phone and frowned. Sarah had been acting a bit strange lately, a bit mysterious. She hoped nothing was wrong.

Sarah walked out into Carlyle Square and got into her car, a 1973 silver-gray BMW CSL. It was a pillarless coupe, built for the road but also for racing. Where possible, the bodywork was aluminum, for extra lightness. It had a three-liter engine, four gears, which it soared through, and a top speed of 140 mph. Only five hundred right-hand-drive models had been built. It had bucket seats, much prized by aficionados. It was a highly covetable, collectible car. Sarah had bought it two years previously to celebrate surviving another year in the City. It was her pride and joy.

She drove around Carlyle Square, right onto Old Church Street, right again onto the Fulham Road, and on to Mayfair. Fifteen minutes later she drew up in Hay's Mews in front of Mosami's house. Mosami heard the car and went to open the door. She stood on the doorstep in a satin kimono over matching pajamas. Her long hair hung loose, making black stripes against the yellow silk of the kimono.

The two women kissed. Mosami gestured to her outfit. "I hope you don't mind. I was kind of lounging around when you rang. You know, Friday nights. I'm absolutely knocked out." She grinned. "I was in bed watching a video of *The Big Easy* when you rang, lusting after Dennis Quaid."

Sarah laughed. "Mmmn. I can imagine. Sounds like bliss."

"It is." Mosami led Sarah into the kitchen. "Chamomile tea?"

"Love one."

Mosami filled the kettle. "So what's going on?"

Sarah spoke to her friend's back. "Why should anything be going on?"

Mosami snorted. "Come on, Sarah. You've been acting quite strange lately. New job all of a sudden, all mysterious. Nothing dramatic, but I know the signs, remember?"

Sarah watched the kettle boil. Mosami took down a teapot from a cupboard and dropped in two chamomile teabags. After filling the pot with boiling water, she placed it on a wooden tray with two cups and carried it into the sitting room, then sat on the sofa and poured the tea.

Sarah sat next to her and sipped carefully, the steam from the tea warming her face. Then she put down the cup on the wooden table before her and turned to face her friend.

"Well, things are a bit strange. I don't really know where to start." She sighed heavily, and her eyes moved around the room as if searching for inspiration. "Like I said on the phone, I need to ask you something. I need your help, but I can't really explain why. At least not in any detail."

Mosami examined Sarah's eyes and the set of her mouth. Sarah raised her eyebrows as if expecting a response, but Mosami shrugged. She sensed Sarah's unease, felt it herself.

Sarah spoke again suddenly. "Look, there's no roundabout way of saying this. It's about Carla Vitale. I need to get into her flat."

Mosami was silent for a while, contemplating the painting that hung on the far wall, a swath of colors, all shades of blue from ice to indigo. Then she turned back to her friend.

"What on earth is going on, Sarah?"

"I'm sorry, Mosami, I really can't tell you. I wish I could. Anyway, I'm not even sure myself. That's what I have to find out. It's all to do with Matthew Arnott. I think he might be breaking the law. And I think Carla might know something about it."

Mosami tilted her head to one side. "So you want to get into her flat?"

Sarah nodded. "I want to install some listening devices."

"Bugs?"

"Yes."

Mosami sat back, letting her eyes rest on Sarah. There was little in their history that had not been shared, either directly or in the telling, sometimes years later. They spoke now in a kind of shorthand; explanations were redundant. What seemed like far bigger requests had been made in the past: for money, for help, for unconditional friendship. This one was strange, but in the litany, it was just a request for a thing, as easy as money, easier. It was nothing. Yet her friend was worried.

Mosami reached for her cigarettes on the coffee table. She offered one to Sarah. For a while they smoked in silence. Then Mosami sat forward and ground out her cigarette.

"Look, I don't understand what you're doing or why you're doing it. No doubt it's better that way. You don't want to tell me and I don't want to know. We'll leave it like that." She paused. "And yes, of course I'll help you. You know I will. I only hope you know what you're doing, that's all."

When Sarah got back to her house, she called Jacob in Golders Green.

"Jacob, it's me. I've just been to see Mosami. She'll help me. So tell your friend we have access."

Jacob put down the phone and called a number in East London. A friendly middle-aged voice answered. Jacob was brief.

"We've got access. To all three targets."

"Good. Come round tomorrow afternoon, say three. I'll have all the stuff by then."

Saturday morning; the alarm clock had been banished to another room. Sarah was freed from its relentless ticking and insidious beeping. She woke up at ten and lay in bed for five minutes, luxuriating in the knowledge that she could stay there uninterrupted for a few more hours if she chose. The sun was streaming through the muslin curtains, and she could already feel the incipient heat of what promised to be a scorching day.

Her thoughts drifted off to Eddie and Alex. She wondered what they were doing. It would be late afternoon in Nepal. Perhaps they were making their descent from a summit climbed in the morning; perhaps they were resting in bad weather. She tried to imagine them huddled in a tent, with snow and gales whirling around the thin canvas. Maybe they lay silently in sleeping bags, thinking of her. She felt a stab of longing to be out there with them, doing whatever they were doing.

She got out of bed slowly, threw on her cotton dressing gown, and walked through to the sitting room. She bent down to gaze at her collection of CDs and picked out Ella Fitzgerald's greatest hits. "Mack the Knife" pealed out at her as she headed for the kitchen and began to prepare the cappuccino machine for its noisy production. Five minutes later she carried a frothing cup of coffee, a quartered orange, a sliced kiwi fruit, and an overflowing bowl of Kellogg's Crunchy Nut Cornflakes covered with chopped banana and whole milk into her bedroom. After laying the tray down carefully on her bed, she squeezed under the covers, carrying in one hand a book she had retrieved from the floor. She ate her breakfast in a leisurely way, reading her book, letting time amble by.

She had nothing planned today. Pierluigi had invited her to join him and some friends of his for dinner. She didn't know if she'd go. Since Alex and Eddie's departure, she hadn't been sure if she wanted company or not. One minute she relished the silence, the next she dreaded it. Other times it just filled her with apathy. It was a pattern, and she knew it well enough. And how to break it. Sooner or later she would create a drama, draw herself out forcibly. Then the drama would ebb, and she would be left with a fragile peace. Tenuous but sweet relief.

Jacob rang at four. Sarah had just got back from a run.

"Ah, sweetie, you're home. Can I pop round? I have something for you."

Sarah grinned. "I'll be here."

He arrived at five, carrying a white plastic bag. Following Sarah into the kitchen, he sat at the table while she made tea. She opened a cupboard to reveal about ten tins and packets of different teas. She took down three, jasmine, Earl Grey, and gunpowder, and dropped equal measures of each into her favorite teapot. A present from Jacob, it had been painted by Clarice Cliff with running antelopes. She took two matching cups, poured out the tea, and sat opposite Jacob with an expectant smile. He reached for the bag lying at his feet. She lit up a cigarette. Jacob put the bag on the table and took out three plug adapters and a double telephone socket.

Sarah stared at them, intrigued. She looked up at Jacob, her eyes shining. They grinned at each other.

"Brilliant, aren't they?" said Jacob.

"They're amazing. Just like ordinary adapters. You just plug them in and they start working?"

"More or less. They're voice-activated—pick up anything in the room, some stuff from neighboring rooms, too. They have their own built-in transmitters, which are good up to about a mile. The transmitters relay everything to a receiver, which then records everything on a digital audiotape machine." Jacob pulled two small recorders about five inches long, three high, and two wide from the plastic bag. "They're specially adapted. The tape runs for a total of twelve hours. I've got twenty tapes. That should do for starters." He pushed on, record, and play. "See. Easy. Just like normal tape players." He reached down to the bag to draw out a handful of tapes. "Oh, I almost forgot. Here's a mini-recorder. Carry it with you, works up to about twenty feet." He handed it over, beaming.

"You're amazing, Jacob. You know that?"

The old man laughed, his eyes bright. "You say you can get into Carla's flat?"

"Think so."

Jacob nodded. "I've checked the distance. Less than a mile. You're perfectly located. All I need to do is set up the receivers. I'll put them on the roof, if that's all right?"

Sarah nodded. "Fine. Anywhere."

"Roof's best. Better reception." He took a long sip of tea, then carried the cup to the sink, returned to the table, and sat down, straight-backed and serious. "My friend has the receivers for the bugs you're going to use at work. He lives in Whitechapel, in a new high-rise block, on the tenth floor. It's perfectly located for picking up the traffic from the ICB bugs. It's less than a mile away, and high up." He paused, glanced at Sarah's face, and continued. "There is the risk he'll listen to the tapes. He's a nosy old bugger, but he's totally trustworthy. If he does listen in, it'll go no further."

Sarah smiled. "If you trust him, Jacob, it's fine by me."

Jacob looked relieved. "I thought it would be all right. Like I said, he's a good man, one of my old pals. He and I used to get up to a few escapades together, I can tell you."

Sarah started laughing. "One of the old boys. Great recommendation!"

Jacob pretended to look hurt. "You're impossible sometimes. I don't know how I cope with you."

"Sorry. It was irresistible," Sarah said, squeezing his arm.

"Anyway, he'll take care of the ICB output. The rest is up to you. You've got two receivers and two recorders, one for the room bug, the other for the telephone bug. Both of those are for Carla. I can easily get more equipment, so let me know if you think you can get to Arnott and whatsisname, Scarpirato's house, won't you?" He muttered the Italian's name with distaste. Sarah registered it, but let it pass. She would not have expected him to have a natural affinity for smooth Italians.

"I will, Jacob. And thanks." She smiled. "Oh, I nearly forgot. How much is all this?"

"I got a special deal." Jacob grinned. "Normally be about eight grand. Got it for four."

Sarah gulped. "God, they're expensive, these things. But well done, though," she added quickly. "Great deal." She walked to her desk and took out the envelope with Barrington's cash. "Here's three. I'll get the rest out on Monday, give it to you then. Will that be all right for your friend?"

Jacob nodded. He had already paid his friend with his own money.

When he left a little while later, Sarah called Mosami.

"Mosami, hi, darling, it's me. Listen, any chance of dropping in on Carla tomorrow?"

———

Carla Vitale lived in Onslow Square, about half a mile from Sarah, in a west-facing three-bedroom penthouse flat. Mosami had been there several times to parties and had dropped by alone once before, for coffee, after a shopping trip along the Fulham Road. She had telephoned Carla the day before and said that she would be having tea at five o'clock with a friend around the corner. Would it be all right if she dropped by for something stronger later? It sounded reasonable enough. Carla obviously thought so too, for she had duly invited her, and now here she was, with a plug adapter and a double telephone socket in her handbag, knocking on Carla's door, wondering what the hell she was doing.

"Mosami, darling, come in." Carla was wrapped in a towel. "Sorry, it's all a bit chaotic. I've just had a massage, all greasy. Got to wash my hair." She laughed and drew Mosami inside. "Help yourself to a drink. There's some white wine in the fridge. I'll be with you in a minute." She disappeared into her bedroom and left Mosami alone.

Mosami went to the kitchen, found the bottle of wine, hunted round for a corkscrew, finally found one, poured herself a glass of Sancerre, and returned to the sitting room. She put down the glass on a side table and looked for a socket. After a while she found what she was looking for: an adapter crammed with plugs, one for a light, one for the television, and one for a VCR. She knelt down, pulled out the adapter, and replaced it with the one from her handbag. Then she sat down on the sofa, glass in hand, trembling very faintly, just as Carla appeared. She sipped her wine and smiled. Conversation came naturally, lightly. She was surprised at how easily duplicity came to her. But then, trading bonds for eight hours a day required almost constant dissembling. It was just that this was more personal. Not that she had any deep feelings for Carla. Carla was an attractive acquaintance, overflowing with fun and vitality, but her allure cut no deeper than a scratch.

Mosami continued to smile and speak, wondering all the while why she was so uneasy. She tested reasons, rejected them. Then, in a flash of insight, she understood: it was fear, Sarah's fear. Sarah had been frightened when she had asked for help. Not of Carla, not of anything obvious or visible. But something, or someone, hidden in the background, was frightening her.

Mosami sipped her wine and stopped her pondering. She had said she'd help, and she would. All she had to do now was get at a telephone somehow or other, to install the second bug. She continued to play out her role, cool, poised, smiling lightly, to the outside eye utterly composed.

Her chance came fifteen minutes later. She glanced at her watch, then sat bolt upright. "Shit, I forgot. I'm supposed to be in Hampstead in ten minutes. Can I make a quick telephone call?"

Carla smiled. "Sure. Use the one in the bedroom if you like." She winked. Mosami smiled and, feeling a pang of conscience, took her handbag to Carla's bedroom.

The telephone socket was under the bed. Mosami squatted on the floor, picked out the telephone line, slotted it into the double adapter, and inserted the adapter into the wall socket. There was now a double telephone socket where there had just been a single connection. But the whole contraption was hidden under the bedclothes draping to the floor. There was no reason why Carla should examine it, or even remark on it in any way if for some reason she happened to notice it.

Mosami sat up with a jolt. She heard voices. She got to her feet and hurried out of the room. In the hallway she saw Matthew Arnott. He swung around as he heard her footsteps. "Mosami. How nice. What are you doing here?" Always the trace of sarcasm in his voice.

"Don't worry. I won't get in the way of a quiet night with your girlfriend. I just came round for a drink." She looked sheepish. "Then I remembered I was supposed to be in Hampstead two minutes ago." She kissed Carla on both cheeks. "Thanks for the drink, Carla. Sorry to rush off like this. 'Bye, Matthew." Before anyone could remark on her flushed cheeks, she was gone.

"I don't think I'm cut out for this sort of thing." Mosami was back home, calling Sarah from the sanctuary of her bed.

Sarah groaned. "Oh, Mosami, I'm sorry. I really shouldn't have asked you."

"Don't be stupid. I said I'd help." She laughed lightly. "I was as keen as you were. It sounded like fun, like a kind of innocent cat burgling." She paused and the laughter faded from her voice. "It just didn't feel like it at the time. I got a really bad attack of conscience."

"I know. I've got one, too."

"Well, I'm sure it's for a good cause." Both women were silent with their thoughts for a few seconds.

"I hope so," said Sarah.

At ten o'clock on Sunday night Sarah drove her BMW to the City. The streets of the Square Mile were deserted. Banks of light still shone out from the skyscrapers all around, but they burned for security reasons only.

During the boom years of the eighties there would have been teams of corporate financiers and lawyers beavering away through the weekend, but that was a rare interruption to today's less lucrative but rather more civilized lifestyle. Occasionally traders would come in on Sunday night to execute business with the opening Far East markets, so Sarah could not be certain the trading floor would be empty, but there was a good chance of it, and anyway, all she really needed was a clear run at Arnott's desk and Scarpirato's office, and that shouldn't be too difficult.

She parked the car in the driveway to the garages directly under the ICB building, walked back to the main entrance, and rang the bell on the marble facade. She felt her pulse quicken and the adrenaline begin to flow. A security guard appeared. Sarah held up her security card for inspection. The guard squinted at it through the glass. Satisfied, he unlocked the door and let her in. She knew the routine and followed him up to the night book lying on the reception desk, where she signed in.

"That your car on the drive?"

"Yeah." He must have seen it on the monitor cameras.

"Wouldn't mind one myself. Beauty, isn't it?"

"My pride and joy."

"You know you're not supposed to park there, don't you?"

Sarah smiled. "I know. But I won't be long, I promise. Ten minutes?"

"Go on, then." As she started to go, he asked, "So what is it? No peace for the wicked, eh?"

Sarah turned and shrugged. "Yeah, something like that. A few trades with Tokyo and I'm free again." He grinned back, not sure what to read into that, and watched her walk over to the lifts, her high heels beating out a pleasing rhythm on the polished floor.

A lift stood waiting, doors open invitingly. Sarah stepped in and rode up to the trading room. She ran her pass through the security check, and the heavy glass doors clicked open onto what looked like an empty floor. The lights were on in places, but there were pockets of gloom, complete darkness almost. It was eerily quiet.

Sarah walked silently across the floor. A bank of clocks suspended from the ceiling watched her pass. She stopped at her desk, sat down, opened her handbag, and took out one of the adapters. She pushed her chair back and bent down, peering under the desk. There was a maze of wires and double and triple sockets, with assorted plugs. She pulled out two, plugged them into the adapter, and stuck the adapter into a socket. Then she straightened up, got to her feet, took a second adapter from her bag, cast a quick look around, and headed for Scarpirato's office. It was unlit, and Sarah's eyes took a minute to adjust to the gloom. She went behind his desk and studied the back wall. In a corner was a double socket, with a plug for the reading lamp on one side and another for a computer on the other. Sarah inserted the plug for the lamp into her adapter and plugged the adapter into the wall. She smiled down at her handiwork for a few seconds, then turned and walked briskly back to her desk. She was about to go when she froze. Walking across the trading floor toward her were Matthew Arnott and Karl Heinz Kessler, the chief executive of ICB. They stared at her in surprise. Sarah smiled, hoping her shock didn't show.

"What are you doing here?" asked Arnott, glaring at her, ignoring her smile.

Thinking quickly, Sarah reached her hand inside her desk drawer and ripped from the top underside of the drawer a spare set of house keys that she had taped there in case she ever locked herself out of her house. She preferred not to have to pick her way in if she could possibly avoid it. She waved the keys brightly in the air.

"Forgot my London house keys." She laughed deprecatingly. "Pretty stupid, eh?"

"Yeah. Pretty stupid."

Kessler watched in silence. Sarah turned to him. "We haven't met. I'm Sarah Jensen, the new proprietary trader."

Kessler shook her outstretched hand. "Yes. I've heard about you." He gave her a cold smile.

Sarah turned to Arnott and smiled again into his hostile face as if expecting an explanation from him. For a few seconds he said nothing, then he snapped in annoyance, "Karl Heinz wants to do a big Tokyo trade. Asked me to put it on for him."

Sarah nodded. "Fair enough." She smiled to Kessler. "Well, goodnight. I'm off."

The two men watched her walk across the floor and disappear through the security doors. Kessler turned to Arnott. "Do you believe her?"

Arnott scratched his chin. "C'mon, she locked herself out. We've all done it before. And I keep spare keys here. I believe her."

Kessler glared at Arnott. "Just watch her, O.K.?"

Sarah took the lift down to the ground floor, signed herself out, and said goodnight to the guard. She walked to her car, let herself in, and lit a cigarette with a trembling hand.

Chapter Fourteen

Monday morning. The finance ministers and the heads of the central banks of the Group of Seven Industrial Nations sat in their high-backed, leather-upholstered brown chairs around an oval table of veneered oak at the massive Bundesbank building in Frankfurt. The room, on the top floor, was high-ceilinged, wood-paneled, decorated at either end by two colored abstract wall tapestries by Max Ernst, the surrealist painter from Cologne. Fifty meters below this room, a great many bank notes, but little gold, were stored in underground strongrooms. The Bundesbank was unique among the world's principal gold-holding central banks in that it kept only a tiny proportion of its bullion on its own premises. About eighty tons, just over 2 percent, lay in the vaults in Frankfurt. The rest was held in the vaults of other central banks—the Federal Reserve Bank of New York, the Bank of England, and, to a much lesser extent, the Banque de

France. The guards who patrolled the Bundesbank were there to protect personnel as much as property. Today their number was swelled by the bodyguards of a number of the men meeting on the thirteenth floor.

There, in the council chamber, seasoned bankers and politicians sat among solid glass ashtrays and bottles of soft drinks. They smiled, chatted, and waited. Anthony Barrington sat next to his opposite number at the Banque de France, Jean-Claude de la Barobisière. Old friends, the two men spoke warmly, blanking out the growing tension.

After a tense two minutes, Herr Mueller, the president of the Bundesbank, wearing a bellicose expression, called the meeting to attention. The representatives from France, the U.K., the United States, Japan, and Canada sat straighter in their leather seats with an air of refined curiosity. After a week of suspense, they would find out why this meeting had been called. The governor of the Bank of Italy, Giancarlo Catania, sat bolt upright, cursing the NO SMOKING signs, desperate for a prop. His feelings of foreboding, stirred up by Fieri's grilling two days before, were intensified by the look on Herr Mueller's face.

The German, who was six-foot-five and intellectually brilliant, rested his forearms on the burnished mahogany and eyed the assembled ministers. As his eyes jumped from body to body like those of a hunting hawk, his chin jutted forward with unconcealed pugnacity.

His scrutiny complete, Mueller was silent for a few moments, setting the stage. Then he spoke. He thanked them all for coming at such short notice; he hoped it hadn't caused too much inconvenience, but a meeting was necessary. He exhaled heavily, like a man overburdened by problems, and his voice seemed to drop an octave.

"We all know the power of rumor in the financial markets, and just how destructive it can be." A round of heads nodded gravely. "Well, a most disturbing rumor has come to my attention." He spread out his hands on the table, and seemed to examine his fingernails.

"We all know the British financier Richard Zender—extraordinary trading record in the FX markets. Well, a couple of journalists are on a fishing trip. They know, or they think they know, two things—first, that Zender is immensely successful in the FX markets, and second, that he is very close to a number of finance ministers and central bankers, myself included. Now these journalists, who work for a British newspaper, are putting together these two facts, and although they've not written anything to date, they may do so soon. From what I have heard, they're implying that there is more than a hint of impropriety in Zender's relationships, that perhaps Zender is just a bit too close to policy."

Mueller paused and looked around at the thirteen taut, silent faces watching him. "I'm sure I don't need to spell out the implications." He paused again, then, improbably, smiled broadly. "Now, I know there is nothing to that. These journalists are purely mischief-makers. I've discussed this with Anthony Barrington, and we both agree that a bit of restraint is needed. All I'm saying is that we should be a bit cautious, perhaps cool our relationships with Zender. The last thing we need is any whiff of scandal, even if we are, as I am quite confident is the case, totally blameless." Round the table, heads nodded sagely, shoulders eased slightly. Mueller continued.

"The other thing is, of course, that Zender is a very useful chap. Huge philanthropist, has given more than a hundred million dollars to various charities. We don't want him embarrassed by the newspapers. He's totally innocent. Just happens to be a genius." He shrugged. "But you know, journalists are creatures of envy, especially the British ones. They're out to get Zender. So let's just be a little careful. For his sake as much as ours." He leaned back in his chair and smiled beatifically. "That is all I have to say on the subject. But since we are all here together, we might as well do something constructive."

The meeting ended half an hour later, with a new policy agreed. Sterling was undervalued; economic recovery was under way in Britain, and the markets were being unduly pessimistic. It would be wise, Herr Mueller had suggested, to give the markets a little push in the right direction. And so G7 agreed to commence limited intervention to support sterling that afternoon.

Everyone agreed that the policy made sense. Barrington was especially pleased at the support for his currency. There were no voices of dissent. No one was in a mood to argue. Everyone was preoccupied with the specter of a financial scandal, wondering if it was real and who, if anyone, was guilty. Perhaps, as Mueller had suggested, it was merely a question of mischievous journalists and idle rumor. Those who knew Zender personally, and there were six people around the table who did, racked their memories to see if they might have been just a tad indiscreet in the past. Trouble was, journalists could twist anything. A bit of mud, and so much damage could be done—careers destroyed, decades of ambition aborted. Each man shot covert glances at his colleagues, wondering, hoping that if there was a problem, it was theirs.

The meeting dispersed. Politicians and bankers filed away, hurtling in the high-speed lifts down to the ground. The black bulletproof limousines were waiting, engines polluting the air. Behind the tinted windows, public smiles were dropped.

Anthony Barrington lingered in the conference room on the

thirteenth floor, waiting for the others to leave. Herr Mueller waited with him. When they were alone, Mueller took a seat next to Barrington.

"Do you think they swallowed it?"

Barrington smiled. "Oh, I think so. Sterling is undervalued. Let's face it."

"Well, we'll start the intervention after lunch. That'll give our mole, if he exists, enough time, don't you think?"

"It should. And if he does exist, we'll flush him out."

"Good. I leave that to you. But what about poor Zender? Everyone's going to think he is up to something now."

Barrington smiled. "As I told you before, he probably is. Not that we can prove it—not that I would want to, particularly. But anyway, he is getting just a bit too important, making just a few too many pronouncements on economic policy. Trouble is, everyone thinks he's some sort of god. They all listen to him. He can move the markets just by opening his mouth." Barrington shook his head. "No. Zender has been getting too big, making a bit too much money at our expense. I can't say I'll be too upset if he's cold-shouldered a bit." Barrington got to his feet. "Anyway, thanks for your help on all this."

Mueller waved away his thanks. "Affects us all, doesn't it? We have to do something."

"We do indeed. I'll just make a quick phone call before I go. These lines are secure, aren't they?" Barrington nodded to the telephones on the conference table.

"Of course," said Mueller, somewhat offended. "Please. Go ahead." He picked up his papers and turned to go. "I'll say goodbye, Governor."

The two men shook hands. Barrington watched Mueller disappear down a spiral staircase to his office on the twelfth floor. Alone in the room, he called James Bartrop in London.

"All done. Everything's primed. Killed a couple of birds, I hope. We act in the markets this afternoon."

"Excellent. Let's hope your girl keeps her eyes open."

Giancarlo Catania watched the Italian finance minister go off to lunch with his French counterpart. He waved goodbye, then climbed into his limousine and sat hunched in the back seat like a cornered animal.

Five minutes later, when his car pulled up outside his ugly high-rise hotel, Catania jumped out and strode through the entrance with all the confidence of his position. To the doormen who sprang forward to let him through, he appeared to be a man without a care in the world.

Catania stalked across the marble foyer in search of a phone booth. After Herr Mueller's comments, he didn't trust the phone in his own room, but it was unlikely that each of the twenty booths that he finally stumbled upon would be bugged. Anyway, he would just have to take his chances, make his calls. Fieri would be waiting. He ducked into a booth, took a few seconds to still his breath, and tapped out the number.

Fieri was sitting alone in his frigid office. He was agitated, and the stolen Matisse looking down from the wood-paneled walls gave him no comfort today. The phone rang loudly and he grabbed the receiver. For security reasons the call was brief, anonymous as always. Fieri listened intently, grunting occasionally. When he spoke, his voice was gruffer than normal, but he sounded pleased. "You'll give me a full report when you get back, eh?" It was an instruction, not a request.

Catania agreed and hung up. He would give Fieri nothing of the sort. He could not afford to. Suspicions formed all too easily in the other man's mind. To feed them would be insane. All right, so this rumor about Zender didn't touch him directly. Thank God he had never met Zender. For once his conscience was clear. But it had occurred to him as he sat there at the gleaming conference table that perhaps Zender was just a red herring, a coded warning. Well, he would take it as such, be on guard. Much more than that he couldn't do. He was trapped, he knew that, felt it just as keenly as if the binds had cut into his flesh. He couldn't stop. He couldn't just smile and say, "Sorry, I don't think I'll do this anymore" and retire gracefully. Neither side would let him. As for pleading security risk, any suggestion that the operation was compromised would be suicidal. For he was the weak link, the security risk. All he could do was to carry on, pretend to Fieri that everything was fine, and constantly prove his own value, alive. That was his only chance. If he could, he would come up with a plan to outsmart them all. It wasn't impossible. But first, another quick, anonymous call.

Three minutes later he returned to his room and called his wife. He spoke to her lovingly, made sure he sounded unworried, completely normal. He was on his way home, he said; he would see her for dinner. He sat on the bed, smiling at his reflection in the mirror opposite. Let Herr Mueller listen to that on the bugs.

Fieri cut the connection with a chubby finger and stared at the Matisse for inspiration. Catania had sounded all right. The meeting had been innocent enough after all, just called to help pull the British economy out of the doldrums. But all that secrecy—it was strange. G7 meetings were normally announced to the press in advance. The ministers and bankers usually enjoyed being photographed flying around the world, busily attending to its finances. But there had been no public announcement of the meeting beforehand, and he was willing to bet there would be no announcement after the fact.

Fieri couldn't make up his mind whether to be suspicious or not. A G7 meeting had been held in secret, but apart from the secrecy it had turned out to be fairly run-of-the-mill. There was no reason to suspect that anyone was onto Catania. But there was always a chance—a stray word, a casual mistake, or even outright betrayal, unthinkable as it was.

He was not happy. His suspicions refused to be banished by logic, and, he reminded himself, he was right to be suspicious. He could not afford for Catania to be discovered. It would do irreparable damage to his organization, and to him personally. He resolved to keep a close watch on Catania. But as long as the man's information was this good, he would do nothing more. Catania justified his existence, for the time being.

Greed having got the better of Fieri's vague suspicions, he switched on his Reuters screen and called his broker, Calvadoro. "Yeah, Giuseppe. It's me . . . Yeah, I'm fine, you? . . . Good. Right, I want sterling, yeah, Cable . . . Oh, I don't know, five hundred million, spot, as soon as possible, like now, but break it up, yeah, between the ten main accounts, and call me the minute you've got it . . . Yeah, I'll be here." Fieri re- placed the receiver and stared at the screens, lost for the moment in the irresistible business of making money.

Antonio Fieri was five minutes ahead of Carla Vitale, who, while he was talking to his broker in Milan, was sitting on her sofa chain-smoking. The peal of the phone when it finally came made her jump. She grabbed at the receiver, announced herself, and listened, a frown of concentration distorting the symmetry of her features. She said a blunt goodbye, broke the connection, and rapidly punched out a number.

The proprietary traders at ICB hung around the floor, waiting for something to happen. They had held their position for two working days. Today was the third, and so far there hadn't even been the suggestion of an upward trend in sterling. If something didn't happen soon, the doubts would begin to set in, pricking away at their confidence. Then one of three things would happen. They would lose faith in the position and cut it completely; they would attempt to convince themselves, and possibly the market, that they were right by increasing the position; or they would hold the position, their nerves growing rawer by the hour.

They all knew the gnawing unease of ebbing confidence. It was a feeling traders dreaded. It could produce paralysis or manic activity, and it was very rarely prudent or profitable. Each trader, in his or her own idiosyncratic way, was trying to keep the doubts at bay. Dante Scarpirato sat chain-smoking in his office, his face a mask of impassivity. Matthew Arnott sat at his desk, listless, his hand in the air, fingers gripping the cord to his handset, his wrist twitching rhythmically, sending the handset spiraling dangerously through the air. Simon Wilson chattered. Sarah Jensen stared at her screens. Since she had arrived at work that morning, she had felt Arnott's eyes on her, scrutinizing every move. She had seen his reflection in her trading screen as he stared at her, a frown knitting his eyebrows, as if he were weighing her up. It made her hackles rise, but she concentrated on the flickering green figures and pretended not to notice. Neither of them brought up their meeting last night—dangerous ground, best avoided. Each wondered at the other's silence.

At five minutes past twelve, line one on the dashboard flashed.

Three fingers shot out to the button. Sarah got to it first. The voice on the other end of the line was female, agitated, high-pitched, the accent Italian. The words tumbled out as she asked to speak to Matthew Arnott. Sarah put the call on hold and swung round in her chair to Arnott, sitting two feet away.

"For you."

He grabbed up his handset and hit the button. He said two words, "yes" and "O.K.," then slipped on his jacket and walked away from the desk.

Scarpirato's voice rang out, stopping him in his tracks.

"Hey, where do you think you're going? In case you'd forgotten, we're running a three hundred million position here. No one goes for lunch until I say."

Arnott glared at him. "Who said anything about lunch?"

Scarpirato came out of his office. "Well, unless you have become civilized and taken to wearing your jacket indoors, which would be a first, I presume you are going out to lunch."

Arnott smiled viciously. "I've become civilized. I'm wearing my jacket indoors. I'm not going to lunch, I'm going to the john. Satisfied?" He walked off, with Scarpirato scowling at his back.

"Stupid excuse," Scarpirato muttered to the desk at large. "He *was* on his way to lunch. He never wears his jacket indoors."

Sarah got up from her desk and walked over to the coffee machine. She read a few office notices pinned up on the board to the left of it, idling away a few minutes, escaping the tension on the desk. She was just about to return to her seat with a steaming cappuccino when she saw Arnott appear through the security doors to the trading floor. As she made her way back to her desk, he turned right, away from the proprietary desk, and headed for a conference room. She walked past and saw him sitting at the table with his mobile phone in his hand. With a jolt of suspicion, she took in the scene at a glance and walked quickly back to her desk.

Inside the conference room, Arnott called eight different brokers. From each he bought £50 million, selling dollars. His voice was low as he spoke, his lips touching the mouthpiece. Safe behind a closed door, he was sure that nobody would overhear him.

Five minutes later Sarah saw him return to the desk and stride into Scarpirato's office. To have it out, perhaps? He was not the type to take public criticism quietly. Sarah watched the office, expecting to hear raised voices and see angry gestures. There were none. The two men spoke intently, heads bowed. Arnott returned to the desk, and pacing out slowly after him, as if on his way to a gunfight, came Scarpirato. He leaned on the desk between Sarah and Arnott, who watched him intently. Wilson sat opposite and fiddled with his tie.

"I want to increase the position. Buy another two-fifty million sterling, spot. Sarah and Arnott get a ton each. Simon, you get fifty. Do it now."

Sarah leaned back in her chair and wedged her hands by her hips. "Are you going to tell us why, or do we just slavishly follow your orders here?" Instructions annoyed her. She wasn't paid to be a functionary, and yes, she admitted to herself, she wanted to get a rise out of him.

He turned on her with surprising vehemence. "Just do what I say, Jensen. You got your explanation before. I don't have to account to you."

"Of course you don't, Dante." She smiled sweetly. "You just go and light up another cigar. Don't worry about me. I'll have the order filled in a flash." Before he could answer, she hit the direct line to the Bank of Paris and asked Johnny McDermott, "Where do you have spot Cable?" Cable was shorthand for the dollar-sterling rate.

"1.4555, 65," he shot back.

"I'll take a hundred pounds at sixty-five."

"Done."

"Done."

She bought £100 million, wrote the ticket, time-stamped it, and dropped it in the settlements tray. Then, with a mean expression, she grabbed up her bag and announced that she was going for lunch and that someone else could cover today. She expected a mouthful of abuse from Arnott. Instead she was greeted by meek acceptance. Fine, he said, he would cover today. *That's a first*, she thought as she headed for the Pig and Poke and half a bottle of Taittinger's.

Chapter Fifteen

Sarah heard her name shouted from across the trading floor as she returned from lunch, an hour late, her cheeks glowing from the champagne.

"Line two," announced Simon Wilson as she hurried to the desk. "Some Kraut."

Sarah glared at him and picked up the phone. It was Manfred Arbingen. He came straight to the point.

"Did you know there was a G7 meeting today?" he asked smugly.

Sarah laughed. "No, I didn't. That's peculiar. The next one was supposed to be in two weeks."

"Very peculiar. Unscheduled, unannounced. I only know because I went to the Bundesbank to pick up a friend for lunch. I had my car—we were going for a drive in the country. Anyway, as I was driving in, I almost got mowed down by a cavalcade of limos, six of them—tinted windows, big aerials, you know. I wasn't sure who it was, so I asked the guards, and they whispered that it was the finance ministers and central bankers. G7."

"What do you think they were up to?"

Arbingen laughed. "What do you think?"

"Well, it couldn't have been policy. That would keep until the next scheduled meeting. It must be some sort of intervention." She paused, weighing things up. "But that hardly warrants a special meeting. They could have worked that out on the telephone, unless it was something really big, controversial, and I don't think that's likely. None of the currencies are that out of line."

"They're not," agreed Arbingen.

"The same goes for interest rates. I can't see them making any dramatic gestures there, either."

"I can't make any sense of it, that's for sure. I suppose we'll all have to wait and see. We'll find out something sooner or later."

Sarah thanked Arbingen for his news, cut the connection, and replaced the receiver slowly on the desk. Sooner or later wasn't good enough in the markets. You had to find out now, before the next man, anticipate the market's conclusions and reactions, position yourself accordingly. Sarah's mind began to race.

She got up and walked over to the coffee machine, hidden in a little alcove on the edge of the trading floor, next to the atrium. It was light and secluded, and you went there for a seemingly casual gossip or, as now, if you wished to think unobserved. Curiosity is endemic on a trading floor, and traders are adept at perceiving secrets fermenting in a colleague's mind, then relentlessly ferreting them out. Sarah had no intention of revealing what was on her mind, and it was impossible to think straight when at least two pairs of beady eyes followed your every move.

She stared at the coffee machine, taking extra time to ponder the buttons before finally punching 146: coffee, white, frothy, medium strength, one sugar. The coffee machine burped and spluttered, a plastic cup dropped into position, and with a noisy squirt steaming liquid rose to the brim.

Sarah sipped carefully, mulling things over, gazing out at the potted plants dotted around the floor of the atrium. Last Thursday Scarpirato decides to buy one-week sterling-dollar futures, selling the dollar, buying sterling—a plausible but highly speculative position. Four days later, an event that might make that position pay off takes place, secretly. And now, no doubt, sterling would start to rise. Some coincidence, thought Sarah.

Insider trading was one of the fastest ways of making money known to the City. It could explain the spectacular profits made by Scarpirato. It was also one of the most difficult forms of fraud to detect and prove. Tracking the flow of information was like trying to catch quicksilver.

Sarah reached for a cigarette from the packet in her shirt pocket. She struck a match and inhaled deeply. If Scarpirato was trading on inside information of G7's currency intervention activities, then he must have a very senior mole. G7's currency policy was one of its most closely guarded secrets. Because of the danger of leaks, it was rarely consigned to paper. It was discussed and agreed by the ministers, the central bankers, and the prime ministers of the member countries, and put into effect by the central banks. It was executed by the trading departments of the central banks, but Sarah thought it unlikely that any leaks would come from there. The traders would be told at the last minute. They would have far less time to pass on their inside information than their superiors would. And the traders would be more exposed. All their calls were taped; any transgressions would be all too obvious. Sarah felt sure that if there was a leak, it would come from the mist-shrouded upper echelons.

She puffed thoughtfully on her cigarette. If her theory was

correct, a top politician or central banker was at the center of a billion-pound conspiracy. The possibility was almost too large to grasp. To a foreign-exchange trader with access to large sums of money and the cover of regular dealings in the market, having a mole in G7 was like having the key to the central vaults at Fort Knox.

The implication hit Sarah like a fist in the face. If there was such a conspiracy, the participants would not give up high office and big money without a fight.

Abruptly, she dropped her cigarette into her coffee and threw the cup into the waste dispenser, then turned and walked to the ladies' room. Locking herself into a cubicle, she dropped the cover over the lavatory and sat down. She leaned forward pensively, her chin cupped in her hands. She sat for ten minutes, till the cold marble floor chilled her feet through the soles of her thin leather shoes and the violent air conditioning raised goose-pimples on her arms. Her nerves gnawed at her stomach. She knew that she had already made her decision, even as her rational mind paraded alternatives before her as if she had a choice.

She stood up and briskly rubbed her arms. It might just be that her imagination had run out of control. It wouldn't be the first time. But she would pursue her suspicions until they were exhausted or confirmed. She would worry about the repercussions when they came.

As she walked back to her desk, she was surprised to feel, not trepidation, but a sense of reckless exhilaration. It made her think of Alex. He had used those words when trying to describe the feelings that swept over him as he ascended a sheer rockface, with thousands of feet of empty space hanging below him. He said that his courage increased when he was faced with a particularly hazardous cliff. Sarah laughed at herself. Alex, in his gentle way, would have ridiculed the comparison. Each time he inched up a rockface, clinging on by fingers and toes, he risked his life. Sitting at a desk in central London was about as safe as you could get.

Back at her desk, Sarah said, "I think I'll join this little punt."

Arnott sat up out of his slouch. Wilson grinned as if it were a huge joke. Sarah smiled grimly. She would test her hypothesis with her own money; in trading-floor parlance, she would put her money where her mouth was. She could do with the money. She could ill afford the risk, but then, she was sure that very little risk was involved. It was as sure as sure things got.

She decided to go into the market and take a spot position. She had capital of £200,000 in cash. That enabled her to trade a maximum of £3 million. The difference would be made up of borrowed money. If her position started to lose money, she could run it until the losses reached £200,000. Then she would be forced to cut the position, and the £200,000 would be raked out of her account to cover the losses. But Sarah felt confident there would be no losses; her capital would be safe. She called Johnny McDermott. Normally someone like McDermott, who dealt with the orders of big institutions, wouldn't take personal account, or p.a., trades as well, but he made an exception with Sarah.

McDermott had started his career executing p.a. trades, and Sarah had been one of his early clients. When he changed banks and began to execute institutional trades, he dropped most of his p.a. clients, but Sarah remained. The compliance departments in their respective banks didn't exactly love the relationship—it could look a bit incestuous—but they lived with it. They accepted the argument that Sarah and Johnny put forward: they just liked to trade together; it amused them, brightened their day; and, more important, both Sarah and Johnny were big hitters, making huge profits for their employers. They had earned a little leeway.

They would sometimes spend hours a day on the telephone, talking, joking, amusing themselves, if the markets were quiet, but they could be equally brusque.

"Johnny, where do you have spot Cable?"

"1.4560, 70."

"I'll take three sterling at seventy, p.a."

"That's done. But you're cutting it a bit tight, aren't you?"

"Don't worry, Johnny. I know what I'm doing."

"I hope so."

It was the biggest personal account trade Sarah had ever done. She had traded over a hundred times that amount many times at Finlays, but other people's money—referred to as OPM, or opium, on the floor—always felt different. It was just a commodity, a series of numbers that moved one way or the other. There was excitement and pain when positions didn't work out, but never the direct, searing hit of emotion in the bloodstream. Other people's money just slid off the surface.

Sarah wrote out her trade ticket, stamped it, dropped it in the settlements tray, and lit up a cigarette. She felt the delicious double edge of the gambler's thrill. If the trade went wrong, her capital would be wiped out, and with it much of her security. But if it went right, she could make tens of thousands of dollars. She would also see her hunch confirmed; it wouldn't prove that Scarpirato was insider trading, but it would substantiate her suspicions. She leaned back in her chair, face raised to the ceiling, and exhaled loudly. Arnott, watching every move, looked at her strangely.

Minutes after Sarah had completed her trade, the central banks of G7 entered the markets simultaneously and started buying sterling and selling the dollar. The word spread like wildfire through the trading houses around the globe: somebody somewhere was buying sterling, in size. First the big banks and currency funds started buying for their own accounts, then smaller buyers jumped on the bandwagon.

At 2:15 P.M. London time, ten minutes after Sarah had taken her position, sterling began to rise. She watched the green flickering figures, dancing more than usual after her liquid lunch. Screwing up her eyes, she felt the first tremors of excitement. Sterling was rising in little hops, minute by minute. She watched the procession, her mind a well of concentration, ruthlessly shutting out all other thoughts, watching the market, talking to the market, feeling the market rise. For every tick that sterling rose, her paper profit grew by $300. And the desk's by around $50,000.

The proprietary traders watched and waited. Dante Scarpirato left his sanctuary, took his trading seat next to Arnott, and peered at the screens. A controlled excitement gripped the muscles of his face as sterling ticked up. By three o'clock it was up three quarters of a cent against the dollar, and the desk was sitting on a profit of over $4 million. Enmities forgotten, they huddled together in excitement. They all agreed it was too early to cut the position and take their profits. The trend was accelerating, with sterling rising in bigger jumps each minute.

By twenty past three, the pound was up a full cent against the dollar. No one they spoke to in the market knew why. No new figures were out, but someone somewhere was buying, in massive amounts. The word was buy sterling; the rumors were rife. Sarah listened only to one: the central banks, led by the Bundesbank, were buying sterling. It was just as she expected. She turned in her seat and caught Arnott and Scarpirato in profile. They looked triumphant. Clearly, she was not the only one who was not surprised.

At three-thirty, sterling had risen one and a quarter cents against the dollar. Sarah's profit was $37,500, large by personal trading standards but dwarfed by the desk's profit. She did a quick calculation in her head; they'd made nearly $7 million.

Arnott and Wilson seethed with pent-up tension. The profits were big enough, astronomical in anyone's book. It would be insane to hold out for more. The foreign-exchange markets were the most volatile in the world. If the prime minister had a heart attack, sterling would tumble in the uncertainty that followed. A hundred things could happen. The variables were endless, the conclusion inescapable. They had to sell, cut their position and take their profits, now.

Sarah closed her ears to noise around her and sat in a vacuum of concentration. She held on.

Scarpirato sat, cigar smoke rising like vapor as he stared, transfixed, at the screens. It was almost as if he were willing the market up. Wilson and Arnott united against him, urging him to cut the position. He quashed them with a raised hand, King Canute holding back a wave of entreaties. Sarah watched, saying nothing.

At four o'clock she decided it was time to sell. She rang Mc-Dermott. "Johnny, where do you have Cable?"

"Ninety-five, figure five." That was shorthand for 1.4695, 1.4705.

She sold. She was nearly $40,000 richer in the space of two hours—her first taste of dirty money. She examined the sensation: it left a certain stickiness, felt unreal. She felt that she was leaving herself behind. Another Rubicon crossed. She deadened herself. It was, she told herself, justifiable, crime in the name of the law. Fragmentary memories came unbidden. She banished them.

Scarpirato watched her cut her position, then relented. He turned to his traders and told them to sell, both the futures and the spot position. They hit their phones like rattlesnakes. In two minutes they had sold out. The position was cut, the profit taken: $6,800,000.

They wrote the tickets and sat back exhausted, euphoric, grinning at each other. Sarah let their mood consume her. The sensation was almost sexual. They felt dizzy, triumphant. They switched off their screens and went to Corney & Barrow on Old Broad Street to celebrate.

In Via Appia Antica, another celebration was taking place. Antonio Fieri slammed down the phone. He had made over $6 million. He leaned back in his chair, folded his hands over his bulging stomach, grinned at the Matisse, and shouted for Federico, his personal assistant. Federico appeared in seconds, listened to his instructions, darted off, then reappeared two minutes later with Signora Fieri, a bottle of chilled champagne, and two glasses.

Fieri poured the champagne out. He and his wife toasted each other. A loving Italian couple, the Fieris had been married for thirty-one years and had been faithful throughout. Antonio had enough other vices to keep him happy. Infidelity was one indulgence he would not tolerate. Apart from anything else, mistresses were bad news, demanding and invariably indiscreet. They were a luxury neither he nor his lieutenants could afford. He wondered about the rumors he had heard, some months back, about Catania's having a mistress. He had looked into it, found no evidence. It was just as well, for all concerned. Catania's information was too valuable, and his involvement with Fieri too intimate, to risk compromising in even the slightest way.

Sarah sat at a small table in Corney & Barrow playing with the stem of her champagne glass. Arnott and Wilson were long gone. She twisted the stem of the glass between her fingers and watched the bubbles rising relentlessly. She knew Scarpirato's eyes were on her. She looked up, met his look. They stared at each other, playing the same game, each unwilling to crack. Sarah wondered at the man before her. He was not conventionally good-looking, nor charming. He lacked humor. He was ruthless. He was intelligent—that was about all you could say in his favor. And, Sarah admitted, well dressed. Not that she cared much about such things; in fact, she tended to be prejudiced against men who dressed too well, especially if they combined that with good looks. But there was something that drew her to him. Perhaps it was all within her, perhaps she had created the excitement herself from experimentation, risk, danger, challenge —all potent ingredients. She was excited by her own risk-taking, as she always had been. The lure of self-destructiveness never completely left her. The characteristics of the other person were almost irrelevant, save that he was unsuitable, flawed, damaged, if not broken, in some way. Why she was attracted to these types she did not know, did not care to analyze. She had thought that with John Carter and now Eddie, that side of her life was over, that she had somehow matured out of it. But as she sat staring at Scarpirato, with every sense sharp, the old compulsions filled her once again, obscuring everything save her desire for him, to lose herself in him.

He spoke finally. "Would you like dinner?"

Her eyes moved to her watch. Nine-thirty. Four bottles between the four of them, and she had drunk her share. Yes, she
ought to eat. She almost laughed out loud. Who was she kidding
with her self-justification?

"Yes, I would."

He got to his feet, peeled off four fifties, touched her shoulder
gently, and led her through the bar.

Twenty minutes later she was sitting at another dark corner
table in the restaurant L'Incontro, on Pimlico Road. She ate little,
pushing the food around her plate.

"Do you always get what you want?"

Scarpirato laughed. "Not always, but in the important things,
yes."

"And do you always know? Is there any question that perhaps
this once you will fail?"

His look hardened, but there were still the teasing eyes, lighthearted but merciless. "That's up to you. What do you think?"

"I think," said Sarah, bending away from the question, "that
you are ruthless, driven by I don't know what, and capable of
switching off your emotions at will."

He laughed again. "Yes, women don't like that, do they? Why
is that?"

Sarah almost grimaced. "They don't like it because it smashes
any illusions they might have about their importance to you.
They are reminded just how ephemeral they are. They leave no
legacy."

He leaned across the table. "And I am responsible for that?"

The arrogance was unyielding. But in the dark eyes there was
desire, a fissure in his mantle of autonomy. And that was enough.
Sarah ran her hands up and down the insides of her bare thighs,
setting off a tremulous shock. She felt her self-control slipping.
Her stomach clenched, and she couldn't eat. She forced her eyes

from him, to the couples sitting at neighboring tables. She tried to watch them, listen to their conversations, but every sense stayed with him.

Watching her, he called for the bill. They stood on the street waiting for a taxi. Several passed. They let them go. Then he reached out his hand, flagged one down.

Sarah sat with one hip pressed against the door of the taxi, glancing across at him, then out the window, torn. He watched her, smiling.

His house was dark, even when he switched on the lights. There was a smell she could not identify. Cloying, it filled her senses. Perhaps it was cigar smoke, cognac, something else too; she didn't know. He gestured to a sofa. She sat down. She felt as though she were holding her breath. Her pose was rigid, as if she were containing herself, or waiting to ward off a blow.

He watched her sit, then disappeared into the kitchen. He returned with two glasses of vodka. The sides were frosted, and wraiths of ice swirled around the surface. He set them on the table and took a seat next to her. She picked up her glass and took a long draw. The cold stung her fingers. The liquid scalded her throat as it trickled down.

She felt dreamy; inhibition, reason, perspective had gone. Her senses took over, so intense that they became almost intolerable. Scarpirato, sitting two feet away, filled her vision. She seemed to see him with a peculiar clarity, every feature delineated, every line on his tanned face so close she wanted to touch and trace it. She was conscious too of her own physical sensations. Her skin felt radiant, ultrasensitive, craving touch. Her physical desire for him, and her mental desire for the risk, uncertainty, and danger that would inevitably accompany an affair with him, drove all thoughts of wisdom and caution, of Eddie and Barrington, from her mind.

She fumbled in her bag for cigarettes, extracted one, and stuck it between her lips. There was a lighter on the table. He took it up and lit the cigarette. She smoked it down almost at once, hardly pausing for breath, holding it to her lips defensively. Finally she stubbed it out and turned to look at him.

In one sweep of motion he was upon her, his mouth on her lips, his hands on her shoulders, pulling her to him. He fumbled at her clothes, his hands shaking. They stood, pressed together, both trembling. Then he guided her backward, through the room, into the hall, up the stairs. She felt a door against her back; it opened behind her. A few more paces, then she felt herself falling onto the soft surface of his bed. Holding her shoulders, he fell onto her. She lay back. He pushed up her skirt around her waist, ripping the fabric of her underwear aside before plunging his lips onto her, tasting her, covering her with tender kisses. He finally made love to her with a passion that left her dazed. But what shocked her, moved her most, were his words. Words of searing vulnerability, of need. When the mask dropped, it revealed a void. She had seen need before, but never like this, a shameless, desperate yearning. She held his face in her hands and answered him, told him what he craved to hear. And he smiled in the darkness as she told him, with a look of triumph and of fear.

Chapter Sixteen

Anthony Barrington sat in his office, morning sunlight streaming through his open window. The silence was punctuated
by the deep ticking of the grandfather clock that stood in
the corner by the door. Barrington was in the middle of review-
ing a speech he was to give the following Monday at lunch with
the Institute of Directors when the phone rang. He finished the
sentence he was reading and picked up the phone in annoyance.

"James Bartrop," announced his secretary.

"All right. I'll take it," said the governor.

Bartrop came straight to the point. "I heard from my Swiss
friend this morning. Account 5376 X200 was active again.
Bought fifty million sterling twenty minutes after the G7 meeting
ended and cleared it out at the end of the day for a fat profit."

Barrington shrugged. "Fifty million sterling is small change to
the Mafia. Hardly worth their while, I should have thought."

"That's in one account, Governor. There could be ten other accounts acting on the same information, for all we know."

"That's always possible."

"What about your girl? Has she come up with anything yet?"

Barrington felt a surge of annoyance. "Give her time. She's only been there two weeks."

Bartrop was not placated. "But she sat through yesterday, presumably. If there is something going on at ICB, and I'm still pretty sure there is, she ought to know about it by now, or at least have some suspicions."

"I'm sure I'll hear about it the moment she does. But in the meantime we'll just have to be patient, won't we?"

Sarah sat listlessly at her desk. Work was a nightmare. The alcohol alone would have shot her concentration. The desk did no trades, reveling instead in yesterday's huge profits. Today was a day off for them. Wilson read the *Sporting Life*, Arnott took a four-hour lunch, and Scarpirato spent most of the day in meetings or out of the office. He did not meet her eye. Once as she passed him there was a look of complicity on his face, but that was all.

Sarah went to the gym. After an aerobics class, some of her energy returned. She swam to ease her aching muscles, then rotated through the sauna, Jacuzzi, and steam room. Finally she had a massage. Emma, the beautician, made polite but mercifully sparse conversation. When Sarah returned to the office, it was four-thirty and Scarpirato had gone. Wilson was preparing to leave, and Arnott was talking drunkenly on the phone. Sarah waved to her colleagues and, with a sense of relief, turned and left.

She arrived home half an hour later. Her silent house disoriented her. A noise had raged in her head all day—voices, emotions hurtling around with no outlet, an amalgam of guilt, excitement, remorse, and fear. At work she had had no chance to analyze the chaos Scarpirato had created in her mind and body. She sat looking out the window, feeling out of control for the first time in years. Every warning light was flashing, had flashed the night before, and had been ignored, shockingly. As she had sat with Scarpirato in the wine bar, it had been as if a decision had been made without her knowledge. Suddenly everything had become explicit. Sarah couldn't think of any one thing that had set it off, no single look or comment. Her desire for him was abrupt, unyielding, irresistible.

She turned from the window to the whisky bottle. The message machine winked furiously at her as she passed. She had ignored it when she had hurtled through her house in the morning to shower, change, and race out again in ten minutes flat. She stopped, sprawled on the sofa, and stared at the phone. Then she pressed the button. The tape whirred wildly back, clicked into place, and began to play its messages.

There were four from Jacob, increasing in intensity to the last one, in which he sounded downright worried. Sarah lit a cigarette and tapped out his number. He seemed breathless when he answered, as if he had run for the phone.

"Didn't you get my messages?"

"Yes, Jacob, all four. I'm responding to them now."

"No, I called you at the office, once in the morning, twice in the afternoon, and left messages." His voice was a mixture of concern, agitation, and excitement.

"That's peculiar. No one passed them on, but it was a funny sort of day."

"I'll bet." Jacob's voice was brisk. "Look, I think you should come over here, I have something for you."

Sarah felt the quickening of excitement. She sat up straight, the sickness and tiredness gone. "I'm on my way."

"You'll have dinner, will you?"

Sarah suddenly felt starving. She hadn't eaten properly for twenty-four hours. "I'd love to."

"Oh, by the way, I came round and took yesterday's tapes from your DAT machine and put in some new ones. I didn't think you'd have time to wade through all that stuff."

"Oh. Thanks, Jacob. No, I didn't, I'm afraid. Anyway, see you soon." She put down the phone, went to her bedroom, changed into jeans and a T-shirt, picked up her bag and keys, and headed for the door. A brightly colored triangle was lying by the door, peeping out from under a buff-colored envelope—a bill, which she had so far managed to ignore. She pushed it aside and picked up the postcard.

It was a scene of mountains, perilously high, gray granite peaks piercing a cobalt sky, mist swirling around the summits. Sarah turned it over. The mountain was Kanchenjunga, the first mountain on Alex's and Eddie's Himalayan odyssey. They would probably be at base camp by the time the card reached her, wrote Eddie. Sarah turned the card back over and looked again at the picture. It was so simple and serene. She felt the sickness of guilt lurch in her stomach.

She slammed the door behind her, unlocked the BMW, which was parked a few feet away, stepped in, turned the keys in the ignition, and accelerated away. In half an hour she was at Rotherwick Road.

Jacob greeted her at the door. Nervously, he led her through into his study, where he had laid out the DAT tape player on an old rosewood desk.

"Would you like a cup of tea, sweetie?" He scanned her face

with a worried frown. Sarah was conscious of her pallor, and of a slight bruising that spread over her lips like inkstains.

"Mmmm, please."

Jacob went to the kitchen. Sarah stared at the tape machine, then forcibly turned her attention to Ruby, who had nosed in through the door and was busy winding herself around her legs. She picked up the cat, sat down in an oversized floral armchair, and smoothed the sleek black fur. Ruby was soon purring, flexing her paws, kneading Sarah's lap in delight.

After what seemed like an age, Jacob returned with teapot, cups, sugar, and milk, all in fine bone china, balanced on a silver tray. He set down the tray next to the tape machine and with careful ceremony poured out the tea. It brought back a fleeting memory of a childhood ritual in which Jacob had given her and Alex tea every afternoon after school.

Sarah told Jacob about the postcard, and they spoke of Alex and Eddie for a while, wondering where they were. Each word gouged at her conscience. Then, putting down their teacups, they turned to the machine.

"My friend sent round yesterday's and today's tapes. There's so much stuff," said Jacob. "Lots of it isn't relevant. I've made notes on where the good bits are, written down the numbers from the tape counter."

Sarah smiled. She had forgotten how efficient and systematic he was.

Jacob nodded at the tape player as it began to play. "This was picked up by Carla's bug on Sunday night. Works like a charm." He grinned.

The voice of Matthew Arnott rose from the machine. "So, another meeting tomorrow?" There was the gentle clatter of knives and forks, as if he were sitting down to dinner.

"That's right," Carla answered, with a full mouth.

"I still think it's peculiar that it hasn't been announced." Arnott again. "Are you sure he didn't say anything about why it was called?"

"Look, Matthew." Carla was exasperated, petulant. "I've already told you a hundred times. He called last Friday, said there would be a meeting this Monday, called by the Germans, that he hadn't been told what it was about, that Herr Mueller or whatever his name is had said he didn't want to discuss it over the phone but it was imperative that he attend. That's all he said, word for word, O.K.?"

There was silence for a few moments, except for the clinking of cutlery, then Arnott continued. "Well, you must admit, it sounds a bit strange. They normally announce everything publicly, well in advance, unless something catastrophic happens and they need to call an emergency meeting." There was another pause. "How did he sound? Was he worried or anything?"

Carla snorted. "He sounded like he always sounds, like he hates me. What do you expect?"

The question hung in the air. Sarah could imagine Arnott doing one of his expansive shrugs. There was an interminable pause before he spoke again. "Love-hate, more likely." The voice was half teasing, half jealous. "Anyway, I'm just a bit worried, that's all. I hope it's nothing to do with us." His voice was pensive, questioning. Even from the tape Sarah could sense the tension.

Carla's voice was suspicious. "What do you mean?"

There was another pause, then Arnott answered in level, measured tones, as if choosing his words carefully. "Well, I hope that no one suspects him. If they do, it all leads straight to us, doesn't it?"

Carla was contemptuous. "He's not going to say anything, is he? It would all come out then, him and me. His wife would divorce him. That's all he cares about." Her voice grew more dismissive. "And none of us is going to say anything, so why are you getting so worked up?"

"You're the one who's getting worked up." There was a vicious squawk from Carla, which Arnott interrupted. "Look, I don't want to argue. It's just that a few things have happened lately."

Carla sounded dubious. "Like what?"

Arnott was hesitant, perhaps wary of further ridicule. "Well, this girl, Sarah Jensen, started work with us a couple of weeks ago. She's very sharp. I almost feel as if she's watching me. There's something about her that worries me."

"So you think she watches you for two weeks, figures it all out, then calls her friend Herr Mueller. Don't be ridiculous."

There was an awkward cough from Arnott, then silence. Finally he spoke again. "Look, I've got to go into the office. I'll see you later."

Jacob hit the stop button, then turned to Sarah. They raised their eyebrows in a look of mutual intrigue, then, staring at the tape counter, Jacob hit fast forward.

"This was yesterday," he announced, hitting the play button, "at twelve o'clock."

They heard a brief hello. A voice asked for Carla, then, reassured, it spoke quickly and briefly in Italian. Jacob looked at Sarah, perplexed.

"I thought it might be important. You learned a bit of Italian, didn't you, in Perugia or somewhere?"

Sarah nodded. "When I was twenty. But I still remember quite a bit." She listened to the deep, angry-sounding male voice on the tape. She turned to Jacob.

"It is important. Our Italian is telling Carla to buy sterling against the dollar, as soon as possible."

They looked at each other in silence, then Jacob turned back to the machine and played the next installment, a phone call from Carla to ICB. Sarah jumped, and squirmed in embarrassment when she heard her own voice leap out from the tape as she passed Carla's call on to Arnott. Carla then spoke six words. "I need to speak to you." Arnott said O.K. and hung up. Two minutes later, Carla made another call. After a single ring her call was answered, but whoever it was said nothing, merely listened to Carla's instructions. Buy sterling, she said. Now.

"That call was logged at seven minutes past twelve," said Jacob, "then at a quarter past twelve Scarpirato's bug recorded a conversation between him and Arnott." He pushed the play button. Arnott announced that he thought they ought to increase their sterling position. Scarpirato asked him if he was sure. Very, replied Arnott.

The final conversation Jacob played was recorded at nine-thirty the same evening. Arnott and Carla were celebrating. There was much laughter and clinking of glasses. They had, announced Arnott, made a profit of $5 million. A million and a quarter each, said Carla with glee.

Jacob switched off the tape recorder. "Well, that's it. We fished for minnows and caught a shark."

Sarah nodded. For a while they were silent. Sarah looked around the room, then back at Jacob.

"I can't quite take it all in. When it all started, it felt like a lark, a diversion, a bit of fun. I never imagined it would turn out like this. It seemed harmless, containable. I thought it was probably just a case of fiddling the books. Nothing more exotic than that. But all this . . . It doesn't seem real. It's almost as if by discovering it, I've made it real. And I have, in a way. If we hadn't discovered anything, I wouldn't have to do anything about it.

Now I know I've got to do something. I'm involved. I can't stop, unlearn it, forget it." She shrugged and laughed nervously. "So what do we do?"

Jacob frowned, saying nothing. He reached under the desk and pulled a whisky bottle and two small glasses out of a drawer. He filled the glasses almost to the brim and handed one to Sarah. They sipped, deep in thought. Sarah broke the silence.

"Well, it all fits together. Yesterday around twelve I took a call for Arnott. Must have been Carla. Arnott said almost nothing, then put on his jacket and got up. There was an argument. Scarpirato wanted to know where he was going. He said, 'To the john.' Scarpirato remarked on his wearing his jacket, as if it were unusual to wear it inside, which it is for traders. I bet he had his mobile phone hidden in his jacket. It's a much safer way to receive inside information than on the ICB phones, where every conversation is recorded. It's peculiar that Scarpirato chewed him out, but perhaps Arnott decided to take extra precautions because of me. Perhaps before my arrival, he just used to swagger off to the loo with his mobile in his hand, or even take the calls on the ICB phones. Anyway, Arnott disappears to the john, and at about that time, according to your tapes, Carla calls someone and tells him to buy sterling. Probably Arnott on his mobile in the loo. Then I see Arnott go into a conference room and get on the phone. Obviously, he was discussing something he didn't want overheard by me or recorded on the ICB phones. Presumably he does his illegal trades for himself and Carla and Scarpirato *and* some fourth person, since your last recording tells us the profit's split four ways. Then Arnott and Scarpirato have their conversation in Scarpirato's office, Arnott says buy sterling, they both come out to the desk, and Scarpirato tell us to increase our sterling position." She paused and half laughed.

"Then, after lunch, my old friend Manfred Arbingen calls, tells me there was a G7 meeting at the Bundesbank. The conversation in Italian was recorded fifteen minutes after the meeting had broken up. It's all pretty clear, isn't it?" Sarah gazed down at her hands. "What a brilliant scam. Insider trading at the highest level, where it's almost unthinkable. And now there's no doubt. I suspected it might be going on when I had my conversation with Manfred. Just to test my hypothesis, I took a position myself—three million sterling. Then I sat back and waited, and of course sterling rose, so I cut my position. I made thirty-seven and a half thousand dollars. The desk made six point eight million, and Scarpirato and his cohorts made another five million." She took a long drink of her whisky. "I saw it all happening, I was right in the middle, but it still seems unreal. I still can't believe it."

Jacob sat back in his armchair and gazed at her. "Well, you really are in the middle of it, aren't you? Did you have to do that trade yourself?"

"Yes. I did. As I said, I was testing my theory. I wanted to do something myself. I didn't want to just sit back and watch from a distance." She looked away and said quietly, "Never have."

Jacob let out a long sigh. "No. You never have." He lapsed into silence and refilled their glasses. He smiled at Sarah as he did so, but his gaze was a long way off, preoccupied. After a while he seemed to come back.

"So anyway, we know who's receiving the information, except our mysterious fourth man. But who's the source?"

Sarah put down her glass. "Could be the Italian finance minister, or the governor of the Bank of Italy, or someone tipped off by them. Perhaps the French or the Japanese are the leak, and their link man just happens to be Italian. But I doubt it. If I had to put my money on anyone, it'd be either the Italian finance minister or the governor of the Bank of Italy."

"It'd be nice," said Jacob, "to get hold of some television coverage of the Italians, compare voices." He was silent for a while, then said, "I've got a friend in Milan. I'll ask him to video the news or something, see if we recognize anyone."

"Good idea," said Sarah. "Whoever he is, it seems pretty clear that Carla had an affair with him. Sounds as if she's blackmailing him. Don't you think?"

"Yep. Sounds like blackmail, all right."

"So he tips her off, she tips off Matthew Arnott, Arnott tells Scarpirato, and they take their positions in the market and make five million dollars." Sarah frowned. "Then they split the profits four ways—Carla, Arnott, Scarpirato. Who's number four?"

Jacob shook his head. "Beats me."

Sarah was intrigued. "A distant mastermind who keeps his hands clean? We need to find out, get some conclusive evidence against Scarpirato, discover who the Italian is. This evidence is brilliant, but it's a bit too close to circumstantial. Our theory relies heavily on supposition. I can't prove that inside information has been divulged, nor that Dante Scarpirato is involved. What we have is not definitive, but it's a good start. I'll type up a report tomorrow—I can't think straight tonight—and ring Barrington the day after."

Jacob nodded. "You tell your Barrington. As soon as possible. It's his problem now." He sat forward in his chair, his face serious. "Listen, Sarah, I'm not sure you haven't done enough. It sounds as if Arnott's already suspicious of you. You'll have to be careful."

Sarah looked up abruptly. "Of course I'll be careful. Why spell it out? That's the second time you've said something. You seem worried. Is there something you're not telling me?"

Jacob stared awkwardly at her, then spoke quickly. "No, no. There's nothing. Nothing beyond what you've just heard. But that's enough, isn't it?"

Sarah studied his worried face. "Yeah, it is enough. But it's only the beginning, isn't it? Something tells me there's a lot more going on. And what's more, having found this much out, I don't think I'll be able to stop, just like that. I don't think Barrington would let me. And I'm not sure I want to."

Jacob let out a heavy breath. "No. I didn't suppose you would. If you want to carry on, then carry on. For the time being. Like I say, just be careful. But as for Barrington . . ." The sentence drifted into space. Jacob stared out the window, seeing a huge financial conspiracy and the governor of the Bank of England in his pristine office. Somehow, the two images refused to gel. He turned back to Sarah. "We're getting a bit out of our territory here. We all are, don't you think?"

She paused for a while and then said softly, "Let me talk to Barrington."

They both went quiet, lost in their thoughts. Sarah sat very still, gazing through the window at the roses outside. Her mind strayed repeatedly to Scarpirato, confusing all other thoughts. She had made a mistake last night. She would not let it happen again. She knew that a prolonged encounter with him would be intensely destructive. As for turning him in, she knew that in her place, he would have no qualms. He would do it with a smile.

Jacob unplugged the tape recorder and went out to the kitchen. Sarah followed him. Supper was ready. They sat at the kitchen table, both in a state of shock. To avoid the enormity of what they had discovered, Jacob talked about old times, reliving his capers. Sarah, happily distracted, laughed till her face hurt. Before she left, she asked if he could get hold of another adapter bug. He gave her a long, hard look and said he would. Exhausted, Sarah drove home and went straight to bed.

Chapter
Seventeen

On Wednesday morning at seven-thirty, Sarah carried her cappuccino and toast across the trading floor at ICB in a little white paper bag with handles. It swung as she walked, and froth eased through the lid on the Styrofoam cup. She took her seat at the proprietary desk, pulled out the cappuccino and the toast, and began to eat. This was a morning ritual, safe, familiar, to be enjoyed in silence.

Seconds later Matthew Arnott took his seat beside her. She nodded in his direction, then turned back to the toast and her butter-stained *Financial Times*. She did not want to look at him, did not want him to see her eyes, for fear they would convey what she knew about him. Simon Wilson arrived, talkative, euphoric still from Monday's successes. Sarah finished her toast and lit up a cigarette.

"God, I feel rough." Wilson groaned. "Went to the Ministry of Sound last night. Up till four."

Arnott laughed. "Still on a celebratory binge, huh?"

Wilson nodded. "Aren't you?"

Arnott smirked. "I just prefer my pleasure a bit more sophisticated, that's all."

Sarah nearly choked. "So what's Mr. Super-Sophisticated got in store?"

Arnott turned to face her. She held his glance, confident that if anything showed in her eyes, it would be disdain.

"I thought I'd go to Positano for the weekend. Take my girlfriend along."

Sarah shrugged. "Positano in July. I suppose it just scrapes through. A bit crowded, though. May and June are much better, I've always found."

Wilson sniggered. Arnott turned on his screens and muttered to himself, "Fucking comedians, aren't you?"

Positano, thought Sarah. *Why is he going there with Carla? Meeting the secret mastermind?*

She watched him carefully that day, her eyes snaking left to study him when she thought he wasn't looking. She found him disappointing. A spectacular crime, committed by one so mediocre. Scarpirato at least made a more convincing criminal. And the secret mastermind, what would he be like? She tried to draw up a psychological profile of him, and failed. The image that filled her mind was a blank face.

Finding it hard to concentrate, she stared distractedly at her screens. Nobody traded. They couldn't be bothered. The lassitude, the anticlimax after the big hit, had set in.

Sarah left at four. She went home, changed out of her work clothes, and typed up her report to Barrington. She couldn't imagine how she would convey her discovery with the spoken word. Writing it down somehow distanced her from it, as if she were a journalist writing an article.

Just as she finished, the phone rang. It was Dante.

"I need to see you." His voice was like a rough caress, and Sarah began to sweat. It was five-thirty, the sun was still high in the sky, and the heat prickled through her jeans.

She was silent for a while, then answered mechanically, "O.K. I'll come round."

She got into her BMW and started it up. She switched on the cassette player and listened to a tape, *Soul II Soul*, volume two. Letting the heavy beat flood through her body, she drove, as if on automatic pilot, down the King's Road to his house in Wellington Square.

He appeared smiling at his door and stood back to let her pass. She walked through the hall. Neither of them spoke. He led her through his house and out onto a roof terrace, then brought out two glasses of white wine and laid them on a wooden table. Sarah sat on the bench opposite him and lifted the glass to her lips, holding his gaze as she drank.

He was wearing blue jeans and a short-sleeved white shirt. This was the first time she had seen him wear anything but a suit. She stared at the thick covering of black hair on his arms and the tanned skin underneath, then reached across the table and took hold of his forearm, circling her fingers round his wrist.

Their conversation was broken, desultory. After a while he took hold of her hand. Neither of them could wait. He led her back through the house to his bedroom, cool behind the closed curtains, and, kissing her fiercely, pushed her down onto his bed. He unbuckled her jeans and pulled them off. She wore nothing underneath. For a while he just looked at her as she lay beneath him, and then he bent down to her and began to kiss her face, his hands clasped in hers.

Sarah lay naked, half covered by a linen sheet. The cool air of early morning mingled with the gentle sun and filtered through the heavy curtains, awakening her. It was a quarter to six. It had been light for over an hour, and the birds were well up, singing in the tree-lined square. She lay still for a while, like the victim of a violent accident, assessing the damage before moving. The purging satisfaction of last night was gone, replaced by an aching emptiness. The solution, Sarah knew, would only intensify the need. Seeking comfort from the source of discomfort was a futile exercise, but one that was, nevertheless, much repeated.

Lying just inches from Scarpirato in his massive bed, Sarah could analyze her situation with dispassion. The futility and the destructiveness of a relationship with this man she could clearly see. But equally clear was the futility of any attempt to break it off. Severance would come ultimately, and soon, she sensed that. She would wait until then. Freeing herself from doomed efforts to leave him, she removed one layer of guilt.

Accepting the power of her attraction to him, she wondered again at its source. He was not the first dangerous, destructive man she had slept with. She had hoped, when she started going out with John Carter, the first decent boyfriend she had ever had, that she had got the dangerous men out of her system. Then with Eddie, so intensely kind, loving, and sweet, she felt sure that she had. And then along came Scarpirato, a throwback, the most extreme case she had yet encountered. Perhaps he was to be her final experiment, catharsis. She leapt on that. Yes, let him be her catharsis. He was using her for his own selfish purposes, but she too would have hers. He was, of course, also her prey in quite another respect. Comforted by that thought, she slipped silently out of his bed, dressed, and left.

She handed her report to Barrington later that day, at twelve-thirty, just before he was due to have lunch with a contingent of visiting German bankers. She sat in his office, next to the tall grandfather clock with its subtle, somber tick. She had ten minutes, he told her.

"I've made some rather interesting discoveries. I've written them up in full, and there's this." She handed over a tape onto which Jacob had recorded all the pertinent dialogue. "It's not courtroom evidence, but it's pretty clear that a crime is being committed, and a quite spectacular one."

Barrington's eyes widened in unconcealed surprise as she related her story. So the trap he and Herr Mueller had set had sprung. He did not mention this to Sarah. His eyes narrowed in scrutiny as she finished, and he tried to think in the silence that followed.

Studying the woman who sat before him, he felt the first stirrings of foreboding. He banished them rapidly. They were inconvenient. He had chosen her, recommended her, and she had produced excellent results in short order. Those were the facts; he would concentrate on them. She had taken him by surprise with her use of bugging devices, that was all, but now that he had the measure of her, everything would be fine. He had given her the scope, and she had proved that she had the ingenuity. She had more than fulfilled his expectations. That was the way to look at it, not that he had underestimated her. He smiled across his desk at her.

"That's quite exceptional, Sarah. Well done. Disturbing, highly disturbing, but brilliant of you to unearth it." He made no reference to her methods. Sarah sensed that he was consciously avoiding this. "I'll read the report, listen to this tape, then get back to you. But in the meantime, just carry on as you are."

Unasked questions lingered in Sarah's mind. Somehow, sitting here in Barrington's office, her discoveries seemed relegated to an almost academic plane, her fears and suspicions melodramatic. She sat in silence. Barrington studied her, then glanced up at the clock. Sarah took the hint and prepared to leave.

"You'll need what's called a digital audiotape player to listen to that tape." She smiled. "But I'm sure you have some of those around."

Barrington held her gaze just a fraction longer than necessary. Her face was without guile, but he could not shake off the impression that somehow she was goading him. They shook hands, said goodbye. He watched her walk away from his office, down the long corridor. Then he shut himself away.

His sentiments were mixed. He did not like revelations or surprises. They were an occupational hazard. The only thing was to turn them to his advantage.

At twelve-forty-five Barrington's secretary, Ethel, announced that the German bankers had arrived and were waiting. The governor walked through the Parlours to his dining room. Smiling sunnily, he opened the door and walked in, tall, cool, calm, and confident—an imposing figure, a charming host, but one whose mind strayed persistently from his guests back to the tape, and to Sarah Jensen.

It was a quick lunch. At two-thirty Barrington shook hands, said his goodbyes, and walked briskly back to his office. He had a brief chat with Ethel, said he was not to be disturbed for half an hour, and asked her to find a digital audiotape machine. Ten minutes later she tapped lightly at his door, entered with the cassette player, then withdrew silently.

Barrington stuck the cassette in the tape deck, pressed the play button, sat back, and listened. Sarah had explained that she had edited the tapes so that all the relevant information was on one cassette. It was, of course, Jacob who had done this, but Sarah kept his involvement to herself. She didn't think Barrington would approve, and anyway, she preferred for Jacob to be invisible, just in case anything went wrong.

Barrington listened in silence for fifteen minutes, occasionally stopping and rewinding a section of tape. Eyebrows raised in shock, he listened to Arnott and Vitale incriminating themselves. Then he switched off the tape and read Sarah's report. Through his fog of shock, he tended to agree with her. Although Scarpirato was not mentioned directly, it did look as if he was the third member of the conspiracy. But he would need some hard evidence before he could move against the Italian. Jensen ought to continue with her investigation until she had more evidence, and until she discovered the identity of the fourth man.

The governor buzzed Ethel and asked her to get him James Bartrop immediately. Bartrop was apparently unavailable. Barrington cursed under his breath.

The two men finally spoke at ten that evening. Barrington was in his penthouse flat above the bank with his wife, Irene, enjoying a quiet evening in.

"Sorry to ring so late, Governor. Short overseas trip. Just got back."

"Quite all right. I called because our girl's come up with something pretty alarming. We were right. ICB is up to its neck in it. Massive insider trading. The other connections, implications, I'll leave to you, but it's a big problem now, for all of us. Jensen's written a report. You'd better read it, pronto."

Bartrop felt his pulse quicken. "How did she find out?"

Barrington paused for a fraction of a second. "Telephone calls, conversations. She intercepted them."

Bartrop's eyes widened. He was silent for a moment. "You mean she bugged people?"

"Yes," replied Barrington curtly.

"Full of initiative, this girl of yours, isn't she?"

"Seems to be, doesn't she?"

"You hinted to her that she might do this." It was more of an affirmation than a question.

"Oh, yes. Obliquely. I gave her the scope. It was up to her then, what she felt comfortable with."

"Like a duck to water, isn't she?"

"Perhaps."

"Any idea where she got her hardware?"

"Come, come, Bartrop. I didn't ask. The less I know about all that, the better. You know that."

Bartrop frowned. *Bit late for fastidiousness now,* he thought.

Barrington broke the silence. "I'll send one of my people round with the report. Where are you?"

Barrington wrote down the address with surprise. Chelsea Square. Most of the houses there were worth over a million pounds. Somehow he hadn't imagined that Bartrop had that kind of money.

Bartrop sat waiting in his house. It was silent, save for the rhythmic purrings of his cat, Trout, who dozed on his lap. He sat musing at his desk in his study, a very old, fine single-malt whisky by his side. Occasionally he could hear the gentle murmur of conversation in his garden: two of his bodyguards passing the time. He had been protected for eighteen months—an unwelcome intrusion, but necessary after a lengthy and dangerous undercover assignment in Colombia, where he had had a run-in with the Medellin cartel. The chances of his being on their hit list were high. Nobody knew for sure, but it was a risk that the Friends wanted to minimize; hence the protection, round the clock, wherever he went. Those men had long memories, but then, so did he.

After half an hour he heard a car pull up; then his doorbell rang. He put down Trout and went downstairs and through the hall to look through the peephole in his door. Munro stood on the doorstep holding a package. He opened the door.

"From the Bank of England, sir."

Bartrop nodded, took the package, and returned to his study. Resuming his seat at the desk, he ripped open the buff manila envelope, pulled out the report, and began to read. A slow smile spread over his face. He listened to the tape. His thoughts traveled to Fieri. He felt sure he was on the right track—that Sarah Jensen, even if she didn't know it, was on the right track. He smiled in satisfaction. It was a good start. He had confirmed that a conspiracy existed. The unnamed fourth man was perhaps Fieri. If that was so, then the fun would really begin.

He rang Barrington.

"This stuff is brilliant. As our American cousins say, we hit pay dirt with this girl. Just ask her to carry on, carefully and quietly. We need to confirm who the third and fourth members of the conspiracy are. The third looks like Scarpirato, but we don't know that for sure. She offered no clues to the fourth, eh?"

"No, she didn't."

"If you get a chance, perhaps you could ask her where she got hold of her equipment. I know it's sensitive, but there might be a way around it. She might even volunteer it."

"I'll do what I can," Barrington agreed with a grunt.

Should have insisted on a cutout, thought Bartrop. If not the deputy governor, then at least someone who was a bit more willing to get his hands dirty. Too late now, he knew, to change things.

"Oh, one last thing," he said. "Today's Thursday. All this happened on Monday. Why did it take so long to get this to us?"

"I just received it this morning. What she did with it in the meantime I don't know. I think it would have been just a tad ungracious, considering what she discovered, to complain that it was late."

"It's not a complaint, Governor. Just curiosity."

Bartrop put down the telephone. For a long while he sat in silence, staring out the window of his study. Tantalizing information. But so many missing pieces. And at the center, Sarah Jensen. He glanced at his watch, then called Miles Forshaw at home.

"Miles, Bartrop here. I know you ran a check on Jensen, but run another one. There's something about her that bothers me. I can't help feeling we've missed something."

A quarter of a mile away, in Carlyle Square, Sarah lay in a hot bath, with the bathroom window wide open. Warm air drifted in, making the steam that rose from the scented water swirl. She had emptied into the bath half a bottle of bath oil, with geranium and lavender, designed to calm and soothe. A candle burned by the side of the tub, its flame flickering in the breeze, sending shadows shimmering up the walls.

She tried to shut off her mind. Her triangle of roles was beginning to pull her apart. Employee, undercover agent, and lover, all mutually irreconcilable. Two, perhaps, were sustainable. Sarah wondered how much longer she would be able to continue with her act.

Sleeping with Scarpirato had shattered her game plan. Now she would be reduced to reacting to events. She felt control slipping from her fingers. She lay in the semidarkness, watching the shadows in the flickering candlelight, her body tense in the hot water.

She glanced at her watch, a waterproof watch. It was eleven. She was exhausted. She stepped out of the bath, toweled herself, and, still damp, crawled into bed. She switched off her phone. She had not exchanged a word with Scarpirato all day. She did not intend to telephone him, and while she sensed that he would not call her, she chose forcibly to shut off expectation, at least for this night.

Chapter
Eighteen

Sarah awoke uneasy, with a sense of foreboding. With heavy footsteps, she headed for work. Jacob called her mid-morning. His voice, slightly awkward, added to her disquiet. He wanted to see her after work. Could he pop round? Yes, of course, said Sarah.

She stared pensively at her screens, seeing nothing. Then she heard Scarpirato's voice at her side. She glanced up to find him standing inches from her. He was talking to Arnott about a position he was running. After uttering a few clipped instructions, he turned to go. As he did, he caught her eye, held it for a second. In his gaze there was a look of desire, but contained, and triumph, which left her oddly excluded. He walked back to his office and lit up a cigar. She turned back to her screens and, breaking all her rules, distracted herself with a few trades.

Careless trading almost always produces losses. When, at the end of the day, she found herself £30,000 down, Sarah was almost relieved by the familiarity of a predictable pattern. She reported her losses to a gleeful Arnott and left for the night.

The traffic on Lower Thames Street roared by in a constant stream. Sarah waited and sprinted across in the break between two huge semis, then walked to Cheapside and caught a taxi.

When she arrived home, Jacob was already waiting, having let himself in with his key. His face creased into a smile when she walked into the sitting room, but the lines around his eyes betrayed concern. She made tea. They sipped and talked. After a while he seemed to wind down, looking for a natural pause in their conversation.

He ran his hands through his thick gray hair. Sarah sat and waited. Jacob's face colored slightly.

"Got some more stuff on the tapes. This Scarpirato fella has a girlfriend—spent last night with her, from what I can gather. And he's taking her to the South of France this weekend." Jacob waved his hand in the air. " 'Course, I don't know if it's relevant. Just thought I ought to tell you, that's all." He didn't tell her what his friend Charlie had told him about Scarpirato and his women, about his reputation for causing pain and cruelty, how he almost seemed to delight in the suffering he inflicted. Jacob continued quickly, absolving Sarah of the need to respond. "By the way, had a listen to all your Carla tapes. Nothing much on them."

He sat pensively, watching her stare at her feet. Averting her eyes from his, she stood, walked over to the line of bottles clustered on a table, and poured two large glasses of whisky. Silently, she handed one to him, walked to the window, and stood, her back to him, looking out. In three mouthfuls she drained her glass, finding reassurance in sensation. She stood motionless as the minutes passed.

She could not hope to analyze her feelings, or to rationalize a way out of the pain, humiliation, and sense of betrayal. That was the worst thing, the betrayal. It filled her with rage and disgust. She had thought she was the betrayer, but her own betrayal by Scarpirato only worsened her crime against Eddie. That it should have been for all this . . . She continued looking out the window, one hand clamped around her glass, the other hanging by her side.

The garden of Carlyle Square lay in front of her, radiant in the evening sun. Mrs. Jardine was watching her children chase each other around the grass. The scene unfolded before Sarah. She observed it with detachment, as if she were watching television.

Jacob rose from his chair, walked over to her, and gently laid a hand on her shoulder. "I'd better go now. I'm seeing some of the boys tonight. I'll ring tomorrow. O.K.?"

Sarah laid her hand over his. " 'Bye, Jacob. Have a good evening." She watched him leave the room, then turned back to her contemplation of the square. The door clicked as Jacob let himself out, and then there was silence.

Monday morning at seven-thirty, right on time, Sarah swung through the security doors at ICB, walked across the trading floor, and took her seat. As usual, rows of eyes followed her progress, but this morning the appraising glances were not rewarded with a sunny smile or a cheery hello. Looking straight ahead, Sarah headed for her desk on automatic pilot. She sat down next to Arnott, nodding briefly in his direction. He watched her from the corners of his eyes. Insensitive as he was to the nuances of human behavior, he noticed a change in her. He made a clumsy attempt at conversation.

"So, how're you doing today?"

Sarah turned to him, and for a brief moment his mouth fell open. He felt as if a mask had been removed from her face. If what was uncovered had been merely blank, it would not have been so shocking. But what he saw instead was a chilling disregard, unaffected and unconcealed. He turned quickly back to his computers. She switched on hers, tapping at the keyboard as if nothing had happened.

Scarpirato appeared and called them all into the morning meeting. Arnott dawdled, fetching a coffee from the machine. Sarah rose to go in. Scarpirato let her pass, then followed her into the conference room. As he took his place at the table opposite her, he met her gaze and recoiled visibly. Contempt blazed in her eyes. Her mouth curled in disgust. Riveted, he watched her face, then blinked and looked away. When he looked back seconds later, her face was blank. Arnott appeared with his coffee, breaking the tension. Wilson, always the last to arrive, scurried in after him. They took their places at the table. Arnott took a cigarette from the packet in front of Sarah and grinned a thank-you at her. She managed a taut smile.

Scarpirato cleared his voice and began to speak in his usual staccato tones. He outlined his suggested trading axes for the week. Sarah listened, saying nothing. Minutes later, they all filed out. Sarah took her seat at the desk, picked up her phone, and got to work.

She stayed at her desk all day. Wilson brought her a Birley's sandwich for lunch. It sat, the bread curling, as the afternoon passed. Her concentration was unbroken. She traded almost incessantly, plunging in and out of the market, building up a position, making a few thousand pounds, cutting the position, and starting all over again. For eight hours she lived and breathed the market, and she made £60,000. After reporting her profits to Arnott, she rode home in a taxi, feeling a grim satisfaction and the first flutterings of relief. Equilibrium was, she knew, a long way off, but at least she was traveling in the right direction.

The phone was ringing as she walked through her front door. Mechanically, she went to answer it. It was Scarpirato. Unexpected, unwanted. She gripped the receiver, then, after a pause, demanded, "What do you want?"

He laughed, in a manner she now recognized as pure device; it was designed to simulate the intimacy of a shared joke, to show fake exasperation at the foibles of a loved one. She nearly hurled down the phone in disgust.

"I would like to know what's going on. Why did you give me that look? What am I supposed to have done?" The voice was pure injured innocence.

Sarah breathed slowly and deeply. She could not challenge him. After all, how could she have known about his infidelity? But the outrageousness of his implied lies, his blithe amorality, were also too extreme to tackle. There was nothing to be gained from confronting a liar who seemed to believe his own fantasies, a psychopathic liar. Perceiving for the first time the nature of the man, Sarah felt a schism, the severance she had been looking for. She felt a wave of relief flood over her.

"I want you to come round now. I want to see you. Sort out this stupidity."

His teasing banter implied that nothing could possibly be wrong, that any slight unpleasantness could be dissipated in his embrace. Sarah laughed. There could be no harm in it now. She felt, she decided, only curiosity. He was mad, insane. If she could see that more fully and understand, it would make it all so much easier. She put down the phone and picked up her car keys.

———

At 7:00 P.M., back at ICB, the trading floor was almost deserted. Matthew Arnott was on the verge of leaving when the phone rang. He picked it up with annoyance.

"Arnott?"

"Yes?" He stiffened, immediately recognizing the harsh voice, which, despite his intentions, always seemed to induce a feeling of fear.

"Can you come up to my office, please?"

Arnott put down the handset and hurried across the trading floor. He walked out onto the fire escape and climbed the four flights of stairs to the seventh floor, where Karl Heinz Kessler had his office.

Kessler was alone, his secretary gone for the night. Arnott paused for a second outside his office. Kessler looked up, noticed him, and beckoned him to come in. Arnott took a seat beside Kessler's glass desk.

Kessler grinned. "Your friend told me the good news. Very profitable." The smile faded abruptly. "Have to look after those profits, though." He reached under his desk and retrieved his briefcase. He opened it on the desk and took out what looked like a small portable radio with an antenna. "This is a little security measure for you. It detects bugs. I'd like you to check around, your home, Carla's, the desk even."

Arnott took hold of the radio. "Why? There's nothing wrong, is there?"

Kessler laughed. "Nothing at all. Simply an exercise in prudence. Our own security people recommend we sweep the most important offices and conference rooms regularly. They gave me this little thing. Thought we might as well use it."

"How does it work?"

"Simple. It picks up a huge range of signals on a wide-band

receiver, like a radio, only more so. You switch it on, walk around, and turn the tuning knob. You wear this earpiece, and if you hear the sounds around you coming back through it, you know you're picking up signals transmitted from a local bug. There's a light-emitting diode here." He pointed to a panel. "A number of lights go on if you are near the source of the signals. The more lights, the nearer you are to the bug. Brilliant, eh?"

Arnott nodded. For some reason, he didn't share Kessler's enthusiasm.

"Seems simple enough. I'll give it a go."

Kessler nodded. "By the way, how's that Jensen girl?"

Arnott shrugged. "Still a class-one bitch."

Kessler laughed. "I wouldn't worry about her."

Arnott took the bug detector back down to his desk. He felt vaguely troubled. He wondered if there was more to it than Kessler's prudence. Was he worried about something, or was it just natural German caution?

He switched on the radio, inserted the earpiece in his right ear, and began to turn the tuning dial, feeling faintly foolish. Suddenly the panel of lights went on, not just one light but a whole column. "Fuck," he muttered to himself. He froze as the word came back to him through the earphones. Bile rose to his mouth. He felt himself panicking. There was a device nearby.

After a couple of minutes he traced the sound to the adapter. He unplugged it with trembling hands and shoved it in his briefcase, then sat for half an hour, paralyzed, at his desk. He thought about calling Kessler but couldn't bring himself to dial the number. Chaos raged in his head. After a while he got up mechanically, walked out, and caught a cab on Lower Thames Street.

He arrived at Carla's flat half an hour later. She knew instantly from his face that something was wrong. His voice was full of fury and fear.

"My desk has been bugged. Kessler gave me a bug detector. Just for prudence's sake, he said. I tested it out and found this." He pulled the adapter out of his briefcase.

Carla turned pale. "Did you tell him?"

"Fuck, no. Not yet."

Carla stared at him in shock. "What are you going to do?"

Arnott looked at her with panicked eyes. "I don't know." He took out the radio detector, switched it on, inserted the earpiece, and began to wave the detector around the room. It took them only three minutes to discover that Carla, too, had been bugged.

Arnott's eyes were wild as he spoke. "I want to know every person who's been in this flat in the last few months."

Carla turned to face him, hands on hips. "Oh, for God's sake, Matthew, I can't remember!"

Arnott walked up to her and pushed her down on the sofa behind her. "Well, we'll start with the most recent and work back." He took a seat opposite her. His eyes shot her a warning. "And no lies."

She glared at him. "My cleaning lady, Maria. My girlfriend Angelica. Her boyfriend Stefano. Another girlfriend, Mosami. A cousin of mine who came over for a few days—it'd never be her." She glanced around frantically, throwing her hands in the air. "I don't know. I can't think of anyone else."

Arnott stared at her, unseeing, turning the names over in his head.

"Wait a minute—that girl Mosami. What's her second name?"

"Matsumoto. You've met her. What's she—"

"She's a friend of Sarah Jensen's. I overheard Jensen ringing

her a few days ago." Arnott grabbed Carla and dragged her to
her feet. He gripped her arms and shouted into her face. "It's that
fucking bitch Jensen! She bugs me at ICB, and Mosami bugs your
flat. Oh Christ, Carla." He let go of her and raked his hands
through his hair.

Carla fetched a bottle of whisky and two glasses from a table
at the side of the room. She poured whisky halfway up, filled the
glasses with water, gave one to Arnott, and sat him down on the
sofa next to her. For a while they both drank in silence. Carla
refilled their glasses.

"So why? Why would Jensen and Mosami want to bug us?"

Arnott's rage began to flare again. He struggled to control
himself, and his words came out slow and distorted. "How the
fuck do I know?"

"What are you going to do?"

Carla's shrill voice was beginning to drive him mad. He
grabbed her arm and pulled her to her feet. "Go and see Jensen
and Matsumoto. That's what." He found the telephone directory
and looked up Sarah's address.

The Mercedes swept into Carlyle Square. Arnott parked it
roughly against the curb, dragged Carla from the passenger seat,
and began to pound on Sarah's door. After ten minutes he gave
up. It would have to wait until tomorrow. He would get the bitch
in the office.

He turned to Carla. "Where does Mosami live?"

"Hay's Mews," she answered faintly. Arnott turned into the
King's Road and blazed off toward Mayfair. Ten minutes later he
screeched to a halt, shattering the quiet of Hay's Mews. He
threw open his door, slammed it with a force that shook the

whole car, marched around to the passenger side, and dragged Carla out. He half carried her up to Mosami's house, held her with one hand, and pounded on the door with the other.

In the cool cream interior, Mosami was sitting on her sofa, reading a book and listening to Mahler's Tenth Symphony. She looked up in alarm at the pounding, clearly audible above the music. She rose, walked out into the hall, paused in front of the door, and looked through the spyhole. She saw Arnott, white with rage, pounding on her door and shouting to be let in, and Carla, clearly drunk. Fear clenched her stomach. She stood in silence for a while. Arnott continued his pounding, roaring at her to let him in. There was no point in hiding. He could hear her music—he would know she was in, and he would be able to get to her sooner or later if he wanted. Better for it to be sooner. And anyway, she told herself, he couldn't have any proof. She would be cool. She lied very well. She drew herself up, opened the door, and studied Arnott with dignified anger.

"Just what do you think you're doing?"

Arnott pushed her back into the house. She let out a little shriek of alarm. He followed her into the sitting room and pushed her down onto the sofa. He sat opposite, twisting his wristwatch between his fingers, his eyes fixed on her. Carla loitered in the background, propped against a wall.

"You know why we're here," he began calmly.

Mosami glared back at him. "I have not the faintest idea why you're here. You come barging in enraged, shouting and screaming. Carla is drunk. I hope you have a good explanation."

Arnott spoke very slowly and carefully, his voice low, taut with the effort of self-control. "It's very simple. I want an explanation. I want you to tell me why you and that bitch Sarah Jensen bugged Carla's flat and my trading desk."

Mosami laughed. "I think you're doing too much coke, Arnott. You need to get a grip."

Arnott stared at her for a few seconds, his face blank. "You've got no idea, have you? No fucking idea what you're dealing with."

"Oh, please. Spare me the big-boy histrionics." Mosami, listening to Arnott's words and watching him compulsively playing with his watch, felt like laughing. It should have been funny, Arnott trying to be frightening should have been funny, but underlying his every gesture, coiled in his tense, controlled posture, was fear. And this fear, reflected from an invisible source, began to fill the room, began to contaminate Mosami, so that she felt her skin turn clammy and her mouth go dry. Mixed in with his fear was a terrifying rage.

His voice came back, low and menacing. "I won't ask you again."

Mosami sat motionless, silent. The room seemed to take on a dreadful stillness. Then, very deliberately, Arnott got to his feet, walked over to her, took hold of her arm, and pulled her to her feet. Then he drew back his right arm and viciously slapped her face. She reeled back. He let her drop, then picked her up and did it again. Carla watched in shock. Arnott returned to his seat.

"Now will you tell me?"

Mosami saw her own fear reflected in his face, but with it a mania unleashed, violence uninhibited. She was surprised by her own clarity of mind. Thoughts came sharply through the pain. He came toward her again, dragged her up. She felt his fingers gripping her jaw, saw his eyes inches from hers. Then she felt herself falling as he pushed her away, felt the crack as her ribs made contact with the edge of her marble coffee table. She lay still on the floor, listening to her own breathing. He would keep going, she knew. With the first strike, his inhibitions had snapped. And whatever was terrifying him would drive him on. Her body began to sweat with pain and instinctive fear, and she began, haltingly, to speak.

"It was Sarah's idea. She was frightened. She thought you were jealous of her, would try to get her fired. She wanted to protect herself, get some dirt on you. She wanted to bug Carla. She thought she might get more dirt that way."

Arnott stared, his eyes bulging. "So that's it? Jealousy?"

Mosami nodded.

"So it was just the two of you. Nothing to do with the police."

Mosami struggle to breathe. "Police? No. Nothing to do with them. Nobody knows. Just me and Sarah."

Arnott stood above her. "Keep it that way. Tell your friend, if either of you tells a soul . . ." He laughed. The sound was high-pitched, with an edge of hysteria. Then he walked out, and Carla followed without a glance behind.

Mosami watched them leave, then slumped back on the floor.

As Arnott and Carla drove off, Arnott considered Mosami's explanation. Jealousy. He felt an overwhelming, exhausted relief. He had been right all along. He had hated that bitch Jensen from day one. Never trusted her. She was just too clever by half. Riddled with jealousy. She should have known what she had taken on. But he had controlled it, would control her. What he had done to Mosami should be a lesson. They would keep their mouths shut. This would not be a disaster. He was in control.

He gripped the steering wheel and drove Carla home. Twenty minutes later, he was in his own house, in Holland Park. He walked upstairs to his bedroom, dropped his clothes on the floor, and got into bed. Lying on his back in the darkness, he opened the drawer in his bedside table and took out a bottle. He removed three sleeping tablets, swallowed them without water, and lay, eyes open, staring at the ceiling, until the narcotics hit and he fell asleep.

Chapter Nineteen

A couple of miles away, in the silent darkness, Sarah lay in Scarpirato's bed. A streetlamp glowed through a slight parting in the curtains; otherwise, there was no light. Dim contours of features were discernible, but not expressions. Sarah could hide in the darkness, ask questions, listen to answers, with no fear of giving away anything beyond that which was already conveyed by her presence. If she did not understand the reasons for that, she felt safe that he could not.

They were talking. They had talked for hours. With her words and her questions, she kept him at bay.

He took her face in his hands. "Sarah, my darling. Tell me. What is it? What's wrong?"

She tilted her head away in the darkness. "Nothing's wrong, Dante. I just want to understand a few things, that's all."

He chuckled quietly. "What's there to understand? I love you, I need you." He paused to kiss her. "What else is there?"

Sarah looked away and tried to keep the tears out of her voice. "Oh, there's a lot more, Dante."

He shrugged. She felt his shoulders move.

"Convention. That's what you're talking about, isn't it?" He laughed teasingly, but Sarah felt that scorn was not far away. "I expected more from you. What would you do with the trappings of devotion? Why would you need to see me every day? This is more intense than a week of encounters for most people. One hour with you is all I need."

Sarah smiled through her pain. "Oh, Dante. You actually believe all that, don't you? Here and now it's true, but in a few hours it won't be. You think you're so tough and hard, but you're just a romantic. In a mundane world, you manufacture your own tragedy and pain and loss. But each time it happens, it kills a little of you, doesn't it? Erodes your capacity to feel. So the next time the pain has to be sharper. It's all right for you. You choose it. But what about your victims?"

They were silent for a while. Then he spoke.

"How do you know so much about me, then? You cannot understand these things without colluding, can you? Why are you here, if not as a willing victim?"

She laughed. "That's exactly what I have been. We fulfilled a need in each other. But I can't do that anymore, Dante. I've had my share of hurt. I keep seeking it out, just to see if I can still cope with it. But I can cope, I know that. I always cope. And so you're futile. You're a pointless exercise. All you can offer me is pain. I don't think I want it anymore."

He traced his finger over her face. His words were heavy. "But I'm here now." He moved closer to her.

She smiled in the darkness. "Just hold me, Dante. That's all I want."

He wrapped his arms around her and held her to his chest. He felt the moisture of her tears against his skin. He stroked her hair and soothed her till she fell asleep. He lay awake most of the night, holding her, quiet and peaceful, in his arms.

Sarah woke the next morning with her head pounding. She heaved herself out of bed and went to the bathroom for a drink of water. When she caught sight of herself in the mirror, her eyes were dull and swollen, her skin sallow.

The alarm was ringing as she went back to the bed. Scarpirato woke, reached out a long, thin arm, and switched it off. He watched Sarah climb back into bed.

"Sleep well?"

"I don't know. I think so. But I feel horrible now." She winced. "I feel a migraine coming on. I don't think I can move."

"Well, I'd better get up and get ready. But you can stay here till you feel a bit better. Then go home and have a good rest." He smiled beatifically. "In my capacity as your boss, I give you a day off."

"Thanks, I'll take it."

He reached into a bedside table and pulled out a packet of pills. "Here. Painkillers. Take a couple." He brought her a glass of water and she knocked back the pills. Then she collapsed into the pillows, trying to sleep as he showered and dressed. Twenty minutes later he kissed her goodbye.

"What shall I do about the security alarm?" she asked as he was leaving. "I don't want to set it off when I leave."

"Don't worry. I won't switch it on. My housekeeper is coming at eleven. She'll switch it on when she leaves."

Sarah slept for an hour, then woke up with a start. She sat up slowly. The pills were working; the migraine had almost gone. She felt weak as she got to her feet and began to dress.

She wondered about Dante. Last night and this morning he had been so tender, so loving. She had seen another side to him, and she found herself wondering if he really was part of the Carla conspiracy. What she had seen before suggested that he was in many ways the ideal criminal: amoral, ambitious, unstable, brilliant, and devious. But capable of massive criminal conspiracy? She had spoken to him of work and Arnott, even mentioned Carla Vitale, but he had shown no embarrassment, awkwardness, or concealment, and Sarah thought that by now she could recognize his lies. For the first time, she began to think that he might be innocent. But if he was, then who were the two unidentified persons to whom Carla and Arnott had referred? Sarah's head began to pound again.

Without conscious decision, she found herself beginning to explore Scarpirato's house, tentatively at first, then with growing conviction. She started in his dressing room, a long, narrow room with a dark blue carpet, lined with mahogany wardrobes. She pulled open a door and discovered rows of brightly colored dresses and stacks of elegant high-heeled shoes, confirmation of what she half expected. Still she winced. Her face set in determination, she closed the door and continued her search. In a drawer in the desk in his study she found a set of photographs in silver frames, showing a pretty short blond woman arm in arm with Scarpirato. She was smiling up at him as he looked at the camera. Sarah studied the look of smug victory, a look she had seen flash across his features many times. Here it was captured. She looked at it for a long while before shutting it back in the drawer.

She found the safe in a bedroom at the top of the house. It

was hidden behind a painting of a mad monkey—oddly appropriate, thought Sarah. Confident that the alarm was switched off, she started to work on the lock.

It was a standard combination lock, probably twenty years old, much less sophisticated than the contemporary versions. It was just like the model Sarah had learned on at Jacob's house. She kept her ear close to the dial, concentrated fiercely, and turned. Years on a trading floor had sharpened her hearing and concentration. Sometimes the noise of traders screaming, phones ringing, loudspeakers hailing, and machines chattering was so loud that it was almost impossible to hear someone on the other end of a telephone line. Years of blocking out the cacophony and concentrating on the whisper now paid off.

After ten minutes and several false starts, the door to the safe clicked open. The interior was about one foot square. It contained a pile of unsealed brown envelopes. She opened the envelopes and examined their contents: share certificates and bank statements from several numbered accounts held at Swiss Bank. The latest balance, for June, showed deposits of just over half a million dollars. For a successful banker in his mid-thirties that was reasonable, even on the low side. The shares, Sarah calculated, were probably worth another $2 million. Scarpirato was rich, yes, but not suspiciously so. Unless he had other secret accounts or hidden assets, then it didn't look as if he could be the third person in Arnott and Vitale's blackmail ring.

His whispered conferences with Arnott looked suspicious, but might be nothing more than typical trading-floor conversations uttered in the usual conspiratorial manner. Scarpirato took advice from Arnott in his trading, but that was not inherently suspect. And as for the desk's abnormally high profits, it would have been easy for him to explain those as simply the product of his own genius.

The rarefied atmosphere of a trading floor could distort perception; it was all too easy to lose touch with reality. Scarpirato's ego and vanity would blur his clarity. He was in all likelihood no more than an unknowing accomplice to Arnott.

Sarah replaced the envelopes, closed the safe, and spun the combination lock a few times to cover her tracks. She walked through the house, glancing around as if for the last time, and left. Ten minutes later the cleaning lady arrived.

Matthew Arnott sat at his desk chain-smoking. Occasionally his eyes would swivel and glare at the empty desk beside him. That bitch Mosami would have tipped off Jensen. Perhaps, knowing what he had done to Mosami, she had gone into hiding.

Jensen's absence worried him. He wanted to see her, hear the explanation from her own mouth, and make sure she kept that mouth shut. He wondered for a split second if she perhaps did have some connection to the police, but quickly ruled it out. No, she was just a banker who got greedy. A scheming little bitch of a blackmailer.

A light flashed three times on his dashboard, then rang loudly, interrupting his thoughts. Wilson got there first.

"Line one, Matthew. It's Carla."

Arnott took the call. After a brief conversation, he put on his jacket and strode purposefully across the floor. He walked into the men's room, discreetly checked that he was alone, and locked himself into a cubicle. He took his mobile phone out of his jacket pocket and waited for the light to flash. Seconds later he hit the talk button and listened.

"I just got a call. He says buy lire. In size. Now." Carla sounded agitated, confused.

"Shit," muttered Arnott under his breath. "Now, of all times."

He weighed up his options frantically. They had to go along with it. To do nothing would be suspicious.

"O.K. I'll do it." He spoke in a whisper. "It will be all right. Don't worry."

She snorted. "It better be."

Arnott switched off the phone and returned to his desk. It would be all right, he told himself. He just had to find Sarah Jensen and get her under control, for all their sakes.

He glanced around. Wilson was nowhere to be seen; Scarpirato was in his office. He walked into an empty conference room, took out his mobile phone, and sold, spot, eight sets of $50 million for lire, dealing with eight different brokers. Arnott's p.a. brokers were dotted around the world, some in the reputable financial centers, some in those areas known for their secrecy. Depending on the time of day, the size and nature of the trade, Arnott dealt with brokers in London, Panama, Liechtenstein, Mexico, Switzerland, New York, and the Caymans and a host of other small, warm islands keen to supplement their tourist revenue. He had more than twenty trading accounts, identified by numbers and names, never his own. His complicated arrangements usually gave him a secret thrill, and a sense of comfort and invisibility, but today he felt for the first time a strange vulnerability. He felt exposed.

He returned to his trading desk and tried to cloak himself in the routine of work. Picking up his handset, he bought another hundred million lire for the desk. Mechanically, he wrote out the tickets, dropped them in the settlements tray, and turned his attention to the screens.

In his air-conditioned office in Rome, Antonio Fieri put down his telephone with a smile of satisfaction. He had just spoken briefly to Catania. Their phone conversations were always curt, cryptic, but the message had been clear enough. Buy lire. Now. In size.

He punched out the number of Calvadoro, his broker. Buy lire, he told him. Spot. Three hundred million dollars' worth, spread around as usual. Calvadoro took the order. Fieri hung up and stared into space.

His fears about Catania had subsided. He had the man watched night and day, in his personal and professional life. Through a trusted intermediary, he had put out feelers, checking inside the government on Catania's standing. After a week the answers came back. Catania was clean, on every count. No one suspected him. That day would probably come, reasoned Fieri, but until then Catania was still his golden goose, and he would make full use of him. So his tone when they spoke had been cordial. He was well pleased with his man.

Catania, sitting in his office at the Banca d'Italia on Via Nazionale, had sensed this and was deeply relieved. His secrets were quite safe. Nobody knew anything about his dealings with Fieri or Vitale. The suspicions of Bundesbank President Mueller were just straws in the wind. Fieri was in the dark. He must be. Catania had no illusions; if Fieri knew, then he, Catania, would be dead. His worries quashed, Catania leaned back in his chair, lit up a cigar, and relaxed.

Nine hundred miles away, Sarah drove home slowly from Dante's house, trying to clear her head. She parked her car, entered her house, walked up to her answerphone, and pressed the button to listen to her messages, undressing as the machine rewound and prepared to play. Suddenly she froze. She heard Mosami's voice, halting and pained, as if she could not catch her breath.

"Sarah, it's Mosami. Make sure you're alone when you listen to this message." There was a long pause, then Mosami continued. "Listen, I have to warn you. Arnott has found out about the devices, the one at work and the one in Carla's house. He came round here last night. I told him I knew nothing. Then he beat me up." Her voice was flat, emotionless. "I had to tell him. I'm sorry. I said you did it because you thought he was trying to get you fired and you wanted to get some dirt on him to protect yourself." She half laughed, and said, "Anyway, that's the truth, isn't it?"

Sarah suspected this was said for the benefit of anyone else who might be listening. Then the line went dead.

She frantically dialed Mosami's number. There was no reply. Immobilized by rage, guilt, and fear, she dug the nails of her right hand into the fingertips of her left till they left deep red indentations. She took a cigarette from a packet on the coffee table, sat down, and lit up. She breathed deeply, forcing her breath into a regular pattern. She thought about calling Jacob and decided against it. More than ever, he would want her to withdraw. More than ever, she wanted to carry on. Her assignment had just turned very personal. Curiosity, novelty, and experimentation were now reinforced by much deeper, more powerful motivations.

She sat very still. It was essential to think clearly now. She had to deal with Arnott and salvage her assignment. If there was a way to do both together . . .

An hour later, Sarah walked calmly across the trading floor. At least she had had time to compose herself, plan a response, what she hoped was a convincing story. If she played it cool, she had a small chance of breaking right into the heart of Arnott's dirty little conspiracy, discovering the identity of the third and fourth members, and obtaining more than enough proof for Barrington. But she would have to temper her desire for revenge for a while and play out yet another role. She took a few deep breaths and slipped into her seat next to Arnott.

He looked up at her in surprise, then rage flooded his features. Before he could say anything, she gave him a knowing smile.

"I think we'd better have a talk, don't you? Shall we take a walk outside?"

She got to her feet and sauntered across the trading floor. Arnott glared at her back, then stalked out after her. From his office, Scarpirato watched them disappear with a puzzled look.

Outside, they leaned against the green iron railings that lined the broad flagstone walkway along the Thames. The ICB building towered behind them, and the river rolled by silently a few feet below. A tug chugged past, its hull deep in the swirling brown water. It dragged a vast hoard of bricks on a floating buttress. Seagulls swirled in its wake, tossing and diving, screaming angrily at the sky.

The walkway was dotted with couples staring into each other's eyes, whispering and laughing, stealing an illicit half-hour. A few glanced briefly at the preppy banker and the beautiful woman at his side. His stance was rigid, hers relaxed, almost mocking—a warring couple, people might have thought, one where the balance of power lay undeniably with the woman.

Arnott looked at Sarah dubiously, his eyes hard, as if to say, *This had better be good.* Sarah calmly lit a cigarette, inhaled deeply a few times, and flicked the ash into the muddy water. Rattled by her silence, he blurted out, "What the hell do you think you're up to?"

Sarah stared at the river, took a few more puffs on her cigarette, then turned to face him. She smiled, but her face was taut,
her eyes glacial.

"I'd like a piece of the action."

Arnott rolled his eyes skyward, took a step toward her, and
grasped her naked forearm like a clamp.

"You stupid bitch. You've just got no idea what you're dealing
with, have you?"

Sarah stepped forward, placed the point of her right heel on
his left foot, and transferred her full weight onto it. Arnott
spread his palm and was about to hit her when something in her
face stopped him. He released her arm and she moved back.

"You forget. I know exactly what I am dealing with. A very
lucrative little blackmail ring. One that I propose to join." She
leaned against the railings and cocked her heel over a lower bar.
"I'll admit, I had no idea I would stumble onto something like
this. I thought your friend Carla might be able to compromise
you in some small way—that I could use it to keep you in line."
She paused, watching the rage flare in his eyes. "I think you
discovered all that yesterday in your conversation with my
friend. But then I came across your dirty little conspiracy." Arnott
began to splutter. She raised her hand, cutting him off. "Don't
worry. I'm not going to tell anyone. Besides, who could I tell? It
doesn't show me in a particularly good light." She spoke casually,
her lips curled in a half-smile.

The tension eased slightly in his body. She continued, her
voice calm and reasonable. "All I want is to share in the information. Nothing more. You give me that, and I'll keep the compromising tapes locked up in a safe-deposit box. They'll stay there
for good. Nobody will ever see them. Unless, of course, anything
happens to me or Mosami. Then they'll go to Chief Inspector

Maynard at the Fraud Squad." She had read about Maynard yesterday in the *Standard*. She dropped his name as an afterthought.

Arnott glared at her, silent for a while. Then he spoke, his voice bright and savage. "You want a piece of the action? O.K. You'll have one. Catania has just been in touch. He says buy lire. In size. Now."

Sarah fought to keep her face expressionless. Catania was the source! And Arnott so careless, letting it slip. Her scheme was working already. Masking her reaction, she drew on her cigarette, watched it burn down to the filter, and tossed it into the river. She stared out across the murky water to Tower Bridge, looming blue in the background, and turned to Arnott with a smile.

"Let's go, then."

They walked across the trading floor, Arnott two paces behind, as if to see that she didn't escape. Sarah took her seat, picked up her handset, and hit the BdP line. Arnott picked up the same line on his dashboard and listened in. Seconds later, Johnny McDermott came on the line.

"Sarah Jensen, my old darling. How are you?"

"Fine, Johnny." She was curt, all business. "Where do you have dollar-lire, spot, in size?"

McDermott consulted his screen and checked the rate. Dollar-lire. Not one of her usual trades. What was going on? "Eighty-seven sixty, eighty-nine ten," he barked out, meaning 1687.60, 1689.10.

"I give you fifty million dollars at eighty-seven sixty."

There was an uneasy pause. It was a large single trade in one of the secondary currencies, the kind of position that worried traders. Some of the pugnacity went out of McDermott's voice as he answered.

"O.K. Done. You sell fifty dollars at eighty-seven sixty." He began to tap in details of the trade on his computer.

"That'll be for me, Johnny. At Cordillon et Cie."

There was an explosion at the other end of the line. "What the fuck are you doing?"

Sarah cut him off. "Just do it, Johnny."

There was a tense silence, then McDermott uttered a strangled O.K. He signed off, muttering that he would talk to her later. Raking his hands through his hair, he glanced around to see if anybody had overheard. Nobody had. His colleagues were all busy, shouting and screaming down the phones. He stared at the screen. The fucking lire better start rising, or they'd all be up shit creek.

"What was that all about?" asked Arnott. "Why was he so pissed off?"

Sarah smiled. "Don't you think fifty million dollars is a rather large punt to do p.a.? It's over ten times my trading limit. My capital's only two hundred thousand pounds."

Arnott went pale. "What the hell d'you think you're doing? That'll have to go through the compliance department. They'll go ape-shit."

She smiled back coolly. "Only if they notice. It's up to me to send them a copy of my ticket."

"So you're just going to keep it to yourself?"

Sarah nodded.

"And what about McDermott? What's he going to do?"

"Draw as little attention to the trade as possible, I should think. He'll probably do upwards of forty trades today. There's no reason why this one should stand out."

"And if compliance still manages to find out?"

Sarah smiled sweetly at him. "Well, then someone will just

have to transfer enough funds into my account to collateralize the trade."

"You don't think I'm going to do that, do you? You're mad."

She laughed. "You wouldn't have much choice. You really don't want compliance to go asking me a lot of hard questions, do you? And besides, it's hardly as if you'd be in danger of losing any money. Unless, of course, Catania's got it wrong, and that's not very likely, is it?"

Shaking inside, she turned back to the screens, watched, and waited.

Johnny McDermott stared at his screens and silently cursed Sarah Jensen. She had done the trade under false pretenses. He had been under the impression that it was an ICB trade, done with ICB's money, underpinned by its vast capital reserves. He was already entering details of the trade on screen when she told him it was for her personal account. He could have disputed the trade, refused to accept it in her name, for her private account. He should have done that. For some reason, he hadn't. Perhaps it was friendship, and something in the tone of her voice. Anyway, it was too late to undo it now. He just hoped that his settlements department would not notice anything untoward, and that the lire would rise. Then Sarah could close her position, make a tidy profit, and meet her payments. If the lire fell, her £200,000 capital backing would be wiped out in a flash, and she would be unable to settle the trade. Then all hell would break loose. He would be fired, she would be fired, and God knows what else. Visions of bankruptcy courts and criminal proceedings flashed through his head.

———

Fifteen minutes later, an announcement ticked across the bottom of the Bloomberg screen: *Italy raises discount rate by one percent.* Sarah and Arnott read it with broad smiles. McDermott read it with horror and relief. The unmistakable stench of dirty money filled his nostrils. But at least Sarah would be able to pay for her trade, and with luck they would all be off the hook.

One minute after the announcement appeared, the dollar-lire rate jumped to 1620.20, 1621.70, a rise in the value of the lire of close to 4 percent. After ten minutes it had risen to 1603.80, 1604.50. Arnott's personal account profit stood at a staggering $21 million. He walked quickly to the conference room, shut himself in, took out his mobile phone, cut his p.a. position, and took his profits. Then he returned to the desk and cut the firm's position.

Sarah's illegal profit stood at just over $2.5 million. Still she ran her position. She felt an almost uncontrollable tremor pulse through her body. Her back dripped sweat. She felt delirious. She stared at her screens, consumed by the illicit thrill. The qualms she had felt a week ago with her first illegal trade had vanished.

The minutes passed. Each second she ran the position she was taking a stomach-churning risk. The lire could fall suddenly and dramatically, just as quickly as it had risen minutes before. Another political scandal or an assassination would send it tumbling, wipe out her capital, expose her fraudulent trade. She should cut her position now, but she couldn't. She stared transfixed at the screen, second by second running the ultimate gamble. The thrill was almost paralyzing, almost sexual.

For fifteen minutes Sarah sat, immobile, keeping her position open. Then she could hold out no longer. She hit the BdP line. McDermott picked up immediately.

"Dollar-lire, Johnny."

"1585.40, 1586.90."

"I'll take fifty dollars." She cut her position and cleared over $3 million.

"Done." Outrage mixed with relief in his voice.

McDermott executed the trade with clinical brevity, then hung up. He would ring her at home, have it out with her to-night, without the tape recording every word. Find out what the hell was going on. He recorded the trade, stormed off the trading floor, and headed for the Pig and Poke.

Sarah leaned back in her chair and exhaled loudly, then lit a cigarette and smoked it hungrily. Arnott watched her closely. She was a fucking lunatic. In all his years on the trading floor, he had never seen anyone take a risk like that. Catania had given the tip, but it was not a 100 percent sure thing; there was always the possibility that something could go wrong. The risk she had taken was hideous. Yet she seemed to relish it. If something had gone wrong, if the lire had fallen, she would have been unable to settle the trade. An inquiry would have been held, their illegal trading ring discovered. She would have taken them all down with her.

Arnott suddenly felt sick. He too reached for a cigarette, lit it with a trembling hand, and inhaled deeply. The nicotine raced into his blood. He breathed heavily, felt calmer. He glanced at Sarah. She sat, quite collected, staring at her screens. Fucking insane. But on his side. The thought gave him little comfort, but it was the best of bad alternatives. He turned and gave her an unsteady grin.

"You're a fucking lunatic, you know that?"

She smiled in silent conspiracy, but her eyes remained cold.

"So how much did you make, Arnott?"

His eyes gleamed as he answered, ego suppressing discretion, "Twenty million."

Sarah let out a low whistle. Arnott grinned but said, "Soros made a billion on Black Wednesday."

"Yes, but legally."

"Yeah, well . . . Just think how much I should be able to make illegally."

"How much have you made?"

Discretion made a late appearance. "Now that would be telling." Arnott glanced at his watch. It was one o'clock. He wanted to escape the trading floor, call Carla, and celebrate. A sudden claustrophobia gripped him. He leaped to his feet. "I'm off to lunch."

"Have a glass of champagne on me."

He walked off, his face taut. Team member she may be, but nothing had changed. She was still a fucking bitch.

Scarpirato came out of his office. Wilson was two desks away talking to one of the settlements girls. Nobody was within earshot.

"How's your headache?"

Sarah glanced up at him, a distant look on her face. "Oh, it's gone, thank you."

He smiled down at her. She looked up at his face, then turned away. She couldn't hold his gaze. Going through his things had felt like a betrayal. Mosami's broken voice rang in her head. She felt dizzy from her illegal trade. She was overloaded. There was no room in her mind for him. She stared, unseeing, at the data on her screens. Scarpirato stood next to her, watched her in silence for a few seconds, then turned and went back to his office.

Sarah watched him leave, then called over to Wilson, "Hey, Simon, you couldn't cover today, could you, please?"

He grinned across the desks. "All right, but your turn tomorrow."

"No problem." She picked up her bag, hurried out of the building, caught a cab, and headed for Mayfair.

Her worries about Mosami had cracked through the barrier of unreality that surrounded her. She had called Mosami on and off all morning, but there was only the answerphone. Sarah was sure she was there, just avoiding calls. Twenty minutes later she stood in Hay's Mews, ringing her bell. After several minutes, Mosami's voice came weakly from the intercom. Sarah spoke briefly, then the door buzzed to let her in.

Sarah pushed open the door and rushed up the stairs and into Mosami's bedroom. Mosami was lying on her bed, supported by a slim pillow and covered with a pale blue cashmere blanket. She smiled at Sarah. Sarah's stomach turned. She was almost unrecognizable. The delicate features and the smooth white skin were gone. On the left of her face from eye down to mouth there were hideous swellings and swaths of black bruising. The whites of her eyes, just visible, were covered with a lattice of red. The finely drawn lips had ballooned.

Mosami reached out a slender arm toward Sarah and gestured to the armchair beside her bed. Sarah walked over stiffly and sat down. She stared at her friend. She didn't know what to say. Her pulse raced with rage and sorrow, and she felt sweat bead her back. Tears rolled down her face. She gave way to them, gulping loudly.

"God, Mosami, I'm so sorry. I had no idea this would happen. I never would have got you involved if I—"

Mosami cut her off. "It's done now. You couldn't have known this would happen." She breathed heavily as she spoke, pausing after every sentence. "As far as I'm concerned, it's over. The doctor came last night and again this morning. He's fixed me up. My face will be better soon enough. In six weeks my ribs will have healed. I won't go to the police. I have a feeling somehow it's better that way." She smiled at Sarah, who sensed that Mosami had guessed there was more at stake than mere office politics, but, wisely, wished to learn no more. She seemed to sense, too, that Sarah did not want the police involved.

Sarah smiled down at her friend and stroked her gleaming black hair. Mosami sighed heavily, one arm folded over her chest as if she were attempting to support her ribs.

"Arnott warned me, Sarah. Not to say a word, and to tell you the same. He's bad enough—he seemed unhinged last night. But you know, I think he was even more frightened than me. Frightened of someone else. Whatever you're doing, for God's sake be careful."

Sarah reached down, took Mosami's hand, and smiled. "No. They'd better be careful. Matthew Arnott, his little sidekick Carla, and whoever else is involved. They'll get what's coming to them. One way or another. I promise you that."

Chapter
Twenty

Sarah spent the afternoon trying to avoid Arnott. Every time she saw his face she wanted to slam her nails into it. So she spent an hour in the library, hidden among the stacks of periodicals, pretending to read *The Economist*, trying to still the clamor in her mind and think.

Returning to the trading floor, she wandered around from desk to desk, chatting idly, smoking, drinking endless cups of coffee. By four o'clock she could stand it no more. She had to leave before her tenuous self-control snapped. She walked back to her desk, switched off her screens, picked up her bag, said as pleasant a goodnight as she could muster, and turned to leave. In her haste she almost collided with Karl Heinz Kessler, who was making one of his rare sorties onto the trading floor. She said sharply, "Excuse me," dodged around him, and walked away. He glared at her departing back, then looked at his watch.

"I wasn't aware that we clocked off at four around here," he said to Arnott.

"Yeah, well, she's above all that, doesn't seem to think that normal rules apply to her."

Kessler paused for a moment, scrutinizing Arnott. "Why do you dislike her so? It's almost as if you're frightened of her."

"Frightened? That's absurd. She's tiresome, that's all. Sitting next to her eight hours a day, five days a week—it's enough to get up anyone's nose." Arnott exhaled heavily and shrugged in what he hoped was a gesture of indifference.

"Anyway, I didn't come here to talk about her," hissed Kessler, lowering his voice. "I was very interested in the rate move today. I thought we might have a chat about it. Tomorrow night. Shall we say seven-thirty, Mark's Club?"

Arnott nodded, forcing a smile.

Outside on the streets, the City was quiet. There was a lull in the traffic, and there were few pedestrians, since most people were still in their offices. The man in the slightly creased suit who loitered outside the gleaming facade of the ICB building was conspicuous. He stood waiting, hands in pockets, glancing nervously around, chain-smoking cigarettes down to the butt. Suddenly he straightened up, as he saw Sarah Jensen walk through the doors and out into the open. He moved toward her. She looked up in surprise. He grabbed her arm.

"Johnny, oh God, what are you doing here?"

Johnny McDermott gaped at her in surprise. "What the hell do you think? What the fuck were you playing at today? Don't you think I deserve an explanation? You could have got me fired, you could have been fired. We could both end up in the slammer."

Sarah shook her arm free and glanced around quickly. She

saw a black cab approaching with its "For Hire" sign lit up. She flagged it down and turned back to Johnny.

"Come on. Get in."

He spoke in a rush, his voice growing high-pitched. "I don't want to get in, I just want to—"

Sarah's voice cut through his. "Just get in, Johnny."

He looked at her for a second, blinking at the tone of her voice, then followed her into the cab. He shut the door. Sarah spoke to the driver.

"Drop us on the Embankment, by Temple, would you?"

McDermott started to speak again.

"Shut up, Johnny. Don't say a word."

He looked at her uncomprehendingly, anger mixing with a strange uncertainty. He leaned back against the seat. They sat in silence for five minutes, until the cab dropped them on the bright open walkway alongside the river.

The water shimmered in the sunlight. The trees, rich in leaf, cast shadows on their faces as they walked. After a while Sarah stopped and sat on a bench facing the river. Johnny sat down beside her and looked at her, waiting.

She turned to him and smiled faintly. "I'm sorry for all of that. I didn't want us to be seen together." She paused and shrugged in a gesture of helplessness. "I know I owe you an explanation, but I'm afraid I can't give you one." He started to speak, but she raised a hand to stop him. "Please, Johnny, listen to me. This might sound melodramatic, but believe me, it's anything but. The less you know, the better. The best thing you can possibly do is to forget about all this, pretend it never happened. Don't try to see me again. Don't speak about this again. It need never rebound on you. If you just let it go, that will be the end of it, as far as you're concerned."

He stared at her face, not smiling now, but cast in a kind of grim determination and, it seemed to him, regret. She spoke again.

"I'm really sorry I involved you in this. I won't do it again. Can we just carry on as before, trade normally, pretend nothing's happened? Please, Johnny. You really don't know . . ." She turned and looked out across the river. "Let it drop, will you?"

He studied her face as she turned back to him, a face he had always found beautiful, composed, in control, but that now looked vulnerable, exposed like a child's. He had wanted to shout, swear, smash through this barrier she was building, but her face softened him, and some instinct that surprised him urged him to agree.

"All right, Sarah. We'll forget it. I'll forget it. But if things really are as bad as you say, then for God's sake get out of this yourself."

He got up, laid his hand hesitantly on her shoulder, then walked away toward the Underground station at Temple. Sarah watched him go, then turned back toward the river. A few pedestrians strolled by, their faces benign in the afternoon sun. Going home early, thought Sarah, to safe houses, normal lives. They were unblighted, free to smile at the sunshine. Johnny didn't have a clue. As if she were free to opt out. She was utterly trapped now, as much by events as by her own determination to see them through.

She got to her feet, walked to Parliament Square, hailed a passing cab, and went home. She arrived back at Carlyle Square at five and phoned Jacob, who came round an hour later. He took one look at her pinched, grave face and sat her down at the kitchen table.

"You've been discovered, haven't you?"

"How d'you know that?"

"Easy. My friend called me last night. Told me one of the devices had gone off the air. Of course, there could have been an innocent explanation—a cleaner might have pulled it out by mistake. I hoped it might be something like that, until I saw your face. So what happened?"

Sarah looked across the table at Jacob's kind, calm face. She almost wished for signs of panic in him. He panicked at small things, but in a crisis he was always calm.

"Arnott found the bugs in his desk and at Carla's flat. He beat up Mosami. Her face is all bruised and swollen, and she's got two broken ribs." Jacob winced.

Sarah continued. "I managed to convince Arnott that all I wanted was a piece of the action. I think he believed me." She laughed grimly. "Italy raised their discount rate a point today. Arnott was tipped off. By Catania. And you know what? He obviously thinks I know more than I do. He let slip Catania's name. He said, 'Catania said buy lire.' So I bought fifty mil for myself, sold out, made three million." She shrugged. "So I have my bona fides. I think Arnott's convinced. The question now is whether or not he tells numbers three and four, and if he does whether they'll trust me too. I thought number three was Scarpirato, but now I'm sure it's not him. If I just hang in there long enough, I'm sure I'll get a chance to find out."

A look of horror broke through the calm on Jacob's face. "These people are dangerous, Sarah. You *cannot* just hang in there." His voice was slow and faltering, full of anger and fear for her and Mosami.

She was adamant. "I have to. For Mosami's sake as much as anything. And don't worry, Arnott's on the hook. He thinks I'm on his side, and anyway, I told him that if anything happened to me, the tapes would be sent to the Fraud Squad. He went all pale. He really believes me, so he's not about to bump me off."

Jacob was angry. "Don't joke about this."

Sarah smiled to herself. She wasn't.

Jacob was beginning to feel out of his depth. He was an old man now, retired. He had expected to leave all this behind a long time ago. He let out a long sigh.

"Look, Sarah, I hope your Barrington knows what the hell's going on, because I don't. I was never too happy about this. It seemed all right at the beginning—a bit odd, the governor's involvement, using an undercover agent, and all that stuff, but it seemed harmless enough. But every day we seem to unearth something more that fills me with horror. And now this. Mosami beaten up and you right at the center of things. Apart from anything else, you yourself have just broken the law in a substantial way. Have you thought about that? Have you thought about what will happen if for any reason Barrington doesn't stand by you? After all, he warned you, didn't he—if you got caught, he couldn't help you publicly. I'm not sure I'd put my faith in him. I'm not even sure that he's the one running things. I can't quite square it somehow. This is turning into a nightmare, Sarah, and what worries me most is that you don't seem to care. You're at risk from all sides." He watched his words rain down on her, watched the quiet set of her mouth, her resistant eyes. He carried on. "You'd better call Barrington, but I'd be a bit careful, even with him. Tread warily."

Sarah looked at him, smiled faintly, and answered slowly and deliberately. "Don't you think I've thought about all this? It's not the first time, is it, that I've walked into a nightmare?"

For a while they were both silent, then Sarah picked up her address book and called Barrington's number. She sat listening to the ringing phone, waiting for him to answer.

"Governor. It's Sarah Jensen."

The flawless voice, jovial, well rounded, answered smoothly. "Good afternoon, Sarah. And how are you?"

"Fine, thank you, Governor. I'm calling to keep you up to date. There have been some interesting developments, bad and good. I planted listening devices in Carla Vitale's flat and at ICB. Arnott discovered them and traced them back to me. He confronted me. I explained that I'd bugged him because I was afraid he was trying to get me fired and I wanted to get some dirt on him to use against him. I told him I knew all about the conspiracy and I wanted a piece of the action. He swallowed it. Started babbling. Told me that Catania is the source." She paused.

There was a long silence at the other end of the line. Barrington spoke finally. "This is quite extraordinary, Sarah." His voice was thoughtful, distant. Then it became more businesslike, brusque. "Look, I'm expected at a meeting—as we speak, in fact. I'll have to call you later."

Sarah stared at the floor. Still the cool facade, the distance. Part of her wanted to scream at him, ask him what the hell she was supposed to do next, make him cancel his meeting and deal with her and what she had told him. But the emotionless, formal voice elicited the same cool, controlled response from her. Emotion and hysteria were bad form, and so she matched his lifeless facade. She also suspected that it would be futile to confront him, to demand answers that he probably didn't have, so she said evenly, "Fine, Governor. Goodbye." She put down the phone, sat back, and lit a cigarette. Her face was taut with the effort of control. She glanced at Jacob.

"I think you're right, as usual. He said he had to go to a meeting, that he'd call me later. It sounded almost as if he were buying time. He seemed out of his depth. But if he's not in control, who is?"

Jacob shook his head. "By the way, you didn't tell him about your three million."

"I didn't, did I? It didn't seem like the right time, somehow."

Anthony Barrington stared at the grandfather clock that towered in the corner of his office. His half-suspected fears about Sarah Jensen had found substance. She was dangerously independent, running away with her role like a bolting horse. And he was supposed to be in the saddle. He had recruited her, but, he told himself, she was Bartrop's responsibility. The whole thing had been Bartrop's idea. Now Bartrop could bloody well take over. He buzzed Ethel.

"Get me James Bartrop, would you. Tell him it's urgent."

Bartrop came on the line; Barrington came straight to the point. "There have been a few new developments, Bartrop. The good news is, Sarah has identified Catania as the source. The bad news is, she's been discovered. Matthew Arnott found her bugs and confronted her. Somehow or other she convinced him that she wants, as she puts it, a piece of the action. She claims he has fallen for it. But I don't know. I feel most uncomfortable. I'm not sure this is sustainable. It's becoming messy, potentially embarrassing, not the cool, clinical affair you led me to expect. I'm wondering if it isn't perhaps time to call in someone else—Special Branch, or perhaps MI5. After all, isn't it partly their territory in the first place?"

Bartrop listened without interrupting. Then he spoke, his voice smooth and carefully modulated.

"You know, Governor, I think this is turning out rather better than I dared hope. I don't see this as a problem. It's a stroke of good fortune. We couldn't have planned it better. Jensen is right at the center now. She has every chance of exposing the whole conspiracy, right from the City through to Fieri, with a bit of luck. She's proved herself to be a very cool operator. If she thinks she has convinced Arnott, then she probably has. Time will tell. But the thing is, Governor, this conspiracy will not go away. It's as much your and my responsibility as it ever was. The question is, who is in the best position to deal with it? We decided at the beginning that we were. In my view, nothing's changed. If we were to bring in anyone else, say Five or the Branch, it would only complicate matters. Their activities would inevitably impinge on our own spheres of responsibility. We would have the worst of all worlds—our control would be compromised, our accountability would be broadened, yet our responsibilities would remain. It would be one almighty mess. Then, of course, there's Sarah Jensen to consider. Now, I will take full responsibility for her, but I will have to remain in the background. I can hardly appear as if from nowhere, mid-assignment. I don't think she'd take kindly to that. It's better for us to stick to our original plan, or she might feel misled and kick up a stink."

Barrington sighed heavily. "I can see what you're saying, but I can't pretend I'm entirely happy."

"I can understand that, Governor. But there's no perfect way to run this case, no free solution. I honestly believe we've hit upon the best way. Look at the results we've got so far. You must admit we couldn't have envisaged that we would have discovered so much so quickly."

"No. I'll admit that." Barrington gazed out the window at the greenery of the courtyard. For a while he said nothing.

"All right, Bartrop. We'll continue as we are. I'll continue to communicate with Sarah Jensen, but you'll assume total responsibility for her."

"I'd be happy to."

"You'll write something for the files, then, would you?" It was an instruction, not a request.

"A sort of comfort letter, as you would say in banking circles?"

"Yes. If you like."

"I'll have it sent round in the next couple of days."

Bartrop hung up with relief. He uncrossed his legs and loped over to the window. He smiled at his reflection in the glass. He was intrigued. Each day his respect for Barrington plummeted while he developed for Sarah Jensen a cautious, almost unwilling regard. She was turning out to be quite an asset—a little unruly, unpredictable, but valuable if properly managed.

Barrington alone could not cope. That was clear. He would need his hand held, but that Bartrop was happy to do. Anything that took him a step closer to Antonio Fieri was worth it.

It was an inspired, if risky, plan. Barrington would run Sarah, and she would lead Bartrop one step closer to Fieri. When the case was ripe, her information would be passed by Six to the Italian authorities. Bartrop would conceal Sarah's identity; she was a deniable, free-lance operative, unavailable if anyone wanted to question her about his methods. Fieri and his lieutenants would be arrested and charged. And Bartrop would achieve his primary objective—when Fieri was removed, his drug network would be dealt a major blow and a myriad of other illegal activities would start to unravel. The Friends would be credited with having played a major part in Fieri's downfall. The plaudits would come thick and fast. *His* plaudits. *His* success. Desperately needed. Too rare to share with Five.

That was his game plan. But he knew he would have to be careful. So much depended on Barrington's continued cooperation and his ability to control Sarah Jensen. It was essential, too, that details of the operation remain secret.

The strengths of the operation were in many ways its weaknesses. Jensen was brilliant—she had penetrated ICB and the Catania conspiracy to great effect—but she was also unpredictable and dangerously intelligent. Barrington was the ideal controller and front man from the standpoint of status, but he showed a tendency to become wobbly under pressure. He had too much to lose if the operation went wrong.

Bartrop would have to keep a tight grip on Barrington and, through him, on Jensen. But it wasn't a problem. Barrington had gone too far to undo his involvement. He had too much at stake. He would cooperate for his own sake if nothing else. And Sarah Jensen . . . well, difficult women were nothing new. He would control her, one way or another. He picked up his telephone and called his deputy, Miles Forshaw.

"Miles, Bartrop. Come up with anything else on Jensen yet?"

There was a slight pause before Forshaw spoke. "Well, yes, we have. Not rock-solid. More surmise. But a bit worrying. I'd better drop by."

Anthony Barrington was unhappy but relieved. He could not undo his involvement. He resigned himself to continuing as Sarah's controller, but it was a role that was becoming more uncomfortable to him daily. At least Bartrop had taken over full responsibility for her. And he, Barrington, would be nothing more than a conduit, passing Bartrop's instructions to Sarah and relaying her intelligence back. If anything went wrong in between, it would not be his problem. Reassured, he called Sarah back in Carlyle Square.

He seemed in a hurry. He spoke almost without pausing.

"Sorry, Sarah. One wretched meeting after another. Anyway, well done. A bit of an upset, but you coped admirably. You are perfectly positioned now, thanks to your own quick thinking. So make the most of it. See what else you can find out."

The old crispness had returned to his voice. Its sudden reappearance was as curious as its gradual waning had been. Sarah began to feel as if she were at the center of two mysteries. Who was the fourth member of the Catania conspiracy? And who, if anyone, was pulling Barrington's strings? She saw him that night in her dreams, a jerking puppet moved by an unseen hand.

At seven-fifteen the next morning, Matthew Arnott parked his Mercedes in the basement car park beneath the ICB building, slammed the door, and pounded up the staircase to street level, metal toecaps beating against the concrete. He sprinted across Lower Thames Street, up Fish Street Hill, and left onto Cannon Street. After stopping at Birley's for his takeaway breakfast, he hurried back to the newsagent's on Eastcheap for his Marlboros. He bought two packets, breaking a rule. He tried to stick to twenty a day. But it would be a long day, and he would need the balm of nicotine.

Sarah was already at her desk, poring over her screens, cigarette in hand, when he arrived. She nodded briefly and turned back to the screens. He spent most of the day trying to ignore her. To his relief, she left him alone. She seemed preoccupied.

He sat and smoked, wondering what he was going to tell Kessler that evening. He could tell the truth, and there would be an explosion, he was sure of that. Or he could lie, cover it up. But he would be found out somehow. He felt equally sure of that.

By five o'clock his head was pounding. Nicotine coursed through his blood, and his fingers shook slightly. He still had two and a half hours to kill. He headed for the library and flicked through newspapers until six-thirty, then wandered back to the trading floor. He didn't go straight to his desk. He took instead a seat at the settlements desk, which ran back to back with his, Jensen's, and Wilson's desks. Trading screens and piles of reports formed a border between the two sets of desks, making the occupants on either side invisible to each other.

The attraction of the settlements desk was the games programs on the computer of the junior clerk, Andreas Rudding. Arnott, like most traders, was addicted to the fast-moving, Nintendo–like games. But he thought game-playing was bad for his image; he was a cut above the herd. So he tried to be discreet.

He glanced around. The desk was empty. The trading floor was almost deserted. Arnott logged on to Rudding's machine and began to play.

Halfway through his game, he was interrupted by voices from the other side of the desk. He took a peek through a gap between two piles of reports and saw Scarpirato walking out of his office with Jensen. Arnott hit the mute button on his machine and listened, silent and invisible, as Scarpirato and Jensen spoke.

"Look, you just can't expect me to sit back and pretend nothing's happened. I need to know what's going on. Decide what to do."

"Oh, Dante, why so many questions?"

"Well, give me some answers, then. Come on, Sarah. I've got a right to know what's going on. So come on. Out with it. Now."

"Keep your voice down, for goodness' sake."

"There's nobody around. So—"

"O.K. I'll tell you. But not here. Let's go outside. Have a drink somewhere."

Arnott froze. He stared at the manic blinking of the screen

before him. Jensen knew, Matsumoto knew, and now Scarpirato. It was getting out of hand. He would have to tell Kessler and face the consequences. Stomach churning, he waited till Scarpirato and Jensen had disappeared from sight, picked up his handset, and dialed Kessler's number. Kessler picked up on the third ring.

"Karl Heinz, it's Matthew. I need to see you now."

"What's so urgent? It's a bit busy up here, not the best time. Can't it wait half an hour?"

"No. It can't."

Kessler's voice was sharp, picking up on Arnott's fear. "I'll come down."

A minute later he appeared on the trading floor. He nodded to Arnott, who followed him into Scarpirato's office.

"Well?"

Arnott told him, from start to finish. Kessler stared at him in silence. Finally he spoke.

"So three people know—Jensen, Matsumoto, and Scarpirato."

Arnott swallowed. "Yes. But Jensen has incriminated herself. She's in with—"

Kessler let out a scornful bark. "What do you mean, incriminated herself? She's done a trade, broken her trading limits, broken some internal rules. That's all. She could say she saw you buying lire, thought it was a good idea, and copied you. There's no law against that. You fool. She has nothing to lose. Don't you see that?"

Arnott looked at his feet. Kessler stared straight ahead. Then he stood up to go.

"Well, it's done now. All you can do is keep your mouth shut and tell me immediately if anything else happens. In the meantime, I'll have to tell Catania."

"What do you think he'll do?" Arnott asked falteringly.

"Something, anything—how the fuck should I know?" spat Kessler. "But he has more to lose than any of us. After all, he's both agent and participant. How much does he have in his account?"

"I've just fed in eight million dollars," said Arnott. "There's probably thirty there already. Enough for anyone who finds it to think he's a full and willing member of the team."

"Well, you have me to thank for that little piece of foresight." Kessler glared at Arnott with unconcealed loathing and contempt. Arnott rose uncertainly. He picked up his briefcase and began a muttered goodbye. Kessler suddenly looked at him with horror.

"You checked this office, didn't you?"

Arnott frowned. "What d'you mean, checked it?"

A vein began pulsating in Kessler's forehead. It looked as if it were going to burst. "The bug detector."

Arnott felt himself go weak. "No. I didn't. I thought it was me she was after. Why would she bug Scarpirato's office?"

"Do you have the detector?" Kessler spoke very quietly and deliberately and with unflinching menace. Arnott reached inside his briefcase. Kessler grabbed the device from him, switched it on, inserted the earpiece, and began to adjust the tuning. Within seconds the light panel flickered into life.

"We're bugged," said Kessler, and heard his voice coming back to him through the earpiece.

Three hundred yards away, in the Pig and Poke, Dante and Sarah sat at a corner table and talked.

"I still don't understand why you don't want to see me anymore." Dante leaned forward in his chair, his customary cool look replaced by one of perplexity.

Sarah looked pained. "All right, I'll tell you. Infidelity. You have a girlfriend, and I have a boyfriend. There's no point in denying it. I've seen you with her." Sarah took a flying guess. Scarpirato must have gone somewhere public with his girlfriend over the past few weeks. She watched his face carefully. He remained silent. "Look, Dante, you might as well admit the truth. It's over between us. My boyfriend has been away. He's coming back tomorrow." God, how she wished that were true.

"So there's no hope?"

Sarah touched his cheek lightly. "No, my darling. There's no hope."

He smiled sadly across the table to her. He took hold of her hand.

"Friends?"

She squeezed his hand. "Friends."

Karl Heinz Kessler sat in the back of his black Mercedes as his driver, Leonard, drove slowly through the rush-hour traffic on Lower Thames Street. Kessler remained silent, brooding, and tense as the car crept out of London.

Two hours later, he was in Wiltshire, approaching Lambourn. The Mercedes passed through narrow country lanes dividing fields dotted with retired racehorses and children's ponies. It slowed before a pair of tall wrought-iron gates set back from the road and swung through onto a long drive bordered by horse chestnut trees. The drive was exactly one mile long. At the end, surrounded by rolling fields, stood a tall white house.

The car pulled up before the house. Kessler jumped out before the driver had a chance to open the door and barked a goodnight.

His housekeeper, Janet, appeared at the door and let him in.

He greeted her brusquely and walked across the echoing stone hallway to the library, where he sat in an old armchair in front of an unlit fire and raked over the facts. Jensen, Matsumoto, and Scarpirato knew. Catania had the most to lose from their discovery. His wife would learn that he had kept a mistress and leave him. He would be unable to plead that he had been set up. Part of the blackmail arrangement so ingeniously devised by Kessler was designed to make Catania look like a full-fledged and willing member of the insider-trading ring; he received a one-quarter share of all the illegal proceeds, paid by Arnott into one of Catania's secret bank accounts. A criminal investigation would unearth the account easily enough. It was in Switzerland, where absolute banking secrecy was now long gone. Investigators who learned that Catania's account was engorged with many millions of dollars would be hard pressed not to believe he was a member of the conspiracy. His political career would be destroyed at a stroke. He would lose his wife, his children, his fortune, and probably his liberty.

Kessler reached his arm behind him to pick up the phone off a side table. He drew it onto his lap. Reaching his hand inside his coat pocket, he withdrew a slim navy-blue address book. He turned to C and dialed. It was Catania's problem. Let him deal with it.

Giancarlo Catania was halfway through dinner with Donatella when Kessler called. Clara, his housekeeper, knocked tentatively at the dining room door and walked in. It was Signore Kessler, she announced. And it was urgent.

Catania glowered at her, excused himself to Donatella, rose, walked out into the hall and through to his study. He picked up the phone and asked in gruff voice, "What's so important that it can't wait until after dinner?" He spoke with a hybrid Italian-American accent, as he had learned his English from American films. Kessler had learned his in the finest German schools. His English was pure, if highly accented, and Catania's Americanisms grated on him.

"We have a problem. A rather serious problem. Our little game is no longer a secret. Three people know—Sarah Jensen, Mosami Matsumoto, and Dante Scarpirato. They know the whole story. Nothing is spared."

Catania uttered a string of guttural Italian curses. "How?"

"Very simple. Bugging devices."

"And you didn't check for that?"

"No. We didn't."

"Who did it?"

"Jensen. She's a colleague of Arnott's. Jealous, by his account. Wanted some dirt on him."

"And you believe that?"

"Yes, I do, actually. She's not official, if that's what you're worried about. Committed a great big dirty trade herself. She's just another greedy little banker."

"Like you," said Catania.

"Like me," agreed Kessler.

Catania clenched the phone, his palms sweating. Three people knew. How long would it take for their knowledge to seep out to the authorities, to Antonio Fieri?

Both men thought of the consequences of discovery. In Kessler's case, ignominy, imprisonment, forfeiture of his illegal fortune. It was hidden away in a variety of numbered accounts around the globe, but they could be found if the authorities were sufficiently determined.

For Catania there could be only one consequence of discovery: death. Fieri would kill Catania before he incriminated Fieri's organization. Catania had too many Mafia secrets he could try to trade for immunity. They would never let him live to talk. Fieri was already suspicious. The president of the Bundesbank, too. Rumors were circulating.

Catania stared at the ceiling and made up his mind. He had nothing to lose. "I'll take care of it," he told Kessler.

Chapter
Twenty-one

The peroxide blonde was naked in bed, coiled around a lean male torso, watching a video, when the phone rang. She swung taut, muscular legs out from under the sheets, wrapped herself in a red silk dressing gown, and walked down one flight of stairs to the library. The phone by her bed had remained silent. It was for personal calls. The phone in the library was for business. She sat in a dark red leather chair and picked up the receiver.

"Pronto!"

It was a man. An Italian, with a gruff voice. He wanted to see her. He had some business to transact.

"Who are you? What's your name?"

"Never mind about that. A friend of Antonio Fieri's. Will that do?"

"For a start." Fieri was one of the few people who had her

business number. Anyone who rang her on it was almost sure to have his blessing. "So don't tell me. You want somewhere neutral and discreet, where you will be inconspicuous. The Hassler, perhaps?" The Hassler was a beautiful old hotel overlooking the Spanish Steps in central Rome.

"That would be fine. Can you make it tomorrow, at two?"

"I'll see if I can make a reservation. I'll call you back with the room number. Then you can just walk straight in without having to talk to reception."

He paused.

"Your number?"

He gave her his number and hung up. She recorded it in her diary. Five minutes later she rang back. "Number 151. I'll see you there tomorrow at two." She replaced the receiver, switched off the light, and sat in the darkness, staring into the night. Who was it? The voice sounded slightly familiar. And what could he possibly want? She smiled at her reflection in the dark window.

When he arrived at two-fifteen she was there waiting for him. A cool blonde. Medium height, about five-foot-four, but powerfully built. He glanced at her elegant calves, the muscles flaring above fine ankles. She stood by the window, shoulders thrown back, chest high, vital and confident. He had never seen her before, but he knew all about her.

She had an astonishing reputation. Antonio Fieri spoke of her with great respect. He said that she had retired, bemoaned the fact. She had, however, from time to time given way to Fieri's persuasion and taken his business, despite her professed retirement. But this was a closely guarded secret, shared only by the two of them; Catania had never known.

She was known as Christine Villiers, an American stunt actress. Not her real name, not her real job, but a useful cover. Years earlier, Catania had discovered her phone number. He had written it down on the off chance, with blessed foresight. Now she stood before him, poised and waiting. He looked at her appraisingly.

She smiled. She recognized him at once.

"What can I do for you, Governor?"

"I will pay you a great deal. Double your usual fee."

She nodded. "I'm listening."

"I want you to kill three people."

Christine arrived back at her apartment on the Passeggiata di Ripetta, an elegant tree-lined street, at three-thirty. She locked herself in, turned off her private phone, and started planning.

Back in London, a few hours later, Jacob sat in Sarah's sitting room waiting for her to return from work.

She arrived at ten past seven. Jacob gave her a worried smile.

"Where've you been?"

Sarah looked surprised. "To the gym. Worked out for an hour. Tried to take my mind off things." She paused and studied his face. "What's happened?"

Jacob walked over to her and laid a hand on her shoulder. "It has all blown up. This whole thing has totally blown up. I got some more stuff on the tapes. Karl Heinz Kessler and Arnott had a conversation last night in Scarpirato's office. Scarpirato's innocent—Kessler is the third man, and Catania the fourth. Kessler and Arnott have rigged up a Swiss bank account for Catania. They feed it with a quarter share of the profits to make it look as if he's a fully paid-up member of the conspiracy. It's another way of keeping him under control."

Sarah clutched at the gym bag still on her shoulder. "God, Jacob, this is too much to take in. I knew Arnott and Kessler were close, but I just thought Arnott was some kind of whipping boy for Kessler. Kessler seemed to be above it all—you know, highly respected chief executive of a top merchant bank. I did wonder once or twice, but I put it out of my head. I couldn't believe it somehow." She lapsed into silence.

"There's worse to come," said Jacob. "Arnott told Kessler all about you and Mosami. He said you both knew about the conspiracy. He thinks Scarpirato knows too. And they discovered the bug in Scarpirato's office. So the game's up. Mutual discovery. No one can hide anymore. Kessler said he was going to tell Catania. That he would have to 'do something.'"

Sarah dropped her gym bag on the floor and sat down on the sofa. She fumbled in her bag for a cigarette and lit up with a trembling hand.

"I knew something had happened. Arnott kept looking at me strangely all day. Not arrogant or hostile like he normally is. He looked scared." She paused and dragged deeply on her cigarette. "I don't think I can handle this anymore." She put out the cigarette, then turned to the telephone on a side table.

She rang the governor in his office and at his bank flat. There was no reply.

Later the same evening, Alitalia flight 286 from Rome landed at London Heathrow with a squeal of rubber on tarmac. It was the last connection of the day, and the flight was full. The two passengers who had booked their tickets that afternoon had been able to find room only in business class. They filed off the plane and on to passport control. Both were traveling with false passports. If they were nervous, it didn't show; they had the best fakes money could buy.

They smiled at the woman in the passport booth as she flicked through their documents. She nodded them through. They moved off to collect their luggage. Anybody watching would have deemed them complete strangers. They had nothing in common, except the ability to kill.

They walked through customs and out to the taxi rank. They took separate cabs. The man, Gianni Carudo, headed for a hotel in central London, the Dorchester, in Park Lane. The woman, Christine Villiers, went to her house in St. Leonard's Terrace, in Chelsea.

The third member of the team, Daniel Corda, was already in London. He lived there, had done so for his entire thirty years. He was Christine's British contact. Although she kept a house in London, Rome was her base, and she needed someone with first-rate local knowledge and facilities. She rang Corda to let him know that she had arrived and that everything was on. She asked him to come to her house at midnight so she could brief him fully.

In the quiet of their rooms, Villiers, Carudo, and Corda thought about their assignments. Christine Villiers was to kill Dante Scarpirato. She didn't kill women. She hired men for that. Carudo would take care of Sarah Jensen, and Corda would look after Matsumoto.

Christine also needed the men because of the urgency of the assignment. Catania had told her that the targets had to be silenced immediately. She hoped to do it within three days, over the weekend. It would take two days to watch the subjects, reconnoiter their homes, and plan strategy. Ideally, they should have at least a week for that, but they had their instructions, and they knew how to move quickly. They had done it before.

A few hours later, in the dark, musty London night, they slipped out onto the streets to take the evening air, and to seek the first glimpse of their victims.

After Jacob had gone, Sarah stayed up reading into the early hours. She sat on the sofa in the sitting room, her book in one hand, a glass of whisky by her side. Restless, every so often she would put down her book and pace around the room. The curtains were open. She stood out against the bright light. She had no idea that dark eyes were following her progress.

Hidden in the bushes at the fringe of the garden, Gianni Carudo watched. She was beautiful. This was going to be pure pleasure. He would return late tomorrow night with his knife and wake her from her sleep. He watched till she rose, switched off the light, and disappeared. A bedroom at the back, he guessed. Quietly, he slipped away.

Sarah awoke exhausted the next morning. She dragged herself to work and sat opposite Dante Scarpirato in the morning meeting. They exchanged a smile of understanding. She had misjudged him. He was innocent, and now, after their conversation of Wednesday evening, she felt she could finally relax with him.

His smile lingered as she sat before him, a few feet away across the conference table, beautiful but untouchable. A memory flashed across his mind. He drove it away. It was better this way. He looked around. Arnott and Wilson walked in. Arnott was looking at him strangely. He shrugged and started the meeting.

Arnott sat, stomach knotted, waiting. Scarpirato seemed disconcertingly normal. Happy, even. He was biding his time, thought Arnott. Perhaps, like Jensen, he wanted a piece of the action. That's probably why he and Jensen looked so tight. They had probably carved things up together during their drink on Wednesday night. He wondered what Kessler and Catania were going to do about it.

Sarah lingered in the conference room after the meeting was over. Closing the door behind the others, she immediately called the governor at his flat. Again there was no reply. She called his office. No one was there. Finally, at eight o'clock, his secretary answered.

"Could I speak to the governor, please? It's Sarah Jensen."

The voice was cold, official. "I'm sorry. The governor is overseas on an official visit."

Sarah tried to keep alarm at bay. "It's urgent. I have to speak to him."

"Well, if he rings in, you can be sure that I'll have your message passed on."

"Can't you call him? What if he doesn't ring in?"

The voice laughed, a tinkle of indignation. "As I just said, Miss Jensen, if he rings in, I'll let him know you called."

Sarah began to panic. "I'm afraid you don't understand. I must speak to the governor immediately."

The voice grew exasperated. "Listen, Miss Jensen. The governor is in the United States. It's the middle of the night there. Like it or not, you will have to wait."

Sarah hung up. She ran her hands along her bare arms. She suddenly felt very alone.

The morning passed quietly. The markets were becalmed. Sarah read the newspapers and tried to put the governor out of her mind. Arnott sat to her left, still giving her strange looks, but she was too tired to confront him.

The offices of Cordillon et Cie lay in a cobbled street in the heart of old Geneva, in a former private house. The sole testament to business was a small bronze plaque bearing the initial C. Only those whose business it was to know would be aware of the presence behind the creamy facade of one of Switzerland's premier private banks.

Much of the interior, particularly that part seen by clients, was furnished as a private house, with fine paintings, elegant reception rooms, and snug studies. The modern face of banking was well hidden. Computers, fax machines, and the odd trading screen were closeted in functional rooms on the upper floors. There the more junior account managers and clerks sat before keyboards, scribbled on the odd ledger, and looked after billions of pounds of secret money. In a further concession to modernity, four clocks displaying the time in Geneva, London, New York, and Tokyo hung on one wall.

Peter Jaeggli, a middle-ranking account manager of twenty-eight, glanced up at the Geneva clock: twelve o'clock. Time for another cup of freshly ground coffee. He walked through the room to the small kitchen at the back and prepared a cup of extra-strong Colombian. Making his way carefully back to his desk, sipping en route, he took his seat and returned his attention to the papers on his desk. They were hard copies, for file purposes, of a series of electronic funds transfers.

Jaeggli frowned and shook his head slightly, as if wanting to disbelieve the fuzzy black type. Words, figures, and instructions shimmered back at him. He did an instant mental calculation. The net effect of these transfers was a profit of $3 million, paid into account LS 236190 X. The trades had been settled the day before, Thursday, two days after the transactions had been executed. Because of their size and slight irregularity, the hard copies of the money transfers had been passed on by a junior clerk for Jaeggli's attention.

Jaeggli took a sip of coffee and gazed up at the ceiling. There must be an innocent explanation. A mistake, perhaps. He must not leap to conclusions. Ask questions first. Judge and act later. Yes, that was the least he could do. He waited till his colleagues with adjacent desks either wandered out of earshot or busied themselves on the phone. Then he briskly tapped out a number.

Simon Wilson shouted across the dealing room to Sarah. "A Kraut. Line two."

Sarah walked back and took the call.

"Sarah. Peter Jaeggli. We need to talk." His voice was grave.

Sarah realized at once why he was calling—her illegal trades, huge inflows and outflows of money, more than she had originally had in her account, leaving a $3 million profit. Cordillon would have managed the flows of money so she wouldn't be overdrawn, but still, her behavior was discourteous to her bankers, not to mention downright suspicious. No wonder Jaeggli sounded so serious. Still, Swiss bankers were supposed to be conveniently myopic, if not blind to suspicious payments. Sarah supposed her payment was simply too irregular to overlook conveniently.

"Yes, Peter. I suppose we do."

"I suggest you come to Geneva as soon as possible. There's a—"

Sarah cut him off. "What! Me come to Geneva! That's a bit melodramatic, isn't it?"

His voice was taut. "Not under the circumstances. I wouldn't ask unless I had to."

Sarah held the phone away from her, and stared down at her desk in puzzlement. She had known Jaeggli for eight years. They had been undergraduates at Cambridge together. She and Alex had stayed with him in Geneva, skied and climbed with him in the Alps. She had never heard this tone in his voice before. She felt worried and bemused.

"Look, Peter, ordinarily I would come. But it's not a good time for me at the moment. I really can't get away."

His voice was unyielding. "I'm sorry, Sarah. I have to insist. You'll understand why when you see me."

She stared pensively up at the ceiling. Finally she spoke. "All right, Peter. I'll come."

"There's a Swissair flight at five past three from Heathrow. I'll pick you up at the airport."

At one-thirty, Gianni Carudo slipped into Carlyle Square. He was wearing jeans, a denim jacket, a white T-shirt, sneakers, and a baseball cap, a uniform guaranteed to lend anonymity on the King's Road.

He walked toward Sarah's house, not too slowly, not too fast. Nothing to arouse suspicion. He glanced up at the empty windows. She wouldn't be home for hours; he had been told that she finished work between four and seven. In the meantime he would just cruise around, study her house from front and back, get comfortable with the lay of the land. Later he would observe from a distance, monitor her arrival home, and see if she had any visitors.

He wondered how the evening would go. Perhaps she would arrive, get dressed up, and go out again? But whatever, she would come back sooner or later, and he would be waiting. He was ready to do it now; a six-inch knife lay under his jeans, strapped to his calf. But nighttime was best. It felt better in the dark.

Keys jingled in his pocket as he walked. He had a selection of the finest skeleton keys on the market. They would get him into her house in seconds.

He walked through the square and out onto Old Church Street. He would disappear in the crowds on the King's Road for a while and redo his circuit later. Now it was time for a different kind of reconnaissance. It wasn't strictly necessary. But he liked to keep a check on the whereabouts of his victims and make contact, however tenuously. He liked to put his marker down.

He slipped into a phone booth on the King's Road. He thought of her face, and his pulse quickened.

Sarah explained to Scarpirato that she had to take the afternoon off for urgent personal business.

"That's fine." He smiled. "I doubt you'd do much anyway, Friday afternoon."

Relieved, Sarah returned to her desk, picked up her handbag, and was just about to leave when Wilson yelled across at her, "Hang on. There's a call for you. Sounds Italian. Line one."

Sarah reached for her handset and picked it up in annoyance. She spoke hurriedly—"Hello! Hello!"—but there was nobody there.

Cocooned in his phonebox, Gianni Carudo smiled to himself.

Sarah Jensen was in the office, as she should be. It was, after all, as far as she was concerned, a normal day. She was not to know it would be her last. Carudo warmed to the thought.

Sarah slammed down the handset in annoyance. Some idiot always called when you were in a hurry. She made a quick exit before whoever it was tried again.

She caught a taxi on Lower Thames Street and told the driver to hurry to Carlyle Square, where he was to wait for five minutes before taking her on to Heathrow. He nodded eagerly; it would be a good fare. He pulled into Carlyle Square thirty minutes later and found a parking space around the corner from Sarah's house. Sarah rushed off to pick up her passport, pack a few things, and call Jacob to let him know where she was going.

The taxi driver parked and switched off his engine. He sat in the cab staring out at the garden and the mass of bright flowers. He saw a scrawny young man approach the cab wearing a baseball cap. There was something unpleasant about him, a sort of hungry leer. He watched, relieved, as the man turned onto the King's Road and disappeared.

He heard a tapping on his window and jumped. The young woman had returned, clutching a small case. She got into the cab.

"Terminal two, please."

He pulled out onto the King's Road. Sarah sat back, head buried in an *Evening Standard* that someone had left lying on the back seat. The taxi driver passed the man with the baseball cap. He was looking straight ahead. He didn't notice the beautiful woman pass by in the taxi, just feet away.

Swissair flight 833 swooped into Geneva airport at five-thirty-five. Peter Jaeggli was waiting in the arrivals hall, as promised.

He greeted Sarah formally and led her out to his car, a metallic blue Alfa Romeo Spyder. The top was down; it was warm and balmy in the late afternoon.

They drove in silence, the wind whipping Sarah's hair against her face until they slowed to a crawl in the evening rush hour. Half an hour later they pulled into a small cobbled side street in old Geneva, half a mile from Peter's office. He parked carefully, backing skillfully into a tight space. Still saying nothing, he took Sarah up to his first-floor apartment, opened the door, and ushered her in. His movements were jerky, awkward. His responsibilities as host and friend jarred with his professional obligations.

He brought her a whisky, poured himself a large one, and took a seat next to her on the sofa, fiddling with his glass. Tension hung between them. Sarah made no attempt at small talk. Whatever it was that he had to say, let him say it and be done. Then perhaps they could talk normally, as old friends.

He cleared his throat. "This is a bit awkward for me, Sarah . . ." He glanced across at her. He looked hangdog, apologetic, but determined. She smiled and gave a slight shrug—absolution in advance.

"The three million you just made in the foreign-exchange markets. I have to report it to my superiors. And I have to ask you a few questions about how you made it."

Sarah sighed almost imperceptibly, leaned back on the sofa, and studied Jaeggli as if seeking an explanation in his eyes.

This was extraordinary. She was supposed to be able to move money into and out of her account as she pleased, without having to answer to her account manager. He was supposed to look after her account, see that payments and receipts were recorded correctly, pay her interest when due, and carry out the usual range of banking services. Yet here he was acting like the guardian of her financial integrity. She felt a flash of anger. She took a long gulp of whisky and felt the anger recede. She tried to think coolly and rationally, but a growing disquiet nagged at the back of her mind, as if offering itself up as a clue.

As far as she knew, only when Swiss bank accounts were suspected of harboring drug money, or perhaps the proceeds of an equally serious crime, were the authorities permitted to ask questions or delve into them. Jaeggli was acting more like a policeman than an account manager, so someone must suspect that her $3 million had been criminally obtained. And obtained not by the mildly illegal means that line so many Swiss accounts without question, but by serious criminal activity. Her mind began to race.

"I think you had better tell me what this is all about."

It was Jaeggli's turn to be surprised. Sarah's face bore an expression of hard resolve, of implacability.

"I'm not really supposed to tell anyone any of this. In fact, I shouldn't even have invited you here in the first place."

"I'm sure. But you have, and you won't find out a thing from me unless you tell me what's going on at your end first, so you might as well get started."

Jaeggli was silent for a while, then began to explain. "It started about a month ago. The general manager, Herr Hoffman, called me into his office and told me that the British and German authorities wanted Cordillon to carry out some inquiries on their behalf. He asked me to monitor my clients' accounts for large movements of cash after certain dates. He didn't explain the significance of those dates, and he wouldn't tell me the background to the inquiries, but after a couple of weeks, it seemed to me that what the authorities were looking for was large cash movements in the aftermath of significant economic events, like interest-rate changes or major G7 intervention in the FX markets." Jaeggli paused for breath. "Then came your three million, two days after the Bank of Italy raised the discount rate by one point."

Jaeggli sighed heavily, as if released from a burden. He got up, walked across to a small table, and picked up a black packet of Davidoffs. He recrossed the room and offered one to Sarah. They both lit up and took a few long draws.

Sarah's mind was racing. The implications of what Jaeggli had just told her were deeply disturbing. The British authorities suspected that there was a leak in G7 and that someone was trading in the currency markets on inside information. The Bank of England must have known. Anthony Barrington must have known. Yet he told her nothing, gave her not even the slightest hint about something that was crucial to her project. Why hadn't he told her?

If he knew but didn't tell her, it made no sense. But even if he didn't know about ICB and Arnott and Vitale, he clearly knew that *someone* was trading on inside information from G7. Realization hit Sarah like a bullet. There had to be more than one insider-dealing ring operating on G7 information. Barrington suspected that ICB was another arm of an operation he already knew existed. But why not tell her that? Did he not trust her, or was there some other reason for keeping her in the dark?

She turned to Jaeggli. "These authorities—was there anyone in particular they were looking for, any particular accounts you were asked to check?"

Jaeggli stared at his feet, but glanced up after a while and spoke slowly and reluctantly. He was breaking all the rules of confidentiality in telling her this.

"Well, I only spoke to Hoffman, of course, and he was very

guarded. He guided me toward certain accounts. I don't think he realized that I knew the identity of some of the account holders. They were secret—just numbers, no names. But anyway, one day several months before this whole business started, I saw some account files on his desk, and I saw him pick them up and take them to a client meeting. I saw the client, too. I recognized the face. I'd seen him in the newspapers. His name is Antonio Fieri. His accounts were some of the ones I was asked to monitor later on."

Sarah looked blank. The significance of the name escaped her.

"He's reputed to be a Mafia boss," said Jaeggli.

Sarah's face became blanker, the features drawn taut, almost like a mask as she withdrew into herself. Inside there was panic, confusion, and fear. Then came rage, slight and tremulous at first, growing in intensity till her mind was in turmoil.

"Now are you going to tell me what's going on?"

Jaeggli's voice came from a long way off. Sarah started. She looked at him with a strange expression of detachment. Then a fraction of the old warmth came back to her face.

"I can't. All I can say is that I, too, work for the authorities." Something in the tone of her voice made him believe her. "That money I made is part of it. It's better that you don't draw attention to it. I know it's a lot to ask . . ."

She watched him in the silence that followed. She waited, hardly breathing. Somehow, she wasn't sure why, it was imperative that he tell no one about her $3 million. The same instinct that stopped her from telling Barrington screamed again, *Keep it secret.*

Jaeggli spread his hands and stared at his fingers. "All right. I won't say anything. If I don't draw attention to it, it should pass unnoticed. But, Sarah . . ."

"Yes?"

"I wouldn't do it again."

She seemed far away. He refilled her whisky. She sipped in silence. He moved closer and ruffled her hair. "Now, since you're here, let's try to forget about all this. Why don't you stay for the weekend? We can drive up to the mountains and do some walking."

Sarah turned to him and smiled. He felt her coming back to him. She thought of a lonely weekend in London, the house silent, empty of Alex and Eddie. She would be rattling around alone with her fears. She set that against two days of snatched normality, walking in the mountains, miles from responsibility.

"Yes," she said. "That sounds wonderful."

Swissair flight 838 from Geneva to London Heathrow took off at five past eight on Sunday evening. Sarah sat strapped in her seat, staring out the window as the plane climbed skyward. The silhouette of the Alps loomed in the distance.

She had spent a wonderful weekend with Peter, climbing, eating, drinking, just like old times together with Alex. For a while she had managed to put out of her mind all of her raging fears. She thought of her brother and her boyfriend, thousands of miles away, out of reach, high in the Himalayan wilderness, wondering how they were, if they were missing her. Again she felt the drift of loneliness and fear.

She arrived at Heathrow at quarter to nine local time. After passing through customs, she headed for the public telephones. She found a free one, fed in fifty pence, and called Dante. He answered on the third ring.

"Dante, it's Sarah."

"So you've reappeared. How was your urgent personal business?"

"Dante, listen. Can I come round? I need to talk to someone. You're alone, are you?"

He laughed. "Yes. I'm alone. Come on round."

G ianni Carudo cursed silently. Sarah Jensen was not at home. She had obviously gone away for the weekend. That much was clear. There was neither sight nor sound of her. The lights were off, the answering machine on. He listened to her voice on the answerphone. It was a good voice, strong and challenging. He liked them like that. He rang every few hours. Still she was not there. After a while he began to hate the voice.

Still, she had to return sometime, this evening most likely, and when she did, he would be ready. His impatience and anger mounted slowly.

Christine Villiers felt the first tremors of excitement snake down her spine. She had monitored the house all weekend. Finally the girlfriend had left. Scarpirato was alone now, she was sure of that. She looked around. The street was quiet. She was ready. She smiled and walked toward his door.

Inside the house, Scarpirato had just poured himself a vodka and lit up a cigar. He sat waiting for Sarah Jensen. He was not surprised that she had rung. He had known she would come back to him sooner or later.

He heard an uncertain tapping at the door. When he opened it, he found a complete stranger standing on his doorstep. He looked at her in surprise.

"Yes?"

She was of medium height, blond, and beautiful. Her long hair was drawn back from her face in a ponytail, which protruded from the back of a baseball cap. Her features were angular—she had high cheekbones, a straight nose, and a chiseled jaw. It was a powerful face, uncompromising even with a smile. The eyes were cold, unmoved by the smile. She was wearing tight jeans and a T-shirt, which made her seem much younger than the look in her eyes suggested. She said that her name was Gabrielle, that she was a friend of Sarah's, and that they had to talk.

He had a weakness for blondes. He could listen, at least. He let her in. The door slammed shut behind her. He led her down the long hallway.

It was perfect. Long and dark. No windows, thick walls. Christine reached inside her bag and took out a .22-caliber Ruger Mark 11, an automatic pistol fitted with a silencer. She planted both feet solidly, took the pistol in both hands, cocked the trigger, and pointed at the skull three paces ahead. Dante turned just as she was pulling the trigger. The words died on his lips. The cigar fell from his hand as he crashed onto the stairs. It fused itself to the carpet, glowing in the dark. The fibers of the carpet began to frazzle in the heat. In minutes, fire would take hold.

Christine studied the gun, then replaced it carefully in the small quilted handbag. She would have to dispose of it now. Still, she'd be able to buy plenty of new ones, thanks to Mr. Dante Scarpirato.

She checked her clothes. No blood. She had stayed far enough away. The wall behind him was sprayed with it, but the blood hadn't reached her. She stepped gracefully out of the house and closed the door behind her, walked out onto the King's Road, and blended with the evening strollers. After a few detours, she was home, in twenty minutes. She made two short phone calls, one business, one pleasure. She smiled in anticipation. She was seeing an old lover tonight.

The taxi sped along the A4 into central London, its engine emitting a high-pitched whine that made Sarah's ears hum. The noise receded as the taxi swung off the Cromwell Road onto Earl's Court Road and slowed in the mass of traffic and pedestrians.

Sarah gazed through the window at the careless bustle outside. In five minutes she would be home. She would change first, have a quick shower, then go and see Scarpirato. She sank back into the hard plastic seat and thought about what Jaeggli had told her. The word *Mafia* ran around her head, making her dizzy.

Catania and Vitale were Italian. Were they somehow connected to the Mafia? Given the spate of scandals linking Mafia, government, and big business in Italy, it would almost have been surprising if the Mafia were not involved. It was almost too much to comprehend. It seemed unreal, unbelievable. Sarah wanted to shut her eyes, close off her mind. She decided to go straight to Dante's house.

She told the taxi driver there was a change of plan, gave him Scarpirato's address, sat back, and closed her eyes. When she opened them minutes later, she saw a scene of chaos. The taxi had pulled up at the junction of the King's Road and Wellington Square. The square was cordoned off, filled with police cars and fire engines. Sarah could see a house in flames. Smoke billowed through the trees at the center of the square. The fire was at the far end. She couldn't see which number. Her stomach heaved against her ribs. She didn't need to see.

A police officer had approached the taxi and was peering through the window at her.

"Are you a resident, madam?"

She kept her voice steady. "No. I was just passing, going to drop in on someone. It doesn't matter. It can wait."

The policeman nodded and turned, distracted by another car that was trying to turn into the square. Sarah felt her control slipping. She leaned forward to speak to the taxi driver. She gave him Jacob's address and collapsed back on the seat.

She knew that it was Dante's house in flames, and she felt, with a chilling certainty, that he was dead.

Jacob heard the taxi pull up outside his house. He saw Sarah hunched in the back seat. He came out, paid off the driver, and led her inside, where he sat her down, poured her a whisky, and asked gently but firmly, "What happened?"

Sarah spoke mechanically, her sentences fractured by silences. "I visited Peter Jaeggli, spent the weekend in Geneva. He wanted to know all about my three million dollars. Told me he'd been asked to monitor accounts for suspicious movements of cash after central bank intervention or rate changes. It was the British and German authorities who wanted to know, apparently. One of the accounts Jaeggli was asked to monitor belongs to someone called

Antonio Fieri. He's a . . ." She paused. Jacob had muttered something. He looked across at her.

"Fieri's Mafia."

"I know. Peter told me." She struggled to control her breathing. After a few minutes she spoke again. "Dante's dead. I just went round there. Fire engines everywhere. House in flames. It was his house, Jacob." The tears began to course down her face, and she started to shake.

"He might be all right. You don't know for sure."

She shook her head.

Jacob stared blankly into space. He got up stiffly and poured out two more drinks.

"We've got to get out of this, Sarah. The whole thing has gone way too far. For some unknown reason you've been thrown into this nest of vipers and, it seems to me, abandoned. There's so much going on around you that you ought to know, yet you discover it by accident, almost against design. There's something very sinister going on, and I'm not just talking about Kessler, Catania, and the Mafia, although God knows that's bad enough. And what's happened to Scarpirato—although he's probably quite all right. But there's something closer to home, with Barrington. Don't you think it's about time you really confronted him?"

His voice was gentle but insistent. There was a controlled anger in his eyes, focused at whoever was behind this.

Sarah sipped slowly at her drink. "I know. I'm supposed to be at the center of things, but I don't have a clue what's going on. I've felt uneasy for some time. Now I'm terrified." She paused and stared into her drink. "I'll call him now. He's been in America. Perhaps he's still there . . ." Her voice trailed off.

Jacob handed her the telephone and she dialed Barrington's

private number. No reply. She spread her hands in a gesture of helplessness.

"I'll try again tomorrow."

Jacob walked across to her and took her hand. "You'd better go to bed, sweetie. Your room's all ready. Your pajamas are laid out, just in case." He kissed her goodnight, then watched her rise, take up her glass, and go exhausted up to bed.

In the quiet of her room, she drained the whisky and fell into a restless sleep. Jacob sat up late into the night, stroking Ruby, who sat on his lap. He had his own ideas, and he was not optimistic.

Eight miles across town, another silent vigil was under way. Christine Villiers sat alone in her house, waiting for news. Her lover, Robert, had come, offered a pleasant diversion for a few hours, and finally left her in peace, just after midnight. The night had grown darker and steadily quieter, until it seemed that all the cars had gone from the streets and everyone was asleep. She drank black coffee and watched the clock on the wall, drawing her solitude like a veil around her.

Corda had called first thing that morning. He had told her everything was fine. So Matsumoto was dead. And Scarpirato. Just Jensen to go.

She felt a tinge of regret, laced with worry. Jensen was an intriguing woman, tough, successful, independent. Someone who obviously played dangerous games. And beautiful. She had seen a photograph, faxed by Kessler to Catania and by Catania to her. It was a portrait in black-and-white, taken from a magazine article Jensen had written. Christine had given a copy to Gianni Carudo and kept one for herself. She took it from a locked drawer and gazed at it. Whatever games Jensen had played to invite the contract, it seemed a shame she had been caught. Regrettable. Christine would have liked to have met Sarah Jensen. But for a million pounds, the woman was more valuable dead.

Abruptly, Christine glanced at her watch and frowned in irritation. Carudo should have called by now. Jensen should have been home hours ago. Carudo should have hit her and cleared out. Perhaps something had gone wrong. She began to worry.

Carudo called finally at 7:00 A.M. His voice was taut. Their "guest"—he used the euphemism derisively—had not come home. He had waited all night. What should he do now? Abort, she said. Go back to the hotel and try again this evening. Their guest had obviously stayed overnight at a boyfriend's place.

Sarah woke, as usual, at six. She lay in the narrow single bed in Jacob's spare room and gazed at the ceiling. The feeling of sick fear and despair gripped her at once. She forced herself out of bed, turned on the radio, and went to have a shower. When she returned, dripping, from the bathroom, the news was on. She hugged a towel around her and went back to bed. The words of the announcer sailed past, unheard. Her mind was scarcely functioning. Then a succession of words leapt from the air and fused themselves to her brain like a branding iron. A suspicious fire . . . last night . . . in Chelsea . . . a thirty-six-year-old Italian. Dante Scarpirato. Police have launched a murder inquiry.

She ran from the room and collided with Jacob, who was coming up the stairs. She took a step back, wrapped her arms around her chest, and hugged herself. She stood moaning, swaying back and forth. Ragged nails cut into the skin of her arms till narrow rivulets of blood ran down to her elbows and then dripped to the floor, unfelt and unseen. Then her face crumpled.

Jacob hugged her to him. Her violent trembling shook him, and his shirt became streaked with red from the blood trickling down her arms. Slowly, fighting for breath, Sarah told him about the radio announcement. Dante was dead. He nodded. He had heard it too.

With great wrenching gasps, she began to sob. She wept until her ribs ached. Jacob held her, letting her weep till the immediacy of the shock had abated and the first slivers of a deadly calm had set in.

An hour passed. She sat, clothed now, at the kitchen table opposite Jacob, a mug of steaming coffee in her hands. A newspaper lay between them. He had just pointed to a brief six-line article in one column. She had read: "A woman was found dead in exclusive Hay's Mews in Mayfair last night. It is believed she was murdered. Police have refused to reveal her name until her family has been notified."

Sarah clenched her hands around the mug till the heat scalded her skin. She looked across at Jacob. Grim certainty lined his face. Both knew it was Mosami who was dead.

Sarah looked at the tranquil scene around her, the china cups and plates hanging on a Welsh dresser, the cupboards full of fine glasses, the worn, burnished floorboards of oak, Ruby curled in the corner. How long would it take for whoever had killed Dante and Mosami to find her and Jacob and wreck their lives?

She pushed herself up slowly from the table.

"They'll have to take us in. Barrington and whoever gets involved now. Take us in and arrest the others. I'll go and call him."

Jacob nodded slightly and watched her go into his study. He walked up to his bedroom and picked up another phone, one with a separate line and number. He punched a thirteen-digit number, spoke briefly, hung up, and made another call, local this time. In five minutes, all the arrangements had been made.

Sarah called the governor's flat. After four rings a woman answered. Sarah's words were slow and deliberate.

"I'd like to speak to the governor, please."

There was a slight pause. "I'm afraid the governor's in a meeting."

Sarah strained to keep her voice level. "I must speak to him now."

Another pause. "I'll see what I can do. If you'd like to hold on . . ." Mrs. Barrington relented and disturbed her husband at his breakfast.

A few seconds later the governor came on the line. Sarah listened to the loud, confident voice. She spoke mechanically, emotions drowned in a sea of nothingness.

"Dante Scarpirato and Mosami Matsumoto are dead. Mosami was my best friend. She helped with my investigation. I tried to ring you on Friday, to tell you that Karl Heinz Kessler is the third man. Catania himself is the fourth—he is given a quarter share of the profits. The Mafia is involved, and I think they're trying to kill me. You have to do something. You have to protect me and a friend. And you have to arrest Arnott, Vitale, and Kessler immediately. You've got enough evidence. This is not just a financial conspiracy. It's murder now. You must talk to the Italians, get them to arrest Catania. And there's someone called Fieri. He must be involved too."

Barrington gripped the receiver in shock. "Oh God, Sarah. This is dreadful." He paused for a few seconds, and when he spoke again, his voice seemed to Sarah to be artificially forceful.

"Of course we'll protect you. I'll arrange it immediately. Just stay put. Now give me your telephone number."

Sarah stared at the ceiling, all her strength concentrated on her voice, on talking, on maintaining some semblance of normality. Mechanically, she recited Jacob's number.

"I'll call you straight back," said the governor.

Sarah replaced the receiver and went out to the kitchen to wait for Jacob to reappear.

Even through the blindness of her pain and fear, it was now painfully obvious to her that it was not the governor of the Bank of England for whom she worked but someone else entirely, someone above him, to whom he looked for advice and instructions. She could imagine them now, conferring, deciding what to do with her. Then Barrington would ring back, continuing the pretense, telling her what to do as if the decisions and instructions were his. She pictured an unseen hand manipulating her. On top of her fear she felt mauled, deceived, and the first stirrings of a familiar anger.

She reined herself in. The governor would call back. She would wait. Give him the benefit of the doubt for just a little longer. There had to be a good reason, a sound explanation for all this. She clung to that, and to her hope that suddenly, somehow, she and Jacob would be snatched miraculously to safety. Then everything would be explained, would become clear. Kessler and his conspirators would be arrested, her role would be over, she and Jacob would be safe.

But she knew that wasn't going to happen.

James Bartrop received the news with equanimity. He already knew about the murders of Scarpirato and Matsumoto. He was thinking through his contingency plans when Barrington called.

His instructions were simple: "Tell her to sit tight. Get her address. We'll pick her up."

Barrington was in no mood to argue, to pick over this nightmare. Jensen had to be protected, urgently, and this was under way. Bartrop would take care of it. The recriminations could begin when she was safe and sound. It was all a disaster—chaos, dead bodies, and for what? He never should have got involved. He thought of the police, of all the questions, and he wondered how Bartrop would control it all. It would leak out, surely; there would be investigations, a public outcry . . . But then, no governor had been forced from office, and Bartrop, surprisingly, hadn't sounded at all despairing. He had been calm, collected. The only trace of emotion had been of excitement.

Barrington called Sarah back. The phone rang once and she snatched it up.

"It's all arranged, Sarah. Tell me where you are and I'll send some people around to bring you in."

"When? Who? How will I recognize them? When are they coming? They need to come now." Her facade of calm began to crack, and words streamed out in a torrent of fear and distrust.

"They'll be with you as soon as possible, Sarah. Just give me your address and they'll be on their way."

Exhausted and fearful, losing control, she blurted out Jacob's address and put down the phone.

Jacob came into the room at that moment.

"What's happening? Who are you giving my address to?"

Sarah sat down, shocked by the tone in his voice. "The governor. He's sending some people for us. To take us in."

Jacob sat opposite her, his soft eyes hard. He listened in disbelief.

"So you were told to go about all this with no protection. You were told that if you were caught, nobody could stand by you, nobody could help you. And you discover, no thanks to them, that what you are actually up against is not some philandering Italian but the head of a major bank, the governor of the Bank of Italy, and the Mafia. Your colleague and your best friend are murdered, and you're sitting here in my house waiting to be picked up by people you don't even know, people who have warned you in the first place that they can't help you."

He saw the tears begin to well in her eyes, saw her furiously biting her lip, raking her hand across her cheek, dragging away the teardrops.

She shouted at him in exasperation, "What am I supposed to do? I don't know what else to do, who else to trust."

Jacob stood up, sat down again, and spoke, his voice gentler but urgent. "Look, I have some friends who will look after us for a while, till we know what's really going on. It's obvious you're not working for the governor of the Bank of England. All this is way out of his turf. He's probably some kind of front man. It's MI5, more likely, and for some reason they are keeping you in the dark, using you as some kind of pawn." He raised his hand to cut her off as she began to argue. "My friends can be here in ten minutes. They'll give us a lift to the airport. You've got your passport. We can be away in two hours, a quick flight. Then we'll be safe where nobody'll find us." He saw the hesitation in her eyes. "Come on, Sarah. Can you really trust them?"

She stared at the dark eyes she knew so well. They looked so different now, alien in their hardness. But he was right. Barrington had let her down almost from day one, and Dante and Mosami were dead as a result.

"O.K.," she said. "I'll go."

————

Back at Century House, James Bartrop scribbled down the address Barrington had just given him and said a curt goodbye. Then he buzzed his secretary, Moira, and asked her to get hold of the chief of MI6, or C, as the holder of that position was generally known, and to send in Miles Forshaw. C came on the line. Bartrop spoke briefly.

"We have a problem with Jensen. Her best friend and her colleague have been murdered. She's found out a lot more, discovered something about Fieri. I'm bringing her in, together with an unnamed friend."

"Bit of a mixed blessing, this operation," said C. "Good intelligence, high price. Not sure about your agent all along, but too late now. I'll have to inform the Foreign Office adviser. He can take it to the undersecretary, warn of trouble ahead. You've got the Branch in, have you?"

"They're with the scene-of-crime people now."

"Good. Salvage what you can, Bartrop."

Bartrop hung up. Forshaw came in seconds later.

"Get a team up to this address in Golders Green." Bartrop reeled off Jacob's address. "Bring in Jensen and whoever she's with. Do it quietly. No one's to see anything untoward. Post watchers around the place, twenty-four hours. Take the Branch. Tell them to pick up anyone acting suspiciously. You never know, we might get one of Fieri's hit men."

"You think it's him?"

"Who else?"

Fifteen minutes later, a team of MI6 agents and watchers and two Special Branch officers were called up and on their way to Golders Green.

———

While Bartrop was talking to Forshaw, Christine Villiers was ringing Giancarlo Catania in Rome. She read him the newspaper reports about Scarpirato and Matsumoto. He cursed wildly and ordered her to get to Jensen immediately. And he doubled the fee—£2 million if she was dead by the end of the day. What on earth, Christine wondered for the hundredth time, did Sarah Jensen know that made her so dangerous, and her silence so golden? She felt, mixed in with the excitement of her task, acute curiosity. She decided to take matters into her own hands. She didn't have time to brief Carudo. She would find and kill Sarah Jensen herself.

When she called ICB, she spoke to a shaken man on the foreign-exchange desk. No, Sarah Jensen had not come in today, she was told. She hung up and paused to think, tracing a finger reflectively around her lips. A haven. Jensen would have found some kind of a haven.

She walked to her safe, took out a bunch of keys, and went upstairs to her bedroom. She unlocked a cupboard and pulled out a collection of wigs and a large metal makeup box. The blond wig she had worn yesterday for Scarpirato lay on top. She rummaged around, drew out a long wavy brown wig, and slowly pulled it over her own short blond hair, tugging at it violently to insure that it would stay in place. Then she opened the makeup box and took out four little tubes of cotton wool of the sort dentists use to soak up blood after a particularly vicious drilling or an extraction. She pushed two tubes high into her mouth under each cheek. Her image in the mirror was transformed. The hard blond had become a sweet, chipmunk-like brunette with a full smile and cheery cheeks.

She picked up her handbag. The .22 was still inside, and she took it out. Later she would give it to Corda and he would dispose of it. For now, she returned it to the safe and exchanged it for a different model, a Browning automatic, an SAS favorite. She wanted no connection to be made between the killings. She relocked the safe and made for the door.

Ten minutes later she was standing outside Sarah's house ringing the bell, a worried expression on her face. A voice from behind made her jump. Mrs. Jardine stood on the pavement with her two young children in tow.

"If you're looking for Sarah Jensen, you won't find her home now. She'll be at work."

Christine looked shaken, upset. "That's just the trouble," she said. "She's not at work, and she's not here either." She looked helpless, on the verge of tears. "I have to find her. It's about her brother, Alex. He's had a dreadful fall in the mountains. He's seriously ill. I need to tell her—she'll want to fly out immediately."

Christine spoke in the jumbled panic of the near hysterical, but underneath she was deadly cool and secretly triumphant. The background information provided by Catania was first-rate. And this woman was swallowing every word.

Mrs. Jardine ran her hand across her mouth in shock. "Oh, God. The poor girl. Yes, of course she'd want to go out there, but—"

Christine cut her off. "I have to find her. Do you have any idea where she might be?"

Mrs. Jardine racked her brains in a silence punctuated by "Well, I don't know" and "I really can't think," until suddenly her face lit up. "Jacob. Jacob Goldsmith. He's a friend of hers. A sort of uncle, looks after her when she's sick. He's in Golders Green, I think. I don't have the address, but he's probably in the book." She raised her hands helplessly. "It's worth a try, don't you think?"

Christine kept the smile off her face. "Oh, yes. It has to be." She gave the other woman a quick thankful look and ran for the phone on the King's Road. Mrs. Jardine watched her go. *What a considerate young woman*, she thought to herself.

Christine dialed 142. The woman at directory inquiries could give the phone number but not the address of J. Goldsmith of Golders Green. She suggested that Christine look for a telephone directory, which would list it. Christine ran to the newsagent across the road. Yes, they had a copy. Could she just wait a second, and they would go and look for it.

Five minutes later the assistant returned. Christine fell on the book. She found two J. Goldsmiths in Golders Green. She wrote down both numbers and addresses, shouted her thanks over her shoulder, and ran out onto the King's Road, where she hailed a cab for the first address, on Rotherwick Road.

She paid off the taxi just before they reached her destination, got out, and walked casually around the corner. The moment she turned into the quiet tree-lined street, she knew something was wrong. A British Gas van was parked opposite number 24, but there was no sign of cable or workmen. Then she saw an old man of about seventy walking slowly toward her, muttering to himself. His glance was casual, but all her instincts were screaming danger.

A cat crossed her path. In a flash of inspiration, she saw her escape. She scooped up the cat and said in a loud voice, "Oh, Tasha, there you are, you naughty thing." She smiled at the man as he approached, and nodded at the cat. "Always trying to escape whenever it's time to go to the vets. Honestly, it's as if she knows." Christine turned, the cat struggling against her chest, its nails piercing the thin cotton of her shirt, drawing blood. She swallowed a yell, shut out the pain, and retraced her steps down the street. She walked about four hundred yards, then, when she was sure no one was watching, released the cat, hailed a taxi, and headed back to Chelsea.

The old man watched her go, muttering all the while. The microphone inside his jacket relayed his words to the watchers inside the van.

"Nothing here. Just some Jewish American princess who lost her cat."

Christine sank back in the seat of the taxi. She was sure her instincts had been right. That was no innocent old man but a police watcher. The gas van was probably bursting with police officers. The police had got to Sarah Jensen first. Too bad. She had done her best. Now it was time to quit, get out, return to Italy. She would pick up two million for killing Scarpirato and Matsumoto. She would give four hundred thousand each to Daniel and Gianni. Sarah Jensen was Catania's problem now.

The watchers waited. The house was in their sights from front and back. There was no way anyone could get in or out without their noticing. But so far they had seen nothing, not even a trace of movement within the house. After half an hour, they began to get nervous. One of the two agents in the van called Forshaw, who called Bartrop. They agreed that if there was no movement within the next half-hour, they should go in and investigate. In the meantime they were to sit tight.

Forty minutes later they reported back to Bartrop. The house was empty. Sarah Jensen and her unknown friend had fled.

Five minutes later a notice went out to all airports and ports. The passports of every woman close to Sarah's description were checked, but there was no sign of Sarah Jensen.

Chapter Twenty-three

The Cessna 500 Citation was thirty thousand feet above the English Channel when the notice was faxed from MI6 head-quarters to Special Branch at Heathrow Airport. Sarah sat in a deep, overpadded armchair, seatbelt slung carelessly to one side. She was slumped against the cushions, chain-smoking, a glass of whisky in her left hand. Her eyes were closed, save for the brief interludes when she ground out one cigarette and lit another or replenished the whisky.

Jacob undid his seatbelt, rose unsteadily, and crossed the nar-row fuselage to her to touch her shoulder gently. He asked how she was. She appeared not to hear. Her eyes remained closed. He stared down at her for a while, then returned to his seat and resumed his vigil, his face wrinkled with concern.

He was taking her to a place of safety, but it would be a flawed refuge. How long could he protect her? How could they even begin to fight their way out of a quagmire they couldn't fully comprehend?

Sarah would be safe for a while, but living in limbo. The restorative powers of starting anew would be denied her. She could try to put the murders behind her, but how could she move on? She would be trapped in a state which at the best of times left her seething—powerlessness.

He knew that somehow or other she would have to formulate a plan, stamp her personality on events. Otherwise she would drown in a mire of nothingness.

The plane lurched as it began a descent through turbulence. Sarah opened her eyes, took a long gulp of whisky, then turned and stared out the window. She saw below her a flat plain ringed in the far distance by mountains, indistinct in the haze of the sun. She saw an airport and a runway. The plane swooped down and with a scream of tires slowed to a crawl on the shimmering tarmac.

In a few minutes it stopped in front of a small terminal building. A uniformed pilot appeared from the front of the plane. He asked Sarah if she had enjoyed the flight. She heard her voice coming from a long way off, disassociated from her, as if it belonged to someone else. "Yes, thank you," it said calmly and politely, before lapsing back into silence. The man smiled, then beckoned her forward. She rose unsteadily to her feet. The muscles in her legs felt like water, impervious to her directions. She felt an overpowering lassitude. She grimaced, willed herself forward, and began to move toward the man in the uniform. Jacob followed behind, watching her walk like a wounded child to the door that had just opened behind the small cockpit.

The captain jumped out onto the tarmac and greeted another

man, who was waiting outside. He was dark and swarthy and wearing a blue uniform. He smiled at the two travelers and said, "Welcome to Morocco." Morocco. Sarah registered mild curiosity, then walked down the three steps onto the tarmac, into an explosion of heat.

The swarthy man picked up the suitcases that the pilot had handed down and led Sarah and Jacob into the terminal building. The floors were a kind of gray-flecked tile, hard and noisy underfoot. The sound of her footfalls seemed unbearably loud to Sarah. She looked around. Impenetrable Arabic script was everywhere. The lettering used to seem joyful to her. Now it was sinister. There were people everywhere, smiling dark men with handlebar mustaches, women carrying what looked like toolboxes. Vanity cases, she realized. Four, five, six of them, hauled around by over-madeup owners. She glanced at her own face mirrored in a glass partition and quickly turned away.

The swarthy man led them toward customs, shook hands, and said goodbye. They showed their passports and walked through to the arrivals hall of the airport and out onto the gleaming forecourt of the pickup point. Sarah squinted as the sun pummeled her eyes. What was she doing here? She turned to Jacob, who took her arm, called out a greeting to a man who was approaching them, and guided her to him.

The two men embraced. Jacob turned to Sarah and introduced Jack Kohl. Kohl was looking at her with a smile, and with curious eyes. Sarah shook his hand and returned the look of curiosity. He was small, slight, and dark, with a perfect circle of baldness on the top of his head. His brown eyes sparkled with an intense vitality. Sarah looked into those eyes and found herself smiling back. At this, Kohl broke into a grin. "Welcome to Marrakesh," he said, taking the cases and leading them to a gleaming white Mercedes.

Sarah looked around and felt as if she ought to be on holiday —the welcome, the sun, the blazing heat. Again she wondered what she was doing here. She thought of work. ICB. The letters stabbed at her. Trying desperately to hold herself together, she stepped into the car.

The seats were leather. Inside it was cool. The coolness swept over her like a glass of cold water, a sensation that raised goose-pimples on her bare arms. She looked out the window and the tears began to flow again, streaming down her cheeks.

Jacob, sitting next to her in the back, watched her out of the corners of his eyes. He saw the tears with relief. It was not the tortured sobbing of a few hours ago but acceptance, resignation.

Jack got into the driver's seat, strapped himself in, and drove out of the car park onto a tarmacked road. After a few minutes he turned onto a dirt road, passing cyclists on rickety old bicycles and carts pulled by scrawny ponies. Sarah closed her eyes and tried to sleep.

She woke some time later, disturbed by the motion of the car, which was weaving and curving around a serpentine track. They were climbing high hills. Fir trees and cacti lined the road in places, giving way to walls of dusty ocher earth on one side, steep drops into invisible valleys on the other. Jack drove skill-fully, occasionally having to squeeze the car in toward the earth walls to let a lumbering truck pass in the other direction.

After driving for over an hour, he slowed to a crawl, took a sharp right, and stopped the car in front of a pair of high iron gates painted white. He reached for a small black gadget on the dashboard, and the gates swung open. He accelerated through and along a driveway lined with vivid flowers, a red, orange, pink, green, and yellow swath stretching for half a mile. Sarah gazed at the flowers, then turned in time to see the gates lock shut behind them. She wondered where the water came from for all this greenery. Lowering the window, she breathed in a roar of hot, fragrant air.

The car slowed again and swung into a wide arc below a large house that was several stories high, built from the local mud and stone. It was a rich ocher color. Shutters of dark wood carved into elegant filigree covered the windows. Flowers and plants filled a border around the house, and a series of terraces led down to the car.

Jack got out and opened Sarah's door. She stepped out and paused before a flight of steps stretching up to the house. A man and a woman appeared at the top of the steps and moved down swiftly to pick up the bags.

"Angelo and Mariella," announced Jack, nodding at the couple. "Worked for me for twenty years, first in Spain. When I moved here, they came with me."

The couple exchanged smiles with Sarah and Jacob and disappeared back up the steps.

Sarah walked slowly up, stopped at the top, and turned to gaze at the view before her. The terraces continued down below the drive, each covered with plants and bushes that spilled over onto stone pathways. Below the terraces was a semi-wild garden with tall palms casting short shadows in the afternoon sun, and again, everywhere, the profusion of flowers. Around the perimeter of the garden, far away in the distance, ran a high stone wall smothered in foliage and flowers. Under the greenery, hidden from view, lay coils of barbed wire. In the middle distance there were mountains covered with green scrubby trees.

Sarah turned to Jack. "Where are we?"

"Ourijane, in the foothills of the Atlas Mountains."

"It's very beautiful."

He returned her smile. "When you've settled in and had a rest, you must go exploring." She nodded slightly. He took her arm and led her into the house. Exhaustion swept over her, and she let herself be guided. Jacob followed behind.

The three of them walked into a large, cool hallway thirty feet high, with stairs to either side. At the far end of the hall was a courtyard filled with flowers and fountains. Jack took Sarah up the staircase on the right. She walked along a cool, shaded passageway lined with windows. The air flowed gently through the delicate shutters, closed to keep out the blazing sun. Jack paused in front of a dark rosewood door, threw it open, and invited Sarah to go in. Jacob smiled in the background.

"If you need anything, just call Mariella. She's on extension five. I'm on one, and Jacob'll be on four," said Jack. He smiled and turned to go.

Jacob came into the room and squeezed her hand. "See you in a bit."

She returned the squeeze and watched him go. The door clicked behind him. Then there was silence.

Sarah studied the room before her. A sitting room, large and cool, with wooden floors scattered with Persian rugs. Books filled the bookcases, paintings and photographs covered the walls. Sarah walked up, examined them. Mountains, flowers, the sea, portraits of unnamed people. She wondered who they were. She squinted slightly in the half-light, a rich sepia daubed by the sun, which filtered through shutters at the front of the room.

She walked through to a bedroom. French windows were open onto a flower-covered terrace. Muslin curtains fluttered in the breeze. The bed was uncovered, exposing sheets of white linen, turned down, as if someone knew of her weariness. It was too inviting. She dropped her clothes on a chair and crawled under the crisp sheets. Sleep came, as always, mercifully quickly.

Jacob sat in the library drinking whisky with Jack.

"It was very kind of you, arranging the plane and everything."

"Pfff, it's nothing. And anyway, in all the years I've known you, you've never asked me for a favor yet. I reckon you've a few owing."

Jacob laughed. If you looked at it that way, Jack was right. His friend was ten years younger and had worked as an apprentice to him, learning all that he had to teach—though in the early days, not quite well enough to avoid a few scrapes. He had turned a few times to Jacob for alibis, or for help in disposing of certain hot rocks that he couldn't quite handle alone. Jacob laughed again as the memories flooded back. He looked around him.

"You've done well, I'm glad to see. Outstripped your teacher long ago."

Jack shrugged and protested, "I've just been more foolhardy. Anyway, you could have something just like this if you could bring yourself to leave your beloved Golders Green."

Jacob's eyes rounded indignantly. "Why should I? There's everything I need there. And while we're on the subject, I've never needed a safe haven in a friendly country with no extradition treaty."

Now it was Jack's turn for mock indignation. "Hey, neither have I. I bought this as a contingency, just in case. Then I decided I liked it better than Golders Green, which is hardly surprising." His face suddenly grew serious. "And besides, bolt-holes come in handy now and then." He paused, slightly uncertain. "You don't have to tell me if you don't want to. And whatever you do or don't say, you're welcome to stay as long as you want. But I might be able to help if I knew more."

Jacob screwed up his face and stared down at his hands for a while before looking up and meeting his friend's gaze.

"It's a long story. Half of it I don't even know. What I do

know is pretty messy. It's a nightmare. Two of her friends have been murdered. She thinks the killers, probably pros working for the Italians, are after her. And she's right—I reckon they will be. There are supposed to be some good guys on her side, but I don't trust them. I keep getting the feeling she's been set up. How and why I don't know. Something very strange is going on, and I thought that until we find out what, it'd be better to get out, just disappear for a while. I don't honestly know what we're going to do, but at least we'll be safe." He quickly bit back his words. He was going to add "for a while." He looked at Jack's questioning face. He had no choice; he knew he had to tell him the whole story.

James Bartrop sat alone in his office, twisting a pencil between his fingers. His eyes flickered, moving with his thoughts. His mouth was set in a half-smile of curiosity.

Sarah Jensen had disappeared and two of her close friends had been murdered, events both dire and promising. The cost to the operation would be political fallout. Bartrop, or C on his behalf, would be on the receiving end of some hard questioning from the foreign minister, the attorney general, and possibly the prime minister. With two foreign nationals dead, his position was bad, but if the murders did lead to Fieri and if he could prove it, it was not irredeemable. The murders were, in their own dreadful way, encouraging. Cool and professional contract killings, they pointed to the Mafia, to Fieri. According to Barrington, Jensen had mentioned Fieri directly, and Bartrop was now convinced of his involvement.

Anything that took him closer to Fieri was a bonus, so the murders produced in him a strange mixture of dismay and excitement. He tried to banish his disquiet. The dead were dead; there was nothing he could do for them now. He caught a momentary image of Sarah Jensen, abject in grief and fear. He felt a pang. But then, she was not wholly innocent. She had overstepped the mark, taken dangerous initiatives, tempted fate. Tempted murder. But then, she could never have known that, and, Bartrop knew, there lay his own culpability. She was a novice. He had misused her. Something had gone wrong, she had been discovered, and now she was running for her life. It was bloody messy, but promising.

Jensen must have discovered a Mafia connection, perhaps linked in some way to Catania, then in turn been discovered herself. Now the Mafia were killing everyone whom they thought she might have told. It was imperative that he get to her first, find out what she had learned. Scores of his agents overseas had been alerted to look for her. Interpol, the FBI, and customs around the globe were monitoring airports and ports.

He would find her sooner or later. And then the delicate work would really begin. For when he did find her, he would not take her in. Instead, he would keep her under heavy but discreet surveillance and, with a little luck and a lot of skill, catch the killers on her tail. He would be risking her life, but it would be a calculated risk, justified by the potential rewards. If the killers fingered Fieri, it would all be worth it.

Moira interrupted his thoughts. "C wants a word."

Bartrop got to his feet and walked to the chief's office on the floor above. C's secretary nodded him in. He took a seat beside the oak desk.

"What news?"

"Jensen's disappeared, I'm afraid."

"So what now? What other live bait do you have?"

"Arnott and Vitale here, Catania in Italy. I'll get the watchers onto them. I've already spoken to the Italian desk. We'll cover

Jensen's house, too." He paused as if thinking things through. "I don't think we would gain anything by getting the Branch to arrest anybody. There's still a lot we don't know. Our best chance of discovering the full story and getting something on Fieri, if he is involved, is to watch. Don't you think?"

C paused, scratched his chin. "Sounds reasonable. Now, what about the Italians? You've just spoken to our own people?"

"For the moment. Best to keep it in-house for now. Too much risk of Mafia penetration of the Italian services. They could blow the whole operation. We'll have to get them involved sooner or later, I appreciate that. But I'd rather delay it as long as possible, if you don't mind."

"I don't mind. I tend to agree with you. We'll keep them out of it for the time being. But you have some of the stations looking out. And Interpol. What are you telling them?"

"Special Branch are handling Interpol. Their line is that it's a criminal matter. As far as the world at large is concerned, Sarah Jensen is a criminal."

C gave a faint smile. "O.K., James. You'll need to give me copies of all the relevant files. I'll have to talk to the committee." The committee was known as PSIS, the Permanent Secretaries' Committee on the Security Services. PSIS discussed general priorities, budgets, potential political embarrassments, and scandals. The Catania conspiracy registered on both the latter counts. The Cabinet secretary, and the permanent secretaries at the Home Office and the Foreign Office, all of whom sat on PSIS, would weigh up what C would tell them and decide whether to draw it to the attention of the foreign secretary and the prime minister.

"Keep me informed, James. This is all a bit tricky. Going to be damage limitation at best if we're not careful. I don't need to tell you, do I? The sooner you find Sarah Jensen, the better."

Bartrop nodded infinitesimally, deigning to accept the obvious. He paused for a second, then said, "There's one more thing I should tell you, C. Of course, it's entirely up to you, but I'm not sure I would share this with the committee, or with anyone else, for that matter." He smiled, his face grave and calm.

C waited. "Well?"

Bartrop looked levelly across the desk at C, holding his eyes, registering and weighing up even the slightest reaction. When he spoke, his voice was cool, reflective, almost academic.

"We've dug a bit deeper into Jensen's history, come up with something a bit worrying. There is a view—and that's all it is, we don't have hard evidence—that Jensen has a somewhat vengeful streak." He paused. The faintest look of disquiet passed over C's face.

"Just how vengeful?"

Bartrop looked down at his cuffs for a second, then back up at C.

"Vengeful enough to kill someone."

Chapter
Twenty-four

Sarah awoke slowly from a deep sleep. She opened her eyes and looked up at the unfamiliar ceiling. Recollection flooded back. Dante, Mosami, Jacob, Morocco, Jack. She reached for her watch, which lay on a table next to the bed. It was 7:00 A.M. God, she'd been asleep since yesterday afternoon. Despair seeped through her. Sleep. Sleep for days, weeks, months. She knew the pattern. Her body would shut down, her mind seek oblivion.

She sat up suddenly, her eyes racing wildly around the room as her mind recoiled from memories. Not again—please, not again. She couldn't cope with it another time. The panic froze as another memory gripped her. She had found a solution then. It had taken years, but it had worked. It would work again. Only this time she would not let years go by. She could not, or she too would be dead. She swung her legs over the edge of the bed and rose, dizzy, to her feet.

She walked across the carpet to the bathroom, a huge room off the bedroom. Cool marble greeted her feet. Marble floors, marble walls, all white, like a mausoleum, relieved only by the gashes covered in wood filigree of three windows, floor to ceiling, along one wall. A large Jacuzzi was cut deep into the marble in the center of the room. To the side was a trio of shower, sauna, and steam room. Sarah stepped into the shower, adjusted the temperature gauge to zero, and turned on the shower full pelt. She braced herself as torrents of freezing water cascaded over her, soaking her hair, flowing into her eyes.

She stepped out, toweled herself dry, and, with a grimace of distaste, put on yesterday's clothes. She combed her hair and walked out through the French windows at the far end of her bedroom into the cool morning air.

The garden was an oasis, deserted save for the birds that sang all around and fluttered back and forth across her path as she walked. There was water everywhere, flowing along little channels cut through the greenery. She came across a large pond full of carp, guarded by a pair of stone cats. As she watched the fat golden bodies of the fish gliding through the water, she wondered if the cats kept the herons away or if the birds stole down and gorged themselves. She walked on, round to the front of the house, enjoying the feeling of solitude.

Hearing a gentle rattle of china, she looked down and saw Jack sitting on one of the lower terraces, having breakfast. She walked down toward him. He looked up and smiled as she approached.

"What are you doing up so early? I thought I was the only one who kept crazy hours."

"It's too beautiful to lie in bed."

Jack gestured at the table. "Well, now that you're up, how about some breakfast?"

Sarah looked at an array of croissants, sliced mango and papaya, and a large jug of fresh orange juice. The smell of freshly ground coffee filled the air. She sat down opposite Jack. "I'd love some."

Jack pushed a little beeper. Seconds later, Angelo appeared. Then Jacob, bent slightly with morning stiffness, limped into view.

"Two more breakfasts, please, Angelo. Oh, and by the way, how are the clothes coming along?"

"Very well, Mr. Jack. Mariella will be finished in about one hour."

"Good. That's very kind. If you'll just leave them in the young lady's room."

Sarah noticed that he did not use her name. Jacob had told him everything, she supposed. And now he was concealing her identity.

"What clothes?" she asked.

"Well, you can't go around in those forever, can you? Mariella's run some up for you from some cloth of her own. A bit basic, but I'm sure they'll look wonderful on you. Better than your having to go shopping in Marrakesh."

Sarah blinked at him across the table. Such incredible caution. So she was to remain hidden away, leaving no traces in the world outside, as if she did not exist. She felt a rush of anger, followed by fear. She saw in her mind an image of nameless faces wandering through crowds, asking questions, seeking her out.

She studied the stranger opposite. How much did he know? she wondered. A worry flashed across her mind, but quickly she banished it. Jacob would not have brought her here unless he could trust Jack completely. She would have to trust him, too.

Jacob appeared at the table at that moment. He was wearing a Panama hat, which he took off and waved with a flourish.

"Morning, sweetie. How did you sleep? All right?"

Sarah smiled at the concern that he tried so valiantly to conceal.

"Yes, thank you, Jacob. I must have had a good fifteen hours."

"Good. That's the stuff." He turned to Jack and shot him a broad grin. "Borrowed your hat. Thought I'd go for a walk—didn't want to fry my brains, what's left of them."

"Can't be too careful, eh?"

"Don't give me too bloody careful." Jacob glared in mock indignation and turned to Sarah. "I tell you, everywhere I went there were eyes on me. You know, those little red lights, blinking away. I made the mistake of going down to walk by the wall, nice and shady. It's like a bloody fortress—fifteen feet high, wire, cameras. Couldn't even take a pee in the bushes for fear I'd set off some alarm."

Sarah and Jack laughed out loud.

"Just as well you didn't," Jack said. "Nothing goes on in this garden I don't know about. I've got the best cameras, infrared, daytime, alarm lights, sensors, the lot. And then I've got Yap." As if on cue, a ferocious Yorkshire terrier appeared, trotting down the steps at the heels of Mariella, who was bringing the two extra breakfasts.

Mariella laid down her tray, scolded Yap, who was jumping about in early morning excitement, and disappeared back into the house. Yap watched her go, then went to examine Sarah. She bent down, ruffled his neck, and cooed at him. Utterly disarmed, he lay down and writhed on the floor, exposing his white tummy for a scratch.

"You've made quite a hit there," noted Jack. "Normally he doesn't go for strangers. Have to hold him back a bit—got a vicious bite."

"Quite right, Yap." Sarah straightened up and smiled at the two men. How sweet, how typical of Jacob to reassure her of her safety here in so light a way, without drawing attention to the danger she was in. And Jack too, picking it up so swiftly, adding his gentle reassurance. Her heart still felt like a stone in her body, crushed by an unbearable weight, but at least the fear that lurked beneath the surface would be kept at bay. And she could laugh still. She had been surprised at that. It was a start.

She woke suddenly from her reverie. Jack was speaking again.

"Mariella's going shopping later this morning—you know, food, groceries. If there's anything you need, just tell her."

Sarah, unable to think of anything she needed, started to shake her head, then remembered.

"Well, yes, just one thing. The newspapers, if possible. I'd like to see if there's anything . . ."

"Yes, of course," said Jack. "Angelo usually goes for them around one. They come in about three, so he goes a bit early and has a drink with some friends in a café. He thinks I don't know about it. Ha! He should know I know everything that goes on in this place."

At four o'clock Angelo returned with a stack of British and Italian newspapers.

"Had a good drink? Your mates all right?" asked Jack, grinning.

"Fine, thank you, Mr. Jack." Angelo grinned back at the joke, which was almost as old as both of them. He carried the papers to a shaded table on the terrace at the back of the house and spread them out like a deck of cards. Jack thanked him and asked him to go and tell the young lady that the papers had arrived.

Jacob and Sarah appeared together a few minutes later. Sarah had changed into one of the outfits made by Mariella, a long white linen skirt and blouse. They were loose, ill cut, but still they could not disguise her beauty. Jack started when he saw her. With her hair tied back and her face white and free of makeup, she looked like a young girl approaching confirmation. But as she drew closer, the illusion disappeared. In place of the lightness of innocence was the burden of experience and the weight of tragedy. Her face was drawn and taut; her arms hung wearily, her step was heavy. But strangely, she did not present a picture of defeat. Her head was held high, and in her eyes there was a spark of defiance.

Together, she and Jacob sat down at the table, and the three of them began to read purposefully. Sarah read *Corrière della Sera, La Stampa,* and the *Times.* Jack read the *Daily Mail* and the *Guardian,* Jacob the *Independent* and the *Daily Telegraph.* No one said anything. All three read solidly, looking for the same story. But there was nothing. Not a headline, not a paragraph, nowhere the slightest reference to the arrest of Karl Heinz Kessler, Matthew Arnott, or Carla Vitale. They knew within seconds of opening the papers that Catania had not been arrested, for that surely would have been trumpeted in the Italian newspapers in banner headlines, impossible to miss. But they still pored over every line.

After half an hour, stacks of crumpled pages littered the ground.

"They've had twenty-four hours. More than that. Why haven't they done anything?" Sarah looked from face to face, seeking an answer in the worried eyes that watched her.

The two men were silent. Then Jacob pointed out, "They

might have arrested them. I don't know what deadlines the papers work under, but it could have happened too late for today's editions."

"Yes. That's it," said Sarah, latching on to hope, trying to banish a latent fear. "If they arrested them yesterday evening, it wouldn't be in the papers until tomorrow. We'd better watch the news. It might be on there."

They watched *Sky News* on a large screen in a dark room. There was nothing. Sarah switched off the television and started to pace around the room. It should have been simple. Evidence, arrest, news. Yet there was silence. Nothing had been done.

"I cannot understand it. I can't bear it. What's going on? Why haven't they arrested them yet?" Her voice was plaintive. The two men exchanged a quick glance.

"It may not be that straightforward. The police, all sorts of people, will be involved. They will all have their own agendas. They may have good reason for holding back," said Jack.

"Good reason!" shouted Sarah. "Two people are dead. What better reason do they need?"

"They might want to tail them for a while, see where they lead," said Jacob. "After all, there's still a lot they don't know. It would make sense."

"Oh, yes, apart from the fact that whoever murdered Mosami and Dante is still on the loose and looking for me." Sarah lapsed into silence. Suddenly her eyes lit up with an idea. "I've just thought of something . . ."

Both men straightened in their chairs and asked in unison, "What?"

"Barrington doesn't have the tapes yet. The ones that mention Kessler and Catania as being the third and fourth men. I told him about them on the telephone, but that's not the same as hard evidence. The tapes will give him that. You brought them with you, didn't you, Jacob? I seem to remember your shoving them into your case."

Jacob nodded.

"So I'll make copies of the tapes. We could Fed Ex them to him. Then we'll see what happens. If he arrests them, I'll trust him, have a bit more faith in his system. If he doesn't, I won't."

Jack and Jacob shifted uncomfortably. Sarah had a point, but they were loath to agree with her. It seemed as if she were setting a test, a trap even, for Barrington, and almost hoping he would fail. It was almost as if she had some kind of hidden plan, for which she was seeking their sanction.

"What'll you do then?" asked Jacob.

Sarah just smiled.

The package from Sarah Jensen arrived on the governor's desk the next day. First thing in the morning, Angelo had flown with it to London, handed it over to Federal Express, paid cash so that it would be untraceable, and asked that they wait two hours before delivering it. Then he caught the next available flight back to Marrakesh. When the package arrived on Barrington's desk, Angelo was over Spain.

The package was marked in handwritten blue ink "Private and Confidential. To be opened by addressee only." Barrington ripped it open. A cream-colored page fluttered out. He read:

Dear Governor,

The enclosed tape will corroborate my evidence. Now that you have this information, I trust you will pass it to the relevant authorities, whoever they might be, and secure the appropriate arrests. You will understand that with these people still free, my fears for my own safety are considerable. I trust, therefore, that you will act with all possible haste. Until then, I will stay where I am assured of at least a measure of protection.

    Yours sincerely,

      Sarah Jensen

Barrington buzzed Ethel. "Hold all calls until I tell you, would you?" With a sense of trepidation he pulled the tape recorder out of his drawer and inserted the cassette.

He listened for half an hour, then switched off the recorder and sat in brooding silence. Sarah Jensen was alive, thank God for that, but her reappearance, albeit by proxy, was inconvenient, to say the least. He had hoped that he might start easing away from this mess, but her latest revelations drew him in once more. That Catania was actively involved was not his problem, but Karl Heinz Kessler was the chief executive of a prominent City bank, under his jurisdiction. If this leaked out, it would savage the reputation of the City and his own supervisory record. He hoped, rather defeatedly, that Bartrop could keep all this out of the newspapers, that there would be no trial but some private solution behind the scenes. But he knew that the murders made that almost impossible. He would have to maneuver very deftly if he were to emerge from this with his reputation and career intact.

He sat deep in thought for fifteen minutes, then called Bartrop. "You'd better come over here," he said. "Sarah Jensen's been in touch."

Twenty-five minutes later, Bartrop was in Barrington's office. He read the letter, listened to the tape, and sat back with a worried frown.

"What do you make of it?" asked Barrington.

Bartrop sighed heavily. "Well, in one respect it's good. She's alive, and she's given us fairly conclusive proof on Kessler and Catania. We should be able to find those accounts that Kessler and Arnott referred to easily enough, and that will tie Catania in nicely. But it still doesn't lead us to Fieri, and it leaves us in a bit of an awkward position."

"What, trying to make her come back, you mean?"

"Well, not so much that. We'll find her. But she seems to be setting out some kind of a bargain—arrest all the conspirators and she'll come back. She obviously knows something about Fieri and a Mafia tie-in, so she'll tell us then, presumably. But if we arrest everyone now, we'll be abandoning some potentially highly rewarding surveillance intelligence, in exchange for some unknown intelligence from her that might ultimately be worth very little. If that is the case, then we've thrown away our best chance of nailing Fieri. That's the problem." Bartrop gazed into the courtyard.

"So what are you going to do?"

Bartrop snapped out of his reverie. "I don't know yet. Think about it for a while."

"What shall I do if she calls?"

"I don't think she will, somehow. She's smart enough to realize we could trace her. That's the other worrying thing. She makes a barbed reference to 'the relevant authorities.' She clearly suspects there's more to this on our side than you told her. She's probably cooked up an almighty conspiracy theory."

Barrington snorted with laughter. "She wouldn't be wrong, would she?"

Bartrop gave him a sour look and left. Before he closed the door, he turned and said over his shoulder, "If she does call, keep her talking. Try to find out whatever you can. Tell her to come back, and we'll sort everything out."

Barrington glared at the closed door as if it bore an imprint of the man. He almost wished Sarah Jensen would stay in hiding, just to frustrate Bartrop. He stared moodily into the courtyard, but found no solace in the cool greenery. His only consolation was that Bartrop's position was much worse than his.

He had spoken to the chancellor this morning, told him of the whole affair. The chancellor had spoken to the prime minister, the PM to the foreign and home secretaries, who had in turn spoken to their own permanent secretaries and the cabinet secretary. So had begun a flurry of telephone calls and frantic face-to-face meetings, which were to culminate that evening when all of these people except the PM would meet with the director general, C, Bartrop, and the attorney general at six o'clock in the cabinet office. Accusations, justifications, and explanations would be kicked around then. His own presence was deemed unnecessary, and it was, after all, prudent that he keep his distance. The flak would be heavy. Let Bartrop and C take it all.

Bartrop sat in the back of the Rover tugging violently at his tie as Munro drove him home. He felt hot and uncomfortable. His tie felt like a noose.

He disliked intensely the sensation of not being in control. The Catania case, which had started off so promisingly, was now slipping from his grasp. First the murders, then the disappearance of Sarah Jensen, and now that wretched committee meeting, from which he had just escaped.

The meeting had lasted an hour. He had seen the quiet satisfaction in the faces ranged against him. His position was grave: two murders of foreign nationals, an extensive international fraud of great political sensitivity, and the ever-present fear that it would leak into the newspapers. When he had relayed Sarah

Jensen's latest revelations, they had produced an audible shock, quickly covered up with indignation at her means of communication. "Going into hiding, sending tapes, giving us veiled instructions. She's making a mockery," the home secretary had spluttered. Bartrop had enjoyed that, the only amusement in a dire meeting.

But the situation was not irredeemable. He could continue his investigation, but he had been warned to play it by the book from now on, had been cautioned not to take unnecessary risks and to insure that nothing leaked into the newspapers. And he had been urged to find Sarah Jensen as quickly as possible.

In the meantime, the Special Branch was instructed to step up its efforts to find the murderers, of whom so far there was not a trace. All it could say was that the murders had been carried out by two individuals, both of them professional hit men.

Neither murder weapon had been found. There were no fingerprints, no trace of the murderers except for two corpses, one with a severed jugular vein, the other with a bullet in the right temple. The bullet had been removed and submitted for extensive forensic tests, which had established that it had been fired from a Ruger Mark 11 that had never been used in a recorded crime to date. Each pistol leaves tiny signature traces on the bullets it fires. Records are kept worldwide, and are matched like fingerprints. But this weapon had no history.

There had been no witnesses. Nobody had seen anything unusual or suspicious. The killings had been supremely well executed.

Bartrop felt a jolt as Munro pulled up in front of his house, got out quickly, and opened the passenger door. Bartrop stepped out, bid Munro goodnight, and retreated into his house. He went up to his study and poured himself a whisky, filling the glass with water from a jug refilled every morning by Mabel, his housekeeper. He opened a cupboard door, revealing four rows of jumbled CDs, and selected a Lester Young. As he sat at his desk, the smoky jazz flowed through the room. The pull and throb of voice and saxophone filled his senses, banishing all thought from his mind. He drained his glass and poured another, swirling it, listening to the sounds, staring out the window.

Then, slowly, the thoughts filtered back. Thoughts, worries, preoccupations, obsessions. He recognized them all, but they were overcome by an unfamiliar sensation: mystification. The invisibility of the contract killers he could understand, but Sarah Jensen's desire, and ability, to disappear without a trace intrigued him. She was supposed to be a novice, but she didn't behave like one. She had behaved from the outset, he realized, with an unnerving sophistication. Now she had bolted, out of either blind fear or fearful deviousness. The more he learned about her, the more his suspicions were confirmed. She was capable of taking her fate into her own hands, with no regard for convention or the law. She had done it once; she could do it again. She had had more than enough provocation.

A gentle tap at his door interrupted his reverie. It was Mabel. "Your supper's ready, sir. Shall I take it through?"

"Yes, thank you, Mabel." He followed his housekeeper downstairs. In the sitting room a table set for one stood in front of the television. Bartrop sat down. Mabel returned with fish soup, shepherd's pie, and cheese soufflé. Comfort food. Clever of her.

Bartrop finished his supper and returned to the library. Moments later, Nigel Southport, head of the Italian desk, telephoned. He confirmed that the watchers were in place, monitoring from a discreet distance the homes of Antonio Fieri and Giancarlo Catania. He had asked for and been given the assistance of the intelligence branch of the carabinieri. This was the only branch of Italian intelligence in which Bartrop had any faith. Realizing that the Friends had insufficient resources to mount adequate surveillance on their two targets, Bartrop had given Southport permission to approach the carabinieri, who, without asking too many questions, had agreed to help out. Favors repaying favors, trust repaying trust.

Chapter Twenty-five

The sun was high in the sky over the foothills of the Atlas
Mountains when Sarah, Jacob, and Jack reconvened the next
day to read the newspapers. They took their seats around the
wooden table, nodded to each other, and began to read. So
began a daily ritual; hope at breakfast, nerves at lunchtime, newspapers at four, disappointment, avoidance, diversion all afternoon and evening, until once again morning brought a glimmer
of hope, weaker by the day.

Sarah tried not to think about it for the next few days. Jack
had a stable of magnificent Arab-Berber stallions, and Sarah rode,
guided by Angelo, up into the foothills for several hours every
morning. When she returned, she lost herself in the gardens and
took long siestas. Meals and the arrival of the newspapers
marked the passage of time.

But on Sunday night, after Jack had gone to bed, she broke

her self-imposed silence. She and Jacob stayed up, got very drunk on old Armagnac, and speculated late into the night.

Jacob repeated his suspicions that MI5 was somehow involved. "After all, what were you? An undercover agent. And who is supposed to be responsible for that kind of thing? MI5." He spoke calmly, patiently. "They held back all sorts of things from you. Like the fact that the Mafia was involved, and that they knew all about the inside information in the first place. But did they tell you that, or at least warn you that it could be dangerous? No. They just told you some cock-and-bull story and you agreed to get involved, to work as an undercover agent for the governor of the Bank of England." Jacob rolled his eyes skyward, and his voice cracked with irritation.

"Who ever heard of such a thing? Why didn't I see it from the beginning? It might just have been plausible, I suppose, if you'd been investigating a nice clean fraud, local, small-time. But high-level blackmail and an insider-dealing ring that includes the Mafia? That's way out of the governor's league." He looked levelly at Sarah. "For whatever reason, he deceived you, and used you. And I'll bet whatever you like that it's all got something to do with the security services, not the governor of the Bank of England at all."

Sarah sat silent for a while. "I don't know about all that, Jacob. I could ring the governor tomorrow and ask him, but if it were true, he'd never tell me, would he?"

Not for the first time in recent days, Sarah wondered why she had been hired by the governor. Why hadn't he used the Serious Fraud Office or more conventional means? He had given her ocean-wide license, never questioned her methods. As long as she got results, he was satisfied.

Self-policing was all very well, but she had broken the law several times in the course of her work for Barrington. At what

point did that become unjustifiable? What would happen if anyone found out about her illicit millions?

The status of Barrington's office and the man himself had dis-
pelled her doubts, but now suspicions were growing like cracks
in a wall. Sarah began to separate the man from his office. She
had always believed herself protected by him and her actions
legitimized by his office. But there was nothing to prove their
connection. There was nothing in writing. There were no witnesses.

She felt a growing isolation. Without the governor's sanction,
she was a criminal. Without his protection, she was exposed,
almost fatally vulnerable. She couldn't stay hiding away here
with Jack and Jacob forever. It was beautiful, yes, but still a
prison of sorts, and claustrophobia was beginning to grip her,
creeping through her fear. She was torn between the urge to
forget everything, disappear, fly away to the Himalayas, join
Eddie and Alex where no one would ever find her, and the desire
to return to London, confront Barrington, and find out what was
really going on.

She had fulfilled her side of the bargain—she had uncovered a
crime, provided the governor with high-quality evidence—but
the crime and the criminals were much more insidious than he
had ever let on. And he must have known. And now there were
the murders. Two so far. And still he did nothing. Why? The
word screamed like a missile around her head.

She remembered her excitement when the governor had
asked her to work undercover for him. She had been flattered by
his position and seduced by the glamour of secrecy. And what
was the result? Death, and the life she had so painstakingly built
up destroyed.

A sense of betrayal, unacknowledged until now, began to seep through her like poison. And a quiet rage began to grow, raising memories, tugging at emotions she had hoped never to feel again. She felt herself in the grip of familiar forces. They had once been irresistible. They were strong now, each day growing stronger.

She said goodnight to Jacob and went to bed, but she lay there all night, sleepless. She rose the next morning with her faith and trust in Barrington in tatters and a new resolution beginning to form.

She had breakfast in her room, paced around the gardens, and took a swim in the pool, thinking furiously all the while. Then, her mind made up, she went to see Jacob and Jack. She spoke with them for half an hour, arguing determinedly.

They persuaded her to wait a few more days. Reluctantly, she agreed.

For two days she lived in limbo, trying to shut off her mind, to live, to enjoy the beauty of the house.

As she expected, there was nothing in the newspapers.

The third day, Wednesday, came, and adrenaline began to pump through Sarah's veins. She felt sick with anticipation. She skipped breakfast, had lunch in her room, made her final preparations, and waited one last time for the newspapers.

The slam of the car door at four o'clock announced Angelo's return. Sarah, Jacob, and Jack came down from their rooms and congregated around the circular table in the shaded courtyard at the back of the house. Angelo piled up the papers on the center of the white tablecloth: the *Financial Times*, the *Times*, the *Guardian*, the *Independent*, the *Daily Telegraph*, *Corrière della Sera*, and *La Stampa*.

Sarah looked at Jacob and Jack. They gave her a look that said "thumbs up" and fell upon the papers. They pored over each page and, with hope fading from their faces, cast the papers to the floor until the table was bare.

Sarah wiped the newsprint from her hands, blackening a napkin. Her voice was cool, almost tranquil among the chaos of crumpled pages.

"One last chance then?"

Grim-faced, they nodded.

Jack shouted out instructions to Angelo, who, moving quickly, brought a mobile telephone to the table. He had bought it in the South of France several months ago. It was registered to a small company owned by a friend of Jack's near Villefranche and was very useful for making calls that Jack did not want traced to his home in Morocco. Attached to the phone was a small recording device, which would record both sides of the conversation and relay them to a master recorder in the house. Jack took the phone from Angelo and asked him to make a copy of the conversation that was about to follow. Angelo nodded and scuttled back inside the house.

Jack handed the telephone to Sarah. She checked her watch. Three-thirty in London. *Please let him be there,* she thought. *Let it be over and done with, and no time to think.*

She dialed the governor's private number. He answered after three rings. She wanted so much to believe in him. It would make things so much easier. She pinched herself, forced out the questions, and knocked him off the fence.

"Governor, it's Sarah Jensen. I think you owe me an explanation. Why have there been no arrests?" She spoke briskly, her voice cold and businesslike.

"Look, Sarah, why don't you tell me where you are? We'll pick you up, take you somewhere safe, and I'll explain everything then."

Sarah snorted in disbelief. "You expect me to believe that? You've lied to me repeatedly since you first recruited me. You expect me to trust you now?"

His voice seemed to harden. "Look, Sarah. This has all gone too far, and—"

Her voice took on a chilling clarity. "Yes, it has, rather. Mosami dead, Dante dead—me next, if I'm not careful. Governor, just answer my question. Why have there been no arrests?"

His voice became slow and pedantic. "It's not that simple. We can't move against any of them yet—there are a few problems with the evidence."

Sarah's patience snapped. "You said from the outset that you didn't need courtroom evidence. So what exactly is the problem now?"

He laughed. "Well, if you must know, you are a bit of a problem. You are up to your neck in it, aren't you, Sarah? We found out about your three million dollars, and there are one or two other things we discovered as well. That's why you have only given me half a case, isn't it? I can't do a thing without all the facts, and you won't give them to me. You can't expect me to act selectively. If I move against Catania, I'll have to move against everyone implicated by him. At the moment, that includes you. Now, there is a way around this, but we need to talk. You see my predicament. There is nothing I can do until you tell me where you are and fill in some of the gaps, and unless you want to come under scrutiny yourself, I suggest you tread carefully. You're not exactly an ideal, unblemished witness."

Sarah listened dumbly, a mixture of horror and rage almost paralyzing her. Barrington continued, his tone suddenly gentler, as if he realized he had pushed too hard. "Look, Sarah, the best thing we can do is get together and discuss all this calmly and sensibly. Don't you think?"

"I think it's gone beyond that, Governor."

She hung up and sat in silence, reeling from his overt betrayal. She forced herself to stay calm, playing his words over in her mind, looking for clues. However she read it, his inactivity made no sense. She could not decipher his real reasons, nor why he was so aggressively hiding them from her. Now he had decided to play dirty. He seemed confirmed as an adversary.

She knew exactly what he was threatening her with. *Let him try*, she thought scornfully. *He can prove nothing*. She smiled to herself through the shock. What a fool. Knowing what he did about her, he should have realized by now that his threats would be impotent, would be likely to backfire. Now she had her own evidence. And she would use it. Her face hardened as she spoke to herself. *Goodbye, Governor, and good luck.*

Jacob and Jack watched the gamut of emotions playing on her face. She told them what the governor had said.

"I think he's had his last chance, don't you?"

Silent nods triggered her contingency plan. She tasted the bittersweet tang of conspiracy in her mouth.

Sarah reached down into the briefcase beside her, retrieved a manila envelope, and laid it face up on the table. The name and address written in flowing strokes of a thick black felt pen leapt up at them.

HILTON SCUDD, ESQ.
THE TIMES
NO. 1 VIRGINIA STREET
LONDON E1 9BD

It was all prepared. The envelope contained a letter, written yesterday by Sarah, describing the Catania conspiracy and her own role, with evidence. Jacob had brought with him all the tapes that incriminated the conspirators. Sarah had duplicated them and rerecorded all the relevant bits onto one tape. After her conversation with Barrington, she added a postscript to the letter. Then she took out her address book and opened it to S. She dialed a thirteen-digit number. The line crackled into life, and she sat back to wait. After twelve rings, the voice of Hilton Scudd boomed down the line.

Sarah and Hilton had been good friends for more than seven years. They had been undergraduates together at Cambridge, where Hilton had edited the university newspaper while pretending to read biochemistry. He was energetic, kind, and uncommonly good-looking: about six-foot-two, on the skinny side. He believed muscles were for lorry drivers. He had a full head of shiny black hair cut short at the back and sides but allowed to fall forward in an extravagant sweep over the forehead.

Sarah announced herself and listened to a tirade of recriminations for various commissions and omissions. She was glad she had not put him on the speakerphone. Finally, through her own laughter, she managed to get a word in.

"Hilton, shut up for a second. You can think up suitable punishments at your own leisure—this is business. I'm sending you a package by Fed Ex. It should be on your desk by eleven A.M. tomorrow. You will find tape recordings and a letter from me. There might be some more stuff I can send you, possibly in the next day or so. Don't let any of it out of your sight."

Her face became grave. "You ever heard of Mosami Matsumoto? You should have, you carried a story about her a week ago. She was my best friend . . . And Dante Scarpirato? He was my colleague, and my lover. He's dead too. The same people who killed them are looking for me. They are killing to protect their secrets. Yeah, big secrets. Just wait for the tapes."

After listening for a moment, Sarah said impatiently, "Don't ask me why I haven't gone to the authorities. I have. They know exactly who's behind all this. They have evidence, but they're doing nothing. Only the press can help me now. If you blow these people's secrets sky high, they will have nothing left to kill for, apart from revenge. I can't tell you any more, Hilton—the package will explain." She could feel him holding his breath. "You won't be able to call me, but I'll call you regularly, don't worry about that. Just print the story, as much of it as you can, and keep me out of it." There was an unusual edge to her voice. "And print it fast."

Hilton Scudd replaced the phone in its cradle, his skin tingling. He got up from his metal desk and loped across the open floor to the office of his editor, Clement Stamp. Stamp was a wiry Anglo-Welshman well endowed with the qualities of both nationalities. He had an instinct for gossip that might have been honed under Milk Wood, but he could be discreet. His best feature was a head of unruly gray hair. He looked like one of those cartoon characters who has stuck two fingers into an electrical socket. Sarah had met him twice and reckoned that it was all the outlandish stories that did it—his hair was some kind of shock repository. He was an attractive character, brilliant and honest but with an engaging streak of deviousness.

Stamp was chewing on a Bic pen when Scudd walked in. He laid down the mangled pen and looked across his desk at Scudd, who took a seat on a broken chair.

"You remember that friend of mine from Cambridge, works in the City now, Sarah Jensen?"

Stamp nodded. "Hard to forget."

"She thinks someone's trying to kill her."

Stamp raised an eyebrow dubiously.

"Do you remember we ran stories last week on Dante Scarpirato and Mosami Matsumoto?"

The eyebrow dropped, and Stamp leaned forward in his seat.

"Matsumoto was her best friend. Scarpirato was her colleague and her lover."

Stamp got up from his desk. "What's going on, Hilton?"

"Sarah's sending us a package. Should arrive tomorrow. Proof of a huge conspiracy, she says. Wants us to blow it out of the water."

Sarah got up from the table, walked round to Jacob and Jack, and stood between them, balancing her hands on their shoulders.

"He's a good boy, Hilton. Let's see what he can do." She looked rueful. "The trouble is, I really need more evidence. The tape of the governor is good, but it's not enough."

Jacob looked at her in shock. "You're not going to use that, are you, with all his implications?"

Sarah shrugged. "Blackmail. That's all it is. Empty threats. He has nothing on me. The three million—well, there is that, but he can't have me prosecuted without having everyone else prosecuted, and it's pretty obvious he doesn't want to do that."

"But if your friend at the *Times* does write an article, expose the whole thing, then there probably will be prosecutions. And you could be trawled in with the rest of them."

"I don't think it will come to that. Besides, the tape of my conversation with Barrington gives me some protection. I don't think he'd want to see me in a courtroom."

"But you can't pretend that a story splashed across the front page of the *Times* isn't going to hurt you somehow."

"No. I know that. But I really don't have much choice. I don't trust Barrington. I was almost willing to reconsider that, but . . ." She shrugged. "Our last conversation blew that out the window. And I can't stay here forever. The only chance I have is to expose the whole story in the papers. Then maybe Catania and his Mafia killers or whoever they are will be arrested and I'll be safe."

The others nodded their heads glumly. Watching them, Sarah felt a sudden wave of helplessness sweep over her. What if the *Times* didn't print her story—what could she do then? She was running out of ideas. What if the intelligence services were involved? Couldn't they stop publication? Wouldn't they put out a "D notice," designed to screen out all stories held to counter national security interests? But then, all sorts of things seemed to leak out these days. She wondered what stories were never seen, what secrets were buried by official sanction or purged from the papers. Who, she wondered for the thousandth time, was she up against?

She looked across at the two men. "You know what I really need?"

"What?" they asked in unison.

"More evidence. What I have is still a bit patchy. I think the *Times* will need more than I've given them."

Jack looked up at her. "Like what?"

"The videos."

"What videos?"

"The ones used to blackmail Catania. I think they're rather explicit. You know, Catania and Carla in bed together."

"Do you know where they are?" asked Jack.

Sarah looked intrigued when she saw the devious look in his eyes. "They're in Carla's flat, aren't they, Jacob? Arnott referred to them on the tapes, didn't he? You didn't play that bit to me, but you mentioned that Arnott had said something to Carla about her performance with Catania on the tapes."

Jacob looked from one face to another. "Yes, he did. They're in Carla's flat, if I remember."

The three of them smiled at each other in silent conspiracy.

"What's her address?" asked Jack.

Jacob reeled it off. He had gone there several times to do some reconnaissance work before ordering the bugging devices from his friend Charlie.

"And what does she look like? You'd better tell me everything you know about her."

They spoke for a few minutes, then Jack got to his feet. "I'm just going to make a few phone calls, if you'll excuse me."

Sarah and Jacob grinned at each other. "I never believed he'd gone into retirement," said Jacob.

"Lucky he hasn't."

"Don't worry. He's glad of the excuse. Crime with a cause. What better?" Jacob gave a particularly wicked grin.

Angelo appeared suddenly at their side. In his hands was a tape cassette with the recording of Sarah's conversation with the governor. She put it into the manila envelope, sealed it, and handed it back to Angelo, who would Fed Ex it from Marrakesh. He took the envelope, which bulged slightly with the extra tape. It was not Queen's evidence, and it never was going to see the inside of a courtroom if she could help it, but it was going to deliver sentence just the same.

The watchers scattered around Onslow Square saw Carla Vitale leave her flat at five-thirty. She was carrying a gym bag. She would be gone for a couple of hours, they reckoned. A few split off to follow her; the others stayed and watched.

A few minutes after Carla had gone, the old gentleman who lived in the flat below her returned from a long and liquid afternoon at his club. Following in his footsteps was a woman in her late sixties with gray hair and an apron—a cleaner, lugging a large vacuum cleaner and a large handbag. The old man gallantly held open the door for her and followed her inside.

The cleaner, Carol Abrahams, walked slowly, stopping to rest a few times on the stairs, and to be sure that the old man let himself safely into his flat and nobody else was around. She stopped before the entrance to a flat on the fourth floor. She knocked on the door and rang the bell, just to make sure. No answer. Nobody at home. She reached inside her handbag, took out a selection of keys, and worked meticulously on the two locks. In under two minutes, she had gained entry to Carla's flat.

She darted in, showing a surprising agility, carrying the cleaner high in the air so it would pick up no threads from the carpet fabric. She took a plastic bag from her bulging handbag, laid it on the ground, and set the cleaner down on top of it, all in about five seconds. She waited for a few minutes, palms sweating, praying that there was no alarm. The seconds passed. Silence. Nothing. No alarm.

She took a few deep breaths to calm herself, then got to work. Her instructions were simple and explicit—rather a shame in the circumstances. She had to remove every video in the flat but touch nothing else. There were, thank God, very few videos around. Four stacked under the television, and another three in the safe, which she picked open in less than five minutes. These videos were in a bag, which also contained a number of cassettes. Carol removed the bag and looked longingly back into the safe at a collection of some of the most extravagant jewelry she had seen for a long time. Wearing her rubber gloves, a bright yellow pair designed for washing dishes, bought that morning in Safeway, she trailed a dozen necklaces through her fingers.

She was sorely tempted, but her instructions were clear. She knew better than to disregard them. She replaced the jewelry, relocked the safe, and slotted the bag containing the videos and tapes along with the others into the main body of the vacuum cleaner. Then, very quickly, she let herself out of the flat.

Resuming her role as cleaner, she wobbled down the stairs and out onto the pavement. A couple of men in a British Telecom van parked outside the building were looking at her. She gave them a spectacular gap-toothed leer and hobbled off down the road.

Around the corner she unlocked her car and climbed in. She laid the vacuum cleaner on the seat beside her. Making sure that no one was looking, she opened it up, took out the videos, and transferred them to an overnight case at her feet. Then she started up the car and set off for Heathrow. Two hours later she was sitting in a Boeing 737 en route to Marrakesh.

Jack met her at the airport and led her out to his car. They both got into the back seat, and with a smile of anticipation, Carol opened her case and handed over her loot.

"There were a lot of jewels," she said, her eyes twinkling. Jack frowned for a second, then his face broke into a grin. Carol had worked for him for twenty years and had been in the game for another twenty before he had been introduced to her. She could never resist teasing him.

"Don't worry," she cackled. "I left them where they were."

"Well done, you." Jack laughed. "Angelo'll be over in a few days. He'll settle everything with you, O.K.?"

"He'd better, or I'm going back after them jewels."

Still laughing, they got into the car and drove to Marrakesh, to Avenue Bab Jdid, where Jack dropped Carol off at La Mamounia, Marrakesh's grandest hotel.

"I might have a package for you to take back tomorrow. It's all right, nothing contraband."

"Better bloody well not be. It's bad enough having to come all this way and then go straight back again tomorrow. Anyone'd think I was a bloody mule."

Jack laughed at her outrage, part mock, part genuine. Carol had set her sights on a couple of days of exploring the souk before returning home.

"I'll call you tomorrow when I know."

"I suppose you expect me to wait in, do you?" Carol stood with legs planted wide, hands on hips, in a gesture of defiance undone by her spectacular grin.

"I doubt you'll be up when I call. Just make sure you're in a fit state to travel tomorrow. Don't hit the old bottle too hard. That's all." Jack winked, closed the door on her reply, and drove off, still smiling to himself.

Professional slights, even delivered in jest, reduced Carol to spitting fury. Despite her ruffled appearance, she was one of the most meticulously professional burglars in the business. In over forty years of crime, she had never had a single run-in with the law. Like Jack, she was in semi-retirement, but occasionally she could be persuaded to undertake the odd assignment, if the money and the client were right. She would have done virtually anything for Jack, and everything for a quarter of a million pounds.

Jack arrived back at Ourijane at one in the morning. Jacob and Sarah had waited up for him. They gathered around him in the library. He opened his case and pulled out the videotapes and cassettes with a flourish, grinning at the others.

"I'm not sure if these are going to be family viewing, but we could give 'em a shot anyway, eh?" Then, as if he had suffered a contagion from Carol, he let out a wicked cackle.

Sarah and Jacob laughed out loud.

"Well, we'd better find out." Reading each other's minds, Sarah and Jacob raced for the best seat, directly in front of the video machine. Sarah won. Jacob looked resigned.

"No respect, this generation. That's the trouble . . ."

They were still laughing, glorying in the sensation, when the first of the videos flickered into life on the screen before them. The laughter continued. Carla and Catania were portrayed in a wide variety of compromising positions, the sex protracted and well documented. The cassettes provided verbal corroboration, recording Catania as he passed on his inside information. Better proof of blackmail they couldn't have asked for.

Jack duplicated the videos and cassettes. Sarah wrote a short note to Hilton, then sealed the note, the cassettes, and the videos into a large Jiffy bag. She handed the bag to Angelo, who would deliver it to Carol Abrahams the next morning. Carol would then return with it to London and give it to a courier who would deliver it to the *Times*. The balance of evidence should now be overwhelming.

Sarah's mind turned to the scenes so graphically captured on the videos. Carla's beautiful features had filled the screen, cold, calculating, and deceitful. But Sarah felt nothing for her other than a mild distaste. It was the other actor who had moved her. For Giancarlo Catania, she had developed an implacable hatred. Watching the flickering of his dark eyes, she had realized that he was capable of extreme ruthlessness. Not that he would soil his own hands, but a killer by proxy, that he could be. Sarah could imagine it all too easily.

She said goodnight to Jacob and Jack and went to her room. She walked out onto the open terrace and breathed in the still-warm night air. The scent of jasmine filled her senses like an intoxicant. She tilted her head and looked at the stars, huge and brilliant. Her face was gaunt—she had scarcely eaten for days—but the features were set firmly. Now she had purpose, and the pain began to recede.

Chapter
Twenty-six

The Federal Express package landed with a thud on the mailroom desk of the *Times*. Leroy Grey, one of the mail handlers, picked up the telephone with a languid twist of his hand.

"Hey, Hilton, the Fed Ex—it's here. Yeah, I'll bring it up, no sweat."

Hilton took possession of the package and headed for Clement Stamp's office. Stamp opened the envelope with Hilton peering over his shoulder. He held it open-ended over his desk and shook it so that the contents clattered out. There were two ninety-minute cassette tapes and a typed letter. The paper had got crumpled up among the cassettes. Stamp smoothed it out on the table. Hilton read over his shoulder.

Dear Hilton,

    Do what you can with this. You can show it to Clement, of course—he is a brilliant editor, and trustworthy. Do not show it to any lawyers or you'll never print it. As we both know, they don't have the balls and would rather lead a quiet life. Do not show it to the police or the authorities. You can see why I have little faith in them, and even if you found a good one, I'd be gray and you bald by the time they did anything. In the meantime, as I told you, I am in hiding and in fear for my life. The same people who murdered Mosami and Dante are looking for me.

My role in all this is as an undercover investigator employed by the governor of the Bank of England. He is working with someone else; whom, I don't know. Possibly the intelligence services. Anyway, I have done my job and furnished them with the guilty parties and evidence, but for some reason they are doing nothing—no arrests, nothing. So the conspirators and the killers remain free. My only hope is that you will write the story and expose them. Then they will have nothing left to kill for, apart from revenge.

There followed a description of the fraud and a list of all involved parties. A postscript suggested that the Mafia might be involved.

Stamp and Scudd stared at each other, eyes glowing. Stamp reached into his desk and brought out a cassette player. In stunned silence they listened to the tapes. Then Stamp returned the tapes and the letter to the envelope and locked it away in a wall safe built into the back of his office. A vein pulsed in his temple.

"What a story. Sex, corruption, and death at the pinnacle of the Italian government, with the City, Threadneedle Street, and possibly the intelligence community thrown in. The conspirators rich as Croesus, and Sarah Jensen set up somehow, on the run."

Hilton rubbed his eyes and spoke into space. "What are we going to do?"

Stamp got out of his chair, came around the desk, and gripped Hilton violently by the shoulders, his eyes bright. "Print it, as much as we can get away with. Write a teaser story. We'll see what reaction we get. Keep it veiled at this stage."

Hilton grinned up at him. "And what are you going to do?"

"I," he answered with a pristine smile, "am going to get the tapes authenticated."

Hilton looked disgusted.

"Arse covering," bellowed Stamp at Hilton's back.

The tapes were being authenticated and Hilton was halfway though his article when the second package arrived. It was delivered by a motorbike messenger clad in black from helmet to boot —Carol Abrahams's nephew. Unidentifiable, said Leroy Grey, who had taken possession and got an illegible signature.

The package lingered in the mailroom for an hour before Leroy sauntered up to Hilton's desk. When Hilton saw the handwriting, he nearly had a seizure. He grabbed the package and rushed into Stamp's office, interrupting a conference. Stamp looked from his face to the package and back again, then dismissed the four journalists grouped around his table. With vaguely resentful looks, they walked out.

Hilton took a seat opposite Stamp, cut open the envelope, and held it over the table. A collection of videos and tapes fell out. He stuck his hand into the envelope and drew out Sarah's letter. It said little; just to watch and listen, and use it all.

Stamp drew the blinds on his glass walls and door, picked up one of the videos, and inserted it into the video recorder that sat together with a television in the corner of his office. A melodious female voice speaking in Italian announced the time, date, and place: 2.45 P.M., October 26, 1992, Rome.

The screen lit up, and a room came into sharp focus. It was a bedroom. There were two people in it. One was the governor of the Bank of Italy, Giancarlo Catania. The other, not known to either Stamp or Scudd, was a brunette in her late twenties, beautiful from every angle. They were having sex. Painful sex.

The encounter finished the first tape. There were four more tapes, shot in London, New York, Geneva, and Riyadh. Then there were a couple of tapes that carried a series of conversations between the melodious voice and Catania. The first set out the nature of the blackmail. Scudd, who spoke passable Italian, translated. Unless Catania cooperated, the video recordings would be shown to his wife. In exchange for keeping the recordings secret, the voice demanded that Catania agree to provide details of G7 and EC monetary policy, such as interest-rate changes and central bank intervention in the foreign-exchange markets. Subsequent conversations were brief, staccato, with Catania instructing the voice to buy sterling, dollars, lire, whatever it happened to be.

"This stuff is incredible. Catania's sunk." Stamp switched off the video recorder and the flickering television screen. He ran his hands through his wiry hair and sighed heavily, as if overburdened by what he had just seen. He stood up and began to pace around his office.

"Absolutely incredible. But it's all there. Cast-iron proof. Wonderful bloody story. But can we print it? The political fallout will be tricky. Less of a problem in Italy—they're used to it, just another scandal. But it's a bit different here, and whichever way you look at it, this thing stinks. The head of a major merchant bank is revealed to be a crook and the governor of the Bank of England is straying into a dangerous liaison with the intelligence services. Together they set up and then abandon their agent, who happens to be one of the most gorgeous creatures I've ever set eyes on. Then they organize a cover-up. The evidence is compelling, but there have been no arrests. It looks like the whole thing's too murky even for them. They'll have little interest in dragging it into a courtroom. A private solution would be more their style, but by the look of it, there hasn't even been that. No sudden resignations because of 'ill health,' no rumors of a search for replacement candidates. I can't make sense of it, can you?"

Scudd shook his head. Stamp continued.

"Then there's Sarah Jensen herself. Barrington describes her as 'up to her neck in it.' And there's this business of three million dollars, and her not being an unblemished witness. And he says he's found out some other things as well. What d'you think she's done?"

"Damned if I know."

"Well, she must have broken the law several times over, bugging people and getting hold of those videotapes, which I'll bet are stolen." Stamp sat down again at his desk. "Still, whatever she's done, two of her friends are dead and the man who is supposed to be protecting her seems more intent on threatening her."

"And she's asking for our help. That's what it all boils down to, isn't it?" said Scudd.

Stamp tilted back in his chair and stared at the ceiling.

"So what are we going to do?" asked Scudd.

"God, I don't know. I want to think about it for a while. But you carry on writing. Take over one of the meeting rooms, password-protect all your copy. Nobody sees this except me. I ought to talk to the governor, but I'm not sure I want to alert him yet. Show me your copy as soon as you've finished. It might give me some ideas." Stamp sighed heavily. "The thing is, I honestly don't know if we'll be able to publish this. We'll probably be hit with a D notice as soon as Whitehall or the bank gets a whiff of it. So in a way I don't want to say anything to them yet. Maybe we can build up such a head of steam that it'd blow any D notices out of the water. I just don't know."

"Well, we'd better do something. I believe Sarah when she says she might be the next one to be killed."

"And you think I don't? The Mafia, Catania—they have every reason to kill her."

"And nobody's doing a thing to help her."

Hilton Scudd rose to his feet, raced out of the office, and locked himself away in a conference room at the far end of the floor. He switched on the computer on the desk in the center of the room, logged on, created a secret password, and began to pound away at the keyboard. His hair fell forward over his eyes. After every few words he whipped one hand through it, sweeping it high over his forehead, only to have it fall forward seconds later.

Giancarlo Catania leaned back in his chair, a look of satisfaction on his face. The waiters cleared away the remnants of an exceptionally good lunch. Bresaola with mustard and parmigiano reggiano followed by piccata di vitello and tiramisu to finish. All washed down with a bottle of Tignorello. Some of the best restaurants in Rome would have been put to shame—not that they would have known. Two first-rate chefs and two waiters were serving in this large, sunlit dining room, but this was no restaurant. It was not listed in any directory, bore no nameplate on its elegant facade. No inquisitive passerby would gain entry. All diners were known by the owner. The politicians and civil servants with whom Catania spent his days never came here, or if they did, they would never admit to it.

The house, located on Via Appia Antica, about seven kilometers from the center of Rome, was a large 1930s villa of pinkish stone. It was low and sprawling, with a swimming pool at the back. At the front was a large garden, ensuring privacy from prying eyes. The house belonged to Antonio Fieri. He and Catania had lunch once a month in the low-ceilinged dining room overlooking the gardens at the back of the house.

Catania was always collected from the Banca d'Italia by one of Fieri's drivers in an car owned by a legitimate Cayman Islands company, just in case anyone tried to trace the license plate. Catania couldn't use his official car; anyone who knew him would recognize the plates. Fieri's car had tinted bulletproof windows, like all his fleet. The driver parked in an underground garage to the side of Fieri's house. Catania could then walk upstairs into the house without being seen from the outside. It was a ritual, but today there had been no comfort in it.

Catania had been dreading this meeting. He knew he would have to act normally while scrutinizing Fieri for any sign that he might know or suspect about Carla, or Scarpirato, or Matsumoto, or Jensen. The list seemed to go on and on. There were too many secrets, almost impossible to keep.

Fieri's intelligence network was vast, and the man was perceptive and utterly ruthless. If he found out, there would be no room for explanations, no second chances, no mercy. If Catania showed even a flicker of nerves, Fieri would be alerted that he had something to hide. Then it would be only a matter of time . . . . Catania had readied himself, knowing that he would be tested. Fieri enjoyed making people nervous, just to see what happened, to see if they crossed the threshold of justifiable anxiety.

But today Fieri was in an acceptably good humor. Anything too good would have smacked of crocodile smiles, but it fell comfortably short of that. He was very pleased with the last G7 operation, which had netted the *unione* $16 million—not a lot compared to their overall take, but not bad for a risk-free undertaking.

As he chatted with the capo, Catania began to relax. Fieri was pleased with business and seemed jovial, unworried. He showed no signs of knowing anything about the Carla business, and with Scarpirato and Matsumoto safely out of the way, that left only the Jensen girl. She had disappeared, scared into silence by the death of her friends. If she had told the authorities, he would have had a knock at his door by now. So far, so good, but he wasn't taking any chances. He kept the contract on Sarah Jensen. Christine Villiers had been instructed to stay in London and wait for her prey. She would get her sooner or later.

As the meeting progressed, Catania's fears subsided and his confidence grew. Fieri was so pleased by business that he was prompted into an uncharacteristic act of largess. He told Catania that he had deposited an extra $1 million in his Swiss bank account. Normally Catania got 10 percent of the profits. That would have given him $1.6 million. Catania smiled—$2.6 million would help to pay off Christine Villiers. He was effusive in his thanks. Fieri received his gratitude with a smile of noblesse oblige, then rose, embraced him, kissed his cheeks, and left for another appointment.

Catania lounged back in his chair. Things were definitely looking up. Lunch had been a success, and his little local difficulties seemed to be under control. He laughed out loud, got to his feet, and called for the driver. He was ready to leave.

———

While Catania was basking in his own well-being, Giovanna Cheri, his junior personal assistant, was chain-smoking and trying to answer two phones simultaneously. Rita, her boss, should have been back long ago, instead of leaving her in the shit. She'd gone to lunch with her boyfriend, Glauco, and then shopping on the Via Condotti, which was impossible to do in less than three hours, and not even that, by the look of it. *Cattiva*. She always pushed her luck when Catania entered "Lunch with Sg C" in his diary.

Catania rarely returned before five from these appointments. Who was Signore C? Giovanna wondered. Perhaps it was a girl. She shrugged. Everybody else had them. Why not him? He was quite good-looking for a man of his age. Giovanna gave up speculating and picked up a copy of *Vogue*. She just had time for a minute's fantasizing before the red phone used by the more important of the governor's callers started ringing.

It was the editor of the *Times*, in London, Mr. Stamp. She had spoken to him once before, she remembered. A very nice man, very polite. Her boss could learn a thing or two. What could she do for him? He wished to discuss very important business matters with the governor. Could she possibly fax him a contact number for her boss for later that evening?

Ma certo. She would be delighted. She took down Stamp's fax number and checked it back. Ten minutes later the fax fluttered onto Clement Stamp's desk.

Across the room, Hilton Scudd was typing feverishly. He had set up a password for his copy, "Cambridge." Only those who knew the password—in this case, Clement Stamp and Christopher Fisch, one of the in-house lawyers—could access it. Normally, all copy went onto the general system and any of the *Times*'s journalists could access it from their own computers. But not this story. The inducements to gossip were strong. For the sake of the story and Sarah Jensen, Stamp wanted no leaks.

Usually a big story filled Stamp with nervous excitement, but here he felt unease, trepidation. It was not just the story itself, but his own role in publishing it, if he ever did. It would take him beyond newspaper editor to catalyst, to dispenser of some kind of justice. It would not be the first time he or his newspaper had played that role, but here it was riddled with an almost intolerable ambiguity. There were too many lies and omissions mixed in with the truth, too many motives swirling around. But in the obscurity, some things were clear: that Sarah Jensen was in grave danger, that a huge financial conspiracy was taking place, and that, darker and almost more sinister, another conspiracy was unfolding closer to home, with Sarah Jensen as victim and the governor of the Bank of England and some unknown parties as orchestrators.

All he could do was start with the obvious, work his way across the spectrum, and see what unfolded along the way. With a heavy stride, he walked out of his office to go see Fisch, the lawyer.

Fisch was not happy. His mouth and eyes sloped down with professional pessimism. Stamp stood over him and peered down at Hilton's copy on the screen. It looked like a battlefield. Whole sentences were highlighted in red for subsequent argument and deletion, with Fisch's suggested modifications typed in bold below. Hilton, Stamp knew, would read the modifications on his own screen, then storm over, argue each point, lose most of them, and storm out again.

Stamp returned to his office. Fisch and Scudd remained in angry debate. Orders were sent up to the canteen, food was devoured, endless cups of bitter coffee were gulped while nerves and tempers frayed.

By eight that evening a compromise had been reached. All three sat at Stamp's desk staring at the copy on the screen. Stamp inserted a headline.

ALLEGATIONS OF BILLION-DOLLAR BLACKMAIL IN G7

Rumors are circulating that a high-ranking banker in the Group of Seven Industrial Nations is being blackmailed by his mistress into revealing details of G7's secret currency intervention activities. It is alleged that this information is then used by parties working with the mistress to trade in the foreign-exchange markets. This is insider trading at the highest level. It does not guarantee profits, but it shortens the odds dramatically. Armed with this information and with as little as $250,000 in capital, a participant could make illegal profits of tens of millions of dollars a year.

Sources suggest that much larger sums have been used to trade and that the illegal revenues earned could be over $100 million.

The article then described examples of malpractice in the foreign-exchange and other financial markets. It was five hundred words long, destined for the bottom left-hand corner of the front page. It said as much as was legally possible and tactically prudent. It set the scene.

Stamp thought of the deluge of telephone calls it would trigger worldwide. Scotland Yard, the Serious Fraud Office, the Department of Trade and Industry, the Federal Reserve . . . and the Bank of England, which had had the evidence all along but for some unknown reason had done nothing about it—nothing visible, anyway. The fallout was going to be huge. Sarah Jensen would pay a high price. There was no way she was going to get out of this unscathed if he printed it. Stamp stared at the copy for a long while. In many ways, it would be so much better if it never went to print.

He smiled at the weary faces, reached for his desk diary, and took out the faxed contact number for Giancarlo Catania. It was nine o'clock in Italy. Stamp dialed the number.

Catania was having dinner at the house of Dottore Nicolo Callabria, his number two at the Bank of Italy. Callabria hated his boss. He thought himself infinitely better qualified for the governorship. He had suffered in silence for three years, and his patience was running out. It was galling to have to socialize with the boss, but it was good politics, so every three months he had Catania to dinner. Catania's wife was the only consolation. He turned his attention back to her. Closeted away in the dining room, nobody heard the ringing telephone.

Callabria's twelve-year-old daughter, Nicoletta, answered it in her bedroom and put it on hold. She loved interrupting her parents' dinner parties. She dashed out of her room, across the hallway, and into the dining room. Twelve pairs of eyes fixed on her.

"Papa, it's for Governatore Catania. It's the editor of the *Times*, in London."

Amused glances turned to Catania.

"Alora, what have you done now, Giancarlo?"

Catania smiled, excused himself. His stomach clenched itself into knots, but he kept smiling as he turned and followed Nicoletta into the hallway. The girl gestured to a telephone on a side table. Catania ignored the gesture and glanced around.

"Perhaps the study?" Fat chance that anyone would overhear there.

Nicoletta pointed toward a door at the far side of the hallway and watched Catania disappear behind it.

A glistening black multi-line phone sat on a table in the center of the room. Catania glared at it as if at an enemy. He braced himself and picked up the phone.

"Pronto!"

He listened in silence, his body stiffening. He gripped the receiver. He didn't deny or confirm anything, just listened. He knew what evidence they had. He had seen it all before, should have taken the necessary steps then. He had miscalculated. Now rage and regret swirled around in his head so that he couldn't think straight.

It had to be Sarah Jensen, but why? Why the newspapers and not the police? He needed time to think; then he would comment. He asked for a couple of hours. They gave him one.

He returned to the dining room. "Pressing business at the bank. Might I be excused?"

Everyone looked sympathetic. "But of course."

Callabria stood and asked if he could be of any assistance. Catania gave him a tight smile, managed a "no, thank you," and left.

He swung the car out of the side street and into the Grand Prix of the Via Salaria. He had given his driver the night off. He always got a thrill out of driving powerful cars, but the protocol of office rarely allowed him the opportunity, so he used whatever excuse he could. He felt the thrill even tonight.

In fifteen minutes he was at the Banca d'Italia. He nodded to the night security guards and walked through the silent hallway to the lift. It took him to the third floor, to fifteen years of familiarity. Was this how it was going to end? What a fucking waste. What a God-awful fucking waste. He unlocked the door to his office and sat down at his desk. He took his head in his hands.

Nothing made sense. Carla had nothing to gain and much to lose from exposing him. It had to be Sarah Jensen. But how had she got hold of the videos, and why had she gone to the newspapers? What could she possibly gain? He would have paid her the sky for her silence, and taken off the contract, if only she had spoken to him.

He sat in the dark, in silence, staring out of the darkened window, seeing all too clearly how his life would fall apart, how the quiet men would one day come for him, how the blood would pump as the bullets ripped through him. And Donatella and the children—would they survive?

Suddenly he gave a start. An idea, a way out, came to him—a chance, slim, but real. He had to try it; he had nothing to lose. He sat up, eyes gleaming. He took the crumpled sheet of paper from his breast pocket and dialed the telephone number. He got straight through to Clement Stamp.

"You're wasting your time, Mr. Stamp. You're not going to print that article. It's all lies. You know that." He paused. "And anyway, all things considered, it's probably better for your friend that you don't publish, eh?"

Clement Stamp laughed in disbelief. "Are you trying to threaten her?"

There was a click, and the line went dead.

Stamp stared in anger at the receiver he held clenched in his hand. He felt a sense of revulsion, followed slowly by the flickerings of relief. Catania was guilty, guilty of fraud and of murder. He picked up a photograph of Dante Scarpirato's burned-out house the police had sent over and stared at it. Scudd and Fisch watched him. It took a long time for him to speak.

"He's guilty. Guilty as hell. Not that he admitted anything. Said it was all lies. Suggested it would be better for my 'friend' if we didn't go to print."

"You mean he'll kill her if we do?" asked Scudd.

"Yes. And spare her if we don't, presumably."

———

Sarah had done almost everything she could think of to pass the time. At ten o'clock she could wait no longer. She dialed Hilton's home number and got the answerphone. She dialed the *Times* and waited. After an age he answered.

"Well?" She listened with growing panic. "What do you mean, you're not going to print?"

Hilton held the phone about a foot from his ear, tentatively drawing it closer after a few moments of silence. "Look, Sarah, Clement's here, and he wants to speak to you."

Stamp came on the line. "Hello, Sarah. It's all very sordid, I'm afraid. In short, Catania implies that he'll kill you if we go to print."

"So it's my life in return for silence, is it?"

"That's about it."

Sarah said nothing. She gazed around the quiet room, so far away from everything. Thoughts whirled around in her head. She was safe now, that was something, but there was still so much undone. She hadn't planned it like this.

Finally she spoke. "I wouldn't worry about Catania, Clement. He won't get away with this."

He laughed. "I wish I could be so sure."

"You will be."

"What's that supposed to mean?"

"Oh, benign worldview, or something like that." She hung up before he had a chance to ask any more questions.

Turning to Jacob and Jack, she smiled weakly. "You probably guessed. I'm off the hook. Clement spoke to Catania. No article in exchange for my life. I'm safe." Her eyes drifted from their faces as she spoke, more to herself than to them. "Carry on as normal. Everyone carries on as normal. Catania, Kessler, Arnott,

Vitale, Fieri, Barrington and his puppet-master. Everyone carries on as normal, apart from Mosami and Dante."

"And you," said Jacob, half in question, half as statement.

She smiled, turning back to him. "Yes. And me."

"What are you going to do?" he asked.

She smiled faintly and turned to the door. "I don't know yet." She bid them goodnight and went to her room, to silence and her thoughts.

The two men stared after her. "What's she going to do?" asked Jack.

Jacob shook his head. "I don't know. I doubt if she does."

"Well, that's all right, then, isn't it? If she doesn't know what she's going to do, then she won't do anything."

Jacob let out a long sigh. "No. She doesn't work like that. She doesn't need to know what she's doing. She just needs to do something. She just launches herself on a course, commits herself, even if she doesn't know to what. It doesn't matter. To her, anything's better than being passive, being noncommittal, paralyzed. That's how she'd see it. So she does something, anything, just to be a catalyst. She makes something happen, then makes something else happen with the consequences. Don't forget, she's a gambler by profession, and a brilliant one. She doesn't just predict the markets, she predicts human nature. I've never met anyone as perceptive as Sarah, when she wants to be. Often she does things blindly, just for the fun. She gets bored with knowing the outcome in advance, closes her eyes, jumps in. But when she really gets down to it, plots, plans, predicts things, and does something, sometimes something so slight, then everything follows just as she planned. It's like dominoes. She lifts her finger and they all fall down."

Jack shifted awkwardly in his seat. "You sound almost frightened."

"I am. I've seen that look on her face before."

"And what happened then?"

Jacob turned away from his friend's gaze and looked resolutely out the window into the night, saying nothing.

Christopher Fisch smiled for the first time that day. Another injunction narrowly escaped. Stamp took the Catania tapes from the manila envelope, threw the envelope in the bin, and put the tapes in a clean envelope. He asked Hilton for Sarah's letter and for the floppy disk on which he had saved his article. He put these in the envelope together with the tapes and locked them in his briefcase. Tomorrow he would transfer them to a safe deposit box, listed by number, not by name. He told Hilton and Fisch to erase the Cambridge file on the hard disks of their computers, and watched them do it.

The story would be locked away physically, confined to a safe. But he knew there was ultimately no closing the lid on Pandora's box.

He glanced at his watch. It was nine-thirty. Time to put the paper to bed. He called in his deputy editor. Let him fill the blank space on the front page. Stamp didn't have the heart to do it himself. He said goodnight to Scudd and Fisch and headed for the Garrick.

Giancarlo Catania sat in his office, savoring his victory. Out of the jaws of defeat . . . Fieri would have been proud of him, if he could have told him. He checked his watch. Ten-thirty. He could be back at Callabria's in time for coffee. But first he had to call Christine.

———

No contract, but $300,000 compensation for wasted time. What was going on? Christine hid her surprise, thanked Catania, and hung up. She felt relieved. She hadn't wanted the contract, didn't like killing women. She opened her safe, pulled out Sarah's picture, and stared at it for a while. It was a disturbing face, beautiful but guarded. The eyes fixed on the camera lens were intelligent and knowing, but, beneath the outward confidence, vaguely troubled.

Christine wondered about the canceled contract. What was the tradeoff? What did Sarah know that had made her death so urgent? And how had she managed to buy back her life? Christine took from her conversation with Catania the impression that Sarah had somehow done a deal with him, could now be trusted to keep her silence. Invaluable intelligence, in the right hands. *I should meet Sarah Jensen,* she thought.

Chapter
Twenty-seven

Sarah awoke the next morning with a sense of determination. She looked out her window at the beauty of the distant hills and felt only restlessness. The calming solace she had found at Ourijane over the past week had gone. She was safe now, supposedly. But there had been no resolution. What she did have was freedom of movement and a slight lifting of fear—a free hand.

She decided to leave, to go home to London, to confront Barrington and discover the missing pieces of the puzzle. She would tell Jacob and Jack at breakfast and leave as soon as possible.

As she expected, they did not want her to go. She was adamant. She told them her reasons, or most of them. For fear of insulting them, she kept to herself the fact that here she felt stifled by a blanket of security which left her impotent to cope with her pain.

She asked Jacob if he would stay. She said she would be happier if he did, till everything was sorted out. He hated the thought of her leaving alone but knew her well enough to sense her desire for independence. He knew too that she was concerned about the consequences of his involvement with her activities. Barrington would know that it was his house she had fled from. It was an almost inescapable conclusion that Jacob had helped her escape and probably knew the reasons for her flight. He cared nothing for the consequences of that, but he realized that Barrington might use the threat of action against him to compromise Sarah in some way. He would be her weak link.

Neither Jacob nor Sarah said as much, in order not to offend the other, but their fears hung unspoken and understood. If Sarah would be happier if he stayed with Jack, that was good enough for him. There was little, if anything, he could do for her now in London, and so he would stay in Morocco. But he hated staying behind, unable to watch over her directly. And he knew she was up to something, even if she didn't know what.

He watched her getting ready to leave. She took Jack aside. He saw them walk into the garden, out of earshot. They paused under the shade of a palm tree.

Sarah said briskly to Jack, "I've made extra copies of all the evidence, and I'm taking one set with me. I'll leave all the others here with you and Jacob. I know it's a lot to ask, but if anything happens to me—you know . . . . Could you see that it all gets out? Either through Hilton or through whoever you think." She smiled. "I'm not being melodramatic. Nothing will happen. It's just my little insurance policy. It worked once, and it could work again."

Jack smiled. "If I ever have to do anything, I will. We both know you won't need it, but it's good to have."

They paused as Jacob walked up and demanded to know what all the whispering was about. Sarah laughed. "You and your suspicious mind. I was just thanking Jack for all his help. Nothing wrong with that, is there?"

Jacob squeezed her hand. "No. Of course not. He's a tricky one, but his heart's in the right place."

Jack thumped him lightly on the back and then bustled around, hurrying everyone up. "Come on. Enough of this. She'll miss her flight."

"All right, all right. Just a minute." Jacob took Sarah aside as Jack went to get the car ready. "Listen. I know you're up to something. I also know there's nothing I can do to stop you. But Sarah, please, for my sake if not for your own, be careful. I know you'll be wanting to even the score a bit, see that certain people get what's coming, but it's not worth it if it destroys you. You got away with it once." He raised a hand in mid-air to silence her as she started to speak. "I know. That was different, and you had to —it had been coming so long. But I don't think you can do it again, do you?" He paused, and his voice began to shake very slightly.

"You remember you asked me to stop, a long time ago—to give up my work. And I did. From the day you asked me, I never did another robbery." He paused again and touched her shoulder gently. "I've never asked you for anything, have I, in all those years? But I do now. Be careful, for my sake. And if you have in mind what I think you do, please, don't do it."

Sarah smiled gently, fighting off tears, and took his hand. "Oh, Jacob, there's nothing I wouldn't do for you, you know that. But you needn't worry. Things are a bit different now. I'm not quite as I was then. You're right, I do want revenge, but not in the way you fear. We all think revenge is a bullet in the brain. It doesn't have to be. It can be just a word, a whisper, and the scales can tip. I might not even need to do a thing. They might do it all for themselves."

They looked up, startled, as Jack tooted the horn. They heard him shouting good-naturedly from the car, "Come on, we'll be late!"

Jacob squeezed Sarah's hand in his. "They probably will destroy themselves. So let them, will you?"

She smiled. "Come on. We'd better go."

Two hours later, the men dropped Sarah off at the departure area. Standing stiff and awkward, they said their goodbyes. Sarah hugged them to her and wet their cheeks with kisses and tears. They watched her disappear into the terminal building—this time she was taking a commercial flight—then turned slowly and made their way home.

Sarah was resolute as the plane took off and carried her to London. For a couple of hours she felt numb. Then, as she soared above the Channel, she felt her emotions coming back. Thoughts that she had kept at bay when miles away tumbled through her like a waterfall. She felt she was drowning in pain, love, impossible longings, and despair. She thought of Dante's face, with his eyes fixed on her. They had always had a look of death about them, but even so, she could not imagine them closed forever. And Mosami, for whom in many ways her feelings ran much deeper. The quiet, smiling face, the wisdom, the uncompromising rebellion, all ripped apart. She fought for breath.

The plane touched down at Heathrow with a jolt. Sarah filed out with the other passengers into the arrivals hall. In her hand, firmly gripped, was a large handbag. It contained lipstick, hairbrush, scent, and the usual assortment of female paraphernalia. It also carried a series of videos and cassettes, copies of all her evidence against Catania and Co., and against the governor.

She passed through passport control, collected her baggage, and walked through customs and out into the chattering normality of the concourse. Weaving through the crowds, she made for the tube. She stood on the platform looking around at the brown faces lined with resignation and depression at the end of a holiday. She thought of them all returning to work—doctors, secretaries, solicitors, shop assistants, bankers. She would never return to ICB. Never return to a normal job.

It was too soon for her to try to analyze her feelings, to try to assess the changes that had taken place within her, but some certainties emerged like concrete in quicksand, and that was one of them: the trappings and restraints of a normal life were for her long gone.

The attendant at passport control moved quickly. He had kept her description—tall, beautiful, and brunette—in his mind's eye for days. And when he saw her, sad and wistful-looking, slowly moving toward him in the queue, he felt sure it was her. He had waited, pulse racing, as she approached. He didn't know what it was she was supposed to have done, but it must have been big. She was classified as a top security alert, a category usually reserved for terrorists and the most wanted criminals.

He had almost jumped when she stood before him, offering him her passport with a tentative smile. He had flicked it open with a surge of excitement. It was her: Sarah Jensen. She didn't look like a terrorist or a criminal, but then, the best ones never did. He had smiled, handed back her passport, and pressed a button under his desk. Seconds later a replacement appeared and took over his post. He hurried away to Security and called his contact at Special Branch, setting off a pulse through the network that was waiting and watching for Sarah Jensen.

Bartrop heard the news with a jolt of surprise. So Sarah Jensen had reappeared finally, strolling through the airport like a returning tourist. She had looked, apparently, weary and drawn, but not fearful.

Her demeanor and her casual reappearance were mystifying, suggesting, among other things, that she was no longer in fear for her life. With a bit of luck and some fast work, Special Branch would get a tail on her and follow her from the airport. Soon the rest of the watchers would swing into action. Bartrop had prepared well; several contingencies had been planned in the event of her return. He would get his answers soon. Curious, he waited for the intelligence to filter back.

The tube rumbled into view, jolting Sarah from her thoughts. She got on and stood shoulder to shoulder, hip to hip, with the other passengers jammed into the end compartment. The compacted bodies sticky with sweat and the foul air shut off her mind. Sweat began to drip slowly down her back, and her hair became damp. In a perverse way, she welcomed the discomfort.

At South Kensington she disembarked and fought her way through the lunchtime traffic. Leaving the station, she walked out into blazing sunshine and heat intensified by glass and tarmac. It was one of those rare summer days when London sweltered like the Mediterranean. The streets buckled in the heat, and slabs of concrete paving cracked in two.

With a slippery hand, she carried her case through the streets, stopping at intervals to switch her grip from left to right, ticking off her own personal landmarks as she passed. Onslow Square— an old boyfriend, early mornings sneaking home in last night's clothes. Sydney Street—Catherine Walker's Chelsea Design Studio, for formal outfits. Chelsea Farmers' Market—long gossipy lunches with a gang of girlfriends on "sickies," all playing truant from the office. And the King's Road, with its faded glamour and rambling seediness, irresistible still. With each step her strength returned.

Carlyle Square was a green leafy haven. Sarah turned into it with relief. The ladies who lunch were on their way in high heels and hose, oblivious to the heat. Small dogs snapped at flies, and the square shimmered in the heat. It was hard to imagine a scene of violence exploding behind the elegant facades of the houses. If she had stayed, perhaps not gone away to Geneva that weekend, not gone straight to Dante's house on her return . . . what would have happened? Would she have been killed here, in Carlyle Square, in her home?

She fumbled with the key in the lock, recalling the fear that had almost paralyzed her, along with grief, but stronger, when she learned of the murders of her two friends. The key turned. Taking shallow breaths, she opened the door and walked in, eyes careening along her hallway.

The hall was empty. The whole house seemed to be sleeping in the sun. The silence was complete.

A pile of mail lay in a heap by the wall, swept there by the door. Strange . . . she hadn't felt the weight of its resistance as she opened the door. A vague sense of unease gripped her. She dropped her case in the hall and walked upstairs to the sitting room.

It was empty. The whole house was empty. She went through it room by room. Sunlight filled it. And silence. She returned to the sitting room, sat in an armchair, hugged her knees to her chest, and cried. She sat there, immobile, for a few minutes, until the phone rang. She got up slowly to answer it. There was silence for a few seconds, then she heard the sound of the receiver being replaced. She put the phone down and returned to her chair. She sat there for half an hour, then glanced around her, went downstairs, picked up her keys, and went out, searching for noise, bustle, and life.

She walked up the King's Road, looking in shop windows. Her head began to pound. She walked into the chemists' to get some Nurofen. Another woman came up to the counter. She turned to Sarah and spoke very quietly. The voice was low, the accent vaguely American.

"My name is Christine Villiers. I need to talk to you."

Sarah turned sharply and studied the woman beside her. She was about five-foot-four, strong-limbed and striking. She had a broad, well-defined face with a strong jaw, a slightly Roman nose, high cheekbones, and large, wide-set blue eyes. Her full lips were painted red. The richness of the features was offset by an austere hairstyle, long blond hair drawn up into a high ponytail. It was an unusual combination. Her coloring was northern European, her features Italian. She was about thirty. She wore a short straight sleeveless cream dress with high heels. She was smiling broadly, infectiously. Involuntarily, Sarah smiled back. The woman spoke again.

"Please, act normal. Pretend that I'm your friend. Let's just walk up the road together, find a café. Then we can talk."

Sarah paid for her Nurofen. "Just tell me, out of curiosity. Why should I?"

"Because of Dante and Mosami and Giancarlo Catania."

Sarah felt her body stiffen. Oddly, she felt no fear. She felt instinctively that this woman, though dangerous, was no threat to her. What she felt was curiosity, anticipation.

"All right. Lead the way."

The two women walked out of the chemists' and up the street.

Christine talked about the weather, about the contents of the shop windows they passed—anything to make it look as if she and Sarah were old, comfortable friends. They headed for the Café Rouge, at World's End. They found a table in the middle of the café, which was noisy, almost full. Christine glanced around a few times, apparently casually. They both ordered cappuccinos. Sarah sipped hers and waited for Christine to speak.

Christine looked across the table at Sarah, her eyes empty of emotion.

"I killed Dante Scarpirato."

Sarah nodded. "I guessed as much."

"He would have killed himself anyway, sooner or later."

"Probably."

"I am sorry."

"You were the bullet. Somebody else pulled the trigger."

"I was supposed to kill you, too, but the contract was canceled last night."

"So what are you doing here now?"

"I figured that with the contract lifted, you would come home. I wanted to talk to you. I was curious. The man who took out the contract doesn't change his mind without very good reasons. That kind of information, whatever it is that you know, can be worth a great deal to me and my friends." The eyes narrowed and the friendly smile disappeared. "I want to know why the contract was canceled."

Sarah sipped her cappuccino and thought for a while. "Assuming I knew, why should I tell you?"

"I might be able to help you. And let's face it, you could do with a few friends."

"Why? Do I have any more hidden enemies?"

Christine leaned across the narrow table. "Your house is being watched round the clock. There's a young couple dressed like a pair of tourists sitting on the pavement eating sandwiches, a technician in a BT van, and an old man in a Panama hat reading a book in the garden. I saw ten of them in a week. Professional, but still easy to spot, if you know what to look for." She paused, letting it sink in. "And they've bugged you."

Sarah stared at her in horror.

"Of course, I can't be sure about that. But I saw them breaking in. They picked your locks very efficiently. Nobody watching would have thought it a break-in." She shrugged. "Anyway, it's a fair assumption they've bugged you. Any surveillance team worth its salt would bug your house."

Sarah remembered the pile of mail pushed up against the wall. She began to feel a sense of claustrophobia, and rage.

"Who do you think it might be?" asked Christine.

Sarah shrugged. She had no intention of telling Christine about her relationship with Barrington or her suspicions about MI5.

"The police, I suppose. My colleague and my best friend are murdered, then I disappear. You can see why they might be just a little bit interested in me, can't you?"

Christine nodded. "I can. So what's it to be?"

Sarah studied the woman opposite her. A plan began to form in her mind.

"Why should I have anything to do with you?"

"I could do a lot for you."

"What makes you so sure I couldn't do it myself?"

Christine sat back and stared at Sarah. She was silent for a few seconds, then asked slowly and softly, "You think you could?"

Sarah didn't answer. She just smiled.

After a while, Christine leaned back across the table toward Sarah. "Maybe you could, but that still doesn't change my point."

"Which is?"

"We could do a lot more together."

"We probably could." Sarah thought for a while, and her own words came back to her: just a word, just a whisper, and the scales could tip. She smiled at Christine. "All right. I'll tell you."

Half an hour later, the two women parted. Sarah watched Christine slip away through the crowded tables and out of sight. Then she walked home, resisting the urge to look for the watchers. She let herself into her house and glanced around. She wondered if whoever was listening could hear her moving about. She walked into the bathroom, dropped her clothes onto the floor, and stepped into the shower. She stood in the pulsating stream of water, slowly arching her body to catch the powerful jets at all points of tension. She switched the dial from hot to cold and back to hot again, flooding her skin with sensation.

She thought about Christine. She was intrigued and repulsed by her. What had started her off as a killer? She hadn't asked. She tried instead to inhabit Christine's mind. She recalled the eyes behind the smile. They were uncompromising, without emotion, the moral faculties long corroded.

There was no doubt or conscience in Christine's cool blue eyes. She made no apologies for her bloody occupation. She seemed to feel sorry for those close to her victims, but not for the victims themselves, whom she regarded with disdain, as if they deserved what they got. Was she a psychopath, or had it started with something personal, a mission, killing with a cause?

Had she perhaps killed out of revenge, then found that she liked it, was good at it? A Rubicon once crossed, never to be recrossed?

Sarah shuddered. Christine was repugnant but still strangely attractive. She had a force of personality that drew you in. Sarah was not immune. And now she found herself waiting, drops of water from the shower mingling with perspiration as she sat on the sofa naked, thinking of Dante and Mosami.

Bartrop received a preliminary report half an hour after Sarah returned home, and updates as news came in. A Special Branch officer had tailed her from the airport. She had taken the tube, he reported; she seemed preoccupied but not uneasy, let alone fearful. He had followed her to her house, where the watchers had taken over.

The watchers reported that an hour after arriving home she had gone out, to the chemists'. There she had met someone she seemed to know. An attractive blonde. A full description was given. The two women went to a café for half an hour and then parted. Sarah Jensen returned home. The blonde they had lost. They hadn't had enough people to watch both her and Jensen. One of the watchers had tried to tail the blonde but had failed.

Bartrop cursed with annoyance. A coincidental meeting, an hour after arriving home? Unlikely. Descriptions of the blonde were checked against files, without success. So far she remained unidentified.

Since Jensen had arrived home, she had made no further contacts. There were two bugs in the house, voice activated, one in the sitting room, one in the telephone. Since her arrival, both had been silent.

Christine ducked in and out of shops, front entrances and back, taking side roads, evading the tail she knew would be following her. When she was certain she was alone, she headed home. She didn't have much time to get organized. It was lucky that Sarah lived close by. She let herself into her flat and ran upstairs to the study.

Sarah's revelations reverberated in her head like a time bomb, ticking on a short fuse. Christine sat, still and quiet, composing herself, trying to impose order and logic on fraying thoughts and myriad possibilities fraught with danger. Excitement, fear, anticipation, and the quiet, deeply seductive pleasure of incipient action coursed through her like a drug. She sat savoring the sensations, plotting, planning, weighing up odds, predicting outcomes, holding life and death in balance until she decided. Whom would she betray? Whom support? What contingencies could she consider? Where did her own interests lie? She was no dispassionate outsider—the consequences of her hurried calculations and the course to which, in the next few minutes, she must commit could prove fatal to her and Sarah Jensen. Yet those same consequences would be impossible to predict with any certainty until she had committed herself irrevocably to a single course and it was too late to change. So she would decide, as always, by that combination of logic and instinct that made her one of the most dangerous and inspired contract killers in the world.

She smiled as the decision came to her, then reached for the telephone and called Antonio Fieri, hoping that he would be there, that she wouldn't have to carry out her plan without his sanction.

Fieri answered on the fifth ring.

Christine, respectful, apologized for disturbing him and explained that the matter was urgent. She told him about Catania and the London conspiracy. Then she told him about the contracts that Catania had authorized and she had carried out. Fieri erupted at this point and asked her why she hadn't told him at the time.

She answered coolly but forcefully. "There was no reason to tell you then. From what I understood, it didn't concern you. But things have changed. I picked up more information. I have strong suspicions that Catania might be in a position to compromise you."

Fieri was silent for a while, then asked her what she proposed to do about it.

"Depends on what you would like me to do. But as it happens, I have an opportunity tonight . . . I could clear things up here very easily."

Again there was a long silence. Christine sat, waiting calmly. Finally he spoke. "I had heard rumblings. You have evidence, you say . . ."

"Compelling."

"From where?"

Christine had anticipated this question and gave him her prepared answer. "From a supremely reliable, well-placed source who has every interest in presenting us with the truth."

"Reliable?"

"Absolutely. You have my word on that."

"And as you see it, there's a real danger that Catania will compromise me?"

"He already has."

"All right. You take care of things. You'll get the usual rate. The same again for the information. Call me when it's done."

Chapter
Twenty-eight

At seven o'clock Sarah dressed: jeans, white T-shirt, and her favorite worn-out Timberland boots. The jeans, normally tight, hung loose over her hips. She threaded a plaited leather belt through the hooks and cinched in the waist.

Outside, the heat of the day still shimmered on the streets. It pricked her skin. She walked into the kitchen, boots squeaking on the marble tiles. She emptied half a tray of ice into a tall glass and filled it with whisky, which she forced down in three gulps. She poured a second and sipped it slowly, watching the ice melt.

At seven-fifteen the phone rang. After three rings the answerphone clicked on. A soft voice, hard edges, the trace of an American accent: Christine. A mechanical clicking indicated that the call was being made from a phone booth. "It was good to see you today. Hope we can get together soon. Perhaps have a drink sometime." The agreed code. Christine hung up.

Sarah rewound the tape and erased the message. The tape ran on unchecked for a few seconds, revealing the remnants of an old message. She recoiled, her face contorted, as a familiar halting voice spoke to her. It was Dante, asking her to call him, telling her he had missed her and wanted to see her soon. Her stomach lurched, and the burning taste of whisky rose to her mouth. She slammed her fist on the stop button, nearly splintering the machine. Her finger trembled on the rewind button. She listened to his voice for the last time. The pain and guilt were like spurs. Then she erased his message, and her doubts.

Scooping up her jacket and baseball cap from the coat stand in the hall, she went to turn off the radio. The first bars of a familiar song drifted across to her. INXS was playing "Suicide Blonde." She laughed out loud, the sound bouncing off the walls of the empty house. Then she switched off the radio and left.

A few hundred yards away, Christine came out of the phone booth and hurried down the street. She passed unobtrusively through the crowds thronging the King's Road. People glanced at her briefly, if at all. They registered little—a blonde with a nice body, possibly a pretty face, though it was hard to tell since she wore a baseball cap pulled down low. She walked purposefully, but unselfconsciously, and kept her eyes straight ahead. She was inconspicuous, unmemorable, unhindered, just as she liked it. She turned a corner and headed for the white van.

It was parked in a side street off Chelsea Green, about ten minutes' walk from her flat. It was a Ford Transit, the kind plumbers used. It was begging for someone to write "Clean Me" with a finger in the thick coating of dust. Its windows were tinted, but otherwise it was unremarkable. It was one of a pack of white Transits that roamed the streets anonymously every day.

Daniel Corda had stolen it six months ago, to order. He had resprayed it, changed the plates, matched it to the logbook of another, legitimate van, and sold it to Christine. A contingency car, he called it.

Christine hadn't gone near it in all that time, except to check that it was still there. She had kept it for an assignment like this. She turned the key in the lock, swung open the door, and jumped in. She was carrying a small backpack, which she locked inside the glovebox, and a plastic bag containing jeans, black T-shirt, and sneakers, an outfit identical to the one she was wearing. She threw the bag onto the passenger seat, strapped herself in, and then, with a quick prayer to fortune, turned the key in the ignition. The engine caught first time. Checking her mirror, she carefully pulled away.

She drove through Chelsea into the cruising streets of Earl's Court, turned left into the blue haze of the Cromwell Road, and went out onto the M4. She passed Heathrow with its legions of jumbo jets hanging in the air. Another twenty minutes and the factories and superstores gave way to open country, hedgerowed fields and farmhouses. She drove in silence, oblivious to all except the road ahead.

She turned off the motorway at Junction 14 and snaked around the exit onto a narrow road. The downs of Upper Lambourn rose above her. Retired thoroughbreds roamed the fields, and children on ponies trotted along the narrow lanes. The smell of drying hay rose from the fields. It was the second cut this year from the rich soil.

She turned onto an unmarked side road. The van lurched down a bumpy track, stones spitting from under its tires. She drove on for five minutes, then turned down a Forestry Commission trail, dusty and deserted. She eased up to a small patch of rough ground shrouded by fir trees. The van disturbed a flock of roosting pigeons, who flew into the sky.

Retrieving the backpack from the glovebox, she opened the door and stepped out onto spongy ground covered with pine needles. She glanced around and stood still for a few minutes, listening. She was quite alone, save for the birds, who gradually returned from the sky to their roosts, their excited chatter easing into soporific cooing. Satisfied, she locked up the van and set off through the trees. She strode, her paces long and easy over the rough ground. The pigeons watched her go: a young hiker out for an evening jaunt.

The setting sun filtered through the canopy of pine trees, dyeing everything orange. It flickered across Christine's face as she disappeared and reappeared in the maze of trees. The forest grew denser as she walked, screening her. After half an hour she felt invisible.

Deeper in the forest, the light grew weak. Christine checked her watch. In less than an hour it would be dark. She quickened her pace. She didn't have much time.

As the light thinned out, she came to the edge of the forest. The trees gave way to a small valley. At the center of the valley, about a quarter-mile away, was a large stone house. The only signs of life were two Mercedes, a black saloon and a red convertible, parked in front of the house at the top of a circular drive.

Christine smiled to herself and walked down the hill toward the house.

Karl Heinz Kessler sat in the study of his country house counting out money. Wads of notes sealed in tight plastic pouches lay in a heap in front of him. In each pouch there was £10,000. He counted out fifty wads, slapping them down on the table. His face was set in a mask of controlled annoyance, as if he were performing an irksome but necessary task. It was an inconvenience, really, sitting here counting out money like some bank teller, waiting around for one of Catania's lackeys to come and relieve him of his money.

Catania's instructions had been explicit: a courier would come to pick up payment for the Scarpirato and Matsumoto contracts —a million pounds in used notes. Catania himself would pay part of the contract, but it was only fair that Kessler should contribute, no? Nobody except Kessler was to see the courier come and go.

Kessler had followed his instructions meticulously. He had sent his wife to stay with her parents in Frankfurt, and he'd given the staff a night off. And he'd raised the money, with a contribution from Matthew Arnott.

He turned to Arnott, who was standing by his side fidgeting, watching him count out the money.

"Now your turn."

Arnott hadn't asked what the payment was for. Kessler laughed at his evasion. Arnott knew what was going on. His refusal to admit it increased Kessler's disdain for him. Arnott picked up the briefcase lying by his feet and put it down on the desk in front of Kessler, who opened it and smiled. It was filled with wads of money, £10,000 in each wad, bound by paper ribbons. Kessler began to count. He removed fifty wads, closed the briefcase, and gave it back to Arnott.

"Don't look so glum. You got off lightly, all things considered."

"Glum? How am I supposed to look?" said Arnott. "You ring me and order me, with no explanation, to bring you half a million pounds in two days. And you sit there counting it out as if it's for a house, a painting, a little investment—cool and calm, as if everything's fine. It's not. It's a fucking nightmare. And what makes you think we've got off? The police have been to see me five times, asking the same questions over and over."

Kessler swung round in his chair and stared hard at Arnott. Arnott waved his hand in the air.

"Don't worry. I've stuck to the party line. I've played my part all right. But I can't stand it anymore. I can't sleep, I can hardly eat . . . I'm thinking of going back to America."

"Don't be a fucking idiot!" shouted Kessler. "That's all they need." He glared up at Arnott. "You will stay at ICB, act like the bereaved colleague, work, keep Carla in line, enjoy your money carefully. If you want to go back in two years when it's all a bad memory, fine. But for the time being you stay put, and for God's sake, stop whining."

Kessler stood up and sat on the edge of his desk, facing Arnott. He spoke more quietly now, with a tight, pinched-lipped control.

"What the hell did you expect? All this was inevitable, from the day Jensen discovered us. She made it necessary. Catania saw that. And I stand by what he did. It's too late to be getting squeamish now. How much have you made, Matthew? Thirty million dollars? Risk-return—the banker's maxim. And don't stare at me as if I'm some kind of monster. I'm fifty-five years old, the chairman of one of the most prestigious banks in the City. I have everything I could possibly want. Do you think I'd let that go, let it be destroyed by Sarah Jensen, or Scarpirato, or Matsumoto?" He leaned closer to Arnott. "We had no choice. They had to be killed. Catania's done it—that was convenient for us. But if he hadn't, I would not have hesitated."

Arnott stared at him in horror. For a while he said nothing.

He turned and sat down in an armchair at the side of Kessler's desk.

"But Sarah Jensen isn't dead, is she? She could still expose all this, and we'd be charged with murder."

Kessler snorted. "Jensen won't say a word. Catania told me he did some kind of deal with her."

Arnott stared blankly at Kessler, who laughed. "Take my word for it, Jensen is not a problem. She'll probably go off somewhere, have a nervous breakdown, and we'll never hear from her again." He glanced at his watch. "You'd better go. The courier will be here in a minute."

Arnott picked up his empty briefcase and began to walk toward the door.

"Oh, and Matthew. For God's sake, keep it together. It's all in our hands now. If we keep cool, there'll be no more problems." Kessler got up from his desk and walked up to Arnott. He stood in the doorway, barring Arnott's exit. Smiling, he added, "Don't forget, Catania has shown his hand, shown what he can do if he has to. He won't hesitate to act again if he thinks it necessary." He took a step closer to Arnott. "Do you understand what I'm saying?"

Arnott stared into the cold, dark eyes almost mocking him. "Yes," he answered faintly. "I understand."

Kessler smiled and stood aside. Arnott walked quickly from the room and out of the house. He got into his red Mercedes and drove off. His eyes, slightly glazed, stared straight ahead. He didn't notice the woman crouching in the gardens thirty feet away.

Kessler bundled up the wads of notes and dropped them in a plastic bag. He closed the library door behind him and walked down the long hallway, his shoes clicking on the wooden floors. Passing a mirror, he stopped to check his reflection. The floor creaked behind him. The smile froze on his face.

He turned, gripped by apprehension. A woman was standing in the hallway. She was blond, pale-skinned, muscular in a tight black T-shirt. A baseball cap cast a pall over her features. She would have been beautiful but for the look on her face, the mocking disdain in the curve of her lips, the grim determination in her eyes. She seemed impervious to all around her, save him. She was looking at him, the whole force of her being focused on him, as if she were a weapon aimed right at him. But what was most disconcerting was the lips, the smile. He couldn't understand that smile; it seemed at the same time bitter and pitying. Fear was not a familiar emotion to Kessler, but he felt it now, corroding his skin. He took refuge, as always, in aggression and bombast.

"Who the hell are you and how did you get in here?" he roared, his voice echoing down the hall.

Christine carried on smiling. "Oh, I just slipped through the front door. You'd left it open. Very thoughtful of you." Her voice was low and contemptuous. Hostility poured out of her.

Kessler said nothing. His unease deepened. His arrogance deserted him, and he started to sweat. Dark stains appeared down the sides of his pink City shirt. There was something sinister about this woman. He glanced at his watch. Catania's messenger boy would be here in a minute. Nobody was supposed to see them together. He began, unbelievably, to panic. He felt ridiculous. Anger reasserted itself. Why on earth should he feel afraid? He took a step forward, toward the woman.

Christine's lips curled into a snarl. "Stay where you are. I haven't finished yet." Something in her voice made him stop, uncertain.

"Your little contract, yours and Catania's. It's incomplete, isn't it?"

Kessler tilted his head slightly, and his eyes widened with recognition. "You're the courier?"

Christine laughed out loud. "Courier?" Catania's little joke, she supposed. "Courier, messenger—yes, if you like."

Kessler's shoulders sagged with relief. "Why didn't you say? Look, I've got the money here." He held up the plastic bag. "Take it!" He was regaining control now, and his voice resumed its arrogant sharpness.

"Oh, I will. But I've got a message to deliver first."

Kessler looked puzzled.

"As I was saying, the contract is incomplete. Sarah Jensen is still alive."

Kessler became impatient now. "Yes. I already know that. But as I understand it, she's no longer a problem."

Christine smiled, humoring him. "On the contrary. She's been most helpful." The smile vanished and the voice took on a deadly softness. "The contract on her is off. It's been replaced." She took a step closer. "By one on you." She watched his face contort with panic.

"We've got to talk about this. You've got it wrong."

She laughed bitterly. "No, Kessler. You've got it wrong. You thought you were so smart, didn't you? You and Catania had it all worked out. Well, I hate to tell you, but Sarah Jensen outsmarted you both. Did you really think she would let you and Catania get away with killing her best friend and her lover, and with trying to kill her?"

"I didn't kill them."

"No, you didn't. I did, effectively. But it all amounts to the same thing. You and Catania wanted them dead, took out the contracts. If it hadn't been me, it would have been someone else.

As far as Jensen is concerned, you and Catania pulled the trigger."

Christine pulled the gun from behind her back and pointed it at Kessler's forehead. He raised his hands. His mouth opened in silent protest. She locked both hands on the cold metal and pulled the trigger. The bullet crashed into Kessler's forehead. The mirror behind him turned red. Kessler fell to the floor. In a second a lifetime was undone.

Christine walked up to the oozing corpse and stared down at it. There was so much blood. There was always so much blood. And the smell, always that smell, prehistoric, electrifying. The hairs on the nape of her neck stood on end.

A plastic bag lay at the feet of the body. It spilled out notes. A red stream ran toward it. With gloved hands, Christine picked it up. She took off her backpack and thrust the gun deep inside, with the notes on top. Her heart hammering, she walked down the hall and out through the back door.

Resisting the urge to run, she walked across the gravel drive and up to the wooden fence. She vaulted over it and began the trek across the narrow field to the forest. The wall of trees spread out before her. From two hundred yards it looked impenetrable and featureless. It would be difficult to pick her way back in the dusk. She quickened her pace and began to jog. Branches whipped her face. Twice she stumbled. She didn't feel the pain of torn skin and knees smashing into roots and stones.

She was sweating heavily as she approached the clearing where the van was parked. Stopping in the trees, she tried to silence her labored breathing. She peered into the darkness. The clearing was deserted. She ran over to the van, took off her backpack, and retrieved the ignition key. She unlocked the doors at the back of the van. Putting down her backpack, she retrieved the cash and counted out £400,000. She placed the plastic wallets of money in a separate bag, which she hid, along with her pack, under a pile of newspapers. She relocked the doors, hurried round to the driver's door, jumped in, and accelerated away.

When she looked down at her torn jeans and bloody knees, she cursed loudly. The jeans would have to be burned. There was nothing she could do about the traces of torn denim and specks of blood on the roots and stones in the forest. Perhaps it would rain and wash away the blood. Christine looked at the clear skies and frowned.

She drove straight from Lambourn to a secluded farmhouse in West Sussex that belonged to Daniel Corda. She parked in front of the house. Corda heard the engine and the crunch of wheels on stone and came out to meet her. He raised a questioning eyebrow. Christine nodded. "So far, so good." She retrieved her pack, took out the pistol, her Browning automatic, and the Ruger she had used on Dante, placed them in a plastic bag, and handed them to Corda.

"Dispose of these, would you?"

He took the bag and nodded. She reached under the newspapers and took out the bag containing the £400,000.

"Your share."

He smiled, thanked her politely, took the money and the pistols into his house, and locked them in his safe. Then he went back outside, drove the van into a garage, and locked it up.

Inside the house, Christine changed into the spare outfit she had brought with her. She bundled her clothes and the old sneakers into a plastic bag and handed them to Corda when he returned.

"Burn these, would you?"

He nodded. He retrieved the guns from the safe and took them outside, together with Christine's bag of clothes, to a small furnace set into one of his outbuildings. He had lit the furnace in anticipation. Christine followed and stood behind him. When he opened the furnace doors, she felt the blast of heat, saw a blaze of amber-red within. She watched him feed the clothes and shoes in one by one, then the pistols. The clothes would burn in seconds. In under an hour, the pistols would melt into a lumpen mass, which he would retrieve when cool and throw into the sea.

He closed the door and led Christine to another outbuilding, where a red Ford Mondeo was parked. He handed her the keys and watched her disappear into the night.

Tomorrow he would take the van to a junkyard belonging to a friend of his. The van would be turned into a hunk of metal one foot square. As a clue to a murder, it wouldn't exist.

Sarah returned home just before nine. She strolled through Carlyle Square, enjoying the evening air. She loved hot summer nights, the lingering light, the smell of lush foliage, dust, and the metallic rasp of exhaust fumes. She stopped before her house as Johnny, the neighborhood tomcat, appeared from the garden and demanded attention. He rolled over onto his back, wriggling back and forth, stirring up a mini-dust flurry. Sarah laughed and stooped to stroke him. He leapt to his feet, preened, and tangled himself around her legs. After five minutes she disengaged herself, bid the cat goodnight, and disappeared into her house. Out of the corner of her eye she saw the profile of a man sitting in a car parked in the corner of the square.

She had given them an easy time tonight, her watchers. She had taken a walk in Battersea Park, strolling through early evening joggers, cricketers, footballers, pedestrians, and boules players. Then she returned to the King's Road, bought a handful of magazines at the Europa, on the corner of Old Church Street, and headed to the Café Rouge for a solitary supper with *Vogue*,

Vanity Fair, The Economist, and the watchers. There were two of them, young women about her age, chatting and smiling, looking not quite carefree. They stood in a queue, waiting to be seated. Sarah kept her eyes on her magazines as, after a discreet but predictable argument with the waiter, the watchers walked past to their table, three feet away from hers.

The waiter appeared, brandishing a menu. Sarah took her time to choose, gave her order, changed it twice, then settled down to enjoy an excellent bouillabaisse, followed by grilled entrecote and french fries washed down by a glass of champagne and half a bottle of house red.

As she sat at her table eating, pretending to read, her thoughts drifted. They were still chaotic, treacherous, and impervious to her attempts to control them. She brooded for a while on Eddie and Alex, long banished from her thoughts. How could she tell them about what had happened? How much should she tell them? Nothing. She wanted to keep them separate, part of a different life. It was too early to think of them now, to get them mixed up in her mind with everything else.

Her thoughts turned to Christine. Should she have dealt with her? Should she trust her? Logic and common sense said no. Instinct said yes.

Christine had been right. She needed friends, however unorthodox, and Christine could help her. Sarah wondered what Christine was doing now, and how she might be using her information. It was valuable, yes, but would it pay off? And for whom?

Sarah had been the catalyst. She could do nothing now but wait. And as for trusting Christine, she had her insurance policy —the package lodged with Jacob and Jack. If it made sense to kill Kessler and Catania, it made sense to keep her alive.

But she would have to wait a while for her proof—bloody proof. She sighed heavily. It disgusted her, but it was the only way. At least this time, if her calculations were correct, someone else would be administering justice. Did that make it better or worse? She didn't know. But she was sure of one thing: she couldn't have done it herself this time.

She shook herself and called for her bill, raising her voice so that her watchers would hear. She took her time settling it so that they too might prepare to leave, and left behind a big tip and a cheery goodbye for the assembled waiters. Nobody who crossed Sarah's path that evening would forget the experience. Should she need them, she would have alibis in droves.

The grandfather clock in the hallway was just striking nine as she walked into her house. It finished, and there was silence. Sarah walked through the hall, up the stairs, into the sitting room, and stood, motionless. The sound of the streets outside, the clock, and then the silence weighed on her. She sat down, picked up a magazine, put it down, and turned to the telephone. For a while she just stared at it. She couldn't call Jacob—she was sure Christine was right and the phone was bugged. She couldn't call Eddie or Alex—they were beyond the reach of telephones. Anyway, she wasn't even sure what she'd say to them. And most of all, she couldn't call Mosami or Dante.

She touched the telephone, then withdrew her hand. She sat very still, looking around the room, feeling trapped, powerless. She couldn't know whether the events she hoped she had set in motion had taken place, would not know for some time. But even if they had happened, were happening now, it was not enough. There was still so much unconfronted, unsaid. The noise in her head was unbearable. Words kept spinning round her mind. She had the same conversations with herself a hundred times, till the words echoed through her sleep. Trapped words, trapping her.

Suddenly she got up, reached into a cupboard, took out a telephone directory, and looked up an address. Then she dropped the directory on the floor and walked downstairs and out to her car. She drove off slowly, glancing in the mirror, smiling grimly. Let the watchers follow.

Ten minutes later she stood before the entrance to Matthew Arnott's house in Holland Park. She rang the bell and waited. After about half a minute Arnott appeared. He opened the door and stared at her in surprise, gaping.

"What do you want?"

She smiled and stepped over the threshold. "I want to talk. What do you think? That I've come to blow your brains out?" She laughed at the look on his face. "You needn't worry, I'm not armed. You're not worth the effort."

She walked through the hall into the sitting room and sat down in an armchair. Arnott followed her and took a seat opposite her. She watched his awkward, jerky movements. He looked strung out, his nerves on a hair trigger. She sat back.

"You look rough, Arnott. Is it all beginning to get to you—beating up Mosami, killing her, killing Dante, dealing with Kessler and Catania, fending off the police? Can't be much fun. Bet you didn't expect it to end like this, did you, when you first started? Whose idea was it, anyway? Kessler's?" She watched him nod feebly. "Yes, I didn't think it was yours. You were just in the right place at the right time. Only now it looks more like the wrong time, doesn't it? Bet you wish you could just stop it all, get out." She got up and walked toward him. He looked up at her and began to fiddle compulsively with his watch.

"So why didn't you, eh? Why didn't you try to get out when you knew that people were going to be killed? And don't tell me you didn't know. You might have taken a back seat, but you could still see what was going on, couldn't you? But it was easier to be passive, to pretend to yourself that there was nothing you could do." She stood feet from him, her body rigid. "You could have warned me about Catania. You could have told me what he was likely to do. I had no idea at the time that he would resort to killing people. But you could have told me, and I could have stopped it. Or you could have told the police. But you said nothing, and Dante and Mosami are dead, and you share responsibility for that."

She was silent for a long time. Then suddenly she laughed. "It's pathetic. The irony is that you, Carla, and Kessler, you thought you were so powerful, so frightening, didn't you? But all along, your power came from someone else. You just happened to get lucky. Catania had an affair with Carla, started to give her a few inside tips as pillow talk, and before he knew it the whole thing was taped on video and he was being forced to hand over the really juicy inside information—all the big currency operations, the interest-rate movements. He only did it to keep you quiet. He was never frightened of you. He just had to keep you quiet. The thing you didn't know is that he could not afford for a whisper to get out, for him to be seen to be compromised. You see, the people he was really working with would have put a bullet through his brain, no questions asked. He feared them, not you." She sat on the edge of a table near him and smiled. "You know who they are?"

He shook his head, silenced by her torrent of words and the tone in her voice.

"The Mafia. That's who. Someone called Antonio Fieri, a Mafia boss, Catania's boss." She got to her feet and began to walk away. "By the way, you don't really think you're going to get away with all this, do you? I don't know about you, but I've always believed that what goes around comes around. Catania, Kessler, you, Carla . . . It's just a matter of time."

She walked slowly from the room. At the door she stopped

and turned to look at him one last time. He sat slumped in his chair, all the old arrogance and confidence long gone. He looked as insubstantial as a husk. She felt pity mixed in with her contempt. She let herself out, closing the door gently behind her. Then she got in her car and drove home.

She felt empty, purged, utterly exhausted. She lay down on her bed and switched on the television, turning to *News at Ten*. She just caught the end of the opening theme tune and was arranging the pillows into a more comfortable position when suddenly she paused and turned to face the screen.

"Giancarlo Catania, the governor of the Bank of Italy, has been assassinated. Reports are still coming in, but it appears that Catania was leaving a restaurant in Rome with his wife and two friends when a motorcycle carrying two people roared up and the pillion passenger opened fire. Catania was hit several times and is believed to have died instantly. However, his bodyguards returned fire, killing the gunman and seriously wounding the driver of the motorcycle. The bodyguards apprehended the driver, who is now in the hospital under police guard. Speculation, as usual, turns to the Mafia, but so far there has been no indication as to why Governor Catania was shot."

The rest of the words passed in a blur. Sarah sat very still, cocooned in her exhaustion as, almost mechanically, events moved toward resolution. If her calculations and suspicions were correct, Catania's would not be the only violent death this evening.

Two miles away, in his house in Holland Park, Matthew Arnott sat cross-legged on the floor in front of his television and listened to the news. He sat for hours into the night, swaying slightly before the television screen. Even when the programs had finished and the screen went blank, he sat swaying in the flickering darkness, his body sweating, his eyes dead.

It was nearly twelve when Christine arrived home, exultant and exhausted. She called Fieri. The instant he answered the phone, she knew that something was wrong. He was curt, cryptic. He told her to read the newspapers, advised her to go on holiday for a while. She told him everything was fine on her end, wondering what the hell had gone wrong at his. He said "Good" but seemed not to care. He said he had to go, he was in the middle of a meeting. Almost as an afterthought, he added "Well done" and said that the usual arrangements would be made. Then he was gone.

Christine turned on the television and switched frantically from channel to channel. At twelve o'clock she heard the news on CNN. Catania had been murdered. The assassin was dead, his accomplice apprehended. When the newscaster mentioned the name of the accomplice, Christine really began to panic: Cesare Romagna, an old Fieri hand, an intimate, who had been used on a number of sensitive hits and had worked on several occasions with Christine. If he talked—and there was always a chance he would turn *pentito*—she and Fieri would be destroyed. She could only pray that he would hold his tongue, or that Fieri would get to him first. It was worth a try; he had nothing to lose. That is what he was probably discussing now in his late-night meeting. But even so, the risk to Christine was unacceptable. Quickly, methodically, she began to pack.

She had a hideout in Rio, bought four years ago for such a time as this. She finished packing, then stood for a long while in the shower, letting the hot water stream over her. She dressed and poured herself a large brandy. She sat in silence, in the dark in her study, planning. She would catch the first flight to Rio, leaving the following evening. She stayed up all night waiting, listening to news reports.

She wondered if Sarah Jensen had heard the news and how she would react. There was no way of knowing. Any contact was impossible, potentially incriminating. But either way, Jensen was a risk. She had shown herself quite willing to play dangerous games. So far, it had suited Christine to cooperate. They had done a deal, and at the time it had seemed tilted heavily in Christine's favor. Jensen had exchanged information, for what? A vague promise of assistance if she needed it. That information, and the events it had triggered, were for a few hours worth over a million pounds to Christine, but now Fieri might never pay, and she might never be free to enjoy her payment. High reward, high risk—she knew that, accepted that. But now it was looking like a poor bargain for her, and an excellent one for Sarah Jensen.

Jensen had secured the downfall of the two men on whom she bitterly wanted revenge, with little risk to herself. All right, at the time Jensen had had no way of knowing that the information she gave would provoke so swift or so bloody a response, nor could she have been sure that Christine wouldn't kill her as soon as she had parted with her secrets. She had taken a calculated risk, and so far as she was concerned, it had paid off. But things had changed. Where did Jensen's interests lie now?

Christine wondered for a moment whether she should have killed her when she had the chance . . .

It was too late to do anything now, and anyway, she didn't think Jensen posed too great a threat. Their interests still coincided—silence, discretion, lies if necessary. She saw in Sarah

Jensen a ferocious instinct of self-preservation. That was her best guarantee of loyalty.

Christine heard a faint sound outside her window. She set down her drink and listened hard. Then she smiled as the sound grew stronger. It had begun to rain, heavily. Blood and skin and fragments of torn denim would wash away.

It was two in the morning, and Bartrop had just heard the news about Catania and was still trying to digest it, when the telephone rang again. It was Special Branch. Karl Heinz Kessler was dead. Bartrop sat stock-still and took in all the details, then asked for an update as information came in.

He walked through his silent house to his study, took a stout glass, and filled it with whisky. He drank it back, put down the glass, and stared out the window into the darkness, slowly and meticulously moving events around in his mind, trying to find the connections. Catania and Kessler dead, Sarah Jensen home and walking around quite confidently, fearlessly. Sarah Jensen dining in a café, establishing a watertight alibi for the time of Kessler's murder. She hadn't done it herself, directly, that much was obvious, but then, she was much too clever for that. But she had done something, Bartrop was sure. He felt again that mixture of anger and admiration that came whenever he learned more of her exploits, of her secrets. Her actions, sometimes so inconvenient to him at first glance, generally worked to his purpose. If his suspicions were correct, she had done him a favor. The murders pointed to Fieri. If the motorcycle rider cooperated, they had a fair chance of substantiating that. But what of Sarah's role? She knew something, had done something, made some sort of bargain. But how, and with whom? The axis had shifted in their invisible relationship. It was apparent now that she knew more than he did, was one step ahead—an untenable position.

On Saturday morning, Sarah woke at six. She lay for a while, eyes closed, listening to the sound of birds and the faint hum and surge of early morning traffic. She let the sensations wash over her slowly: sound, smell, the feel of her own bed. She opened her eyes and shifted around. She gazed at the white wall, white linen, pale muslin curtains billowing in the breeze, windows open to a terrace of flowers. The air was cool, moist, with the promise of warmth. It had rained last night, breaking the prickly, suffocating heat.

She sat up in bed and hugged her knees to her chest. She felt, for the first time in weeks, months, the beginning of a fragile calm. Events were moving toward resolution, albeit bloodily. There was little left for her to do. Soon she would be free to pick up what was left of her old life. She felt her energy returning, and suddenly she felt starving. She jumped out of bed, threw on yesterday's clothes, grabbed her keys and bike from the hall, and set off.

One of the few shops open at that time was the misnamed 7-Eleven on Gloucester Road, open twenty-four hours a day. Sarah cycled through the streets, deserted but for a handful of

committed joggers and rubbish collectors doing their rounds.
The shop was empty. She wandered around with a wire basket,
stocking up: eggs, milk, butter, bread, fresh orange juice, newspapers—everything she needed for her favorite breakfast. She
loaded her purchases into her green panniers and cycled home,
taking a winding route, enjoying the early sunshine, the peace,
and the sensation of effortless movement.

Back in her kitchen she set to work, interrupting the task of
cracking eggs to put some music on—k.d. lang, mellow, relaxing,
comforting somehow. She kept the volume low—she didn't want
to wake any neighbors with open windows—and returned to the
kitchen. Her hands sticky with eggs, she beat in flour and a
pinch of salt before submitting the mixture to a quick blast in the
blender. Five minutes later, fresh coffee was brewing on the stove
and pancakes were sizzling in a frying pan.

She looked around her ingredients shelf, finally finding a red,
gold, and black tin of treacle. When she pulled it off the shelf,
she turned it around in her hands, gazing at the picture of a lion
with bees in its dead belly. She read the inscription: "Out of the
strong came forth sweetness." She stopped for a moment as the
memories came. Her mother had made her pancakes with black
treacle as a treat, or to boost her up before exams. Sometimes she
had added a slug of rum; Sarah had been drinking the stuff since
she was four years old. And every time her mother had showed
her the magnificent treacle tin and read the inscription.

Strong and sweet—so long ago. But now, what of everything
else . . . ? How long would that take to wash off? She shook
herself, piled up the pancakes on a plate, carried them on a tray
with the coffee and orange juice to her sitting room, half lay on
the sofa with the newspapers, and began to eat. The treacle
oozed out of the pancakes, running down her fingers. She licked
it off and it was gone.

The phone rang a while later, just as she was stepping out of the shower. She walked, dripping, to her bedroom, sat down on the bed, and picked up the receiver tentatively. It was Barrington, a little earlier than she had anticipated. This time there were no formalities, no transparent small talk.

"I think we had better talk, don't you?"

Sarah turned his tone back on him. It was he who owed her an explanation, not the other way around. "Yes, Governor. I think we had better."

"Someone will come round to see you in half an hour. All right?"

"No, not all right. I'm not going to open my door to anyone who strolls up. And if anyone is coming to see me, it had better be you. Oh, and while you're about it, why don't you bring along your boss, or whoever it is that pulls your strings? Then perhaps I'll get some honest answers. Or is that still too much to hope for?"

There was a long pause. Sarah could imagine Barrington breathing deeply, tempted to make some acid remark but not wanting to be seen to be rattled. Finally he spoke, patiently, laboriously, as if to an unruly child. Sarah had to stop herself from laughing.

"Someone will be with you later this morning, as I say. I'm busy, you're busy, we're all busy."

"Yes, I'm sure it's very inconvenient, having your weekend disturbed, and yes, you have to stall for a while, don't you, Governor? Of course you can't commit him, or is it her, without checking first. So why don't you call me later and tell me what you've managed to arrange?"

"Look, Sarah. I can tell you're angry. I can understand that."

Sarah cut him off. "Understand? No, Governor. I don't think

you could even begin to." Fingers trembling with rage, she hung up and sat down to wait.

Barrington called Bartrop. "She's angry. Wants to see you."

Bartrop's eyebrows shot up in surprise. "What do you mean, wants to see me?"

"Well, not you exactly." Barrington shifted awkwardly in his seat. " 'Whoever's been pulling my strings'—that's how she put it."

Bartrop let out a loud guffaw. "Sorry, Governor. I can just imagine her saying that. So she's angry, is she?"

"Yes, but it's no temper tantrum, so I wouldn't laugh it off if I were you. But she was also very open, blunt, with no pretense, as if the game were up."

Bartrop chuckled softly. "Is that what she thinks?"

"Look, Bartrop, I don't pretend to read her mind, or yours, for that matter. You asked me to telephone her and I've done that. Now I'd rather like to leave it there, if you don't mind."

"No, I don't mind. I think it's better that way. We don't both need to dance attendance."

"You're going to see her?"

"I think it's about time, don't you?"

Barrington smiled to himself. "Well, I wish you luck."

"Will you telephone her again and tell her that someone will be on his way?"

"Telephone her yourself. I'm not your messenger boy."

Five minutes later Bartrop was in his car, Munro at the wheel, heading for Carlyle Square. He arrived just before ten. He told

Munro to wait, stepped out of the car, and walked up to Sarah Jensen's house. He gazed at the facade. He knew she was in; the watchers were giving him regular updates on her movements. He paused a few seconds before ringing the bell.

He was curious. He wanted to prepare himself to distill his first impressions. He knew what she looked like—he had seen the surveillance photographs and video recordings—but most important, he had never seen her in the flesh, never seen her animated, watched her think, react, move. She was still an enigma to him. He had spent hours dissecting what he knew of her character. He had learned that she possessed a bizarre mixture of qualities, each of an intensity that alone would have defined a character. But they combined in her to produce a dizzying complexity. She was extreme in so many ways, so many conflicting ways, it was a wonder she was not pulled apart. But it seemed rather that the extremes provided a balance, albeit tenuous, demanding.

No wonder she sought security and stability with Jacob Goldsmith, her brother, her boyfriend. It was as if she knew that if she allowed one part of her life to tip out of balance, the other parts would have to swing wildly to compensate. If his theory was correct, and it was solidly based, extreme events in her life forged extreme reactions. That was what made her so dangerous, and so valuable. But there were other conflicting currents. She combined a self-destructive streak with an acute instinct for self-preservation. Above all, she was unpredictable.

Bartrop rang the doorbell.

Sarah heard the bell, looked out, saw a black Rover with a man in the driver's seat parked outside the house and another man standing on the steps before her door. Flunky and official, she de-

cided. Special Branch, the Met, the intelligence services of Jacob's theories? She studied the man on the steps—tall, straight-
backed, confident; brown hair swept back; distinguished; slim;
powerful stance. She couldn't see the face, he was standing too
close. All she got was the top of his head. Like the man she was
studying, she felt a surge of curiosity. *Whatever he is, let him not be
like Barrington, weak, evasive, and impotent. Let him be a target, solid,
unyielding.* She went downstairs and opened the door.

The man stretched out his hand. "James Bartrop. A friend of
Anthony Barrington's."

Sarah took his hand, returned the handshake with equal force.
"You'd better come in." She moved to lead him through the open
door.

He stayed still. "If you don't mind, I'd rather we talked in the
car." It was an instruction, not even couched as a request.

Sarah paused for a second, looking at the car and back to him.
"All right, just give me a minute." She went upstairs and collected
her handbag and the micro-recorder Jacob had given her, which
she switched on and hid in the handbag. She came back downstairs, picked up her keys, and locked the door behind her. Bartrop led her to the car. She was about to get in when Mrs.
Jardine appeared.

"Sarah, good gracious, you're back."

"I am. By the way, Mrs. Jardine, this man here says his name is
Mr. Bartrop, James Bartrop. He claims to be an estate agent
taking me to look at a house. So just in case I don't reappear,
remember the name and the face, won't you?" She said it lightly,
with a smile.

The other woman chuckled. "Buying another house—I'm glad
someone's doing all right." She nodded to Bartrop and went on
her way.

Bartrop held open the door. Sarah stepped into the car and he sat beside her. There was a glass partition separating the front and back seats.

"Just drive around for a while, would you, Munro?" Bartrop closed the partition and turned to Sarah. "I wasn't planning to abduct you."

"Well, that's just in case you change your mind."

He smiled. The watchers had been using Mrs. Jardine's house as a base. The woman and her husband, a former army officer, were being fairly rewarded for the inconvenience. There was no question of where their loyalties lay. Still, it was quick thinking on Jensen's part. She was clearly deeply distrustful, but he couldn't blame her for that.

"I think it's about time we had a talk, don't you?"

She glanced across at him. "I'd say it was long overdue. But first, perhaps you would tell me who you work for and what your role is." She stared out the window, watching pedestrians on the King's Road, catching a blaze of color from the windows of the rows of boutiques. The images skimmed across her consciousness. She was concentrating her senses on the man next to her, trying to decipher him, as she supposed he was trying to decipher her. She could feel the force of his resistance, sense his determination. This wasn't going to be easy.

"Well, we'll get to that in good time. There are just a few things I'd like to take a look at first."

Sarah turned her head to him and looked him in the eyes, waiting for him to continue. For a while there was a tense silence.

"The first thing that puzzles me is why, after disappearing, you suddenly reappeared? With hindsight, it doesn't seem to be a particularly safe time. After all, Giancarlo Catania and Karl Heinz Kessler have been murdered."

"What?" It came out as genuine surprise. Catania she knew about, but Kessler . . . It removed her doubt. Her words to Christine must have been the catalyst. She registered her shock, kept it, primed it so that it shone from her face.

Bartrop studied her. She was either a bloody good actress or she genuinely didn't know, hadn't expected it. She sat in silence.

"Why did you come out of hiding, Sarah? Did you do a deal? Did you do a deal with Fieri?"

Sarah stared straight ahead for a moment, then turned slowly to him. "How dare you." Her voice was low. Rage ripped through it. "You sit there, self-righteous, unrepentant, accusing. Two innocent people have been murdered because you set me to work on this assignment, or at least I presume it was you. Or do you too have a puppet-master?"

His face was taut. "No. I have no puppet-master, as you put it."

"Well, then, the responsibility is all yours." She paused, steadying herself. "Two dead. So many lives destroyed. And for what? Who was your real target all along? I presented you, or your flunky Barrington, with all the evidence you could possibly have wanted, and you have done nothing. No arrests, not even a quiet resignation. No measure of justice, no reason. Nothing." Inspiration came to her quickly. "Unless you're going to tell me that you had Catania and Kessler killed."

Bartrop laughed. "That's more your domain, isn't it? Revenge." She bit back her words. She watched him.

"You killed that lorry driver, didn't you? The one who crashed into your parents' car."

They stared at each other. She didn't flinch. Her eyes were dead, unreadable. It was as if she had closed herself down.

He spoke again. "Cold-blooded revenge. No compassion."

Nothing prepared him for her reaction this time. Her words came like blood spit from her mouth.

"Compassion. Don't talk to me about compassion. I'm flayed by compassion." She stopped just in time. She so desperately wanted to explain, to let the words come tumbling out. *Don't you see? That's behind everything. Revenge and compassion, the only things that bind me together. I did it once, for my parents, directly, and I did it again, with words, for Mosami and Dante. And yes, I admit, I did it for myself too. It's the only way I can look at it, live with what's happened. Do you know what it's like? To see dead bodies? To imagine how they got that way? When I think of it* . . . For a while she fought back sobs. Then she continued her silent soliloquy. *Revenge is the only way I can deal with it. It's radical, imperfect, I don't enjoy it, God knows what it does to me, but it's a resolution, some form of justice. Don't you see that?* She turned to look at him. His face revealed nothing.

He watched her quietly, guessing at the conflicts raging through her mind, gripping her body. She sat tense, as if to ward off physical blows. He decided to change tack.

"You realize that I must have had very compelling reasons for starting this investigation."

"I hope you did." Her voice was cold, controlled now.

"What would you say if I told you it was aimed at a Mafia don who controls the importation of huge amounts of heroin and cocaine into Britain?"

"I would say you should have told me that in the beginning, or involved someone who knew the risks, who wouldn't have put innocent people at risk, as I did, unwittingly."

"I suppose we underestimated you."

"Cheap compliments veiled as honesty. Why don't you tell me what you want?"

"All right, I will. I want you to help me get this person. You know who I'm talking about, don't you? Antonio Fieri." He paused and smiled reasonably. "That's all. Anything else that has happened—well, as far as you're concerned, it's not relevant to me."

Sarah stared at him, trying to take the measure of him. "I'm not interested in what is or is not relevant to you. Why couldn't you just ask for my help honestly? Instead you wheel out oblique threats. Suspicions, that's all you have. And after all that's happened, do you really think I can be swayed so easily?" She almost choked on contempt. "Stop the car."

Bartrop drew back the partition and asked Munro to stop. The car slowed. Sarah opened the door and moved to get out. She turned first to him.

"You don't need my help. You ever heard of the domino theory?"

He nodded, curious.

"Well, watch them fall. They'll do it all by themselves." She got out of the car and slammed the door behind her. When she was several paces away, she reached her hand into her bag and switched off the micro-recorder that was hidden within.

Inside the car, Munro shot a questioning look at his boss.

"We'll go back now," said Bartrop.

Bartrop sat in his study and stared out the window. Miles Forshaw telephoned.

"Worthwhile?"

"I think so. In a strange sort of way."

"So what did you learn?"

"Patience."

Forshaw said dubiously, "What happens now?"

Bartrop smiled. "Nothing. We do nothing. We watch, and we wait."

"And what about Jensen?"

"Well, she seems to have decided that her role is all over."

"And is it?"

"Of course not."

Chapter
Thirty

That afternoon, at the house in Morocco, Jacob and Jack lounged around, out of sorts in Sarah's absence. They knew she couldn't call. She had warned them that she wouldn't make telephone contact or write. She wanted no trail to link her to them, just in case her bargain with Catania didn't work out. She had worried too about Barrington and whoever he was working with. She didn't want Jacob or Jack dragged into it. This they knew, and had accepted reluctantly at the time, but three days later they were finding it impossible to live with.

For distraction they went to Jack's study to watch the lunchtime news on CNN, a welcome diversion. They wouldn't have to talk to each other for a whole hour. Jack switched on the set by remote control. They sat side by side on the sofa and listened as the newscaster launched into his report. After reading the main items, he returned to the news that had come in late the previous night. His tones were measured, calm—casual even. His words lanced into Jacob and Jack. Giancarlo Catania had been murdered in Rome. As they sat, silent in shock, the announcer reported that another prominent banker had been murdered in London: Karl Heinz Kessler. The two men looked at each other in horror.

"I'm going back to London," said Jacob.

"I'm coming with you," replied Jack.

They booked themselves on the first available flight, which left Marrakesh the following morning.

Christine walked across the concourse of Heathrow's Terminal Three to the Varig ticket desk and smiled at the woman in the blue uniform. She spoke in fluent Portuguese.

"I've reserved a seat on tonight's flight to Rio. Julia Rodriguez."

The woman smiled. "O.K. Let me just find you." She punched rapid instructions into her computer terminal. "Yes, that's fine. One first-class ticket, paid for by Visa. If I could have your card and passport, please."

Christine drew out a gold Visa card and a passport in the name of Julia Falla. The ticket woman—"Mrs. Costa," it said on her badge—glanced at the passport and discreetly back at Christine. Apparently satisfied, she busied herself with the credit card. She swiped it through a machine, which printed out an invoice. Christine signed and took the card and passport back. The woman handed over the ticket.

"Boarding at gate forty-nine. Have a good flight."

Christine returned the smile. "Thank you. I will." She turned and walked briskly across the hall and up the stairs to the departure gate, an attractive woman, typically Brazilian—of medium height, with a taut, muscular body, gamine-style black hair, brown eyes. Christine smiled at her reflection as she walked along the glass-bordered walkway to her gate. She had spent two hours that morning perfecting the role of Julia Rodriguez—the hair dye, the haircut, the fake tan, the brown contact lenses, the false passport, and, most difficult of all, a different gait, busy, hurried. She walked fast, tensing her stomach muscles, and wore tight shoes. Of Christine Villiers there was no sign.

The plane took off half an hour later. It swept up through the air, turned in a long, slow arc, and began its climb to cruising altitude. Christine unfastened her seatbelt, a glass of champagne in her hand. She gazed out into the blackness blanketing the English countryside far below. She didn't know when she would see it again, but she wasn't wistful. At that moment she was exultant. Like a lizard who had lost its tail, she gloried in her freedom.

When Varig 747 was high over the Atlantic Ocean, Cesare Romagna, the motorcycle driver, weakened by his wounds and by the drugs administered to him in his hospital bed, turned *pentito*. He began slowly and methodically to inform on everyone he knew. He had no choice. His lawyer, coerced by the intelligence branch of the carabinieri, told him that he had heard the don didn't trust him not to speak, had arranged a hit. His only chance to stay alive was the Witness Protection Program. He was forty-two. He had no family. He could disappear, oh so easily, with the aid and protection of the state. He could live a new life, maybe in America.

The police at his bedside took down his statements. They were transcribed and typed up and given to the magistrates in Rome. The magistrates pieced the evidence together and began to prepare their official papers. By midnight the arrest warrants were issued. Among those named was Antonio Fieri. He was picked up in the early hours. News reports around the world carried the story later that morning.

Bartrop sat up through the night, alone in his house in Chelsea Square. The dominoes were falling. Where would they stop? Antonio Fieri had been arrested. Finally, after years of trying, the Italians had coerced one of his henchmen into testifying against him. Cesare Romagna's revelations should send Fieri to prison for life. His drug operations would be interrupted, possibly even smashed altogether if Romagna implicated more of his lieutenants, and there was a good chance he would.

Bartrop smiled faintly. All this as a result of his operation, of events he had set in motion. In the corridors of his secret world, he would receive great credit. But his satisfaction was incomplete, more that of voyeur than of participant. Much of what had come about he felt sure was the result of Sarah Jensen's veiled actions, which remained infuriatingly hidden from him.

What exactly had she done? How had she done it? She wouldn't tell him. That was clear. She despised him. He had what he wanted from this operation, not because she wished to cooperate but because her agenda had partially overlapped with his. She regarded herself as invulnerable to his threats against her, and by attitude alone had neutralized their power. But despite what she thought, she was not invulnerable. She had her Achilles' heel: Jacob Goldsmith. He had harbored her. That was not a crime, but he was an old man trying to enjoy a quiet, simple life. If events turned and focused on him—well, given what Bartrop knew of Sarah Jensen, she would find that intolerable, and she would talk.

And that was essential. One *pentito* wasn't enough. One life, so fragile. Bartrop and the Italians needed more substance to reinforce the case, to provide for contingencies. Bartrop needed Sarah Jensen, needed to know what she knew, and he intended to find out. He went to bed and dreamed of Sarah.

He received a spur to his plans the next morning. Special Branch at Heathrow telephoned at eleven. Jacob Goldsmith had just arrived back in the country. Bartrop took the call and smiled in anticipation. All the pieces were falling into place.

Jacob and Jack took a taxi straight to Carlyle Square. They paid off the driver, stood nervously in silence on the threshold, and rang Sarah's bell. They waited, heard a noise from above, looked up, and saw Sarah's head appear out the window.

"Jacob! Jack!" she screamed in delight. "I'm coming down."

The two men grinned at each other. "I knew she was all right," said Jacob.

Sarah came downstairs. She hugged and kissed them both and wiped a tear discreetly from Jacob's cheek. They dropped their cases in the hall.

She smiled at them, then held a finger to her lips. "Let's go for a walk." She stared at them firmly.

They nodded, slightly perplexed. They walked out into Carlyle Square, into the sunshine. Sarah unlocked the gate to the garden and took them in. All three sat down on a bench. There were a couple of children in the garden, laughing and playing, with a woman watching over them, but they were out of earshot.

Sarah sat between Jacob and Jack. "It's so good to see you both, I can't tell you."

They all spoke at once for a while, words, laughter, and relief bubbling over. Then the laughter abated and the questions began.

"My house is bugged," said Sarah.

Jacob, terrier-like as usual, snapped out questions, driven by worry, by a need to understand, to keep tabs on her, even retrospectively.

His inquisitions had driven her mad in the past. Today they were a relief—to see him again, to be home in London, to tell him the answers, to rationalize everything by the act of putting it into words, into conversation. There was no one she could tell but him. And Jack. She was happy to tell him, too. He deserved it, and it took some of the burden off Jacob.

"What have you been doing? What's happened? Did you have something to do with Catania and Kessler?" asked Jacob.

Jack looked shocked and glanced back and forth between Jacob and Sarah, expecting incredulity on her face or irony on his. There was neither. She answered heavily, wearily, but matter-of-factly. But what surprised him most was the look that passed between them—a look of knowing, a sparkle of conspiracy.

"I haven't done much. I told one person something, and another nothing. I should probably have told the first person nothing and the second everything. But I didn't, and I'm glad. And in answer to your last question, yes, probably."

Jacob looked exasperated, Jack bemused.

Jacob said, "Would you mind telling us that again, without the riddles this time?"

For the next ten minutes she told them. The two men sat in silence for a few minutes, digesting her news.

"And this Christine Villiers—where is she now?" asked Jacob.

"Hiding, I suppose. She hasn't contacted me again. If she did pass my information on to Fieri and kill Kessler for him, she's not going to hang around now, is she?"

"Do you think she did?"

Sarah sighed heavily. "God, Jacob, I don't know. But I think it's likely, don't you?"

"And what about James Bartrop?"

Sarah frowned. "He asked me if I had done a deal with Fieri. Can you believe it?"

"Well, you did, didn't you?"

Sarah glared at Jacob. "No. I didn't. I told Christine Villiers about Catania. And yes, I hoped she would use that knowledge to discredit him, to kill him, even. I suspected that Catania might be involved with Fieri, with the Mafia—it's a fair assumption— and that if he were, they would not appreciate his being black-mailed by a group of outsiders, or his ordering hits on people. What they did about it, if they were involved, was up to them. And Christine Villiers—how am I to know whether she has any Mafia contacts? She's an assassin. She lives in Italy. Again I made a reasonable assumption, so, adding up all these things, it made sense to tell her. I told her, and now Catania and Kessler are dead. Did she have anything to do with it? How can I know? But they are dead, some Mafia drug pusher's in prison, and the con-spiracy is over. Dante and Mosami will never come back, but this is the best I could have hoped for. A measure of justice. It's not perfect, but I've done all I can."

Sarah sighed, then continued. "As for Matthew Arnott and Carla Vitale, I don't think their prospects look too bright. I saw Arnott the other day and he looked about ready for a crack-up. And Barrington, and James Bartrop—yes, I hate them. I feel con-tempt for them. I hold them responsible for Mosami and Dante. Not so much Barrington—he was just weak. But Bartrop, he's the real culprit. He seems to think he can justify everything that's happened by saying that it was regrettable, that he underesti-mated me and that was his sole mistake. Now he threatens me, tries to blackmail me." Sarah glared. "I'm never going to tell him anything."

Jacob said very gently, "But he won't let up, Sarah, if he thinks you know something you haven't told him."

She smiled. "No. I'm sure he won't. But I won't be here when he next comes to question me."

Both men sat up in shock and asked in unison, "Where are you going?"

Sarah smiled. "I'm going to Katmandu, to join Eddie and Alex. I've been checking their itinerary. They are in Katmandu now, buying supplies. It's perfect timing. I've sent a telegram telling them to meet me at the airport. I've booked myself a ticket. I'm flying out this evening, Royal Nepal Airlines, from Gatwick."

Jacob and Jack sat looking at each other, at Sarah, then off into the distance, as if trying to see Katmandu. Jacob was the first to speak.

"I think it sounds like a good idea. I'll miss you. I'd come with you, but I'm a bit old for that." He laughed and glanced at Jack. "I've also been missing the Green. It's about time I got back, picked up Ruby, checked on the garden. All the flowers are probably dead." He looked rueful. Sarah squeezed his arm.

"I'll be back, Jacob. Probably not for a while. Apart from you and Jack, there's not much to come back to. And I can't help feeling that the longer I stay away, the better." She smiled. "The next stage of Eddie and Alex's trip is taking them into some pretty remote areas—Bhutan and Ladakh. Not easy places to get to, or to look for someone. And beautiful. So beautiful. I've always wanted to go there."

"So we had better take you to the airport, then?" said Jack.

"Oh, would you?" asked Sarah. "But we might have to take a

funny route, do a bit of fancy driving. I don't particularly want to alert Bartrop."

Jack said gleefully, "No problem. Haven't done it in years, but it's like riding a bike. You never forget."

Jacob looked skeptical. "Well, we'll see about that." He sat thinking for a few minutes, then got up from the bench, excused himself, and went off in search of a telephone. Ten minutes later he returned, grinning broadly.

"All set."

Sarah laughed. "What have you got up your sleeve?"

"Wait and see," he replied.

They set off in the late afternoon. First they took a taxi to Jacob's house in Golders Green. They went in through the front entrance, and then, very quietly, following Jacob's instructions, they filed out into the back garden. At the far end of the garden was a low fence, which separated Jacob's garden from that of the house in the parallel street. They stepped quickly over the fence, walked up to the back door of the house, and tapped lightly. A wrinkled face appeared at the kitchen window, grinned at them, then disappeared.

Seconds later the door opened and Vera Watkins stood smiling in welcome. Vera had known Jacob and Sarah for nearly twenty years. Like most of Jacob's neighbors, she had a soft spot for them both and was only too pleased to help out without asking any questions. They introduced her to Jack and chatted briefly. Then Vera turned to Jacob.

"Your friend Charlie came by half an hour ago. Left his van in the drive." She reached into a pocket of her voluminous skirt. "Here's the keys."

Jacob pocketed them and gave her a broad wink. Sarah and Jack smiled at the exchange, thanked Mrs. Watkins, and followed Jacob through the house. The party said a brief goodbye at the door. Jacob handed the keys to Jack.

"You'd better drive, since you like it so much. Give you a chance to show off."

Jack laughed, took the keys, and got into the driver's seat. Sarah and Jacob climbed into the back and sat on the floor. It wasn't comfortable, but the windows were tinted and they were concealed. The windows at the front were also dark, concealing Jack. Unless the watchers were observing the front of Mrs. Watkins's house, they should have a clear run to the airport. Jack turned the key in the ignition, the engine caught, and they slipped out of the drive and away. Bouncing around in the back of the van, Sarah smiled at Jacob, filled with the sensation of escape.

After a long, bruising journey, they arrived at the airport. Sarah stepped stiff-legged out of the van and glanced around nervously. Jack got out of the front seat and smiled.

"Nobody. I did a bit of roundabout driving, just in case, but, believe me, I know what to look for, and there was nothing on our tail."

Sarah grinned. "Brilliant."

Jacob laughed. "Brilliant—is that what you call it? I left half my stomach whirling around the back streets of South London and you call it brilliant?"

Laughing, they walked toward the departure hall. Jacob and Jack kept up a lively patter, distracting themselves and Sarah from the imminent farewell. They paused outside on the tarmac. Sarah hugged them and kissed them both goodbye. Laughter gave way to tears. Sarah studied their brave faces and gave Jacob one last kiss. Then she reached into her pocket and pulled out a small cassette, about one inch by two inches. She handed it to Jacob.

"My conversation with James Bartrop. Recorded it yesterday on the micro-recorder you gave me. It doesn't show him in a great light. I'm sure he wouldn't like it to get into the public arena, or into the hands of his superiors, or the politicians, for that matter." She smiled. "Just in case he tries to be bothersome."

Jacob returned the smile, pocketed the cassette, and hugged Sarah one last time. Then he watched her nod to Jack and turn and walk away.

He and Jack stood watching until she had disappeared from sight. Then, not trusting themselves to speak, they returned to the car park, collected the van, and drove away.

Back in Golders Green, the watchers sat patiently in a van on Rotherwick Road. They had no suspicions that Sarah was at that moment passing through Gatwick Airport, miles away.

She was lucky, too, because Bartrop hadn't expected her to leave the country again so soon. No one was looking out for her at the check-in desks or passport control. Sarah moved through the airport unobserved. She stopped to buy the Sunday newspapers, a packet of cigarettes, and some chocolate, then made her way to the departure gate.

She sat down on a molded plastic seat beside a window overlooking the runways. She glanced around. She saw a few people look away. People were watching her, but that was not unusual, and she saw nothing suspicious in their eyes. She felt almost invisible, as if slowly she had been able to wrap herself in a cloak of normality. She had the sensation of having reclaimed her life.

She smiled to herself, ate a few squares of chocolate, and lit a cigarette. Then she opened her copy of the *Sunday Times* and began to browse.

Suddenly she froze. At the back of the paper, tucked away in the late news section, was a small item, one paragraph. She read and reread it till every word was fixed in her memory.

> Foreign-exchange trader Matthew Arnott was found dead last night in his million-pound house in Holland Park. He was discovered by his girlfriend, Carla Vitale, an Italian, who immediately called the police. It is understood that a note, believed to be a suicide note, was found by his body. A postmortem will be conducted today.

Sarah stared at the newsprint until it went fuzzy before her eyes. Arnott dead. Suicide. She was not surprised. It reflected the look she had seen in his eyes: hopelessness, despair, fear, and self-disgust. She suddenly felt a lacerating pity for him. She stared at the newspaper until the departure gate was almost empty. Then she got to her feet and walked very slowly through the metal corridor and onto the plane.

She smiled at the flight attendant who welcomed her aboard and made her way to her seat halfway down the cabin. After fastening her seatbelt, she sat patiently, waiting for the plane to take off. Ten minutes later she felt the engines rumble beneath her. The plane taxied onto the runway, the engines roared and began to throb, and the nose lifted into the sky.

In the empty seat next to her lay the *Sunday Times*. She glanced at it, then away. Arnott was dead; one paragraph, less than a hundred words. There was so much more that could have been said—about his working for ICB, about Kessler, about Dante, about her. Late news, sparse facts, or the hand of James Bartrop and a D notice? What did it matter? There was much she didn't know, didn't want to know. Better to be left in ignorance of that world, which had had her in its grips, which she had left behind physically. All that was left was the mental transition, and that had already begun, was growing with the sense of resolution that now filled her. Kessler, Catania, Arnott dead. Only Carla was left, rootless, terrified, exposed. She had her millions stashed away. Perhaps they would be found, perhaps not. She would find out now what a sterile comfort money was.

Barrington and Bartrop had got off lightly, but then, their only real crime was poor judgment, and arrogance in Bartrop's case. It was just that the consequences of their errors were so huge. Sarah thought of Mosami and Dante. She filled her mind and senses with memories of their smiles and warmth and love. She faced them fully in her mind for the first time since their murders, and then she let them go.

She gazed out the window at the English countryside, fast disappearing in the summer haze as the plane gained height. The flight attendant brought her a glass of whisky. She sipped it and felt the warmth diffuse through her body. Her limbs felt light. She thought of what lay ahead. In a few hours she would be with her brother and her boyfriend, and everything else would be a memory.

Ten hours later, on Monday morning in Katmandu, the plane began its perilously sharp descent to the airport. Sarah watched the peaks looming in the distance, huge, magnificent, unlike anything she had ever seen. Then they gave way, seemingly reluctantly, to the plains, as if they had lost territory in a ferocious turf battle. The beauty and the power of the landscape thrilled her, and her heart quickened in anticipation, as if she had started to climb the mountains in her mind. The plane swooped down to the tarmac and shuddered to a halt on the short runway.

Sarah undid her seatbelt and got to her feet, eager to disembark. She ran down the steps and into the terminal building. Her heart pounded as she waited in queues: passport control, baggage collection, customs. Finally she was through. She walked out onto the concourse, her eyes darting through the crowds.

They were standing some way back, apart from the rest—Alex and Eddie, tall, brown, smiling in delight. Sarah smiled back at their open faces and walked toward them, leaving everything behind.

Epilogue

"I've already told you, I don't know where she is. And you can threaten me with whatever you like. I don't care. I'd only care if Sarah worried about it, and she won't. She's gone away, and she refused to tell me where for this very reason. You're not going to get anywhere with me. And don't forget, I know all about your dirty games. They'd make a damn good story . . ."

Bartrop leaned forward in his seat. "You also have to cross the road every day."

Jacob laughed in Bartrop's face. "I'm seventy-three years old. Do you think I care about threats like that?"

"She'll come back sooner or later, or I'll find her in the mean-time."

"Don't count on it. She'll stay away for as long as she needs. When she comes back, the case will be over and tried. It will be closed, and there will be nothing you can do. You might not even be around then. Forget her, Bartrop. You've done enough damage. You've got what you wanted. You've got Fieri, thanks to her. Now leave her alone."

"And what happens if I decide not to take up your kind advice?"

Jacob laughed again. "I've got enough to sink you. And it'll get out, one way or another. Don't think you can just sit on it, slap a few D notices around. Things filter out—people get to hear. Perhaps it will never go public, but someone will get to hear. And a man like you has lots of enemies, inside government and out. You wouldn't want me to give them any ammunition, would you?"

Bartrop smiled. "Well, let's wait and see. If she's gone, she's gone. Things have been stirred up a bit. Perhaps we should just let things go."

"So you'll leave her alone?"

Bartrop got to his feet and nodded. "I'll leave her alone." He added silently, to himself, *For now.*

About the Author

After graduating from Oxford in 1985, Linda Davies moved to New York and worked for a year on Wall Street in the heyday of takeover mania and the cult of money. She then returned to London and spent several years as a merchant banker, working in areas ranging from leveraged buyouts to Eastern European venture capital to bond sales. In 1992, she left the financial world to write *Nest of Vipers*. She is currently at work on her second novel.